C000126263

Detyen Warriors
One

Featuring: Soulless, Ruthless, & Heartless

By

Kate Rudolph

and

Starr Huntress

Want to ready new chapters and get books before they're available to the public? Join my **Patreon** today.

More Detyen Warriors

Soulless

Ruthless

Heartless

Faultless

Endless

Soulless: Detyen Warriors

By

Kate Rudolph

and

Starr Huntress

Prologue
One Hundred and Three Years Ago

Detya

The morning burned hot and bright and the people of Detya awoke to a pleasant summer day, just like all the summers before. Birds flew from tree to tree and small animals scampered through the forest. The defense monitoring stations sensed no threats and even the summer monsoons were a month away from threatening the peace of the planet.

But two million miles away, at the interstellar gate at the edge of the solar system, trouble brewed. A dark ship slipped through the black sky, setting off no sensors and communicating with nothing. It did not identify itself to the Detyen crew monitoring the galactic shipping lanes and it silently crushed a small pleasure craft which crossed its path.

No insignia identified the origin of the ship and the design could have come from a hundred different civilizations.

As it sped closer to the planet, no one sensed the danger. A military ship launched an hour before the silent threat passed Detya's final moon and did nothing to defend the planet.

With a single shot, the mystery ship destroyed the planet and the billions who lived on it. Fire coated the land and the seas dissolved. The damage ate through everything, leaving nothing but a burnt-out husk, incapable of sustaining life.

And before the few survivors who'd managed to make it off planet prior to the destruction could even begin to fathom what had happened, the ship was gone.

The kingdoms and republics of Detya were dead.

The military was destroyed.

And from a planet that had once hosted billions of lives, fewer than a million remained.

The Detyens were extinct. They just didn't know it yet.

No matter where they went, home was gone, and there was no way to know who had stolen it away.

Chapter One

Sierra didn't know why she'd agreed to family dinner. Her father sat ramrod straight with a glass of whiskey clenched in one hand and studiously ignored the insignia on the sleeve of her uniform. She ate her peas one by one and only spared him glances when he shifted or sighed. Three years of this shit and she still hadn't learned.

"I talked to Commander Mitchell about the training course I told you about. Two years of officer training and then you'll have a command. Say the word and it's yours." He wasn't using his General voice, which Sierra appreciated. But it also made her want to cry. He'd given up ordering her around. How long would it be before he gave up on her all together?

It was moments like these that she could still smell the stench of the Wastes where she'd spent her first years sticking to her skin. Her father, General Remington Alvarez, had saved her life. And all she was to him was a disappointment.

"I like my job, Dad." She forced herself to look up. Even though he was in his mid-sixties, her dad barely had any gray hair and his muscles made her think he could lift a tree if he had to. He'd been stationed behind a desk for more than a decade, but none of the work had made him soft. No, Remington Alvarez was all hard edges and strict rules.

"The job that means I have to spend every night you're in the field wondering if you're safe? The job that I can't talk about to any of my friends? The one that will steal away your future before you even realize it?" He jerked his glass up to his mouth and threw the whiskey back, hissing as the liquid burned its way down his throat.

"I wouldn't be any safer in the fleet," she felt the need to point out, even as his other statements flayed her alive. "And if it weren't for the work I did, the fleet would be flying blind." He made it all sound so *sordid*, and not a necessary part of any defense apparatus.

Her father sucked in a deep breath and Sierra had to look away, staring at a still photograph her father had taken at some fancy event with an alien with bright yellow skin and sharp teeth. They'd had this fight a hundred times before and the only sure thing about it was that both of them would be left hurting and resentful by the time the night was over. "I'm—" she cut herself off before the apology could flit across her tongue. That was the problem. She *wasn't* sorry.

"Sneaking behind enemy lines, lying to people. It's not honor—" he, too, choked on his words.

Sierra still flinched. *It's not honorable.* Yeah, she'd heard that one plenty of times too. This had to end now. If they spoke for any longer, it would lead to more months of silence and shitty tempers.

She placed her napkin on the table and scooted her chair back. "Thanks for dinner. I'll give you a call when I get back and we can do this again." Emotion lodged in her throat and she swallowed it, unwilling to break in front of this man.

"Back?" her father demanded, throwing his own napkin down. "Where are you going?"

"A mission. Classified. Dishonorable stuff, you wouldn't want to hear about it anyway." Her eyes itched and if she didn't get out of there in the next minute she'd end up crying. Sierra didn't cry in front of her father, not ever. That was even worse than dishonor, that was weakness.

"Erra—" he tried to stop her with her old childhood nickname. Sierra didn't even pause as she scooped up her jacket from where she'd laid it on the back of his couch. She made her way through the narrow hallway of his quarters and to the front door.

Something that might have been regret danced in his eyes as he met her at the door. "Be safe," he finally said, grabbing her in a tight hug and yanking her close. "Come back in one piece, I still need a date to the reception for Ambassador Yormas of Wreet."

Sierra squeezed her eyes shut, but when she opened them again, her eyelashes were wet. Her dad said nothing. "I'll give you a call," she promised, not ready to agree to anything when her emotions were so raw.

He just nodded and let her go.

The hallway outside of his apartment was the same boring gray as the walls inside her father's quarters. He shared the floor with three other units, but she saw no one as she made her way down the faded carpet to the stairwell beside the elevator. She took the stairs at a fast clip, as if speed were enough to outrun everything on her mind and in her heart. She hated disappointing her father. He'd saved her from a short, hard life of unspeakable cruelty and darkness. She doubted she would have made it to twenty-nine if he hadn't adopted her. But Sierra had long ago realized that being grateful for her existence didn't mean she owed her dad her entire future.

He saw it all for her: officer training, command, rank. Everything he'd doggedly pursued for his entire life. The only life he could conceive of. She'd taken one look at the training manuals and run screaming. Sierra was no stranger to discipline. How could she be when her father was General Remington Alvarez? But if she made that life hers, she'd be extinguishing herself. And as much as she loved her dad, she couldn't do it.

He'd give her that derisive laugh of his if he knew she thought that way. How, he'd ask, could she be more true to herself as a spy than as a soldier?

She didn't have the answer, but he wouldn't care to hear it even if she did.

Her vehicle was located in the parking garage under his building. Sierra scanned the area, noting the android attendant near the entrance and a flickering light near where she'd parked. Awareness prickled at the back of her neck and her muscles loosened, her stride long and confident as she waited for the threat to make itself known.

A cat darted out from a dark corner and Sierra's blaster was out, her finger on the trigger before she even registered the movement. When the animal jumped on top of her vehicle, she laughed and put her weapon away. She needed a damn vacation.

But vacation was the last thing she had to look forward to, not when planetary defense had to come first. Sierra gave the cat a gentle pet and then shooed it on its way before sliding into the car. As soon as she was on the road, her communicator lit up. She engaged the call without video and didn't bother to glance at the identification to see who was calling. Anyone who had her code wouldn't call if it wasn't an emergency.

"Joyce is calling us in," her friend and navigator, Mindy Branch said in lieu of a greeting.

"Right now?" A glance at the clock showed it wasn't even close to midnight, let alone their 0500 call time.

"Yeah, Jo's already on her way." Mindy sounded about as pleased with that turn of events as Sierra was, but neither voiced their concerns.

"I'll be there in an hour."

"Got it. Drive safe." She disengaged and the communication's display went dim.

Sierra sent a silent prayer of thanks to anyone who was listening and turned her car around to head to the rendezvous point. She needed to get the fuck off of Earth to remember why it was worth saving in the first place.

***

Raze's indicator alerted him that his required physical exertion period had come to an end. He glanced at the readout on the machine to see that he'd improved his last run time by three seconds and noted the statistics for his file. A quick swipe with the cleaning pad took care of the sweat that had dripped onto the machine, and he used a separate towel to take care of the moisture beading on his forehead and at the base of his neck.

The material was rough and cheap, but sturdier than anything else the legion had been able to purchase. He dragged it slowly across his skin and nearly couldn't suppress the shiver that tried to climb up his spine from the almost painful friction. A moment later he pulled the towel away and disposed of it in the laundry chute. He mechanically stripped himself of his clothes and they followed the towel down to where they'd be laundered and returned to the rotation.

He nodded to Kayde, one of his fellow warriors, as he walked naked to the shower station. The cold water hit his skin with bruising force and this time he couldn't stop the hiss from the sensation. The water quickly warmed to a sufficient level and he cleaned himself in his allotted time. Another swipe of a different abrasive towel saw him dry, and he barely spared a glance for the marks it had left on his green skin. He pulled on a clean uniform and exited the shower station before the next warrior to finish his training could be delayed.

Though Raze knew he was scheduled to join his team for the final briefing before their scheduled mission, he consulted his schedule before heading toward the administrative building in case the plan had changed. The legion and its soldiers were slaves to their schedules, especially those like him. To eschew routine was to eschew control, and when the soulless lost control, there was only one solution.

If he could still feel fear, Raze might have felt the shiver in his spine. But just like everything else, those emotions had been taken away from him, given up, two years ago, just before his thirtieth birthday. He couldn't regret his decision, and he chose not to dwell on it. The legion had saved his life, he owed them his loyalty and his service.

A quick walk through one of the service tunnels brought him to the administrative building. The entire compound was connected through underground tunnels and elevated walkways so that no soldier or staff member would need to brave the harsh weather of their home moon by walking between buildings outside. The moon was habitable, but the weather extremes made it less than ideal, and for that reason, it had been sitting uninhabited after a failed colonizing attempt six decades before. The legion had bought the rights to the land and had spent years making their own little colony into a fortress.

No one would be able to do to them what had been done to their ancestors.

Something that might have once been sorrow clenched in his chest, but Raze paid no attention to it. If he chased the phantom emotion, he could easily find himself out of control and scheduled to be executed within the hour. Punishments were harsh and final for the soulless, but it was the only way to protect the legion.

The familiar path inside the administrative building centered Raze with the comfort of routine. He walked down the brightly lit hallway and spared a glance at the Detyen art that decorated the walls. When he was younger, it would have brought to the forefront all of the sorrows and joys of a home he'd never seen. Now he merely noted that one of the frames hung slightly askew.

He entered the assigned meeting room and took his seat, nodding in greeting to Toran NaLosen, a younger Detyen warrior who smiled at him in response. Unlike Raze, Toran still possessed his soul. He wouldn't need to choose between death and soullessness for a few more years. "Kayde and Sandon should be here soon," Toran said. He tapped his fingers against the table, the small sound loud enough to fill the room.

Raze let his eyes rest on those moving digits. Toran's clan markings climbed down both of his arms and covered parts of each hand, making his golden skin appear almost spotted. The door slid open and two more men walked through. Toran pulled his fingers into a fist and stilled as he studied the newest entrants. Raze spared them a glance, nodding at Kayde and Sandon before settling his gaze on the holo projector in the center of the table. Kayde settled in beside him and Sandon took his place at the front.

With a flick of his fingers, Sandon brought up a projection of the planet they would be heading to and their target. "The planet is called Fenryr 1," Sandon said, calling up the basic climatological and population statistics as he spoke. "It technically sits at the edge of the Oscavian Empire, but has no native population and no Oscavian development. Flares from the dual stars at the heart of the system make it difficult to monitor the planet and it's become a haven for pirates and slavers. Our intelligence has detected a small gathering here," he pointed to a peninsula on the globe. "There are few other inhabited pockets near the southern pole, but we have no interest in them. Your target is the *Lyrden,* which is located a hundred kilometers away from the peninsula. It was brought to the planet two years ago and we think it is meant to be scrapped. Due to the extensive number of scrap ships collecting there, the *Lyrden* is not heavily guarded and we have no reason to believe that it will be destroyed before you can find it. We need all of the data that you can scrape from the onboard computer. Questions?"

Both Raze and Kayde glanced at Toran, who was reading through the mission parameters on his personal tablet. "This says the *Lyrden* is a XA-1. That's more than a hundred years old. It's possible, if not likely, that the system can't be scanned or recovered.

Do we have the authority to bring parts back? Or do we not want the inhabitants to know we were there?"

"This is a high priority mission. Use any means necessary to recover the data," Sandon pierced Toran with his steely gaze. "The *Lyrden* was recorded in the Detyen system the day of the attack. We have reason to believe the information on that ship could lead us to whoever attacked us or supplied the weapon. Are we clear?"

They were. Sandon left them alone to plan. If Raze weren't soulless, he'd describe the blood coursing through his veins as excitement. He sat forward, ready to talk the mission through. They couldn't save their home, but they could get revenge, and this was the first step.

***

Within two hours of her disastrous dinner with her father, Sierra was on a ship and off planet, speeding towards the jump gate. The mission had suddenly moved up when a gap in scheduling provided her team with a quicker route to their destination, but the gap would be closed by the scheduled launch time. She could still hear Jocasta Nelson, her pilot, grumbling about missed sleep. Sierra kept her distance, opting to spend the time from Earth to the gate strapped in one of the chairs in the kitchen.

Mindy had shot her a glare and taken her position at the navigator's station beside Jo. The two traded barbs as they worked through the checklists that would see them safely out of the solar system and on their way to Fenryr 1. Fucking pirates were stealing women from Earth and selling them off as slaves... or worse. Hundreds abducted over the course of a decade, and it wasn't until the niece of a US Senator disappeared that anyone paid any attention to the victims. Sierra was trying *really* hard not to be angry about that, but she had three days to get her emotions under control. By the time they reached the pirates, she'd be ice. Until then, she wanted to hit something and not stop until it bled.

Deep breaths. Deep breaths.

A warning alarm buzzed and the lights flashed as they approached the gate. The interstellar passageways were seeded throughout the galaxy and made it possible to travel throughout inhabited space in a relatively short amount of time. Humans hadn't put them in place, but the Sol system had free use of one gate and that gate opened to a highway of other passageways that led anywhere a person could want to go. Not that Sierra particularly *wanted* to go to Fenryr 1, but she'd do the job, gather the intel... and leave any women behind.

She clenched her jaw as her ears popped. Pressure built in her head as they slipped through the portal and out the other end. An all clear alarm sounded and the first leg of the journey was complete.

A minute later, Mindy came bounding back and plopped into the seat beside Sierra, pulling her legs up to curl into a ball of fluffy woman. She wore a gray sweater that was soft enough to pet, but it was covered in soft balls of an unfamiliar fabric. The ensemble was matched by tight, synth leather pants and a bright green headband that held her long blue hair back. She didn't look like a spy, but she was one of the best navigators in the entire Sol system.

"We'll save them all," Mindy promised.

Sierra wasn't surprised that her friend had read her mind. The parameters of the mission hung heavy over all of them, even the standoffish Jo. "It's a lot easier when we get to go in and steal data from rich assholes or plant a bug in some government official's communicator." Sierra unbuckled her safety harness and turned so she could more easily face Mindy. As her body shifted, the chair reshaped itself to accommodate her new position. They were designed for comfort on long journeys, something regular military vessels didn't need. Though she'd never use that point in an argument with her dad.

"But you might actually get to shoot someone this time," Mindy countered. She glanced back toward the cockpit and then lowered her voice. "Dinner not go great?" It was more of a statement than a question.

Sierra shrugged. "Could have been worse. We're still talking to each other, so that's good. I think he's still kind of pissed off that I grew up." Feelings weren't something that they talked about in the Alvarez household, and Mindy was one of the few people who didn't let Sierra get away with deflecting the discussion.

"And he knows that you're doing dangerous shit," Mindy pointed out. "My parents think I work in accounts receivable. They'd be terrified if they knew what I really did. But it's not like this is a secret you can keep from the great General Alvarez. No one keeps secrets from the man who singlehandedly saved a city from alien destruction."

Sierra groaned. "Don't talk about Mumbai, please!" She covered her face with her hands and burrowed further into the chair. The trouble with being a hero's daughter was that she could never escape his heroics. No one saw Remington Alvarez as the guy who'd panicked when he needed to help her buy bras. No, he was the man whose astute observations and quick thinking had turned a would-be massacre into a minor skirmish.

"He wishes you had your own Mumbai," said Mindy. "It's not that he wants destruction, but he wants you to be recognized. And as long as you're doing *this*, recognition is the last thing you can have."

"I don't give a shit about medals and ceremonies. *This* is what I'm good at." She'd been nine when her dad had swooped in and saved her from the Wastes, but that was old enough to already know how to wear a dozen different faces depending on what she needed. A safe home and years of therapy had given her the opportunity to live a fulfilling life, but she couldn't escape those early years, not completely. They'd given her the tools she needed to survive and now that she could control her own destiny, she wanted to use those tools to help others, to help her people. Anyone could hold a gun, but only someone like her could lie to the face of the head of the Oscavian Diplomatic Corps and get away with it.

"You ever regret what we have to give up?" Mindy asked. She grabbed a blanket from the storage bin overhead and wrapped herself up, adding to her already high level of fluff.

"Like what?" She still had her dad, the money was good, and when she was home she was pretty much safe. What more could she need?

Mindy scoffed. "Really? You know, a guy? A family? It's kind of difficult to maintain a relationship when we're called off planet for months at a time with no way to communicate."

"I don't think I've ever met a guy worth more than a few weeks of my time, and even those are rare. What's wrong with having some fun? We've got plenty of time for families later." Though now that Mindy mentioned it, Sierra tried to remember the last time she'd been on a date. Had it even been this year? She had a feeling her friend wouldn't count a hookup with one of the marines they'd been briefly stationed with.

"So you don't want any of it?" This truly seemed to baffle Mindy, whose face screwed up in a look of confusion and something approaching pity.

"Not enough to give all this up."

A slew of curses followed by fevered hammering came from the cockpit as the ship did something Jo didn't like. Sierra and Mindy shared a look and both bit their bottom lips to keep from bursting out laughing. A moment later, footsteps pounded down the metal catwalk leading from the cockpit to the kitchen and Jo stomped through. She paused to look at both of them.

"One of you babysit the damn autopilot. I need to take a shower." Without waiting for either of them to agree, she headed off towards the bathroom, muttering more curses.

For once, Sierra said her silent thanks to the temperamental pilot. A few more minutes of Mindy's questioning and they'd be talking weddings or babies or some shit like that, and Sierra was not in the mood to discuss things that weren't going to happen, at least not anytime soon. Unless there was some man out there who could respect what she did and appreciate her for the woman she was and not some perfect princess that he wished she'd be, she'd rather be single and fulfilled than paired off and miserable.

And she hadn't once met a guy who wouldn't want to change her. So single it was. And that didn't make her regret anything.

Not at all.

Chapter Two

An uncharted topographical disturbance derailed the initial plan to land near the *Lyrden* and quickly retrieve the data. Toran directed Kayde to a secondary location and within the hour, they had the ship hidden among an outcropping of rocks and were hiking over the stony terrain down the windswept peninsula. The gusts beat at Raze's hair, sending some of the longer strands into his eyes and mouth. He normally kept it cropped short, but his scheduler had malfunctioned and deleted his appointment for his last haircut. He smoothed his fingers through it and the slight mist in the air was enough to wet his hair and keep it slicked back.

From space, it hadn't been obvious why Fenryr 1 remained mostly uninhabited. The weather seemed moderate, despite what they'd been warned of, and green covered huge swaths of the planet, both over land and sea. But once they set down, the inhospitality became more apparent. The green that looked like trees from space was actually a dense and malodorous moss that covered everything and stuck to their boots where they walked. A few small animals darted out from the cover of the moss, only to be snatched up by birds that swarmed in dense black clouds.

There was no sign of the pirates and slavers, and the path that they'd charted to the ship was meant to keep them out of range of whatever detection devices and patrols they used.

After several hours of walking, Raze's legs burned and his lips cracked, parched for water. He took a drink and surveyed the area around them. There was little cover, other than some stone outcroppings, and if he hadn't been tracking their coordinates, he might have believed they'd been walking in place. It all looked almost the same. The suns were setting on the far horizon and a chill froze the air around them. His clothes were meant to withstand subfreezing temperatures, but he suspected that Toran would soon stop them for the night.

In another setting, Toran, as the youngest of the three of them, might have been the junior member of this team. But among the legion, it was those who still had their souls who led in the field. They had the ability to adapt and follow instincts that Raze and his like had surrendered in the name of survival. And it was only soldiers who still had their souls that could make the choice to put down one of the soulless if he went over the edge. They could see the danger long before he would, long before the bodies hit the floor and blood coated the walls.

Toran held up a hand to stop them. Kayde and Raze came up beside him and waited for him to speak.

"Those rocks look like they'll give us some cover. I want the two of you to set up camp. I'll see if I can round up food or water. Don't break into the rations until I'm back." He handed off his supplies to the two of them and took off.

Kayde followed Raze toward the area Toran indicated and they worked in silence to set up tents and ignite the warming block that would act as a heat source and a way to cook any potential food Toran hunted down. It gave off no scent and little light, which helped with stealth.

More than an hour later, Toran returned with two small animals in hand. They were covered in fur with large ears and looked to have a good amount of meat on them. He handed them over to Kayde with instructions for him to clean the kills and test them for digestive compatibility before taking his place in setting up camp.

"I've set up the drones to monitor a perimeter," Toran told him. "Kayde can take first watch, but I'll want us to keep to the camp in case we need to make a quick retreat."

Raze nodded and finished adjusting the final strap of the tent he was working on. Once he was finished, he stepped back and looked around the little camp. Tents, warming block, refuse pit, everything was set up. He took a seat on a fallen log and stared into the dim glow and let his hands soak up the heat as night fell around them.

"You can't get bored, can you?" Toran asked as he set up one of the portable chairs beside Raze.

Raze thought about how to answer that for a moment. "Not like you mean, I don't think. I could sit here until it's time for me to sleep, but my mind is sharper with stimulus." The first week of training after becoming soulless had been all about how not to fall into ennui now that he couldn't desire anything. The warriors who survived were the ones who found a way to keep engaged, even when engagement no longer seemed to matter.

Toran studied him for several moments, his form quickly disappearing into shadow as the suns finally set. He was little more than the outline of a Detyen, the soft glow of the warming block not enough to discern details. "Can I ask what it's like?"

Raze didn't need to clarify what he meant by 'it.' Most people back at the base wouldn't ask, but there was only one thing he knew that they didn't. "It isn't like anything," he said after taking another few minutes to gather his thoughts. "I can remember emotions, remember desire and goals and everything else. It hasn't completely vanished. But it's the difference between a steaming hot spring and a tepid bath. Water surrounds me no matter what, but now it merely serves a function. I neither like nor dislike it." Raze paused for a moment and then unexpectedly added, "I would not have chosen this if it weren't for my debt."

"Debt?" Even in the shadows, Raze could see Toran jerk his head in his direction and lean a little closer.

"For surviving," Raze explained. "My brother and I were saved by the legion, not born into it. And we owe it to our people, as the last link to Detya."

He could almost feel Toran's stare boring into him. "Do you really believe that?"

"I used to." It was hard to believe anything these days. He hadn't realized just how much emotion went into belief until his life dissolved into the nothing of soullessness.

Toran said nothing for several moments after that before changing the subject. "I hear chatter."

Raze stayed silent.

His teammate let out a small huff that might have been a laugh. "I'm going to talk at you until you tell me to stop."

Raze had realized that. "We're outside of surveillance range, I have no reason to stop you."

This time he was *sure* he heard the laugh. "You know about that Detyen colony in the Consortium?"

14

"Yes." The Consortium was a system of several planets mostly ruled by humans. They'd been abducted from their home world over centuries and set up their own civilization which welcomed almost any race. Raze had never been, the legion tended to stay in less populated areas of space unless a mission called for something else.

"They say that one of the leaders there found his denya." Toran spoke so quietly that Raze almost had to strain to hear.

"It does still happen." Even among the legion, a few had found their mates.

"She's human."

Those two words froze Raze in place, rooting him to the ground. "What?" Something like curiosity nipped at his mind.

"A human denya." Wonder filled Toran's voice at the thought. "Mated to a Detyen. I don't know if it's just a fluke. Maybe she's not all human. But wouldn't that be..." he trailed off.

"Why now? Detyens have had some contact with humans for a long time. Why did none find a mate among them until now? This sounds like a story, a legend." Though humanity's expansion into space hadn't begun in earnest until after the destruction of Detya, there'd been some level of contact for centuries, whether through the Consortium or humans abducted from their home planet. Raze had never heard of a human becoming mated to a Detyen in that time.

"You mean like warriors who give up their emotions to live longer than a biologically mandated death sentence?" Even he could recognize the sarcasm dripping from Toran's words.

"Toran... don't get your hopes up." If he'd heard this story three years ago, Raze could only imagine how he would have felt. And how he'd have been crushed as his birthday approached and that hope was snuffed out again.

"Aw, I'd almost think you were worried for me." Toran placed a hand on his shoulder and gave him a friendly squeeze. Raze sat still and took it. Contact didn't exactly hurt, but it reminded him of things that were no longer his.

"I would be." If he still had the capacity.

A beep cut through their conversation and Toran's wrist communicator lit up. He sighed. "I need to go check on Kayde. He's due for an eval."

"And me?" He and Kayde needed to be closely monitored to ensure that they didn't compromise the mission. Toran would run through basic diagnostics on a daily basis while they could spare the time.

But his fellow Detyen only shook his head. "You're good. I'll see you later."

Raze let him go without another farewell. He sat there for a long time staring at the warming block and considering everything that had just been said. Thankfully, he could not hope and he could not regret. He didn't know what he'd do with the information Toran had given him if that were the case. And the hollow core in his chest might have ripped open and bled if he could feel anything other than the mildest pang of longing.

***

"I've got us landing by this piece of crap old ship," Jo said as they orbited Fenryr a final time. "Should give us good cover from any surveillance. This craft is small enough that they'll just think we're another piece of debris."

Unlike the departure from Earth, Sierra was strapped to her seat in the cockpit for their entry into the potentially hostile planet. She had her blasters strapped to her sides, communications devices secured, and a first aid kit within reach if they needed it. All signs indicated that the slavers and pirates had no idea they were coming, but she liked to be prepared in case the cold mission turned hot. That was a lesson she'd only needed to learn once.

"Entry path is clear," Mindy confirmed. The navigation visor covered half of her head, feeding her information from the hundreds of sensors studded to the outside of their craft.

"Affirmative. Entering orbit in thirty seconds."

Anticipation bubbled in Sierra's veins. A feeling of restless uselessness had been dogging her for the entire flight. She could take over either Jo's or Mindy's position and do an adequate job if the circumstances called for it, but everything had gone off without a hitch so far, leaving her sitting on her ass for the past three days. That was a *good* thing, she reminded herself. Still, it was just about her time to shine.

Best navigator. Best pilot.

And now, it was time for the best operative to get into position.

She didn't say anything while Jo concentrated on getting them through the atmosphere at a blistering pace. They came in hot in the hopes that any sensors would read them as a meteorite, rather than a hostile ship. Once they were in place, they'd split, with Jo guarding the ship, Mindy finding high ground to run surveillance, and Sierra getting up close and personal with the kinds of assholes who thought it was okay to steal and sell people. Well, as up close and personal as a person could get without actually being seen or sensed in any way by the enemy.

With a final jolt, they punched through the atmosphere and crashed down in what felt like a free fall. Sierra gripped the armrests of her chair hard enough to hurt her fingers and her jaw ached from being clenched so tight. *Jo's the best,* she reminded herself. *This is all going to plan.*

That didn't make the semi-controlled landing *feel* any safer though. But in a matter of minutes they were out of the sky and nestled into a rocky outcropping within sight of the shipyard.

"They must be stripping these pieces of junk," Mindy said as she leaned forward to get a better view through the screen. "That guy over there has to be more than a hundred years old. God, the tech must *suck*."

Jo started to scoff but the noise lodged in her throat.

"What?" Mindy demanded.

"That's an XA model from the Oscavian Empire. It's not some dinky Earth ship that could barely make it out of the solar system without a malfunction. Some of the best ships in the galaxy are old as fuck. Just because humans haven't been travelling for millennia doesn't mean the rest of space is so far behind." Jo, too, leaned forward, but from what Sierra saw of her face, she wasn't disappointed by the old ships. She looked like a kid in a candy store.

"We don't have time for sightseeing," Sierra reminded them as she undid her safety harness. "I want our scans done ASAP. The sun is getting low and I don't want to lose the light."

Both women whipped around and glared at her. Sierra sent them a smirk. Not much could get her navigator and her pilot on the same side, she'd need to remember this for the future.

Despite the glares, they got to work while Sierra got ready. While her goal was to remain unseen by any of the planet's inhabitants, she knew she couldn't count on it. Most of the human women on Fenryr would be caged and possibly collared. But Sierra wasn't about to dress herself up as a slave. While media shows back home liked to portray slavers and pirates as barbarians, from experience Sierra knew they didn't look all that different from the mercenaries she'd worked with on various jobs. Knives went into sheathes on her arms and around her waist. She pulled an old synth-leather jacket out of her luggage and slid it over her shoulders. Heavy, tight pants and thick boots gave her protection from the elements and some weapons, and a dark knit hat covered her hair, disguising the burnt umber tone. If they'd been on a space station or some civilized place, she might have taken the time to do up her makeup and play up the sexy vibe. But Fenryr 1 wasn't designed for socializing, and she was here for business.

When she came out of her quarters, Jo looked her up and down and gave a licentious whistle. "If you showed up at a bar back home looking like that, I might just buy you a drink."

Sierra laughed and shook her head. "You just like that I look like I could kick your ass."

"Well, yeah." When Mindy came up behind Sierra, Jo's face shuttered and she turned back to the console. "Scans are finished. There's activity to the south, but we should be out of their range. If anything comes up, I'll follow protocol to evade them and protect the ship." She handed over two bracelets. "The locators are working well. If the light turns red, I'm heading your way. Standard call procedure if you need a pick up."

Sierra slipped on the bracelet and saw Mindy do the same. "Good luck, be safe," she told her team. "Let's get this done."

Chapter Three

Something about what Toran said the night before nipped at Raze's conscience, but when he woke up the next morning, he pushed the thoughts aside. So what if human mates had been discovered? It couldn't change his situation. He'd given up the part of himself that could sense or care for a mate, so even if she did exist, he'd never know. That, at least, was a small comfort. If he could sense his mate and never claim her, he'd go over the edge for sure. And while he had little life to live, his will to survive still pushed him forward every day.

The three Detyens took down their camp and covered any hint that they'd spent the night in the area. Once that was done, they took off on foot, heading closer to their destination in silence. Raze kept his mind alert as they moved. In the distance he saw a ship flying, but it headed away from them. Even if its sensors detected life, it was unlikely to check them out.

As the suns rose high overhead, sweat dripped down Raze's neck and clung to his top. Removing a layer would be more comfortable, but he couldn't risk it when they could come under enemy fire at any moment. Even Kayde seemed bothered by the heat. He placed his fingers in the collar of his shirt and pulled, trying to circulate some air. Though his face remained impassive, his lip twitched and he gave up the effort after a moment.

They came to a rise in the land and moved carefully, unable to see the path ahead of them. The caution was warranted. As soon as Toran cleared the hill, a shout rang out and he cursed, dropping down low and waving at Raze and Toran to do the same. They did without question.

Crawling on his elbows and knees, Raze moved closer until he could see what Toran saw. He would have cursed too. Ten pirates, armed to the teeth, were running their way. One of them clutched something that might have been a perimeter drone, specifically, one of the drones that Toran was using to ensure that they weren't seen. They were almost impossible to detect.

Almost.

"Engage your camouflage and try to flank them. We can't let them call in any backup." Toran kept his gaze glued to the pirates while he gave the command.

Raze slunk back, making space for Kayde to take up his position. Under other circumstances, they may have been able to get away from the engagement without any bloodshed, but the drone changed things. It was military grade and didn't belong on this planet. If the pirates called for backup, the mission would be compromised in no time. They were too close to the shipyard to be discovered now.

The camouflage in his uniform made him blend in seamlessly with the area around him, but the battery wouldn't last more than an hour before needing a charge and constant use caused the tech to overheat and malfunction. Raze noted the time he'd engaged and moved slowly, following Toran's orders. As he got closer, he counted the pirates again and confirmed that there were ten, all armed and ready to shoot at anything that moved. Raze couldn't use his own blaster until he was in position, and he spotted at least two las cannons among the pirate's weapons. They wouldn't need to see him to kill him with those. One blast in his vicinity and he'd be cut in half by the searing flames.

Shouts rang out as the pirates climbed the hill where Toran and Kayde had waited. He didn't spare a glance, his men needed a distraction to handle the problem. He couldn't take out the enemy before anyone else was in danger. All he could do was his own job. And to do that, he needed cover. The moss all over the place was no good—even if he laid down he'd still stick out. But the territory here was even rockier than where they'd bedded down for the night. He found what he needed a short jog away. Three towers of stone, close enough to dart between if he was spotted while giving him room to move if the pirates had any friends coming up behind him.

He disengaged his camouflage and grabbed his weapon. Rather than aim for the men still rapidly climbing the hill, he sent a charged shot to a moss-covered rock behind the men. It exploded, the wet moss smoking wildly and making visibility hazy. He sent another shot and watched it blow a hole in what he'd thought was a rock but must have been a fallen tree of some kind.

The pirates didn't scatter, instead falling into a formation that suggested they had some sort of training and discipline. It wouldn't save them. Not against three warriors of the Detyen Legion on a mission to finally discover who or what had destroyed their homeland.

Raze aimed his weapon, but the smoke was too much for him to risk firing. He couldn't get a shot, could barely see the outlines of bodies scattered on the ground. When the blaster fire subsided, he engaged his comms, calling up Toran for confirmation of his next move. But his comms were strangely silent, the barely audible hiss that indicated an open line too quiet.

"Toran, are you there?" he requested.

Toran didn't respond and Raze tried to call again. Still nothing.

The smoke began to clear and Raze counted the bodies lying on the ground. The number was difficult to discern. Someone had lost control of a las cannon and body parts were flung about. He counted seven heads on the ground. Potentially three survivors. And no response from Toran or Kayde. Raze waited a few minutes more to see if the clearing air revealed any more heads or if he saw movement from the pirates or his fellows. But all was still on the hill. The bodies needed to be hidden before the pirates and slavers could find them, and he needed to find Toran and Kayde to ensure they were safe and continue the mission. There weren't enough Detyens left in the legion, they couldn't afford to lose anyone else.

That was his only concern, he tried to tell himself. But the warring priorities buzzed in his head, freezing him in place. *This* was why the soulless didn't lead. Both objectives were equally important: hide the bodies, find the men. And Raze didn't know which one he should do first.

Calm down, Raze. He could almost hear his younger brother, Dryce, speaking to him. *You can do this, just pick one.* He'd said that at their first meeting after Raze lost his soul when he'd needed to choose a meal in the mess. Raze had frozen in place, unable to choose between one dish and another since neither held any significance to him. He didn't crave the taste or texture and they had the same nutritional value. Neither was better or worse than the other.

Bodies first.

Toran and Kayde could be right there, injured or simply with malfunctioning comms devices. If Raze went to deal with the bodies, then he could find out whether that was true or not. And if it wasn't, he'd use any information he found on the bodies to hunt down Toran and Kayde and recover them before continuing with the mission.

Plan in hand, he took off at a fast clip, almost choking on the rotted stench of the smoke as he ran through it. Whatever that moss was made of, it smelled terrible, like fish guts and bile that had been left out in the suns for weeks.

He climbed the rise with care, weapon in hand and senses alert. But the only sound was of the gentle breeze and the dying fire. He didn't hear Kayde or Toran, and there was no sign of the surviving men. Raze studied the spot on the hill where they'd crouched only minutes ago. A small patch of green caught his eye and he knelt down, placing his hand in the sticky fluid.

Detyen blood. Not enough for a killing blow, but one or both of the men was injured and in the hands of the enemy.

The mission had just changed. The ship and data on it could wait. He needed to find his men, make sure they were okay, and kill whoever he needed to make sure that they posed no threat to any of his people ever again.

***

Sierra cursed and dove for cover when the weapons started firing. She tried to call Mindy over the comm, but something was up with the signal and all she heard from her ear piece was silence. The moss that seemed to be everywhere didn't offer much in the way of cover, but a large boulder was enough to squat behind to wait out the firefight. She tried to get a look around to see if she was in anyone's sights, but the band of pirates climbing the hill off in the distance seemed more concerned with the blaster fire coming from their front and the explosive charged shots aimed at their rear.

Trouble in paradise? Intel hadn't said anything about factional violence, but pirates and slavers weren't the most forgiving bunch.

She'd keep her eyes peeled for any other signs of trouble, but this could just as easily be some dumb squabble.

Smoke stung her eyes and the stench made her gag. What the fuck was the damn moss made of? She was far enough away that she didn't have trouble breathing, but that didn't help when she still wanted to throw up from how bad it smelled. While the smoke grew thicker, the sound of blaster fire cut off. A few strangled moans echoed eerily across the rocks near her, but otherwise it was silent. She tried her comm again, but still nothing. She was still close enough to the shipyard that she suspected something there might be causing interference.

Sierra waited to see who came out the winner of the firefight. Her fingers itched to grab her blaster and finish off the unsuspecting champions. Chances were, anyone who found the bodies would think they'd all done each other in. But she kept her hands off her blaster. That wasn't the mission and she wasn't going to screw this up and endanger the women who'd been captured. The information she gathered out here could be instrumental to freeing them.

Minutes ticked by and nobody moved. Maybe they *had* finished each other off, but something was bugging her, something was *off*. Sure, pirates fought all the time in space, but whoever was living here had to be living under some sort of organization. They might not have any law or military, but they wouldn't have lasted a year if gangs of a dozen men got into fire fights with any regularity. And that had been some heavy duty weaponry. Despite the stench of the smoke, she caught a hint of the burning ozone smell of las fire. That shit meant business. It could eat through just about anything and had only one use: destruction. A blaster fight between rivals? That she could understand. But bringing a las cannon to this kind of battle showed they meant business.

Maybe this was all part of some leadership challenge and the place was on the brink of war. Given the intel they had, that might be why the pirates were moving on. But one fight wasn't enough to think that was true. Not yet. She pushed the thought to the back of her mind with a note to keep an eye out for anything that might be relevant, and then she was on the move.

She didn't make it far before darting back behind her boulder as some of the survivors started moving. She grabbed binoculars from her belt and slipped the sleek glasses on. She spotted three men in gear not that dissimilar from her own. One had a blaster out while the other two dragged two other men, one with golden skin and the other a greenish blue. Two of the slavers were human, the other a humanoid with purple skin and no hair. Oscavian if she had to guess from this distance. She couldn't identify the species of the guys being dragged, but that didn't matter for the moment.

They moved with the slick efficiency of those accustomed to stealing people, and though Sierra was watching them closely, they disappeared between one blink and the next.

What the hell?

She refocused her binoculars, but it was like they'd never existed. All that was left in their place was the haze of smoke and a pile of dead bodies. Curiosity urged her closer. Though it was a trait that served her well in her line of work, Sierra forced herself to stay still. Unless there was a hidden entrance or a stashed vehicle of some kind over there, those slavers hadn't just disappeared. There were types of camouflage that could disguise people like that, and she didn't want to march on up there if she couldn't see them. Besides, it wasn't her problem.

Just as she was ready to move again, she caught movement coming from the other direction. Though most of him was obscured by his clothing, she caught a hint of light green skin on his face and hands. She pressed the button on the side of the binoculars to take a recording. If the AI system couldn't identify him, maybe Jo or Mindy would recognize his kind.

Something rooted her in place as she watched him cross the killing field and climb the short hill with the self-assurance of a man who thought he was invulnerable to blaster fire. He barely spared a glance for the dead bodies of his fellow slavers, but why would he? Pirates and slavers were a heartless lot, and he'd been one of the guys firing at them. Hell, she was surprised he wasn't grinning from ear to ear. She couldn't quite make out the details of his face, but there definitely wasn't a grin. She couldn't see any expression at all.

Her heart clenched and Sierra shook her head to clear the unwanted thought. She could barely see the guy, let alone read his emotions from almost indecipherable expressions. For all she knew, he'd eaten a bad sandwich for lunch and was trying to keep from throwing up.

He crested the hill and froze in place. Sierra wanted so badly to stay and see what he did that she forced herself to turn away. She needed to continue on to the coordinates where the slavers were keeping the women and plant her surveillance gear. The sooner she had that information, the sooner they could work to get the women to safety.

The first step was the hardest, when something in her chest was tugging at her to turn back around and... well, she wasn't sure what she was supposed to do. She only knew that she didn't want to leave. But that was too bad. He was just some pirate, better off dead or caught in a power struggle. And there was no reason for her to tell him that his buddies had been dragged off by survivors. No reason to offer help.

That was crazy talk, and finally got her feet moving away.

Chapter Four

Nothing. No scent, no tracks, no more blood. Nothing that would tell Raze where Toran and Kayde were. He recounted the bodies they'd left behind and was sure that only seven of the ten pirates they'd encountered were there. He spared a minute to dig out his information tablet to try and call up the trackers that Toran and Kayde were both wearing. Neither of them came up, but neither did his own, which meant that whatever was interfering with the signal in their comms was also interfering with the tracker. He stuffed the tablet back in his pocket and turned his attention to the bodies.

It was grueling work to make them disappear. The ground was too rocky to easily dig a pit, but he got lucky. A little more than a hundred meters from the hill there was a moss covered bog and a quick scan showed that it was deep enough to make seven men disappear, at least for a little while. It didn't matter if they were discovered after he'd retrieved his men and they'd completed the mission. The bodies just needed to stay gone long enough for them to get off the planet without being found.

By the time he finished he was covered in sweat and his muscles ached. Each of the slavers was covered in muscles and many of them were just as big as he was. The work took hours and the suns were beginning to set. But he couldn't take the time to find a place to camp. He needed to get a signal and see if he could call up information on the trackers. If not, he'd need to figure out another way to find them. Raze called up his scheduler and set the time. Protocol gave him seventy-two hours to act in his own capacity without reporting back if Toran and Kayde were incapacitated. If he didn't find them before that, he'd need to return to the ship and get orders from HQ.

But as soon as Raze put the scheduler away, he let that thought slip from his mind. He would find his fellow soldiers.

He searched the area methodically after setting a drone to scan for any other hostile forces in the area. But it seemed that the group they'd encountered was the only danger for the moment. He covered every centimeter of the hill and the area beyond it, what would have been out of sight when he was shooting from beyond the rocks.

Nothing.

No more blood. No tracks. No clues. If he hadn't been nearby for the entire encounter, he might have believed that a stealth ship of some kind had taken them hostage. If that were the case, he had no prayer of finding them. He had to examine his other options, the ones he could do something about.

Raze turned around. Night had fallen, but the moon in the sky overhead was bright enough to see by. His bones were heavy from the long trek and the exertion of disposing of the pirates, but he could go for a long time before collapsing, days perhaps. He let the pain and weight of the day lay heavy on him and held the physical sensation close. It wasn't emotion, but it was as close as he could get now.

He gave up on the hill and fanned out. While there were no clues at the abduction site, that didn't mean that all hope was lost. A few hundred meters away he found tracks that had pressed hard into the mossy ground, as if a heavy vehicle had sat there for some time. The tracks headed toward the hill before disappearing, he discovered as he walked alongside them a second time. They disappeared so quickly that the vehicle must have engaged its hover mode.

It wasn't enough evidence, not yet, but he was willing to think that *this* had been the vehicle used to take Kayde and Toran.

He took out the mostly destroyed drone that the pirates had discovered and checked to see if any of the memory or display function had survived. They were sturdy beasts, meant to work through the toughest conditions that a habitable planet could offer. And while they could be destroyed by a determined person, it took a little know how to truly damage them beyond use.

The pirates lacked that know how.

It wouldn't fly again, not without significant repairs, but the memory drive and holo display had survived well enough that Raze could view what the drone had picked up before and during the fight. He found a boulder that came up to his waist and set the drone down, engaging the display and quickly navigating through hours of data that were useless to him.

There.

The drone shook as something struck it and air whooshed by in a dizzying drop as it felt to the ground. He didn't get a good look at the pirates, not with the machine so unstable, but he'd found the time he needed. He let it play through slowly and shut off any thoughts he had of the battle. This was an entirely new, if disorienting, perspective and he didn't need his preconceived thoughts interfering.

At some point in the fight, the drone had fallen out of the hands of the pirate who was holding it and the angle was all wrong to see what happened to Toran and Kayde. But Raze let the holo play through in case there was anything that could help.

It took several minutes, though at the end of it all, the fight had taken less than a quarter of an hour. Skirmishes were always shorter than he'd thought they'd be before he became a warrior.

He didn't see the survivors who took Toran and Kayde. He didn't see most of the battle. But the holo feed gave him something just as important. A witness. It was a brief hint of a moment. She— and he was almost certain the pirate he saw was a she—ducked out from behind a stone pile and made her way closer to the fight. Raze enhanced the display, making it larger in hopes of getting a better view of her.

Dark leathers, bound hair, pale skin. Human, he thought, though the image was blurry enough that he could be wrong. His gut said he was right, though. A human female pirate who'd witnessed the whole thing.

She seemed to freeze after the fight, watching out for something. Did she see the pirates take his team? She walked away after several minutes of watching and he could not see any emotion on her face. Did the sight of her dead fellows make her feel... anything? Or was she just another heartless pirate bent on destruction and pillage?

This was a slave colony, he reminded himself. The pirates and slavers worked together to sell people to the highest bidder, which made this woman, this witness, one of the worst scum in the universe. He could do whatever he needed to get the information he was after.

His focus sharpened, noting the path she used to escape. He found it easily after stashing the drone away where it was unlikely to be found. It was too big to be easily carried.

Before setting off on the journey to find the pirate woman, he forced himself to eat a nutrient bar and take a half an hour to rest. Night was all around and if Toran were here, he'd be ordering Raze to take the entire night. But Toran was gone, captured and possibly undergoing torture or worse. The longer Raze waited, the longer they suffered and the longer it would be before they could complete their mission.

The time passed in silence with no animals or insects crying in the night. Once upon a time, he might have found that eerie, but now he merely noted the fact as he sat as silent as the night. Once his food digested and his limbs no longer threatened to give out from the stress of the day, he pushed himself to his feet and continued on, chasing down his lead.

Tracking a stranger on a strange planet at night was no easy task. But he'd find her or die trying.

***

She was so close she could taste it. As night fell, it got trickier to move around, but Sierra used the cover of darkness to her advantage. She moved with stealth, cloaked in shadows, unseen and unnoticed, taking stock of her surroundings and looking for points of attack and extraction that could be used when a team came in to recover the stolen women.

The static crackling in her ear was a welcome reminder that she'd made contact with Mindy after getting away from that dead zone. Dead in more ways than one. She idly wondered what had happened to the surviving pirate that she'd seen. Had he called help for his friends? Or was he now gathering allies to make a move against some weakened faction on this hell planet?

That kind of information needed to go in her report. She wouldn't add that she'd wondered what color eyes he had or if he was as strong as he looked from a distance, wondered if he could lift her up with little effort while he—

Nope, she wasn't going there. Pirate, she reminded herself. Pirate. Evil, bad, slaver, killer. Not a sexy alien dude who could fulfill some of the fantasies she didn't even let herself think about while she was still on Earth. Besides, he probably wasn't nearly as hot as he'd seemed from a distance. His teeth were probably all rotten out and he might have been all slimy and gross.

Alien-human relationships were becoming more common on Earth as more aliens migrated to the planet, but Sierra was going to have to draw her personal line at gross alien-frog man slavers.

She didn't know why she couldn't quite get him out of her head. Every step she took, every time she dodged away to hide from a patrol, every crevasse she hid in to get a better vantage to spy on the slaver settlement, he was squatting in the back of her mind, uninvited and unwanted, but she was unable to get rid of him.

Night had fallen in truth now and Sierra needed a place to hide for a few hours. At the moment she was close enough to hear the moans and screams of the captured women and her heart tore in half at the sounds. She wanted to rush in, open the gates, and set them free. But that would only end up with her dead or captured, doomed alongside them.

The slavers were enjoying dinner and... entertainment. She tried not to think too hard about what that entertainment consisted of, even as the screams gave her little doubt. But given a few hours of revelry, they'd be at their weakest, the watches minimal, the alcohol and drugs consumed, and the men, women, and other beings tired out from the partying. All she had to do was stay hidden for long enough and then she'd have plenty of time to gather data at the safest point of night.

She ended up on the middle branch of a squat tree on a hill near the settlement. There hadn't been tree cover for most of her journey here, but around the settlement, there was a veritable forest of new growth. It might have helped with the air quality, or maybe they just liked the decoration, she neither knew nor cared. She took a few surveillance photos and settled in for the wait.

Would her— no, not *her*, what the fuck—*that* pirate show up here? Would she see him again? For a moment she imagined him showing up, guns blazing, in a reveal that he'd been a double agent all along. She shook her head with an embarrassed smile. There had to be something weird in the air here to have her thinking such crazy thoughts. She'd never before caught a glance of a dude on a mission—let alone an enemy—and started daydreaming.

But she wanted to know his name, and his species, and if they were biologically compatible. She wanted him to not be a pirate, to be an ally she'd never imagined finding. She wanted...

Okay, when she got back to Earth, she was going to get laid. This was fucking nuts. Thank every god out there that neither Mindy nor Jo could see her now. They'd be giving her so much shit. And she would 100% deserve it.

Crazy space air. There was probably sex pollen here, or sex moss, something that made her think of sex when it was beyond inappropriate. Something beyond hormones denied for far too long.

"I've detected movement three hundred meters away," Mindy came in over the comms, almost like she could detect what Sierra had been thinking.

"Heading this way?" Sierra whispered back. The night wasn't silent; wind whipped around her and the revelry and terror from the settlement was carried with it. But she couldn't be too careful. A tree didn't provide *that* much cover.

"Affirmative. Suggest you find a different position to the north of your current location." Mindy was monitoring everything through a mix of a hijacked satellite feed and drone footage. They could have gathered most of the relevant information from her surveillance alone, but there was no use in wasting a trip of so many light years and not getting human eyes on the location.

"Copy that." Sierra climbed to the edge of the branch and tried to see if she could spot the patrol that Mindy had warned her about. It was too dark and they were too far away, but that gave her the advantage. She clambered down quickly and made her move, keeping to the deepest shadows cast by trees, rocks, and buildings. Either drone and electronic security was too expensive, or the slavers just didn't care, but it was her saving grace. She could evade people far more easily than she could technology.

But she couldn't defend against a blow that she didn't see coming. The skin on the back of her neck prickled, but before Sierra could even think to turn around and scan her surroundings, something punched her spine and she fell to her knees, the world around her blotted out to darkness.

***

She came to with a splitting headache and her nerves crackling from the stun blast. It wasn't the first or the tenth time that she'd been shot, but it hurt like hell every time and she wanted to turn over and curl up into a ball to stop the pain. But Sierra held herself still, trying to keep her breathing even. One eye opened a crack and she saw everything through a veil of eyelashes.

Everything wasn't much. The stars sparkled in the sky above. She'd need to move her head to see anything more than that sliver of freedom. The silence in her ear wasn't a good sign. Normally she couldn't feel the communicator that rested snugly against her skin, but it always gave off a faint noise when she was in range, like a very subtle ringing in her ears. She wanted to reach up and feel if the device was still there, but if she was under guard, she didn't want *that* to be what alerted her captors to her consciousness.

Not if she could find a weapon.

For some reason her hands weren't bound, and she hoped that was a sign of general incompetence. She let her fingers dig into the ground at her sides, searching for a rock or a piece of glass or anything she could use to bludgeon a slaver bent on making her his. All there was under her fingers was loose dirt and gravel. She curled a fist around some, deciding it was better than nothing.

She didn't hear the sounds of the revelry, which meant it was either later than she thought, or she'd been dragged far away.

A shuffle to her right caught her attention and she gave up the pretense of unconsciousness and opened her eyes as she turned. Shock rocked through her as her eyes locked with the green alien slaver she'd seen earlier that day. He was tall, at least six inches taller than her. He kept his dark hair short, but her fingers itched to touch it, which was one of those crazy impulses that was going to get her killed one day. Under his thick clothes, he looked built enough to bench press a small car and he carried himself with a predatory grace she might have found attractive back on Earth. But not from a slaver. She had to be suffering from a concussion or oxygen deprivation to be thinking like this now. He froze, a length of rope in hand, his dark eyes intent on her. For a moment, she thought she saw a flash of red, but it must have been a trick of the moonlight.

I know you.

What? No she didn't. He was a fucking slaver who was about to tie her up and have his way with her. That was *not* how she was about to spend this mission, especially if she couldn't rely on her comms.

She flung the dirt and gravel straight at his face and sprang to her feet, taking off in a run. She'd figure out where she was later, she just needed to get away, out of range of his blaster. She expected shouting or a curse and the silence was so unnerving that she had to turn around to make sure he was actually on her tail.

Yup, there he was, right behind her, his long legs eating up the distance between them like it was nothing.

She sped up, but despair blossomed in her chest. There was no way she was going to make it to safety. She was screwed.

***

A shock of *something* ripped through Raze in that moment when their eyes locked. He faltered and pain scored his chest as if claws raked him from shoulder to hip. In a blink it was gone as the pirate woman flung grit at him with astonishing accuracy and was off running like an Oscavian hound was on her heels. He stumbled for a moment, heart pounding so hard it threatened to beat out of his chest.

He clenched his fists and for one crazy second his claws threatened to slide out of his hands as something they couldn't define washed over him.

Find her, that foreign urge demanded. Protect her. Claim her.

33

He could almost feel it, could almost recognize what it was, but his mind rejected the impossibility even before his feet moved and the chase was on. He didn't pull out his blaster. Though the pirate had quickly recovered from the stun, far more quickly than he'd thought possible, two shots in such a short amount of time might do permanent harm to her. Why he cared about that, he wasn't sure, but his gun remained in its holster all the same.

She glanced back and that was her undoing. He had height on her, and endurance. He could run for days and not give in to exhaustion or pain. No pirate training was a match for a Detyen warrior.

Though he wondered why she hadn't cried out, hadn't tried to raise an alarm. Surely she must have some allies in the nearby settlement. They were probably too far away to be heard, but didn't creatures such as she rely on hope like that for survival? Or were her enemies too numerous that she doubted help would come?

He closed the distance between them in easy strides until he could almost reach her with a swipe of his arm. Just as he launched the final step, she dropped and rolled to the side, her hand coming up with a small knife he must have missed on her person.

"Fucking pirate scum," she spat as she rolled to her feet, knife held confidently in her hand and absolute disgust written across her features.

Pirate scum? "You're the pirate," he replied without thought, keeping his distance. His claws should be out now, with her on her back at his mercy, her cheeks flushed and breath coming in hard as she panted under him. What *that* stirred froze him in place, his body rocking with sensation he hadn't known in years, sensation he could barely remember.

The distraction cost him and she took advantage, swiping in with the knife in a move that showed practice and training to rival his own. His instincts took over and he rolled with her, taking her arm and flipping her as she cut a ragged wound across his shoulder. The hot flash of pain brought his focus back and they rolled together, neither able to take a position of advantage on the ground.

The woman—not a pirate?—sprang back up and jumped on the balls of her feet, those cheeks flushed like he'd imagined and her eyes glinting bright in the moonlight. "Of course a giant like you isn't going to make it easy for me. What are you, anyway?" The run and the fight hadn't winded her and as his subdermal translator worked, he realized she wasn't speaking IC, interstellar common. His translator identified her language of origin as English, an Earth language. Strange.

Remaining silent would frustrate her, but Raze couldn't stop himself from answering. "Detyen." He should have kept it hidden in case she escaped and reported back, but he found himself wanting to talk to her, and he hadn't wanted anything in so long that he couldn't deny this one simple thing.

She blew at an errant strand of hair, ruby red in the moonlight, as her eyes narrowed. Her eyes flicked down to his hip, where his blaster remained holstered. The distance between them wasn't long, both of them standing just out of reach of one another, but it might as well have been a deep chasm. "Why aren't you shooting me?"

"I don't—" he couldn't finish the sentence. He didn't know *how* to finish the sentence. In the last ten minutes, he'd been more alive than he'd been in two years and his control was shot. If Toran or Kayde saw him, they'd order him put down in a second, and he'd deserve it. He wasn't thinking clearly, wasn't operating at acceptable capacity. He wanted to... he *wanted* and for a soulless Detyen, there could be nothing worse.

That narrowed gaze of hers relaxed a fraction and she took a step back, her knife still out, but the hold not quite as threatening as it had been only a moment ago.

They stared at one another, neither sure of what action to take. No, Raze knew what he should do, what he must do. Anything that would give him the information he needed about his men so that he could retrieve them and complete the mission, find the data they'd been assigned to retrieve and return home to his bleak existence, where nothing awaited him except years more of gray emptiness until he came to his natural end by his own hand or that of his fellow soldiers.

And that should bring up no reaction in him except acceptance. He'd chosen the path when he let his soul be ripped apart in the name of the survival of his people.

But in this endless moment between him and this strange woman, he wished that he'd taken another path, one he'd never realized was there in the first place.

The woman broke him out of his daze. "You're not a pirate, are you?"

Before he could answer, he caught a hint of movement and light out of the corner of his eye. He moved without thought, launching himself at the woman and tackling her to the ground, his hand clasping her wrist and keeping the knife away from anything important. For a moment, their hands met, skin to skin, and agony ripped through his body and he held it close with a silent scream.

Chapter Five

Now would be a good time to start fighting back against the too big, too sexy alien laying atop her like they'd just gone a sweaty round in her quarters and he was gearing up for round two. Or three. She shifted her hips, her legs splaying for a moment in something that might have been invitation before her brain caught up with what the fuck was going on.

What that fuck was? She had no clue, but it was all kinds of wrong and it had her heart beating and her body on fire in a way it had never been before.

An unwanted thrill went through her as she struggled against him, trying to wrench her wrist, and her knife, back under her own control. But this alien held her down like she was nothing. If it weren't for her training, she might have been scared, but fear had no place in a fight like this. That was for later, for when she was evaluating everything that had gone wrong and right, everything she could do better.

And that evaluation of this encounter was going to be one hell of a doozy because she still had no idea what the hell was going on.

"Patrol," he hissed in her ear. "Stay still if you want to live." And, no, an excited spark didn't race down her spine from his gravelly, strangely flat, voice. He almost sounded like one of the androids she'd worked with back home. They never quite got the emotions right on those bots, making them hollow simulacrums of real people. But this guy was real, she could feel almost *all* of his reality pressed up against her and if she shifted just enough, he'd be cradled between her thighs.

Well, provided they were biologically compatible. Which she kind of thought they were. Damn tactical gear getting in the way made that impossible to tell.

No, focus. She needed to get a damn grip. A light flashed off in the distance, one of the patrols doing its rounds. If her comms were working she could have known they were coming, could have used that distraction to her advantage. She tried to move her hand, the one not clamped to the ground, but her captor captured that one as well.

"Not going to hit you," she spat out on a sharp whisper.

His face was flat, unreadable, nothing but darkness swirling in those black eyes of his. What would he look like in daylight? Why did she care?

The light went away, the patrol not finding them. Still, her pirate didn't give up. But if he was a pirate, why had he hidden her from the patrol? "Who *are* you?" she asked, and there were so many questions piled into that word that she wasn't sure what she wanted him to answer first. Detyen wasn't enough. She wanted, no, *needed*, everything he could give.

And that meant she'd gone crazy. Maybe she was still unconscious and this was all some weird, blaster-induced fantasy. She was going to wake up in a few minutes and never speak of this again. Not at all. Nope. Mindy would want the details and Jo would laugh at her. But even as the thought flitted against her mind, she knew it was wrong. This guy was *way* too solid to be some kind of fantasy.

"Raze," he said, and that must have been his name. "Who are *you*?" Something flashed in his eyes there, that hint of red that disappeared between one blink and the next, so quickly that she might have been imagining it.

She wasn't supposed to give her name. What kind of spy would she be if she went off telling her identity to anyone who asked? But she couldn't have stopped the sound from slipping out if she tried. "Sierra."

He loosened his grip on her hands, paying little heed to the knife she still gripped. "Not a pirate," he said quietly, sitting back on his knees.

Sierra crawled backward and hid her own weapon away. "Not a pirate," she agreed. She shouldn't take his word for it. The only people on this planet were pirates and slavers, and that made them all consummate liars and thieves. But she couldn't *not* believe this guy, and that was the crux of the problem. They stared at each other, at a loss for what to do now that the fight had left them. She wished the light were better, sunlight instead of the moon. Even as bright as it was, the alien before her, Raze, was more shadow than person.

"Since we've settled that, I'll be on my way. I assume you won't tell me about your business." As long as he was working against the pirates, she didn't really care what he was doing. Their paths wouldn't cross again.

"No," said Raze. At first she thought he was agreeing about the business, but when she went to stand up, he grabbed her arm and pushed her back down. "You're staying."

Like hell she was. "I have my own shit to do. Let me go now or my knife comes back out." She should have never put it away in the first place, but that weird *something* about this guy made her not want to hurt him.

He ignored the threat. "I saw you earlier today. My men disappeared. Did you see anything?"

Was that what this was about? "There was no need to stun me for that," she said sharply. Though she would have never given the information to someone who actually was a slaver. "Three men took your guys. Two looked human, one might have been Oscavian. They were walking away and disappeared. Literally disappeared in the blink of an eye. That's all I saw."

He studied her for several seconds and it felt like she was under a microscope. Or being stalked by some jungle predator that had gone extinct a hundred years ago. His gaze was unnerving, too level, without a hint of what he was thinking or feeling. She was getting that android sense again, like he *didn't* feel, and that wasn't possible. How could a person not feel? Then again, he wasn't a person, he was an alien.

"Get up," he ordered.

She wanted to resist just because she could, but Sierra needed to be standing if they were about to fight. "Is that all?" she asked, unable to stop poking at him.

"You're coming with me." He said it like that was a reasonable request.

"Afraid not." He might be a big sexy alien who could throw her over his shoulder and have his way—or whatever—with her, but that didn't mean she was going to abandon her job when she was halfway through it.

39

"My men need to be found." Was he trying to convince her? Maybe if he didn't sound like an encyclopedia bot, listing off dry facts, then she might be swayed.

"And I wish you the best of luck. But that's not my job." Something compelled her to take a chance, to believe that he wouldn't do her harm if she walked away, despite all evidence to the contrary. Sierra took a step back and turned on her heel. She wasn't surprised when Raze caught up. He grabbed her hand to pull her back, but the damnedest thing happened.

A strangled sound caught in the back of his throat and he froze, pulling her in place. She glanced back and saw his eyes flare red, this time *definitely* not a trick of the light. His knees locked and he fell forward, into her, taking her down with him.

***

Agony. Blinding hope. Darkness.

Raze gasped and curled into himself as Sierra jerked her hand away from him. He couldn't move, couldn't defend himself. If she chose at that moment to stab him in the back, he would bleed out before he realized that he was finished. But her shadow came over him, blocking out the light of the moon. Her hands fluttered around, never touching him for more than a second and careful to avoid his bare skin. It was the most exquisite torture he could imagine, to be in reach of her, of that indefinable, impossible thing and to have it taken away before he could realize what it was.

His mind circled around a word, but it was so outlandish that he wouldn't let himself think it. He couldn't hope, and in this moment, that was more blessing than curse.

His hand burned where their fingers had met, but he had a driving impulse to reach out again and lace their fingers together and hold on through the pain, to ride it to the other side and see where that left him. Instinct blazed bright, demanding he take that path. But instinct wasn't the territory of the soulless, it was some vestigial limb that served no purpose.

After several long moments of searing pain, his breathing evened and the sensation faded to a dull ache inside of his chest. He sat up slowly and stared at Sierra, the human woman who'd witnessed his men being taken, the human woman who wounded him with a simple touch, the human woman who *almost* made him feel. His emotions were so close to the surface that if he reached out a hand, he thought he might be able to grasp onto them and gather them back. Instead, he turned away from that insanity, that instability.

The mission came first.

She studied him closely. "Does... that... happen a lot?" she asked after he had recovered himself. If it weren't ridiculous for her to care, he might have thought she sounded concerned for his safety.

"No," Raze responded, his voice back to its normal neutrality where it belonged. "I apologize if I disturbed you."

She gave a harsh laugh. "I was more concerned about whether I could find a place to hide your corpse, to be honest." That note of concern he'd detected before seemed even stronger. "And the last patrol came even closer, if I didn't have a dark blanket in my pack, they might have seen us."

"Patrol? When?" He couldn't have been in that strange condition for more than a few minutes.

"You were out for nearly half an hour. I think we're both lucky that you didn't scream." Now she sounded just as neutral as he did, and in someone with a soul, or whatever humans called that essential part of themselves, that was always a front. But why did she care?

"I can't scream," he found himself saying.

"Can't?"

Raze shrugged. "It is physically possible, but I no longer have the motivation." No fear, no anger. The only reason he had to raise his voice was to be heard in a loud environment.

"Motivation?" Sierra asked on a high note.

These were secrets of his people, things never spoken to outsiders. They couldn't understand the soulless and why a man would walk that path. But he could not stop himself from trying to explain to her. "I no longer feel emotion. It was a sacrifice made to lengthen my life."

She gasped and took a deep breath, letting it out slowly. "I..." she tried to speak, but trailed off.

Raze himself didn't know what else to say. His nerves were raw from the contact and the night grew short. "Come, if we start now we can make it back to the hill by daylight." He waved his hand at her, but was careful not to touch.

Sierra sputtered a laugh. "You may be emotionless, but you're also crazy. I'm not leaving here."

He should have brought the rope with him when he chased her. He could stun her again, but he didn't reach for his blaster. For some reason, he needed her to come with him willingly. "Please," he tried the request, though he could not remember the last time he'd said that word.

Sierra sighed. "Your little... freak out gave me time to think. If they were going to take your guys anywhere, wouldn't it be to the settlement?" She nodded her head towards the town. "I'm doing some recon. I can keep my eyes open, tell you if I see anything."

"And how would we communicate?" He didn't want to let her go, but she had a point.

"Set up a signal? Or a rendezvous? I don't like the idea of *anyone* being at these guys' mercy, and I know how to look for things. We can plan to meet up tomorrow night, right here. You can go back and see if there's any more evidence at the scene of the crime, I'll find out if they're being held in the village. Then we go our separate ways, no questions asked." She leaned back, sitting on her calves, her posture deceptively calm. He almost wanted to insist again that she come with him, just to see what she would do.

But no, he didn't want anything. He couldn't.

"I could go with you," he countered. He doubted there was anything more to see back at the hill, especially if she wasn't there with him to give him more detail about what she'd witnessed. "If we find the men, I'll help them escape and we go our separate ways."

She breathed deep, watching him for several seconds. Finally, her shadow nodded in the moonlight. "If we don't find them by tomorrow, we're done," she insisted.

He wasn't supposed to lie, that was one of those early lessons from his soulless days. But Raze nodded and said, "Very well," as if there was anything on this planet that would allow him to let her go.

Chapter Six

Okay, she was officially crazy. It took a little time to get ready to head back to the settlement, but when they crested the first hill, static crinkled in Sierra's ear and she almost pumped a fist in the air in celebration. Raze walked half a step in front of her and she wasn't sure if it was because he trusted her not to stab him in the back, or because he didn't trust her to lead him back to the village. How could *she* trust *him* based on his word alone? If she were actually one of the pirates, she would have lied her ass off to save her life.

He hadn't given her an explanation, hadn't told her what he and his men were here for. No, all he'd said was that he'd "sacrificed his emotions," whatever that meant, and now he was in search of his people.

"Sierra, do you read me?" Mindy said into the comms. It was so loud in the night that Sierra was concerned Raze would hear it. She might have believed that he wasn't going to hurt her, and she could believe that he wasn't a pirate. That didn't mean she was going to give up any weapon without a fight. She cleared her throat, hoping that Mindy would pick it up.

Raze glanced back at her. "Do you require hydration?" He spoke in that flat tone that was really beginning to grate.

"I'm fine here," she replied, hoping the response would work for both of her listeners.

He looked at her for a long moment, face completely placid, before looking away.

"Do you have company?" Mindy asked. "Do you need extraction?"

Shit. "Under control," she mumbled as quietly as possible.

Raze looked back at her again. "What was that?"

"I said that we have this under control. We'll find your men, I'll complete my mission, and then this will all be a less than pleasant memory." Exactly how bonkers did she sound repeating all this information? Now she almost wished that he had found and removed her comms, at least then she wouldn't be talking in circles.

"What's going on?" Mindy asked, somehow still not picking up on the fact that Sierra couldn't speak freely.

Raze had already begun walking, so Sierra caught up with him. She could wing this, and maybe get some necessary information. "Raze, wait up." He slowed a step until they walked side by side. It was quiet in the night, the sounds of revelry dampened by distance and the late hour. "You said you're Detyen, right? I'm not familiar. What's your home planet?"

"That is irrelevant to this partnership." He walked beside her silently, and if he hadn't claimed to feel no emotion, she would have said that he was tense.

"Detyen," Mindy said over the comms. "I'll look it up. Give me the sign if you need help. Going quiet."

Finally. Sierra hoped the relieved breath she let out didn't sound too weird. That breath turned into a yawn that she barely choked back and her jaw cracked when she got her mouth shut.

"Would you like to rest for a moment?" Raze asked, too conscious of her for her liking.

"I'm fine." Tired, but she'd live.

"You keep saying that."

"It keeps being true." She'd never been so talkative on a mission before, especially not in a mission in enemy territory. But something in her liked speaking with Raze, even if he was a granite block of unresponsiveness.

"A human yawn indicates exhaustion. If we are to succeed, you need to be in optimum condition. We should rest," Raze insisted in that infuriatingly flat voice.

"Do you have an encyclopedia entry on humans memorized?" she asked.

"Yes."

Oooookay. "I'm a little tired, not exhausted. You see, I was supposed to get some shut eye before some hulking beast of an alien decided it would be fun to fry me and drag me away to his little lair to have his way with me." Why did she have to go and say it like

45

that? Now all she could imagine was him looming over her in the dark, those intense black eyes of his drinking her up as he discovered her body with his hands and mouth.

There was a long pause before he said, "I don't have a lair." It came out quietly, almost confused. Definitely not flat.

Sierra kept her eyes straight and thanked the darkness. Unless he had super night vision he couldn't see her blush. "You still wanted to have your way with me." If she had one iota less training, she would have slapped her hand across her mouth to try and grab those words back. Was she *flirting* with him? The emotionless alien who was happy to kidnap her until she suggested a better plan? The man who would probably kill her if it seemed like the logical thing to do, whether she deserved it or not?

"I needed information," he said, "so, yes. I supposed I did have my way."

Thank God for translators. Whatever she'd said must have lost the playful tone, or maybe he just couldn't hear it. The smart thing now would be to just let this all lapse into silence, but something inside of Sierra couldn't do that. She wanted to know more, and since she'd only know him for a day before leaving this planet and never seeing him again, now was the time. "What did you mean when you said you sacrificed your emotions? Did you used to be able to feel?" That had to be too personal for a near stranger to ask, but the night and the mission fostered a false sense of intimacy and Sierra had always had bravado in spades. Still, she didn't expect Raze to answer. If she'd been asked something as nosy as that, she would have shut the conversation down in an instant.

But maybe the emotionless thing meant that Raze didn't sense those boundaries. He was quiet for a moment before speaking, his tone even and unbothered as it always was. "Yes, I felt emotion until I turned thirty. Two years ago. I made the choice of my own free will. There is nothing to regret about it. It simply now is."

She tried to imagine what it would be like to feel nothing and couldn't. But pity would be wasted on Raze. "Why did you need to do it? You said something about lengthening your life?" Lifespans differed among species, but given what she could see, Raze didn't look like he was on the verge of keeling over.

"It isn't something to be spoken of."

Of course not, not when she got to the interesting bits. "Got it." The dim lights of the village at night were becoming clearer and brought the conversation to a natural end. "We'll cover more ground if we split up. How about I come in from the west, you from the east. We'll meet in the middle before dawn and find a place to hole up once activity gets too much for us to do any more searching. Sound good?"

Raze looked at her like he wanted to open her up and scan her to see if she was being honest. She was sure he was going to nix the idea, and as the seconds marched on, it got harder and harder not to fidget. A full minute passed and he finally nodded. "Very well. Good hunting."

Sierra took off without giving him a chance to have second thoughts.

***

It was unwise to let Sierra go alone. Raze didn't doubt her ability to take care of herself, she'd more than proved capable against him. But as she trotted off, he knew that she could easily disappear and he'd never see her again. Toran might say that was for the best. She brought something out in him that he couldn't understand. He'd spoken more to her in an hour than he had to most of his fellow Detyens in the past two years.

And every moment he spent by her side *hurt*. It was a soul deep ache that he shouldn't be able to feel, and yet it was there, ripping him in two as surely as a finely-honed blade. If there was any sense in the universe, the pain would let up the more distance they put between themselves, instead, it only transformed into a harsh pull, urging his feet west towards her. In two years, he hadn't felt any urges, and he'd forgotten how hard they were to deny, when his body screamed at him to do one thing and his mind knew he must do another.

He needed his control back, needed to stabilize before he found Toran and Kayde. They couldn't know about Sierra and what she did to him. What if Kayde had the same response, these strange, impossible pseudo-feelings and excruciating pleasure and agony from physical contact? He'd cut off Kayde's hand before he let him touch Sierra. And if Toran saw her as a threat to the legion, he needed to protect her, to keep her hidden before some other warrior hunted her down and took her out before she could weaken any others.

He knew. He *knew* that these responses were irrational. Knew that if he chose not to take the human out, he should at least keep his distance. But that wasn't going to happen. There were a few hours until sunrise and anticipation licked through him, excitement thrumming at the thought of seeing her again.

A human denya.

He recalled the wonder in Toran's voice as he relayed the story. Was that what Sierra was? The denya of some unknown Detyen? He'd never reacted this way to the denyai at headquarters, but none of them were human. Perhaps he'd react this way to any of the alleged human denyai.

Or perhaps she is yours.

That way led to madness far beyond instability, and Raze refused to consider it. Whatever pull he felt towards Sier—the woman, it was because of the abnormal situation and had nothing to do with her. He set aside thoughts of why he'd reacted so poorly to her touch and why a part of him longed to reach out and see if a second round would be just as painful. He wasn't even certain whether he wanted it to hurt or not.

Want. No, he could not want anything. He had his mission and his people. That was enough, it had to be.

As agreed, he entered the village from the east. There wasn't much to the place. Three roads ran more or less parallel and were crossed by another three roads. Housing was a mix of poorly constructed buildings and broken down space ships that had been recycled into houses. A few pirates still caroused, but given the late hour, they paid him little mind, more focused on mind-numbing substances and sex. But the woman with one of those carousing pirates caught his eye. She studied him for several long seconds, watching him walk in the shadows. She wasn't there by choice. Her clothes were threadbare and torn, her hair dirty and knotted. A bruise covered half of her face. But her eyes had a hint of defiance he'd seen in survivors.

And she looked at him like she knew he didn't belong. He stared right back at her, practically daring her to raise the alarm. But the pirate dragged her into one of the buildings and the moment was lost. At another time, on another mission, he would have followed after to stop whatever was about to happen. But he had no place to hide her, no way to save her. And saving her would only hurt whatever other women they'd captured and decided to keep. Raze didn't need intel from home to tell him that the slavers brought the women here for... entertainment. It was what slavers did, and Raze found some measure of satisfaction in destroying them out in the black of space.

But on Fenryr 1, the slavers' home turf, with no team and only a small ship, Raze could do nothing to help. Not yet.

Was that why Sierra was here? He'd told her nothing of his mission, and she'd done the same. She had no reason to be after the data on the *Lyrden,* but the woman he'd seen was human. Maybe the humans were doing something about it. Or perhaps she was some sort of mercenary on a rescue mission. *It doesn't matter*, he told himself. *Find Toran and Kayde and get out.*

He couldn't recall ever being so distracted before. He took a deep breath and brought his mind to a sharp point of focus, imagining his meditation chamber back at headquarters and the equilibrium he could find there. When he opened his eyes back up, the world righted itself, the colors more muted and sounds tamer. He could breathe again, even if now he was conscious of some missing piece he'd never before noticed. It didn't matter. This was what he was supposed to be. Temperate, focused, alone.

Given the layout of the settlement, he took the streets methodically. The shadows were long in the bright moonlight and there were nothing like streetlights to illuminate his path. Some of the ships and houses had lights attached to the outside, but this late, most of them were extinguished. He could almost imagine that this was a simple traveler settlement without the dark underbelly of rot, but the occasional pained moan or scream disabused him of that notion.

They deserved to be burned to the ground.

That wasn't why Raze was here and he pushed those thoughts to the back of his mind. The first street he crossed yielded no clues to the whereabouts of his men. He doubled back to make sure and ended up where he'd begun with no more information. On the second street, he heard a group of pirates talking and stood in the shadows to listen, but they spoke of a past raid on a faraway planet and made no mention of two captured Detyen soldiers.

He'd just passed one of the cross streets when something caught his attention. A larger space ship that didn't look as decrepit as the rest stood ringed in light with two guards at the entrance. *That* seemed to have potential. From the shadows, Raze couldn't make out much, but he couldn't get a closer look from the ground without being seen. He surveyed the surrounding area and made a choice.

There were no men on the roof, so if he couldn't go on the ground, he'd go through the air.

He scaled the side of an adjacent building, slipping twice as the shadows played tricks with the hand and footholds that he could make. His arms began to burn as he pulled himself up onto the roof of the building and he walked with light feet to the other edge, feeling exposed by the openness of the roof. But none of the guards were looking up and he crouched low to try and keep the attention away from himself.

The structures sat close together and a few running steps and a jump saw him on top of the old ship. He could hear sounds coming from the inside and for a moment he let himself believe that he would find Toran and Kayde, barely worse for wear. He took a moment to steady himself before entering and pushing all expectations aside. This was the job, it was time to do it.

Chapter Seven

The amount of sleeping pirates and slavers that Sierra snuck past had her on edge. From the way the buildings were set up, she got the idea that most of the activity, whatever passed for entertainment around here, happened at the center of the settlement. Most of the residents lived on the outskirts. Though *outskirts* was a misnomer. She could sprint from one end of the village to the other without running out of breath. The place was little more than a way station, a place where these terrible people could take some time to rest and re-energize before heading back out to terrorize innocent people out in space.

A few old-fashioned torches serve as the light sources for some of the more dilapidated huts and her fingers itched to tip them over and burn this place to the ground. But that would only send them fleeing, rats scurrying for survival. She and the agency would lose the lead they had on the abducted women and the way things worked out here, those women would never be found again. So she left the fires burning and didn't stab anyone in their sleep, no matter how much she knew they deserved it.

Now would be a good time for her to check in with Mindy and catch her up on the situation, but Sierra remained silent. She didn't want to risk making any unnecessary noise while she was so close to so many potential hostiles. And, if she were being honest, she didn't want to listen to Mindy telling her to run away or take Raze out. Mindy couldn't *order* her to do it, but there would be a notation about it in the mission log and that could complicate things. And things in Sierra's head were already complicated enough, she didn't need to add job troubles to the list.

She cleared her half of the town with no sign of the men that Raze was looking for and too much evidence of the women. She hadn't found where they were being kept, but she could hear their screams and see them sleeping beside some of the pirates, dirty and unkempt. Her soul lurched and ached with every one that she walked past, but saving one now would doom the rest and Sierra wouldn't do that. They were getting everyone out of this mess. Soon.

Dawn threatened on the horizon with no new clues. She'd used her journey to get a more accurate map of the town, but she'd need to return the next night to find the women. The longer she and her team stayed here, the longer it would be before the abducted women could be rescued by an extraction unit. Sierra promised herself that she'd find what she needed tomorrow and be done with this place. She'd stick the strange encounter with Raze into a box in the back of her mind and never think of it again. Or, well, maybe if she wanted to fantasize about what ifs, she'd think on it from her own place on Earth, many light years between them, which seemed like it was probably a safe distance.

They hadn't specified the rendezvous point, but Sierra found Raze waiting for her at nearly the exact center of the town. His face gave away nothing, but his body thrummed with energy and she would have called him excited if he hadn't said that thing about not feeling emotions. They slipped out of town in silence and she let Raze take the lead. She knew of a few places that would serve as decent hiding spots during the day, but she didn't want to give them away if she didn't have to.

But great minds clearly thought alike, as he led her past two hills and into a little cave that was obscured by bushes and moss. It was at the top of her list for potential hiding places. She was glad to see no signs of life on the inside; it didn't seem like the pirates knew about the place and there weren't any droppings or remains of animals. She might actually get a few hours of almost pleasant sleep, despite the company.

Or because of it.

"Any luck?" she asked as she settled herself into a little corner, trying to get comfortable.

Raze didn't need to fidget like she did. He swept an area large enough for him to lay down and sat still as a statue. "Why are you here?" he asked in lieu of an answer.

"Why are you?" He didn't get to know without a little quid pro quo.

"I found Toran and Kayde," he said instead.

He hadn't said their names before, but there were only two people he could be talking about. "Do you need help to get them out?" Now why did she have to go and offer that? She'd offered recon assistance, that was it. She couldn't afford to get even more side tracked. Mindy wasn't going to be silent for long.

"They're being kept with about a dozen human women at the center of the settlement," he said. "I can get them out by myself. But if I do..."

If he did, he risked the women. And if he did, the women wouldn't be there for long. "They've been taking women from Earth," she said, no longer playing games. "They finally nabbed someone important enough for the government to give a damn. I'm here to get the information we need to send in a team to get them out."

"That seems like a lot of work for twelve abductees."

"I thought there would be more." Anyone saved was worth it, but space bound missions cost money, *a lot* of money. And part of her assignment was to confirm that the senator's niece was among those held captive here. Sierra had been trying to ignore what that meant, but she knew. If the girl wasn't here, these twelve women would be abandoned to whatever fate the slavers had in store for them.

"You are concerned for these women." It wasn't a question, thankfully. She might have slapped him if it was.

"If..." Sierra shook her head. "Every day they're here is another day they suffer. And if—when—I leave them here, I'll feel... complicit in this whole thing. I can't guarantee that the follow up mission will be approved. I can't guarantee that they'll still be here if it is. The only thing that I *can* be sure of is that they'll be abused every day until someone intervenes. And I want that someone to be me so bad that it hurts."

***

Those psuedo feelings were getting to him again. Raze was torn between leaving this little cave to go and slay every pirate and slaver out there in Sierra's name and closing the small distance between them to wrap her up in his strong arms and give her the support that she seemed to need so desperately. Her arms had started to cross in front of her, like some sad imitation of a hug.

He needed to stay where he was, needed to keep his distance. He'd found Toran and Kayde, and when the time was right he would retrieve them. He could not deviate to rescue the human women and he could not offer them a place on his ship if transportation was an issue for Sierra. But there was a flicker deep inside of him, one he'd extinguished so long ago that now relit, it burned like an inferno. He shifted to his feet and closed the distance between them, slinging an arm over her shoulders and pulling her close, careful to avoid contact with her skin.

"What are you doing?" she asked, not pulling away. In fact, she leaned in closer, letting her cheek rest against his chest where his heart pounded faster than the occasion called for.

That abnormal bodily reaction was one he should have noted in his log for further investigation of destabilization later, but sitting beside Sierra, he'd never felt more whole. He tried to come up with the proper thing to say, the words that would make this connection between them make sense. But nothing in his experience could explain it, and nothing short of immediate attack could make him let her go. "You need comfort," he finally murmured, her hair soft against his lips.

Her own fingers danced across his stomach until she had a hand wrapped around his side. "How do you know that if you can't feel anything?"

With you, I can. He didn't say it, couldn't quite believe it was true. This had to be some anomaly or some sign of degradation to himself. "You're from Earth?" he asked, instead of going down the path of questions he couldn't answer.

Sierra seemed to sense the conflict within him and accepted the change in topic. "Born and raised. Where do you call home?"

"That's not something I can answer." The location of the legion was one of the most closely guarded secrets they held. That, and the process to make the soulless. But Sierra stiffened in his embrace and he could sense she was about to pull away. To stop that, he had to say something. "It is not my home planet. I was born and raised there, but we have no home."

She tilted her head up to look at him and their cheeks almost brushed. He pulled back enough to give them space, but that impossible part of him wanted to lean forward and see what would happen if they touched once more. What would she do to him? How would she change him? Would he survive it? Could he be whole?

"No home?" she prompted after several seconds.

"My race, Detyens, are originally from a planet called Detya. A little more than a hundred years ago it was destroyed, completely uninhabitable. Now there are survivors scattered throughout the stars. But there is no place that can really compete with where we're supposed to be." He'd seen the images of the planet in the run up to the final day, and he'd seen footage of what happened. An entire planet gone in minutes, with no explanation or foe to fight.

"Were you at war?" She settled back against him and something in Raze's chest eased at her acceptance of the contact.

If he didn't know better, he'd say that she was comforting him as much as he comforted her. But that was impossible. "No, it had been a long time since my people made an effort at anything besides peaceful exploration. Our military existed to protect our ships and our home, nothing more. Then one day a weapon was dropped from space. It incinerated the land, boiled the oceans. And whoever dropped it never claimed credit, never left any evidence of where they'd come from. And as far as we know, no one has ever used such a weapon again. News of a planet killer would have spread fast, and yet almost no one has heard of Detya or what happened to us."

"That's terrible." Now she looked up at him with an unreadable expression in her eyes.

An awareness swelled between them, something too big for Raze to understand. It had him leaning in a little closer, breathing deep and catching the warm scent of her skin. He found himself saying more, even as he drew nearer to dangerous truths not meant to be shared with anyone. "Tens of thousands, perhaps even more, survived the attack. Mainly those who were away from the planet or on one of our space stations. A few craft managed to escape land before it was too late. But that was not the end of our suffering." A strand of her hair had come undone from the braids she'd styled to tame it. Raze wrapped it lightly around one finger, careful to avoid her skin. The soft texture was a knife against his flesh, but he couldn't make himself let go. "Every Detyen is meant to have a denya, a mate. They are the person who completes our souls. With billions of Detyens on a single planet, finding matches was no issue. Very few people were left alone. But when we scattered, we lost that connection and that hope. And if a Detyen doesn't meet their mate by the time they turn thirty..." She stiffened against him slightly and he surmised that she knew the direction of this conversation. "We die without our mates. So the bomb may not have destroyed us in one instant, but we will not survive for many more generations as we live now."

"So what does your mate think about that?" she asked. "You said that you turned thirty-two years ago, so you have a mate since you're alive."

He could say no more. Raze let go of her hair and pulled away. "My decisions are my own. Sleep now, I will take first watch."

    ***

Oh, so he was going to do the stoic warrior thing. Great. Before the mission, Sierra would have said she preferred that attitude to the cowboys and bravos that she sometimes had to work with from the Earth military, but Raze cutting her off like that made her wish for a dozen of those guys from back home. She knew how to handle them. Raze, though? With his emotionless act that she was starting to see through and his heartbreaking story and the pain he couldn't keep hidden? No, he was making her want things that she couldn't afford to want. She'd never see him again after tomorrow.

Besides, he had some mate or something to go back home to. He wasn't her problem in any way. Why that sent acid coursing through her veins, her stomach clenching with an emotion that *was not* jealousy, she wasn't going to examine. She watched as he stalked away, each move dripping with the fluid grace of a jungle cat as he settled into position near the entrance to their little hideaway. He didn't look back at her, but every cell in her body was attuned to him.

For a second back there, she'd thought he was about to kiss her. And she would have let him, no questions asked. Maybe emotion meant something different to the Detyens because she could no longer believe that Raze didn't feel anything. She'd even begun to distinguish little inflections in that flat tone of his, micro-changes in pitch that she would have never noticed if they hadn't been speaking for more than an hour. And that time had just flown by, seconds bleeding into minutes and more, without ever dragging on into awkward pauses and boredom.

She wanted more than a night with him, wanted to see what he'd do if she laid her hands on him, wanted to taste him and memorize the shape of his lips under hers. She *wanted* with such a fury that it frustrated her, lodging a sound of longing in her throat as she tried to find a comfortable position to rest in.

What was his denya like? Was it a mate for life sort of gig? Or did they have kids and then separate for good? Did *he* have kids? No, she decided, she didn't believe that he did. She couldn't imagine someone like him sacrificing the love he felt for his children in order to do whatever it was he did without his emotions. So maybe the mate thing was just a onetime deal, not a woman he had loved and given up to be a warrior for his people.

"If you would prefer to take the first watch, I can take my rest now," Raze interrupted her thoughts. "You seem restless."

No shit. "You gave me a lot to think about." Her training usually meant she could fall into a light slumber in a blink and wake up alert with no issue. But not with her mind racing like this. "How does the denya thing work?" she asked. He had angled his body towards her and she chose to believe he'd answer some more questions, but she had to be careful because he would turn away in an instant, she was sure.

He was silent for so long that she started to think she was wrong about him being willing to answer, but after several moments he spoke and it was clear that he'd been putting his thoughts into logical order. "There is supposed to be a moment of recognition, when a Detyen knows his denya on sight. Then, commonly, they will bond as quickly as possible. Many choose to remain together, choose to love and have children. Some, though, find mated life not to their tastes and separate. Once bonded, they are safe from the Denya Price and may go on to live long happy lives, whether with their mate or not."

Supposed to, commonly, many, some. But nothing about what *he* did. And then she remembered what he'd said earlier. He'd sacrificed his emotions to lengthen his life. "You don't have a mate, do you?" There was no woman back home, no passel of children. If she had to guess, he had a small, cold cot with neutral colored sheets and no decorations wherever he slept. A cold, lonely little existence.

"No, I don't."

"Was it worth it?" If she were facing the prospect of death at her next birthday, would she make the same choice? Some days she felt ancient, but twenty-nine was so young, she didn't want to die. But was Raze really living anymore?

She didn't expect an answer, but she could feel his gaze on her, the weight of it as heavy as an emergency supply pack. "If you cannot sleep, you should take the first shift."

That was it then. Sierra settled back into position. "It's alright. Wake me when it's my turn." She flipped over and faced the wall, her mind strangely more at ease, even as it roiled with questions she knew Raze wouldn't or couldn't answer. Static crackled in her ear and she hoped that the signal had been disturbed and Mindy hadn't heard their conversation. It wasn't pertinent to the mission, and if he wanted to share his secrets with her, she'd gladly take them.

She drifted off to sleep with the weight of his gaze weighing her down and dreamed of darkness.

Chapter Eight

Could a Detyen without a soul find his mate? And if he did, what would claiming her do to him? What would claiming *Sierra* do to him? He hadn't felt the stirrings of desire for two years, hadn't yearned to share his body and his space with another for even longer. But in a handful of hours, he'd craved things he'd long thought impossible.

A soulless Detyen could not crave. Could not lust.

And yet, here he was. If he touched her again, would he collapse? Or had that been a onetime reaction? She'd flung a hand out above her head, her pale skin almost glowing in the dim light of the cave. Moonlight streamed in through the opening and some of the moss had a bio-luminescent effect, making it possible to see, even in the dark. He could reach out and brush his fingers over hers, just a kiss of skin, just a test. If he had no reaction, she would never know he'd done it.

But she was asleep and even that minor of a touch seemed like a liberty he could not steal. It would be one thing to touch her to move her from harm's way. To do so just because her hand was there and looked so soft that his fingers ached to find out? No, that he could not do.

He paced around the perimeter of the space, giving his body something to do, some way to burn the excess energy that seemed to have come from nowhere. He could list the exact amount of calories he'd eaten in the day and the standard effect that they had on his body. Today was far from standard.

His alert went off, signaling it was time to change the shift. Raze silenced the alarm and his eyes snapped right back to Sierra's hand. He'd promised to wake her up. Would she think it strange if he touched her to do so? He took a deep breath and leaned forward, but before he could do it or stop himself, she turned over and her eyes snapped open.

"If you were thinking any louder you'd call the pirates down on us," she mumbled as she rolled into a sitting position. Her eyes followed the line of his gaze down to her hand. "Was something crawling on me?"

Raze shook his head. "It is time to switch."

"I got that." She pulled her pack up and grabbed a bottle, taking a deep swig. "Do you need water?"

"I have my own."

Sierra nodded and stuck the bottle back in her pack, settling it back on the ground. She looked over at him and dragged a breath in, as if to speak, but after several moments remained silent.

She wasn't going to ask him about the staring. He could say nothing right now and they would both go on pretending to one another that there was nothing between them but this temporary partnership. He would gather Toran and Kayde tomorrow and leave her to do her own job. Space was so big that he could almost guarantee that they would never see one another again. Besides, his chances of not being put down after the mission debrief were slim. He would need to report on his instability. He doubted that anyone of influence would trust him to continue in his function. Two years as a soulless member of the legion was at the lower end of average. There would be no shame in ending once he returned.

And that realization, that his survival was once again limited to days and weeks rather than years and decades, freed him from something he hadn't known was holding him back. It didn't matter if touching Sierra damaged him or did strange things to his mind, he wouldn't be around long enough for it to hurt anyone but himself.

"I found myself curious," he said, voice barely whispering the word. The soulless should not experience curiosity at all.

If Sierra realized that, she didn't mention it. "About?" Her tone was cautious, the word drawn out over more syllables than necessary.

"I wondered if the effect that came from our physical conduct last night was a onetime occurrence or not. And I wished to test the hypothesis."

She pressed her lips together like she was holding back a smile. "You didn't state a hypothesis there."

The teasing loosened something within his chest. He wished that he could remember how it felt to smile, just so he could return the one she hadn't given him. "My hypothesis is that physical contact a second time will not have the same effect."

"Why?" This time the smile couldn't be held back.

Raze didn't know the answer to her question. "Why belongs to another experiment, I think."

"This is about the most convoluted way a guy has ever asked to feel me up. So, congrats to that." Sierra shook her head a little from side to side, still smiling. She held out a hand towards him. "Give it a go." Raze raised his own hand up, but at the last moment, Sierra reared back, eyes wide. "Wait!"

"What?"

"Do you have a med kit, you know, if things are actually worse?" She flashed her hand open and closed a few times before leaving it fisted.

Raze nodded. "In my bag."

She nodded again and loosened her hand, bringing it forward. "Okay."

***

She was more nervous than she'd been on the night she first had sex with her first boyfriend. She hoped that this experience, whatever it was, wasn't as disappointing as that one, even if they were just touching hands. Her body thrummed with anticipation, like she stood at the edge of a cliff, ready to jump off as soon as she got the go ahead.

The light in their little cavern wasn't great, but a fanciful part of her mind wanted to call it romantic. Moonlight streamed in through the opening and the moss glowed. The memory of Raze screaming and convulsing on the ground made her want to scurry back and stay out of reach, but the intensity in his posture kept her rooted in place, stretching one hand out to close the distance between them.

I wish I could be what you needed. He didn't need anything, that was his problem. He'd gone beyond need years before he met her, and there was no way to help him. Besides, he couldn't even want help anymore.

His hand moved in slow motion, each second stretching out into five until, almost suddenly, warm fingers brushed against her palm. The pads were work roughened, a warrior's hands, used to holding a weapon and firing with ease. For a moment he flinched and Sierra leaned forward, ready to jump into action. But he didn't back down, his fingers tracing over the lines of her hand until he bumped up against the juncture of her fingers. He crawled up, his digits easing their way into the gaps between her own.

She shivered, the skin there more sensitive than she'd ever realized. He sucked in a deep breath and she jerked her eyes from their interlocking hands up to the shadows that ringed his face. And there she saw twin glowing orbs of red where his eyes had been. They glowed in the darkness, demonic but not terrifying. No, she saw them as a challenge and a confirmation of something she couldn't define. Something she was scared to approach.

But they only had tonight, and she couldn't let go of this *thing* until she knew more. Need roiled within her, not just need for his body, but to know him as completely as one person could know another.

"What's happening to your eyes?" she whispered. The distance between them had shrunk to a few hand spans. All she had to do was lean forward a little and she could capture his lips and take this experiment to another level.

"My eyes?" His fingers curled around hers, gripping tight, almost painfully so.

Sierra didn't let go, even as shivers raced up her forearm. It was almost like the tingling sensation she got before a limb fell asleep, but not painful. No, it woke her body up in a way she didn't know she could feel. She was more *alive* than she'd ever been before. "They're red."

His hand squeezed harder. "Impossible." They were both whispering now, the words faint kisses in the air.

Sierra held up her other hand, offering it to him. "More?"

Raze reached out, this time skimming one finger across her palm until she shivered. He sucked in a harsh breath and his finger stilled. Sierra wanted to ask, but she was afraid to break the spell between them. He seemed to be teetering on a tightrope of decision. One wrong word or move and he'd pull away. And why that felt like the biggest tragedy of all, she couldn't say and didn't want to examine. Not tonight. Doubt and regret could belong to tomorrow.

He took another deep breath and scraped a second finger against her palm. Sierra's skin tightened and she practically moaned. The last time she'd checked, her hands were *not* an erogenous zone, but the sensual assault he was waging against her was almost enough to make her reconsider. His fingers trailed the same path he'd crossed on her other hand until all of their fingers were laced together, connecting them palm to palm on each hand.

They *fit*.

They'd been born hundreds, maybe thousands, of light years apart. They belonged to different species. They had only met hours ago and would soon never see one another again. And yet, it had never been more right with *anyone* as it was in that moment. It was the single most sensual experience that Sierra had ever undergone, and all her clothes were still on. They hadn't even kissed.

She couldn't fix it all, but that one thing she could. "More?" she asked again.

Raze nodded, those glowing red eyes moving up and down with the shadow of his face.

She leaned in, giving him more than enough time to realize her intent. He pulled on her hands, helping her close the distance until her lips ghosted over his, barely a breath of a kiss. She wanted to seal their mouths together and taste him until sunrise, but she held herself back, reading his body. They'd somehow managed to sit side by side without her realizing, and as much as she wanted to drape herself over him, she kept to their three points of contact: right hand, left hand, and lips.

He leaned in close, returning the innocent pecks with something unpracticed and carnal, even though their tongues weren't involved. Yet. He closed his lips around her bottom lip until she could feel his teeth, not a bite, but something more forceful than she'd expected from him. Her fingers squeezed against his, silently urging him to take control of the kiss, control of this encounter. Right now, she'd give him anything, as long as he wanted it.

With a gasp he pulled back, tearing his hands away and falling backwards, hitting the wall with a hollow *thunk*. Heavy breaths echoed around them as he tried to regain his equilibrium. And though Sierra wasn't suffering from exactly the same confusion as him, her entire world still felt off-kilter, changed with a single kiss.

She wished the light was better so that she could see if he was okay. He didn't seem to be convulsing this time and either his eyes had stopped glowing, or he had them closed. How long had they embraced? She glanced at the cavern opening and hoped they hadn't left it unattended for long. A rookie mistake if they got caught because they were too busy making out to look out for their own personal safety.

That thought alone sent a cold shiver down her spine, dousing the desire that had been coursing through her. Had he felt it too? Or was he putting off some weird sex pheromones that made her forget herself and her duties? She scooted back, putting a little more distance between them. What was *wrong* with her? Even back on Earth she couldn't remember ever getting hung up on a guy so quick. She didn't do the love thing, and relationships were a thing of the past. So why was she all caught up on the fact that this guy would be gone tomorrow? That was a *good* thing. She could get her mind back in the game and get the damn job done. Her team was waiting for her, the women held prisoner were waiting for her. And she was wasting her time making out with some alien who said he couldn't even feel emotion?

She stood up. "I'll take the watch. Get your sleep." If it came out gruffer than intended, she wasn't going to care. The experiment was over, it was time to get back to real life.

Chapter Nine

The pain was gone by dusk. In the minutes after that life destroying kiss, Raze had almost said something. No, he didn't collapse this time. But every nerve was on fire and pulsed with the unbearable agony of wakefulness. It was like he'd woken up after a centuries-long sleep, only to find all his muscles atrophied and every movement full of pain as he tried to use a body unaccustomed to any movement.

Everything was brighter as the suns set; the weak rays of light streamed into the cave and illuminated the green moss. He'd known it was green, had seen plenty of it since they landed. He could have described the color exactly in his report. But he'd forgotten what that green really looked like since he'd lost his soul. But not today. Today the green glowed with a depth that reminded him of dense forests and fresh spring. He could imagine what soft grass felt like under his fingers and remembered an agility exercise that had taken him high into green leafed trees until sitting on the limbs had felt like flying.

By every god, he *felt*. And it hurt. Not physically. His body had rested and adjusted to whatever those touches and that kiss had done to it, but his soul ached, even as he knew it was impossible. But he remembered. Once upon a time he'd held this ache close and promised himself that he would hold the memory close through the dark years to come. As soon as he made that promise, it had dissolved along with love and fear and hope and regret until he was nothing left but an automaton doing tasks assigned by his superiors to support a cause he knew that he'd once loved.

And Sierra shone in a way that he'd never before realized. She'd taken her hair down to readjust her braids. Sun glinted off the red strands, radiant as a gem. Despite her days outdoors, her skin was a pale cream and he remembered soft, full lips that had tasted like hope and impossible dreams. She held herself with a refined strength, both physically and mentally, though he wasn't certain if it was strength or fear that had made her pull back the night before. He recognized a retreat and respected her decision.

They worked in silence to cover the few signs that they'd stayed the night.

"So what's the plan?" Sierra finally asked, breaking through the quiet.

He'd had hours to come up with a way to get Toran and Kayde out, but simplicity in this scenario seemed best. "I need you to make a distraction away from where they're being held. That should draw away some of the men. I'll retrieve my men and the business will be done. You have my thanks."

Sierra bit her lip and glanced outside before looking back at him. "Can you do the retrieval without drawing attention to the women? If the slavers think the location is compromised..."

Then her mission would be for naught, and it would entirely be his fault. Raze nodded. "I will make every effort."

She nodded. "Good then." She hitched her pack over her shoulders and checked her weapons. "It's been... interesting. Good hunting."

No mention of the kiss, or the charged intimacy of the night before. Raze wanted to step close, circle his arms around her, and taste her once more before they walked into danger. He wanted to keep her by his side and shelter her from harm, not send her into it in the name of his mission. A mission that had nothing to do with her. He could grow tired of wanting, especially if he were parted from Sierra, the impossible woman who might have been his in another life.

"You could..." He almost made an offer he couldn't promise.

Sierra looked at him like she knew what he wasn't saying. She gave the slightest shake of her head and that was it, the moment gone. They named a time for her to make the distraction and went off their separate ways, and an ache in his chest bloomed as it became more and more clear that he would never see her again.

***

This was a terrible idea. Unless Raze was holding onto some serious tech that he'd kept hidden from her, she was about to charge head first into the heart of pirate territory with little more than a blaster. Weren't people without emotions supposed to rely on logic? Because logic was telling her that he was about to embark on a suicide mission of epic proportions. And that was not only going to get him dead, which she was trying hard not to imagine, but it was also going to fuck up her mission and get those women transported somewhere else, somewhere they'd never find.

"Mindy, are you there?" she asked, finally engaging her comms. She was moving towards the settlement with the most stealth that she could manage, but if she kept her voice low, no one should be able to hear her.

"I was beginning to think that you ran away with some alien hunk." Mindy sounded chipper, like she'd slept in a soft bed and was relaxing with coffee and a warm pastry. She had the bad habit of waking happily, no matter the time of day or what planet she was on. "Care to fill us in on what the hell that was about?"

"Jo's on the line?" Normally those two kept communications as brief as possible.

"We got curious about your little adventure," came Jo's droll reply.

At least her stupidity seemed to bring her teammates closer together. That had to count as a win... or something. "There was a bit of a mix up," she explained. "Raze thought I was a pirate who kidnapped his guys. I thought he was a pirate who was trying to kill me. It's all cool, we're friends now. And we found out where the women are being kept."

"Wait, back up. There's another team on planet? What's the mission?" Now Mindy was all business. "I managed to get the basic info on Detyens, I've relayed it to both of your tablets. If this guy's not a pirate, he must be a merc. Detyens don't exactly have a military... or a planet."

"He's not a merc." Not that Sierra had anything against mercenaries, but she'd listened long enough to determine that whatever organization Raze worked for, it was Detyen in origin. Who else would have come up with some way of prolonging their lives, no matter how horrifying? She kept that info to herself, it wasn't relevant. "He came here with two men, also Detyen. I saw them myself. They were nabbed by the pirates yesterday morning." Was it really only yesterday? "They, along with our women, are being kept in a central building. I agreed to provide a distraction at a specific time so he can extract the men. Whether he's successful or not, we're back on track after that."

"You mean except for the part where he's announcing that there are hostiles on the planet, right?" asked Jo, voice dripping sarcasm. "What the fuck, Sierra? Since when do you fuck up like this?"

Sierra decided to take that as a compliment. She usually didn't fuck up and Jo knew it. "It will be fine. They'll know that Raze and his team are here, they know nothing about us."

"Unless Raze barters information about you," Mindy pointed out.

He wouldn't do that. She choked back the words before they had a chance to slip out. Any agent with the barest competence would trade information like that for safety. One mostly chaste kiss and some hand holding weren't enough to cement loyalty. "He doesn't know about the two of you," she said after a moment.

The silence on the line said volumes of what her team was thinking of her right now. But Mindy gathered her wits and got back to business. "So where does that leave us?"

"I was able to set the crawlers yesterday." They were small pieces of tech that could map out a location and gather data about the number of people and calculate where they were likely to cluster. She'd left them in the settlement while she helped Raze search. "I'll gather them today. Once we ensure that Raze's mission hasn't compromised ours, we can call it and return home for phase two."

"And if the mission is compromised?" Jo asked, because of course she would.

"Then we deal with it." Sierra infused steel into her words. If they sounded hard, maybe her team would stop asking all these inconvenient questions. "We won't know until it's done. I'll get back to you in a few hours. Out." She cut off the comms and let out a frustrated sigh. They were going to give her so much shit when she got back to the ship, and Sierra would deserve it. But she couldn't beat herself up about it right now, not until the job was done.

Covering the ground back to the settlement was easy, but more nerve wracking in the fading daylight. Her instinct was to hide whenever she caught sight of pirates and slavers in the distance, but that would only draw more attention to herself. From afar, she looked just like any one of them, no one that needed any special attention paid.

When she got to the village it was a different story. There were only a few hundred people living there at any given time, and most of them would know each other, at least in passing. Around them, she couldn't afford to be seen. No cover story could explain her presence, unless she wanted to pretend that she was one of the captured women who'd somehow stolen a slaver's outfit and was now pretending to be one of her captors, just taking a walk around town like nothing was wrong. Yeah, no one was going to buy that for long.

The key to staying hidden was to play it cool. She stuck to the shadows and alleys created by the dilapidated structures and grounded craft, but she didn't hunch over or try to look like she was staying out of sight. If someone caught a glimpse of her, she couldn't panic. Running would call way more attention to herself than ducking around a corner or keeping her head down.

She engaged the sensor on the crawlers and called them back to her. Three little black balls, each fitting comfortably in the palm of her hand, rolled towards her. She scooped them up and turned off the data collection module, sticking them in her pack without going over the data. They had the capability to transmit information back to Mindy, but the encryption wasn't as strong as she'd like it to be and she didn't want to risk the signal getting picked up, not when it was just as simple to walk the data back to the ship.

Sierra checked the time; she still had more than an hour before Raze was ready to make his move. A slither of apprehension snaked through her. This must be what operatives in the old days felt like, before they could stay in contact with teammates and ensure absolute synchronization. The only way she'd know if he was successful was if there were no Detyens aboard the prisoner ship when she set a crawler to do the final check. And even then, she couldn't be certain. All she'd know is that they were no longer on the ship, not if they'd survived or been slaughtered or been left to die.

She'd pine later, right now she had a job to do.

"Get that merchandise back to the pens," she heard a gruff voice from around the corner. Sierra's first instinct was to peek and get a look at what they were talking about, but her training kept her in place, hunched behind a short wall that acted as a gate between structures. "Krend's moved up the schedule."

"He said I could have one until midday," came the plaintive, nasal voice of the second pirate. She guessed he was young and human, but couldn't be certain. He sounded like all of the boys she'd gone to school with who complained when the cafeteria ran out of their favorite food.

"Plan's changed. He said something about a buyer. We need to move." The first pirate was a man used to being obeyed, and she wouldn't be surprised if he was the second on one of the fleet ships. Definitely someone with responsibility, and a person had to have a lot of blood on their hands to hold one of those positions for long in a group like this.

Damn it. A buyer changed the stakes. Even if a recovery team came for the women as soon as Sierra got back to Earth, there'd be no way to get back in time to save them. The protocol was to place a tracker so they could chase down the ship, rather than engage here, but Sierra's entire soul rebelled. Even with a tracker, they wouldn't be able to retrieve them all. No way would a buyer keep the women together. In a matter of days they'd be scattered across half the galaxy, sold into slavery with little hope of rescue.

She noted the information and pushed it aside. That was something she'd need to look into later, *after* she'd provided the distraction for Raze. He was counting on her, and she didn't want him to end up dead because of her negligence. She left the pirates be to find what she was looking for.

The key to a good distraction was to walk the line between danger and fascination. She needed to pull the men away from the central area of the settlement, but she didn't want them too afraid to approach. And given the layout and building materials that were

70

scattered everywhere, what she had to do was obvious. Her first stop was to find the three nearest maintenance bots and take them out. Then she scouted the area, looking for the perfect place to do what she promised.

Three little huts, practically leaning against each other, were the perfect candidates. She smiled and rubbed her hands together. It was time to heat things up.

***

Raze got into position and watched the clock. At some point in his journey back to the settlement, his mind had settled down from the chaos of his earlier thoughts. The more time spent away from Sierra, the more he felt his equilibrium returning. He could not rejoice at the reassertion of normality, but he knew he should find it satisfactory.

But he wanted Sierra back. He was finding that he hated to want, hated the roiling churn in his guts every time he remembered that he would never see her again. They'd spent perhaps twelve hours together, and he was already certain that those were the most important twelve hours of his life. He'd sacrifice most of his tomorrows for another twelve hours with her, though he'd hope that they were both awake for all of them this time.

He wanted to explore these newfound feelings and figure out *why* he could feel them. Were they the same as he'd felt before he underwent the procedure to remove his soul? Or was this like the phantom pain some felt after the amputation of a limb? A soul could not simply grow back, and if it did, wouldn't that mean that he should be dead? After all, he was thirty-two and without a mate.

Unless Sierra was his denya. Now that he could want, he found he wanted *that* more than anything else. To taste her again, to claim her as his own, to keep her by his side. If she were his, the stars would open up for the two of them, anything would be possible. It would be an unknown, impossible hope for his people. Even the soulless could find their mates, regain what they sacrificed.

Their people might no longer be on the brink of extinction.

He hadn't been ready to believe Toran when he spoke of human denyai, but now the possibilities seemed endless. The main thing holding him back was certainty. Every account he'd heard of a Detyen meeting his denya spoke of certainty. From the moment they first met, they recognized one another as mates, unwavering in that single fact. And Raze wasn't sure. He *felt*, and that alone might be a sign, but more importantly, he wondered *if* Sierra was his denya. Was that because he had lost his soul? Or was it a symptom of her humanity? Maybe if she were a Detyen, he would have known for sure. No woman of any species had ever provoked feelings like this in him. Something about Sierra was special.

If he had met her while he was alone, he would have taken every risk to see where the thing between them led. But his responsibility to his people was still the bedrock for his very being's existence and he could not turn away from that. If he did, he would be worthy of no one, least of all Sierra.

He would do his duty here, retrieve his men, and continue the mission. And then... then he had things to consider. If he let her go, all hope for him, and possibly for his race, was lost. But if he could find a way to stand at her side, strong and whole, then it could be a new day for the legion and every Detyen survivor scattered across the galaxy. And he could find out if he and Sierra's bond was true.

His alert vibrated against his wrist as the hour for action ticked by. As soon as he began to question whether or not Sierra had been able to make the distraction, a shout rang out and the acrid smell of smoke tickled his nostrils. He let his gaze follow where the pirates were running and saw dark clouds blotting out the bright sky.

A fire. Perfect.

Though his muscles were primed to spring into action, he held himself back, waiting to see if anyone ran out from inside the building to see what the commotion was about. When a group of three black clad figures came sprinting out, he knew he'd made the right choice. Another two quickly followed, prompting Raze to make his move. He didn't want to wait too long and have the entrance to the holding cells closed off while the guards went off to fight the fire.

He pulled the hood on his jacket up, casting his face in shadow. On his hands he wore black gloves which would tear easily if he needed to unsheathe his claws. Most of the pirates and slavers on Fenryr 1 were human, and with his skin covered, he would pass on first glance. Detyen height and musculature were similar to that of muscular humans.

It soon became apparent that the pirates didn't give a shit. This wasn't a prison planet with strict protocols and highly trained guards. No, these were slavers and pirates, people who thought cruelty and deprivation were more than enough to keep people cowed. Perhaps that worked for the humans who'd never experienced any hardship. For his men, he knew that they'd be ready, if they hadn't already formed an escape plan.

The craft the prisoners were being held on was largely concentric, and as he walked inside, he saw that it was made of several loops, each connected by hallways that ran to the center of the ship. He passed two elevators and several ladders, but stayed on the main floor until he found an information hub. There was no helpful listing for "Prisoners" or "Enemies" but just below the mess hall he saw a listing for "Live Storage." The ship was relatively small, for a long-distance star craft, and he doubted that prisoners would be kept in separate places on the ship. That would require too many guards and double the work. And from his experience, pirates avoided extra work like the plague.

Footsteps echoed down the hall, heading his direction. Raze closed out of the map and ducked behind a pile of unsecured crates, out of sight of anyone walking down the path. As they got closer, he realized two people were walking towards him, rather than one. If he were a lucky man, it would have been Toran and Kayde, successfully escaped. But as they got close enough for him to make out what they were saying, it became clear that it was two pirates speaking to one another.

"Did Krend tell you about the buyer?" One asked. He had a raspy voice, like he'd taken damage to the throat at some point. He spoke IC with a strange accent that Raze couldn't place, and his translator was no help.

"Like the boss ever tells me anything," was his surly companion's reply. Raze's translator had to translate this man's words and identified his language of origin as an Oscavian dialect. "We shipping out? Or do we have visitors?"

"You see any grunts getting this place into flying condition?" Raspy asked. "Rumor has it some big shot from out your way is coming by to see the merchandise."

The Oscavian sputtered out a laugh. "The meat is much better back home. Why would anyone waste their time with those scrawny nothings?"

Slavery was illegal throughout most of the Oscavian Empire, Raze remembered. But the empire was huge with plenty of petty princes lording it over their own planets, and the emperor couldn't police everything. The pirates wandered further down the hall and their conversation faded. He went in the other direction, further into the heart of the ship to his destination.

The first thing that hit him was the smell. The slavers clearly didn't care about the general state of their prisoner holding cells. Unwashed bodies and other, fouler scents assaulted his nose and Raze breathed through his mouth to avoid most of it. He tried to ignore the sounds coming from the center of the room where it was clear that several people were being kept. But his eyes were drawn that way with laser focus and they connected with the gem green eyes of one of the abducted women. Her blonde hair was a nest on her head and a bruise marred one of her pale cheeks.

Every single slaver on this planet deserved to die painfully.

Her mouth dropped open when she took in his shadowed form and she drew back from the bars of her cage, as if that would have saved her if he were a pirate. There weren't any guards standing near the cages. Either they believed this area to be secure enough, or they'd all been called away to deal with the fire. No matter what, he didn't have much time, and it would take too long to get the women freed.

He turned away from the central pen and circled the room until he found what he was looking for.

Kayde was slumped against the far wall, hands manacled above his head. He looked up and a shock went through Raze as their gazes locked. Kayde's eyes were dead, no pain, no hope, nothing lurked in them. Was that what people saw when they looked at him? Toran was next to Kayde, his hands bound and chained to the wall, but with enough give that he could lower them by his side and walk a meter or so from where he sat to the corner where a little hole in the floor might have acted as a latrine. His eyes flashed red as he caught sight of Raze and he stiffened before looking around and realizing that no one was with him.

Wasting no time, Toran jerked his head to the left. "That panel controls the cell. The code is 0041752."

"How—"

"I heard one guy tell another when they brought us food."

At least they'd been fed. Good, they'd have the strength to run. He entered the code and a menu came up afterward. He selected to disengage the bars, chains, and manacles, freeing his teammates with the swipe of his hand. The computer processed his request and Raze found himself holding his breath as the request went through. When the door slid open and metal clanked to the floor, he looked up and saw Toran and Kayde standing, both stretching cramped muscles for a moment before moving out.

Toran glanced at the pen in the center of the room while Kayde stood beside them, eyes on the exit. Toran turned back and studied Raze for a long moment, but whatever he was thinking, he let drop in favor of getting off the ship. "Weapons?"

"Just my blaster. Most of the slavers are dealing with a fire on the other side of the settlement. We need to hurry." He didn't look at the pen in the center of the room, taking his cue from Kayde. Before he'd met Sierra, he wouldn't have known he should look, should care. And until his men were out of harm's way, he couldn't afford to slip.

"Please don't go!" one of the women in the pen cried as they began to move. "Let us out."

Toran took a step closer to the pen, but Kayde put a hand on his arm. He shook his head slightly and Toran turned away from the central pen.

Footsteps echoed in the metal interior of the ship, making it sound like they were surrounded by slavers ready to force them back into a cage and kill them or sell them, whichever was easiest.

Raze grabbed his blaster and looked back at his team. It was time to get out of here and back on track.

Chapter Ten

As soon as the fire grew to a raging inferno, Sierra made her escape. She wanted to run to the center of town and either help Raze or make sure he'd survived, but she forced herself to leave the settlement and put some distance between her and the soon to be enraged pirates. Raze wasn't her responsibility, and she couldn't even really call him her friend. All he could ever be to her was a stranger that she'd never forget.

Still, she found an out of the way place to gather her wits after leaving and waited in the shadows for movement headed out of town. It didn't take long for her to spot the three men running like their lives depended on it. She let out a breath she didn't realize she was holding when she saw that they weren't being followed.

Have a nice life, Raze.

She let them run off and stayed in place for another hour to make sure that no one followed, even if she couldn't do much to help them if they did end up being pursued. But her hiding spot was nice and she still had to go back into town and determine exactly how much damage Raze's little extraction mission had done to her own information gathering pursuit.

"Mindy? Jo? You there?" she asked, engaging her comm.

"Oh, so you're talking to us again?" Mindy asked, ready for a fight, or as much of a fight as a person could have over comms.

"We're back on track now, just keeping you updated." Sierra wasn't going to do this now. She needed to get the job done, especially in light of what she'd heard those pirates talking about. "It sounds like they're going to have the women on the move soon. There's a buyer."

"Are they packing up shop?" Jo asked.

"Don't know. Let's rendezvous back at the ship at 2300. Shit's about to go down, and I don't want to be here when it does." It was something she could feel in the air, a sense of tension just waiting to be released.

"We're not going to have any trouble from your new... friend, are we?" Mindy asked, just when Sierra thought she'd get away with saying nothing about Raze.

"That's done. We're good. See you tonight. Out." Maybe it was cowardly, but she cut the comm back off and sank back against the rock she'd been hiding behind. She only had a few more hours that she could avoid talking about Raze. As soon as she was back with Mindy and Jo, they'd be on her like jackals, ready to tear the story out of her physically if they had to.

Sierra took the path back to the settlement and found an abandoned hut to hide in. A fine layer of dust coated everything and a nest in one of the corners looked like something a wild animal had made. She doubted that anyone would be coming home anytime soon. She let the crawlers do most of the work, sending them out for a final scan of the area while she set up an audio enhancer in the window that allowed her to hear anything said within fifty meters of her hut. It took a bit of skill to filter, but she was up to the task, listening for more information about the mysterious buyer and what the slavers planned to do with their captives.

The hours slipped by and in no time she was calling the crawlers back and heading out, ready for the rendezvous. After all the excitement of the first day, it was almost a letdown to exit the settlement with none of the pirates the wiser. She crossed the terrain back to her ship without coming anywhere close to the hostiles, though the raised eyebrow that Jo sent her when she climbed back aboard their ship almost sent Sierra running back out to find someone to bloody. Her partners were going to give her *so much shit* for how this all went down.

Mindy wasn't far behind her, climbing in the hatch and sealing the door behind her. "Engage deflectors," she told Jo as soon as she spotted Sierra. They wouldn't be invisible, but it would be a lot harder to spot the ship on any tech or with the naked eye.

"Engaging," Jo confirmed, jogging back to the cockpit. The lights dimmed around them as the power was rerouted and Jo came back a few seconds later. "So what's the news?" She grinned at Sierra and shared a look with Mindy that could almost pass for friendly. Had they really mended fences over a little gossip? Sierra would take that win.

She dug into her pack and pulled out her crawlers and handed them to Jo. "Get these loaded up into the reader while I wash off some of this grime. We'll do a scan of the data and make sure that we don't need anything else." She turned to Mindy. "Get us set up for takeoff, we need to get back home quick if we're going to recover anyone."

"Did you confirm that the senator's niece was there?" Jo asked, rolling the crawlers between her fingers like they were some kind of toy.

"Not yet." Sierra nodded at Jo's hands. "I suppose we'll see. Get facial recognition running so we can see if we can get ident on anyone."

Though a long soak in a giant, warm bathtub sounded like heaven, Sierra didn't have time for more than a quick scrub down. She shot her hair a mournful look in the sliver of a mirror provided by the ship bathroom and promised herself to clean it as best she could once they were safely on their way home. As a stopgap, she covered it in a bit of cleaning powder to soak up some of the oil and dirt that had managed to accumulate during her days outside and sleeping on the ground. She'd been through worse, and she would have worse in the future, but after every mission she craved cleanliness like a woman stuck in a mud puddle for days.

By the time she was in a clean set of clothes, Jo had the crawlers loaded and scanning and Mindy was busy working on a flightpath. Sierra picked up a tablet and started scanning through some of the data that had already been analyzed. There wasn't a hit on the girl yet, but they'd only gone through fifteen percent of the data, she still had hope. That senator's niece had to be out there, if not, none of those women were getting saved. She knew that there was no way that Sol Intelligence or Defense would authorize the expense of a second trip for a group of a dozen nobodies. The thought made her grit her teeth.

"Proximity alert," beeped the ship's warning system.

Sierra sat up straight in her chair and switched the tablet view over to the security feed, expecting to see a group of pirates coming their way.

"Three hostiles," Jo read out, scanning through the security reading. "On foot and armed. Two hundred meters away and closing. It appears they haven't seen us."

Sierra's heartbeat kicked up as she zoomed in on the feed, trying to get a better look, even as she already knew in her heart who it was. And when the picture on her viewer resolved, she was right. Standing two hundred meters away from her ship was the man—alien—she'd never planned to see again.

Before she could even think to say anything, a second alert blared, this one much more urgent than the simple proximity monitor. Mindy cursed and docked her tablet before running behind Jo into the cockpit. Sierra put her own pad down and followed them, standing behind the navigator as she called up the complex view screen that could give them more data.

"We've got a military grade ship breaking atmo with three scouts. They're doing a scan for enemy ships and the deflector won't hold up to it. We need to power down. It's our only shot. The scan *might* read us as one of the junkers down there. But those guys outside will definitely spot us. We'll need to take them out."

"Don't worry about that right now. Power down." Sierra put her hand on top of her blaster as she watched Mindy and Jo work in concert to take the systems offline one by one, every second ticking by like an eternity in her mind. She was praying whoever was coming in fast was the buyer she'd heard about and not some new hostile. Their ship wasn't equipped for battle.

And right now all she could do was wait while the two people on board with experience did their best to save their asses. She walked back to the exit hatch and waited. No way were Raze and his men going to ignore a ship appearing out of nowhere. Here was to hoping that they were still on the same side.

   ***

Something tickled the back of Raze's senses, like an electric charge in the air. They'd made it back to the shipyard in record time, even with a short stop to make sure that Toran and Kayde ate as well as a quick scan for injuries. They hadn't been with the pirates long enough for symptoms of hunger or thirst to set in, and lucky for them, the pirates hadn't been interested in much beyond a little rough treatment.

Kayde seemed completely unaffected by the detour, as he should. Toran kept shooting glances at Raze like he didn't expect him to notice. Only momentum had stopped the talk that was coming from happening, but Raze knew the second they made it to wherever they were bedding down for the night, he'd be subjected to some kind of test of his stability. And he didn't know if he could pass.

He'd always expected the fall to be more violent. Soulless soldiers who failed in the field usually went out under explosive blaster fire and screams of sorrow and rage. But while he couldn't stop thinking of Sierra and how it felt to be in her presence, he'd never been more focused, more stable. But he didn't know if he could make Toran believe that. A soul didn't just grow back overnight.

They came to the *Lyrden* just past midnight, the moon bright in the sky. "Scan for threats," Toran told Kayde once they came to a halt.

Raze took the opportunity to look around. Their intelligence had called this a shipyard, but there was so much space between the ships that it was hard to see the organization. And it made guarding the ships more difficult, which worked well for them.

"There's some static north of here," Kayde reported, consulting his scanner, "but I think it's just planetary feedback. Something in the atmosphere has been causing issues."

Toran nodded. "Remain here to guard while Raze and I find a way in."

Kayde nodded and took his position, scanning around them for threats. Raze followed Toran as he circled the ship, waiting for him to say something. He didn't have to wait long.

They'd made it twenty meters from Kayde when Toran spoke. "Did you have difficulty deviating from the set mission?"

"Nothing significant." That was a question he could answer honestly, at least.

"Is there anything you want to tell me?" Toran was using a density scanner to search for a place to cut through the ship if they couldn't get a door open, he studied his device intently instead of looking at Raze. He knew something was up.

"Want?" Raze asked. The soulless couldn't want anything.

Toran let out a frustrated sound. "I'm speaking colloquially." He muttered something about Kayde that Raze couldn't quite make out.

"Is it strange to be around us?" It was suicide to ask something like that, but with the knowledge that he wouldn't survive for long sinking in, Raze found many of his self-preservation instincts had abandoned him to curiosity.

From the way Toran's shoulders stiffened, he knew that something was wrong too. He looked over at Raze, eyes narrowed, studying him for a long time, the silence stretching out between them like a river. "What happened to you?" he asked, instead of answering Raze's question.

"I'm still not sure." He couldn't lie to Toran, even if he was willing to engage in a little bit of misdirection. The soulless had no reason to lie, were, in fact, forbidden from doing so unless ordered otherwise. Raze had forgotten how to make it believable to a man he should have considered his friend.

"I'll need to report any deterioration in your mental state. You *know* that." Why that statement sounded like an accusation, Raze wasn't sure.

Before he could answer, Kayde let out a warning cry, sending Toran and Raze running back towards him, weapons in hand.

"Report," Toran demanded.

Kayde nodded to the north of them. "That ship just appeared out of nowhere."

"It landed?" Toran asked.

Raze looked over and saw a small craft whose origin he couldn't identify. It looked like a small, long range craft and he spied an FTL engine not unlike the one on their own ship. That meant it was built for speed and stealth, not battle.

"No," said Kayde. "It *appeared*. Shields dropped."

A whizzing sound overhead caught Raze's attention and he looked up to see a large craft in the distance flanked by three smaller vessels. One broke off and began flight in their direction. He touched Toran's shoulder and pointed at the ship headed in their direction.

Toran cursed. "I don't like the look of that. We need to get out of sight."

They redoubled the effort to find an entrance to the ship and in a matter of minutes, Kayde called out that he'd found a hatch. Toran and Raze ran around to find him slamming the butt of his blaster against the age roughened metal, trying to weaken the seal. From where they were standing, it was impossible to see the ship headed their way, but the toxic anticipation tied Raze's stomach in knots.

A chunk of rust fell and Toran surged forward, grabbing onto the door handle and heaving. It creaked open slowly, but only a handful of centimeters.

"It won't seal shut again once we get it open," Kayde warned.

"I'll worry about that later," Toran panted as he pulled. Raze got next to him and found a grip, pulling alongside him. The gap widened, millimeter by agonizing millimeter, until with a sudden shudder, the door gave and swung out wide enough for all three of them to get inside. They pulled it shut behind them as best they could and made their way into the heart of the ship that could finally give them the information they needed to find out who destroyed their home.

Chapter Eleven

The scout ship hovered over the area for long enough to make Sierra sick to her stomach. She sat with Mindy and Jo, checking the one window that had a good view of the sky. They couldn't power back up until the ship was out of range, so they had to rely on visual contact to see where the enemy ship was.

Though the likelihood of that ship being able to pick up anything inside their vessel was almost impossible, they sat in silence, waiting for the all clear. Sierra bit her lip as she watched the scout hover over the edge of the shipyard long enough to do several scans. What was it looking for? There were enough ships in the yard for decent scrap money, but a military vessel wouldn't need to bother with that. Not unless they needed something specific. She wasn't the praying type, but she sent one out into the universe, just in case.

Watching for the ship meant paying little attention to Raze and his men. Mindy and Jo had to be going crazy about them. In the excitement of powering down, Sierra hadn't told them that they probably weren't in danger. She added a footnote to her prayer for anyone out there listening to keep Raze and his guys safe too.

Jo tapped her on the shoulder and Sierra stepped back from the window to let her teammate take over the watch. They'd been switching between themselves every fifteen minutes or so, just to have something to do. With the ship powered down, it was a dark tomb inside, so there wasn't much to do but sit and wait.

Sierra took her seat in the kitchen and smoothed her fingers out over the table, trying to make as little noise as possible. She wanted to tap out a rhythm, but she didn't dare. Mindy took a seat next to her and took her cue, drawing little circles against the grain of the faux wood covering. Nothing in the mission brief had prepared them for an Oscavian warship. This was supposed to be a place forgotten by the empire, safe from military intervention, for better or worse.

"They're not going to send anyone back," she whispered, her words loud and clear in the silence of the ship.

Mindy's fingers stilled and she looked at Sierra and quirked up a brow. "Hmm?"

"If the empire is monitoring this place, no way would they risk angering them. Not even for a senator's niece. And that's *if* that warship isn't here to collect the women." Failure was a heavy weight on her shoulders, making her slump down until her head hung low enough for her hair to fall over her face. She waited for some hollow platitude from Mindy, but her teammate remained silent.

The whole situation sucked.

"I saw some of those women," Sierra said, emotion gathering in her throat, making her words thick. "They look so... defeated. They've given up hope. And they're right."

"The scout is moving on," Jo said, her normal tone like a shout in the silent ship. She took the seat on the other side of Sierra. "It would be tight, but we *could* fit twelve more people on this craft for a short journey. It's rated for up to twenty passengers."

Sierra snapped her head over to her surly partner. "You are *not* the person I expected to make that suggestion."

Mindy made a snorting sound but remained silent.

Jo shrugged. "This location is burned. We had a reason to hide our presence when we thought the empire didn't give a shit about it. But no way are humans coming back here. I just don't see how we pull an extraction op with three people."

"True." Against just the pirates and slavers out there, the risk might have been worth it. But add in highly trained Oscavian warriors? No way. "What if we had six?"

"Would that include three who have seen exactly where they're holding the women?" Mindy asked with a grin. Then she shook her head. "It's still pretty much suicide."

Sierra pushed back from the table and started pacing. "Yeah, in an ideal situation, this wouldn't be the setup. But they won't expect us."

"And if they put in greater security measures after your new friends escaped?" Mindy asked, keeping her part as the group's new downer. "This isn't a training sim. If we die here, we're just dead."

"There's nothing new. I'd bet my life on it. This isn't a military grade operation. They think because the women are stranded on this planet with no way off, they don't need to bother with high tech measures." That much had been clear from the data she'd pulled off the crawlers before the ship powered down, and from what she'd witnessed in the settlement.

"Okay." Jo held up a hand and Sierra stopped moving, leaning back against the storage cabinets behind her. "Say we get the women out, how do we get them across twenty kilometers of rough terrain without being seen. We can't exactly land the ship right outside of town."

Sierra grinned. "If we time it right we can."

"You're fucking crazy." Mindy gave a mirthless laugh. "If we risk the ship and lose, we're stranded here."

"On a planet with hundreds of ships just ripe for the taking," Sierra gestured with a hand, as if she were looking out a window instead of in the enclosed kitchen. "One of these babies is probably flight worthy, if it comes to that."

"No." That wiped the smile off of Jo's face. "We can't make a plan based on maybe and probably. You should know better than that. What is it about this one that's gotten to you?" she demanded. "You've lost objectivity."

She'd never had it in the first place, but Sierra kept that part to herself. She took a deep, calming breath, and then another for good measure. It did little to calm her nerves, but her heartbeat started to settle, at least. "I was born in the Wastes. If I hadn't been lucky, I could have been one of those women. Either abducted from Earth for sex slavery, or forced into it the old-fashioned way. If it weren't for my dad..." She shook her head. "Twenty percent of the women in the abduction files came from the Wastes. No one gives a damn about them. And I know these women represent barely a fraction of the ones who have disappeared, but we're their only hope. Leaving them isn't an option for me. Not one that will let me look myself in the face in the mirror, not if we don't even try." Her past wasn't exactly a secret, but Sierra didn't like to spend time dwelling on it.

Neither Jo nor Mindy had a response to that. The three of them stayed looking at each other for several moments until Jo broke the silence. "So... how would we even find our new friends, if we were willing to try this?"

At that Sierra smiled and pointed towards the hatch. "Last I checked, they were about two hundred meters away."

***

Powering up a hundred-year-old ship held together with more rust than metal was a challenge, but Raze trusted Kayde to do his job. He was there to provide any support his partner needed while Toran took the first watch outside. They were wary of more ships like the scout they'd spotted, but they couldn't afford to be caught by the pirates who guarded the ship yard this late in the game.

Kayde worked in silence and Raze respected that. They had nothing to say to one another, so there was no reason to fill the space with idle chatter. He found that he had to keep reminding himself of things like that, things that would have come naturally two days ago. Standing near Kayde did more to confirm that the impossible had happened than anything else.

Raze's emotions were back, to some degree. What that meant for his soul or the Denya Price, he wasn't sure, and he doubted that he'd have time to figure it out. At least Toran was keeping his distance for the moment. Kayde could not care if Raze acted slightly strange, and as long as he didn't do anything drastic, the man probably wouldn't even notice.

"Please grab me a second battery pack from the case," Kayde requested without looking away from his work, the words muffled by all of the wires and metal in front of him. Raze dug through their tool kit until he found the part and handed it over silently.

He looked toward the door before he realized that he heard a commotion. A moment later, Toran came in with a bound and hooded woman. Raze's spine stiffened. *Sierra.* He took a step closer, his hand clenched in a fist and claws pricking his skin, begging to be let out. "Let her go," he gritted out before he did something rash, like attack his leader to free a woman he barely knew.

"Raze?" Sierra asked. She was curious, not scared, which did a little to settle his nerves. "Want to explain that we're friends?"

87

Friends? Like it was that simple. When Toran made no move to unhand her, he stepped forward and reached for her. Toran stepped in front to block his path and Raze growled, this time unable to stop his claws from shooting out. "She's the reason you're free," he managed to say around the protective anger in his throat. "Unhand her. Now!"

A tool clattered to the ground behind him and Raze had to take half a step back to keep both Kayde and Toran in his sight. If they took him out, there was no telling what they'd do to Sierra.

Sierra held up her bound hands. They seemed to be held together with Toran's belt. "Easy there, buddy," she said, her words only for him. Even without sight, she managed to step around Toran and close the distance between them. She placed her hands on his chest, right over his heart, and some of the fighting edge lessened to the point where he could think. Raze covered her hands with his own, careful not to prick her with his claws, even as they rested against her skin. He heard her swallow hard. "Um, are those claws? When did you get claws?"

With a flick of his wrist he retracted them. "Sorry," he said. "They're gone for now." Carefully, he pulled the hood back. It was a spare bag that came standard with their supplies in case they needed the extra room. He placed it beside the toolkit before unwrapping the belt from around Sierra's hands, her hot skin burning his flesh in exactly the right way. No risk of seizure here.

Her red lips pulled into a smile and their eyes locked.

Denya.

Recognition tore through him, sweeping uncertainty out of place and replacing it with the driving need to claim Sierra as his own. He cupped her cheek with one hand, unwilling and unable to break eye contact with her as he pulled her close enough to taste.

"What in all the hells is going on?" Toran broke through the spell and Sierra jumped back, suddenly coming back to herself. Raze let his hands drop, but took a step closer to her, ready to protect her if his men turned on his mate.

"She's mine."

"We need your help."

They spoke at the same time and Sierra shot him a confused look. She mouthed something at him that he didn't understand, then subtly pointed to her chest and then to Toran. He nodded, letting her speak. Toran narrowed his eyes at Raze for a moment before turning back to the human in front of them.

"From that welcome, I'm guessing that Raze didn't mention me." She smiled brightly, but her tone lacked sincerity. She leaned back against a wall and kept her hands loosely at her sides, deceptively casual and quite unlike the woman he'd spent the night with. What was she playing at?

"Raze has yet to give his report," was Toran's reply.

Sierra nodded. She glanced back at him, one eyebrow slightly raised as if asking him a question. He nodded, even if he had no idea what she planned. If she needed help, he'd do anything to see it done.

"Right." She nodded. "So, let's talk."

***

Sierra had *really* hoped that Raze would be the first person she met when she crossed the distance between her ship and the place he and his men seemed to be investigating. The old junker couldn't be theirs. It was more than a hundred years old and covered in rust, completely grounded. When she ran into the golden alien that she'd spotted before he was abducted, she knew some portion of her luck had run out. He didn't give her much time to talk, but at least he didn't shoot her. She'd been blasted enough for one mission.

And she really hadn't expected Raze to make such a fuss about it. Jo and Mindy would have done the same, or worse, if one of his guys had shown up unannounced. This was just business. And she had to keep her head in the game.

No focusing on this *she's mine* nonsense. No matter that it sent a thrill through her and had her crazy to know exactly what he meant by that. The guy could barely kiss her without freaking out, and she'd walked away knowing there was nothing between them. But relationship—or whatever—conversations would need to wait until later.

Right now they had some lives to save.

"Please have a seat," the leader said. "I'm Toran, and that is Kayde." He pointed to a man practically wrapped up in wires. "You clearly already know Raze."

Toran was different from Raze and Kayde. Though his expression was more or less neutral, there was a tightness to his eyes that gave away frustration and his tone was nowhere near as even as the infuriating way Raze had of talking. Maybe he hadn't given up his emotions yet, or he had a mate. Either way, it was clear that he was in charge.

She's mine.

Raze's voice sure hadn't been neutral there. And every time she looked at him, his expression held layers that hadn't been there when they first met. A conclusion tickled her mind, but if she let herself think about it, she just might panic, and shit was about to get way too dangerous to allow panic.

"I'm glad you're safe and more or less unharmed," she offered, which Toran acknowledged with a polite nod. "I came to you because I need your help." She didn't call it a favor, but from the look Toran gave her, he could read between the lines. He and Kayde might be dead if it weren't for her. She didn't look at Raze as she spoke, she didn't want to know what he thought of her leveraging his teammates' lives like this. "I have a team prepared to extract the women being held for transport in the heart of the settlement." An exaggeration, but they didn't need to know that. "Our mission parameters have changed and we need backup. We'd like to offer you the opportunity for a little payback."

"Who is 'we'?" asked Toran. "Where are you from?"

"We're a team of three, all well trained on Earth." There was little use hiding their origin, since Sierra was speaking English rather than Interstellar Common. The Detyens' translators would have been able to pick that much up. The fact that they were Sol Intelligence, on the other hand, couldn't get out.

Toran opened his mouth to speak, but Raze interrupted him. "A word?" he asked his leader. The two men exchanged a look and walked down the hall silently, leaving Sierra alone with Kayde.

She watched him for a minute, waiting to see if he'd say anything, but he was an animated statue, breathing and watching her silently, ready to take her out if she gave a hint of danger. She hadn't brought weapons with her as a sign of good faith, and Toran had patted her down, but Kayde didn't seem to care that he was bigger and apparently had claws sometimes, he respected her as a threat.

She liked that.

Though the claws thing was freaking her out a bit. Green skin? No problem. Muscular enough to hurl boulders? Great. Weird biological imperatives to mate or die? Well, that was kind of fucked up, but not in the same way. Claws were scary. It meant that a Detyen always had a weapon and she'd have to remember that and warn her teammates in case this idea went south.

The longer Raze and Toran were away, the more concerned Sierra grew. She couldn't hear a hint of what was being said and as the seconds ticked on, her optimism for her plan working plummeted. Kayde's hard stare was starting to get to her, making her want to cover herself up even though she was fully clothed. It wasn't that he was being lecherous or anything, but he seemed to see through her, analyzing her like some kind of interesting scientific specimen.

Had they been gone for five minutes? More? Jo and Mindy wouldn't wait forever, no matter the assurances she'd given them that Raze's crew wasn't likely to kill her. She knew that Raze wouldn't, but Kayde would pull the trigger, no questions asked. Toran was the wild card.

A door somewhere in the back of the ship rattled open and out came Raze and Toran. Raze had on that mask of emotionless calm that had started to look fake to her eyes and Toran looked ready to tear something apart. Sierra's heart sank. So much for that plan.

Toran ignored her and asked Kayde something in a language that her translator couldn't process. The man responded in the same language. Raze looked at her, but his face gave nothing away. She gave him her best blank look, but compared to Kayde, she knew she gave away far too much.

A moment later, Toran turned to her and Raze looked away. "You will have our help," he said. "We will rendezvous at your ship in four hours."

Chapter Twelve

"What you're suggesting is suicide." Toran sat beside him and Kayde in the small kitchen on Sierra's ship. They'd exchanged greetings with her crew: Mindy, a human woman with an explosion of brightly colored hair, and Jo, a much more sedate human woman with a hard expression. These weren't soldiers, that much was clear. No matter the planet of origin, soldiers held themselves with a similar bearing. Sierra, Mindy, and Jo all seemed relaxed, even in the company of three strangers who could easily prove to be hostile.

Spies held themselves like that.

They hadn't given much information on what they did, but Raze had spent enough time around the legion intelligence agents to recognize the signs. Not to mention the plan they'd put together.

"It's risky," Mindy conceded, "but none of *us* have a death wish." That 'us' clearly just meant the humans.

Raze shot Sierra a look and she rolled her eyes at her teammate. It wasn't a common Detyen expression, but he'd seen plenty of humans make that face to understand what it meant. "We can't guarantee that the women will be in the settlement beyond tonight," Sierra added. "In the time since we last spoke, we were able to gather a little intelligence. Despite the size of the ship that breached orbit this afternoon, there are fewer than thirty Oscavian soldiers on the ground. We have no intel on how many are in reserve on the ship, but that shouldn't matter. The ship is docked fifty kilometers away in a large canyon. The scout ships are near the settlement, but they're all powered down. The Oscavian in charge is keeping his men close. As far as we can tell, the women are still in the central holding pens where Toran and Kayde were imprisoned. As long as they're there, we can extract them."

"What makes you think they'll still be there after midnight?" Toran asked. He hadn't spoken to Raze in the hours since their private discussion and even Kayde seemed to understand that there was something wrong.

"A payment dispute," said Jo. "They've been arguing about it all day. The slavers are trying to extract every credit they can from their buyer, while the buyer is trying to bargain since the women are *used goods*." She sneered out the last two words.

"Where is your intel coming from?" was Toran's next question.

"We're relying on electronic surveillance," Sierra admitted. "It's too risky and time consuming to get one of us back in the settlement. Something on the planet has been doing strange things to our signal, but we're confident of everything we told you. We are these women's only chance of a rescue."

"Why these twelve?" Kayde shocked Raze by asking. "There are billions of humans. If you are so opposed to slavery, why not hit a place like the Slave Markets?" He referred to a notorious planet which made all of its money in the slave trade. "There are thousands of humans there that will never be rescued."

Mindy recoiled as if he'd slapped her and both Sierra and Jo glared. Kayde didn't seem to notice the response.

Sierra was the first to recover. "It would take an army, or billions of credits, to rescue anyone from the Slave Markets. We're here. I'm not sure what's so complicated about that." Her tone was harsh enough to cut, but Kayde merely nodded, satisfied with the answer.

"If you're out, tell us," Jo commanded. "This is our only shot, so we either need you beside us, or out of our way. Which is it?"

Toran studied the three humans for several moments, and Raze knew he must be weighing the pros and cons of the plan. This was far outside the mission parameters and he could be disciplined for offering his assistance. But he still had a conscience, and both he and Kayde had listened to those women's screams for hours. Though he still had his soul, his leader could be cold. Could he really leave those women to suffer? He finally spoke. "As payment for the assistance that you provided to us, we will be your distraction. But we cannot risk engagement or discovery. And I need your promise that you will not reveal who we are or where we are from to the enemy on the ground here or to anyone from your world. Can you do that?"

"Yes," Sierra said without hesitation. "No problem."

"Then we have a plan."

***

Raze was *right there* and Sierra couldn't find an excuse to say anything to him. And even if she had an excuse, she wasn't sure *what* she'd say to him. No, that wasn't right. She'd ask him what the hell he'd said to Toran that had the man practically glaring at her every time his gaze swung her way. Then she'd ask him what he'd meant by that 'she's mine' comment. His what? Friend? Acquaintance? Responsibility?

Mate?

Ugh! She was beginning to wish that she'd never come up with this harebrained idea in the first place, if only so she didn't have to examine her weird thoughts and emotions when it came to Raze. He was a piece of adhesive that she couldn't tear off, sticking to her every time she thought she had him removed. And the longer he stuck, the worse getting rid of him would hurt. It didn't take a genius to figure that part out.

"We need to leave now if we're to make it to our ship in time to be of any use to you," Toran told Jo. He'd been addressing most of his comments to her, rather than Sierra or Mindy. Why he ignored Mindy, Sierra wasn't sure, but at least Jo didn't seem to mind the de facto leadership position she'd been pushed into.

"If you give us the coordinates, we can take you there," Jo offered. "The scouts haven't flown since their initial scan and we haven't attracted any pirate attention so far." The Detyen leader made a sound like he was going to refuse, but Jo threw a hand up before he could say anything. "I insist."

Their gazes locked and something ticked in Toran's jaw, but he relented after a moment and gave her the coordinates. She thanked him with a falsely bright smile and left for the cockpit, Toran right on her heels.

Mindy caught her gaze, then flicked her eyes to Raze and then back to Sierra. She didn't cock her eyebrow up, but she didn't need to. Sierra got the message. She still didn't have an excuse for why they needed to be alone, but with Toran gone, it didn't seem to matter as much.

She placed a hand on Raze's shoulder and nodded to the hallway towards the back of the ship. "Come on," she said.

Raze stood with her and followed without a word to Kayde or Mindy. Maybe that whole 'emotionless' thing could come in handy sometime, if it meant she didn't need to make meaningless small talk or excuses. She could get used to that. They passed by the door to her quarters and for one insane second Sierra considered opening it up and yanking him inside, but that choice only led to madness and embarrassment the second they were discovered. No, she wanted enough space between them and the crews that they wouldn't be overheard, but no doors between them. No temptation to do things she knew she shouldn't.

That thinking was what ended with them squashed into the little alcove beside their fresh food storage closet, standing not quite close enough to touch, heat from their bodies boiling between them. Sierra stared at Raze, trying to look in his eyes, but her gaze kept dropping down to his mouth. She had questions, she needed answers.

But when he leaned forward, her hands went to his waist like they were being pulled by magnets and her lips found his, swallowing his breath as they crushed themselves together. There was nothing tentative, not like the first time they'd done this back in the cave. This was an affirmation of everything they'd felt, everything they'd known was impossibly true from the moment they'd stopped trying to kill one another.

Raze let out a groan strong enough to reverberate down through Sierra's toes and she forgot about anyone else on the ship, forgot about anyone else on the planet. As far as she was concerned, she and Raze were the only two beings to exist in the entire galaxy. His fingers reverently cupped her cheek and she didn't care about the claws she knew lurked under his skin. He'd never hurt her, that certainty ran bone deep.

His tongue swiped at her lips and she opened for him with a gasp, swept under the spell of the kiss as he ensorcelled her with sensation. A shudder ran through him, his body vibrating under her fingers. She tightened her hold on his hips, hard enough to bruise, even through the thick material of his clothes, anything to keep him close. But Raze showed no signs of pulling back. His other hand cupped the back of her neck, his fingers teasing the hair at the base of her neck until it came undone from the tie she was using to hold it back. It wrapped around his fingers and every movement of his hand was enough to pull it just a little, not quite painful, but a rattling sensation through her body.

The floor under her feet tilted, sending Sierra sprawling forward and pulling her mouth off of his. She buried her face in the dark material of his shirt, afraid to look up and see the expression on his face. God, she was nuts, throwing herself at him like some sex-crazed teenager going through her first crush. Her actions were the opposite of professional, and they were setting a horrible example of human-alien relations.

She placed her palms on his chest, as if she could push away from him and put some needed distance between them, but he covered one of her hands with his own and tilted up her chin with his fingers. In his eyes she saw the dazed wonder that was surging through her, not something she understood but something she wanted to explore further and see where it went.

But there was no 'further' for them. After tonight they'd be off the planet and heading in different directions and only Mindy and Jo would ever know that he'd existed in her orbit.

"What is this?" she asked, afraid that if she spoke louder than a whisper she'd break the spell between them.

"It's right," said Raze, his volume matching hers.

"You're different than you were." Maybe it was too soon to say something like that, but it was true. She'd seen him next to Kayde, and there was no way to believe that Raze was just as emotionless as his cold partner.

"You're—"

She cut him off, placing her fingers over his lips. "Don't say it."

He kissed her fingers and she slowly pulled them away, tracing a path along his cheek. "Say what?"

"What I think you're going to say." If he said she was his mate, his denya or whatever, she didn't know what she was going to do. But she wouldn't be able to let him go, and neither of them had another choice.

"I'll find you," he promised.

"How?" She didn't know where he was going, and Earth was a backwater, far away from everything.

"Meet me somewhere."

"Where?" It was a dream, but she wanted it so bad she could taste it.

"Honora Station, on the interstellar new year." The hope in his voice and eyes was enough proof that those emotions he'd claimed to have sacrificed had come back in full force, and Sierra couldn't be the reason that hope was quashed.

The interstellar new year was months away, and though Honora Station was far away from Earth, plenty of transports took passengers there. She could make it happen, somehow. "Okay," she agreed.

He kissed her again, this time hope and desperation mixing into something she was afraid to contemplate, but as the ship glided through the air, taking them closer to Raze's destination and their parting, she knew she had to find a way to make this work. They came from different worlds, but nothing had ever felt so right as his lips on hers. And no matter what happened, she needed to feel this again.

***

Toran's silence continued once they left Sierra's ship and boarded their own. Raze could still taste Sierra on his lips and feel the imprint of her fingers on his hips. Toran had no idea that they'd sneaked away to steal a moment for themselves, and Kayde didn't seem inclined to tell. How Raze would keep his promise to meet her, he didn't know. The soulless didn't have permission to leave the legion by themselves, and he would need time, money, and transport to get away from home. But no matter what it took, he'd find a way to get back to her. He'd somehow survive the next months until he could claim her, his existence lonely and cold, but with a bright spark of hope held close to his heart.

His stomach roiled, not for the first time, and Raze gripped the armrests on his seat as Kayde engaged the launch sequence. A similar sharp lance of pain had shot through him while he held Sierra in his arms, but he'd been able to push that aside, years of training at working through the toughest conditions perfectly applied to experience a pleasure he'd never thought possible. He'd thought the pain came from physical contact, his soul, or lack thereof, reacting to its reawakening under Sierra's touch. But she was far away now, back on the other ship with her own people.

And Raze thought he was going to vomit. Sweat beaded his brow and his vision went a little hazy. He clenched his fists tighter, almost hard enough to leave in imprint in the metal beneath his fingers. It didn't do much to help, other than make his fingers hurt nearly as much as his stomach. Would this be what he felt like now when he was away from his mate? Would it go away once he claimed her? He'd never heard of this kind of sickness from anyone who'd met their denya, but he'd also never heard of one of the soulless finding a mate.

Another thought occurred, one chilling enough to freeze him to his core and momentarily make the physical pain flee. He'd met his denya, his emotions were back in some capacity. What about his soul? And if his soul had grown back, did that mean his life was at stake? He hadn't claimed her, hadn't bound her to him. Without that bond, he was living on borrowed time, over thirty with no way of knowing if he might fall over and die at any minute.

The stomach ache began to recede, stabbing pain gentling into something manageable. He wiped the sweat from his brow and didn't sweat anymore. The physical effects of distance from Sierra, or from exposure to her, were letting him go and he could feel the calm returning to his mind, blotting out the peaks and valleys of emotion until he had his equilibrium once again. But unlike their parting before, he did not mistake this for an emotionless state. His feelings were still there, a present threat to his safety among his people and something he would need to hide until he could find a way to get away and claim Sierra as his own.

"Do you require medical assistance?" Toran asked, finally breaking the silence between them with a concerned look.

"No." He was under control now and he wouldn't endanger the mission. Wouldn't endanger Sierra.

Anger simmered in Toran's eyes and something that might have been betrayal, but Raze wasn't sure how he'd betrayed them.

The conversation they'd had when Sierra came to them with her plan hadn't revealed much. Raze had given Toran a more in depth report about what he'd done in the hours between Toran and Kayde's abduction and their rescue—leaving out the parts about kissing and emotion—and he'd argued that they owed it to the humans to help them. But nothing they were doing now, provided they were successful, was a betrayal of the legion.

"We need to talk before we get home," Toran said, his voice devoid of all inflection.

Raze just nodded and kept his eyes forward.

Kayde cut through their discussion. "I'm patching in to the humans' communication. We're coming up on the settlement in thirty seconds."

"Engage cloaking," Toran ordered.

It was time to fight.

Chapter Thirteen

The rumble of the engines from the Oscavian warship made the ground under Sierra's feet shudder and she had to remind herself that it was almost fifty kilometers away and would take several minutes to go from parked to flying. Plenty of time for a nimble crew to get away. Plenty of time to pull off the heist of the century.

"I have contact with our friends," Jo's voice came over the comms. "Are you in position?"

Sierra glanced over at Mindy, who blended into the night with her dark cap, black clothes, and face paint. "We are in position," Sierra confirmed. She'd been here before enough times that she was beginning to feel more like a tourist on Fenryr 1 than an infiltrator. They crouched in the same abandoned hut that Sierra had used as a base of operations earlier, the space a little cramped for two people.

Unlike the previous night, the settlement was subdued, a hush of anticipation laying heavy over everything. She hadn't seen any of the prisoners out with the men, which was good for them. Unfortunately, the central ship was under heavy guard and locked up tight. They didn't want anything to happen to their prisoners until the sale was completed. Too bad for them, Sierra wasn't about to let that happen.

"Counting down one minute until go," Jo warned them and began to count backwards from sixty.

Sierra closed her eyes and took a deep breath, leaning back on her heels and centering her focus. She couldn't think about what would happen between her and Raze. She had to push all thoughts of what this mission would do to her career aside. All she could worry about until this thing was done was the twelve women who needed her help, who would be forced into slavery for the rest of their lives if they failed. Beside her, Mindy chanted a prayer under her breath, the words too faint for Sierra to make out.

"Three, two, one, engage." As Jo cut out, a blast rocked the hut, sending a loose piece of wood to the floor and forcing Sierra back a step.

"Damn," she muttered. That was some firepower on Raze's ship.

Adrenaline coursed through her veins and she wanted to shoot off running for the center of the settlement, but they had a plan, and she and Mindy had to wait. If they moved too early, they would be caught and could end up sharing the same fate of the women they were trying to rescue. A second blast, this one from the opposite side of town, reverberated through the hut. This one wasn't as big, but Sierra knew it would make a lot of smoke and fire, causing confusion even if it didn't cause that much damage.

Today, they needed confusion more.

Slavers went running down the street outside the door to the little hut. Sierra resisted the urge to fall back further into the shadows of the hut; at this point movement was more likely to grab their attention than anything else. Another pack of men rushed past them and once they were clear, Sierra risked sticking her head out the door to check their path.

She gave Mindy the signal and they took off running towards the center of the settlement. Both of them were dressed in dark colors with their hair covered by dark caps. Given a single glance, they'd pass for pirates or slavers, but Sierra hadn't seen many women pirates on the ground, which meant their costumes weren't likely to hold up under scrutiny.

The guards in front of the central ship had mostly run to investigate the blasts on either side of town, leaving three to stand watch. Sierra held up her blaster, but Mindy put a hand on her arm before she could fire and pointed at the door.

The *opening* door. Maybe Mindy had a point with that prayer thing.

Two more men ran out of the ship and the door began to slide shut behind them. This was the chance. Sierra and Mindy opened fire, setting their blasters to the highest stun setting they could. Blasters normally weren't fatal, but they hurt like hell and could knock a person out for hours. The guards went down before they realized they were under fire and Mindy and Sierra sprinted for the door, shouldering their way in before it could close behind them.

The inside of the ship was lit with eerie red lights that put Sierra's teeth on edge. Thanks to Raze, they knew exactly where the women were being kept and the code that had freed his men. The only way they could quickly get twelve unarmed, potentially injured women out from the pens was to make sure that they didn't come under fire on the way out, which meant that Sierra and Mindy showed no mercy. The first handful of pirates went down easy, not expecting to be attacked inside the central fortress of their settlement.

"I have visual on the information console," Mindy said as they made their way further into the ship. They couldn't risk a security alarm giving them away and calling the rest of the pirates back. Sierra hated to stop where they were and sweat beaded along her brow as her blood pumped too fast in her veins, but they had to take down as much of the security system as they could.

"Say a prayer of thanks for me that this place looks retrofitted as hell," Sierra muttered to her partner, who shot her a smile while she got to work. The ship itself was solid, but it hadn't been built for containment or security. The lights flickered and Sierra looked at the screen, but it was still brightly lit with a glowing map of the ship. "Was that you?" she asked, tapping a foot to keep from bouncing with spare energy.

"Give me a minute," Mindy muttered around a piece of wire in her mouth. "Almost there."

Footsteps echoed ahead of them and Mindy pressed herself flat against the wall, making herself as small a target as she could. Sierra ran up to a thin pillar and used it for her own cover, waiting for the pirates to turn around the bend. Her blaster was warm and heavy in her hand, carrying the weight of salvation and pain in one compact package. Two heads came into view and she fired, blasting off shot after shot until they went down in a sad clatter of bodies.

While Mindy worked, Sierra stripped them of weapons, disabling their modified blasters and confiscating enough knives to slay an elephant. There wasn't a good place to hide the unconscious bodies, so she stashed them as best she could down a narrow hallway, angling a stack of crates to hide them from view.

Coming back up to Mindy, Sierra peered over her shoulder. "Does that give us any idea of how many slavers are in here?" she asked.

"Lights are powered down on most of the ship," Mindy replied. "There's a central command center and a mess hall that have activity. Based on our crawler count from earlier and the men we've already taken out, I estimate we've got ten more hostiles on board."

"Wonderful." Some of the tech they had back home would have given them exactly the information they needed, but given the parameters of the mission, there'd been no reason to requisition it. Then. Now Sierra was kicking herself for not thinking ahead.

Mindy let out a bark of laughter, startling Sierra. "Oh that's just perfect," she said.

"What?"

Her partner looked about ready to kiss the machine. "Someone forgot to disable the admin controls," she practically sang. "I can lock the control room and mess halls down from here. The most likely override of that little trick is to completely power the ship down, which will take them a while to figure out. Especially since I can power down their admin terminals from here." She cackled. "God, I love idiots."

"Get it fucking done." Sierra's feet itched to get on the move. They didn't have much time.

A minute later, Mindy stood. "We're good. Let's get this done and get out of here."

***

Ten minutes into the operation and every single one of Raze's newly awakened nerves was on edge. He felt like a green recruit, scared of his own shadow and ready to fire his blaster at anything that moved, whether friend or foe. But neither Toran nor Kayde were paying attention to him at the moment, which gave him the time he needed to at least pretend he had something like composure.

"Cloaking reserves at seventy percent," he reported. "Dropping as expected."

Their ship had some of the best cloaking tech available, but the engine burned out fast, which didn't give them much time to engage with the slavers and Oscavian soldiers who had come to join the party.

"What's your status?" Toran asked over the comm line they had with the humans.

"We need more time." Jo came back, cool as any Detyen. "Approaching position three."

"Get higher," Toran told Kayde. "We can't maintain fire for much longer."

If their cloaking reserves dropped below fifty percent, they wouldn't be able to make it off the planet undetected. Instead, they'd need to find a place to hide, which had just become much more difficult between the Oscavian military vessel and its scout ships. Escaping at the same time as the humans was their best opportunity.

Raze jolted in his seat as one of the ground to air blasts made contact with their ship. "Shields intact," he reported, "glancing blow." Unless the Oscavian ships got involved, their defensive shields would hold up to the slavers' offense. But every second that ticked by made it more likely that the Oscavians would come out to play.

A blaze of fire flashed at the edge of his peripheral vision. Raze changed his view and saw the roaring flames coming from the other side of the settlement. "Position three is lit up," he told his team before switching his viewer back to the scene below them.

Pirates had taken cover in the buildings at the farthest edge of the settlement and under the rocky outcroppings nearby. They used blasters and a few surface to air weapons to try and find their ship, but with the cloaking, it was almost impossible to score a hit. Their ship wasn't built for war and their firing capability came from a modified tractor beam. Rather than pull things to the ship, they used it to blast a weak laser at the ground. It was useful for breaking through rocks on land and pushing space debris out of the way without damaging the ship, but it was no match against actual blasters or las fire.

The minutes ticked by and Raze kept flipping between watching the forces on the ground and monitoring the sensors. He summoned all the discipline that he'd learned in his thirty-two years to keep thoughts of Sierra out of his mind. Being on this ship was helping her do her job, and he could not afford to worry about her status and keep his men safe at the same time.

"Reserves at sixty-five," he warned. The more they flew, the faster they burned through the cloaking engine. Evasive maneuvers like Kayde was pulling were the most taxing use for the cloaking drive, but they still had time. The humans just needed to hurry up.

As the reserves dropped lower and Toran got a lucky shot, hitting some kind of fuel tank and sending fire spurting up in a blooming burst, Jo's voice crackled over their comms. "The team is returned. All safe. Thank you for flying with us. Out."

"Best of luck, out," Toran replied before cutting off the comms. He looked over at Kayde and said, "Get us out of here."

Kayde nodded and flicked several switches on the control panel. "Fasten restraints and brace," he ordered before taking a hold of the controls and tilting back, shooting them straight up towards the atmosphere, leaving a blast of dust from the thrusters in their wake.

Raze braced and watched the cloaking engine reserves steadily shrink. He switched views again to study the path ahead of them. "We're clear, space is empty and open overhead." As the last word left his mouth, a blast rocked the ship, sending them spinning. Something rattled around, a loose piece of equipment that Raze couldn't see, focused as he was on his monitors.

"What in all the hells was that?" Toran demanded as Kayde righted the ship.

A yellow warning light flashed over his screen and Raze brought up the schematic. "Something hit a panel. Heat shielding is intact, FTL is intact. Defensive shields compromised, cloaking reserves at thirteen percent."

A second blast rocked them, but Kayde managed to avoid the spin this time. He kept his focus on steering the ship while Toran barked out orders.

"Is something locked onto us?" he demanded.

Though Toran held control of their reverse tractor beam, Raze had more detailed viewers. He checked every sensor he could and ran a report on the ship's status again. "Sensors aren't showing anything," he reported.

"Then check it again!"

A second check had Raze biting back a curse. "One of the scouts is in the air. It's shooting randomly. I don't think it has us on its sensors yet."

"Fifteen seconds to atmo," Kayde warned.

"We need to take out the scout," Toran said. "Change course."

"We won't have cloaking if we do that," Raze warned.

Toran took a deep breath and nodded once. "Get us out of here, Kayde."

Raze watched the rear sensors and stared at the scout ship as if he could attack it with his eyes. In the last seconds before the sensors blacked out, the scout veered off their course and headed west. "It's off our tail," he reported.

Toran acknowledged him with a second nod and Kayde guided them off planet through the thick atmosphere of Fenryr 1 and into space.

Raze thought they were safe and ready to hop to FTL to head home when the emergency lights flashed on. He brought up the ship schematic again and hissed as he watched their systems go offline one by one. "FTL offline," he reported, "cloaking exhausted. Heat shielding compromised, defensive shields down, main life support system down, back up life support compromised. Fuel reserves at eight percent."

Toran stared at Raze for several seconds, processing the news. "How far can we get?" he asked.

Kayde was the one who answered. "With no FTL, we'll barely make it past the next moon."

"And," Raze added, "our air will run out long before then. We have three hours." And that was if the scout ship didn't break atmo and find them first.

Chapter Fourteen

Settling a dozen women onto a tiny ship fleeing from a hostile planet in a matter of minutes was almost more difficult than extracting them from their prison in the first place. Sierra turned down the extra seating in the kitchen, folding down benches that normally laid flat against the wall. She guided the women to the seats, using her most comforting voice, but after the fight and the run to freedom, she was riding high on adrenaline and she knew she sounded more excited and high strung than competent.

"Buckle in, buckle in," she commanded a short blond woman and a woman with short, wiry black hair and brown skin who wouldn't let go of the blond woman's hand. "We need everyone secured before we break atmo."

"Who *are* you?" the black woman demanded. The other women around her all nodded.

There hadn't been any time to exchange pleasantries as she and Mindy ushered them out of the holding pens. "My name is Sierra Alvarez. I'm from Earth and we're taking you home." The women just stared at her, one a few seats away daring a small smile. Sierra reminded herself that these people had been held for months, maybe longer, and forced to endure great hardship and abuse. Of course they weren't going to cheer the second a human showed up to take them away. Hell, most of the pirates out here *were* human, so there was no reason to trust her more than anyone else.

She'd deal with winning them over later. She confirmed they were all secured safely and climbed up into the cockpit with Jo and Mindy, who were already completing the pre-flight checks.

"Do we have any company?" Jo asked as she pressed several buttons on her control panel and slowly pulled back on one of the joystick controls.

"We have clear skies," Mindy replied. "Take us home."

Sierra strapped herself in and braced for takeoff. Their deflector shield wasn't as good at cloaking as the one Raze and his men had, and the Detyens had agreed to draw the most fire while Jo snuck into the settlement to gather Sierra, Mindy, and the prisoners. That meant they had an easier escape path and Sierra would need to find a way to thank them, somehow. She'd have months to figure it out, months until she saw Raze again. Months until she'd find out if anything went wrong on their end.

What would she do if he didn't show up at Honora Station?

"Are you with us, Sierra?" Mindy asked, jolting Sierra out of her spiraling thoughts.

She was so out of it that she hadn't realized they'd broken atmo. "The women are buckled up," Sierra reported. "They aren't happy, but I can't blame them for that. We just need to prove that we actually did rescue them. It will be okay."

Mindy offered her a smile and then jerked her head back to her screen as a proximity warning blared. From where Sierra was sitting, she couldn't see anything. The warning could be anything from a little space debris to another Oscavian warship. She bit her tongue to keep from barking out orders. This was Jo's show now.

"What have we got?" the pilot asked, steady and calm.

"Looks like an abandoned craft. Might have been too damaged to reenter atmo," Mindy speculated, scanning her screen intently.

Sierra leaned forward as if that would give her a better view, heart hammering. "You're sure it's a pirate craft?" she couldn't stop herself from asking.

"Since everything they have is scavenged, there's no way to be certain." Mindy wasn't any comfort.

Jo glanced over her shoulder. "What are you thinking?"

Raze. "The Detyen ship. If they were under fire while leaving..."

"Are you willing to risk the women we just saved to check it out?" Jo's eyebrow quirked up and her gaze held the weight of fourteen lives in the balance.

"They didn't have to help us. We just need to get close enough to scan for life forms. If there's nothing, we move on." It killed her to even think it, but she couldn't risk the women on her ship if Raze and his men were already dead. She ignored the stab of pain in her chest and the bile in her throat, doing her best to tamp down her emotional reactions.

"Wait!" Mindy held up a hand. "We patched in to their comms. If the line is still functioning, we should be able to hail them."

A wave of relief washed over Sierra and she let out a heavy breath. Though it was on the tip of her tongue to give the order, she looked at Jo and waited.

"Do it," the pilot commanded.

She opened the line of communication and sent out a signal. Seconds ticked by and Sierra's pulse beat hard enough for her to hear it in her eyes. She clasped her hands together and bit her lip. She wasn't sure what she was hoping for, but as long as Raze was alright, she would call it a win.

"This is Toran," a voice finally crackled over the comms. "We could use some help."

***

Raze could see his breath in the dim light of the ship. He'd lost feeling in his fingers, but his arms pulsed with a pain that radiated out of his chest and had been getting worse since the moment he stood up from his chair. The systems had failed in a cascade and now the only thing keeping them alive was the ambient air and the human ship coming to their rescue. It would take a few minutes to set up the dock, and in that time, he, Toran, and Kayde packed as many of their belongings as they could. Though, in truth, the only thing that they needed to take with them was the copy of the hard drive from the *Lyrden*. As long as that tech made it back to the legion, they had done their duty.

Coming back from his quarters, Raze slung his gear bag over his shoulder and watched Toran place the drive in a secret compartment in his own bag. "No one on that ship can know about this," Toran said, and waited for Raze and Kayde to nod their understanding. "Unfortunately, this," he gestured to the powerless ship around them, "will set back the mission by months or more. I don't know when we will get this data back to the legion."

"If it weren't for the humans, they'd never get the data," Raze commented. "Dead men can't deliver anything."

"True," Toran agreed. He turned to Kayde. "Set the self-destruct sequence for thirty minutes."

111

The seconds ticked by slowly, but soon the welcome sound of grinding metal reached their ears as the human ship docked with them. The airlock engaged and in no time they were through the hatch and safe on a ship full of air, light, and too many humans. Sierra met them at the air lock, her smile as bright as the sun on the snowiest day back home. He bit the inside of his cheek to keep from smiling back while Toran was looking. Some of the pain he'd been feeling dissolved under the warmth of her gaze.

"Welcome," she said, giving them room to step completely onto the ship before shutting the seal behind them. Sierra hit a button on the wall beside it and the lock unhitched from the other ship and began to retract. She touched her ear and spoke to her crew. "Our guests have arrived. We are clear."

"Prepare for jump," crackled a voice over a loudspeaker. "Two minute warning."

Sierra glanced up at the ceiling where one of the speakers was installed and muttered something that Raze couldn't make out. "We'll get you set up with somewhere to sleep once we've made the jump to FTL. Right now, we need to get buckled up before we get thrown around like rag dolls. Please follow me."

They walked down a narrow hallway with Toran right behind Sierra and Raze taking up the rear. He didn't trust himself not to try and touch his mate if he stood too close, but he wanted to surge forward and step between Toran and Sierra to keep the other man away from her. The need to claim boiled in his blood, the need to declare to all that Sierra was his and he was hers. But with the imminent jump to FTL and his crew all around, all he could do was bide his time.

Sierra came to a sudden stop and Toran almost ran into her, making Kayde almost run into him, and Raze brushed the back of Kayde's uniform before he realized what was going on. Sierra let out a curse under her breath.

"One minute warning."

She turned around and looked past them before shaking her head and steeling her shoulders. "All of the women we rescued are in here. We have extra seats for you in there and I don't have time to set up anything else. *Please* don't scare them." She stared for an extra second at Kayde and Toran, as if she trusted Raze to behave himself. He couldn't stop the small smile that tugged at the corner of his mouth. Sierra caught it and her eyes brightened for a second before they both got themselves under control.

"We will do our best," Toran promised.

Sierra held up a hand. "Do better than your best. These women are traumatized and terrified. They can handle you all being emotionless robots or whatever, but..." She shook her head again. "Just be good."

Toran shot Raze a look and Raze was suddenly happy for all of the people around them. He'd have to answer for Sierra's knowledge later.

"Thirty seconds."

Sierra opened the door and pointed to four empty seats, two on either side of the central aisle. She took one closest to one of the human survivors and before Raze could sit beside her, Toran took that seat. Raze slid in across from her and didn't say anything about the arrangement, instead focusing on buckling up. A human woman sat next to him and he could feel her stiffen and stare, but he kept his eyes forward, uncertain if looking at her would cause even more fear. Sierra murmured something to the women around them, but the final countdown to FTL crackled over the speaker and the ship jolted to high speed, making communication momentarily impossible.

Once his senses adjusted to the shift, Raze tried to meet Sierra's gaze, to speak in glances if not words, but she was lost in thought and not looking at him. A few minutes later, the lights flashed twice and Sierra looked up. She unbuckled her belt. "I'll be back later, please stay seated," she told everyone in the room. Finally, she spared him a glance, but quickly looked away and headed through the rescued human women up to the cockpit.

They might have been rescued from certain death, but with each minute that went by, Raze knew this was going to be torture.

***

Sierra had no clue how to treat Raze when he was in front of his men. He went to that stoic, emotionless place that left her feeling cold, but then she caught him flashing her a smile when Toran and Kayde weren't looking. Did they know that he was feeling again? Did it matter? And would the humans freak out too badly if she sat on his lap and stuck her tongue down his throat? Okay, maybe she shouldn't do *that*, but mostly since she wasn't sixteen, not because he wasn't human. They all just needed a little time. It had been one of the busiest days of her life and she couldn't remember the last time she'd slept.

She slid into the cockpit and closed the door behind her, taking her seat behind Jo and Mindy. "The aliens are sitting by the humans. I didn't have time to set up any other seating. I warned them to be cool, but I don't know if that will last for long. Since you're both busy here, I'll get sleeping arrangements settled and do an inventory on our food. We should have enough not to starve, but it won't be a pleasant couple of days. I wish that I could give them more than the most basic health scan, but we can't even look for tracking or control chips. No one ran away, so I'm thinking the slavers didn't risk taking control. I know those chips blow up half the time, so why risk the cargo, right?" As for tracking, Sierra didn't need to add, once they got close enough to Earth, they wouldn't be in much danger. It didn't matter if the pirates knew their destination, they wouldn't follow the women down to such a densely populated planet. Any tracking chips could be removed by the medical teams back home.

"Right. Get the arrangements made," said Jo. She leaned back from her controls and spun her chair around to face Sierra. Mindy did the same. "Any ideas so far?"

She'd only been thinking about it nonstop since Raze came aboard, but putting him in her quarters seemed a little obvious. He didn't have to sleep there... officially. "I want to put the Detyens in Jo's quarters and have the two of you share." At the start of the mission, she would have never suggested it, but her crew seemed to be getting along better now. Though from the sounds of protest they made, a person would have thought that Sierra suggested the two of them sleep in a vat of acid.

"What? Why?"

"No way!"

The response could have been worse. "Jo's quarters are biggest. Three people won't fit in mine or Mindy's." That, at least, got Mindy's nod. "The women will panic if we put the guys in with them, and they're already going to be squeezed like sardines into the unused crew barracks. They'll have to sleep two to a cot."

"That's still not explaining why I have to share with Mindy," Jo bit out. "This better not be just so you can get laid."

"What? No!" Sierra sputtered, completely unconvincingly. "It's not that," she protested, "really. I promise." Mostly, it *mostly* wasn't that. "You and Mindy will be working in shifts and neither will be sleeping at the same time. With managing our guests, I could be up at all hours and in and out of the room all night. I don't want to disturb your sleep."

Both of her crew mates looked at her skeptically. But finally Jo looked at Mindy for a long second and nodded. "Fine, move my bag over into her room. You owe me for this."

Sierra owed them both a lot, and given the risks they'd put their lives and their jobs in, she could never repay them. After talking logistics for nearly an hour, she left the two of them in the cockpit and went to get the ship in order. Some of the women had unbuckled themselves from their seats, but they seemed to be staying in the kitchen area, so Sierra didn't tell them to sit back down. If walking around made them more comfortable, she'd let them walk all night.

She grabbed Jo's bag out of her room and tossed it into Mindy's before heading further into the ship to get the beds ready for the women. Time flew by as she worked, and by the time her muscles were straining from cleaning and set up, she was done. Food was another issue. They had a limited supply of fresh produce which wouldn't be enough for even a single meal. Between canned goods and protein bars, Sierra could stretch their food to last until they made it to Earth, but they didn't have much room for error.

At mealtime, she passed out the first batch of protein bars to everyone. A few of the women muttered complaints, but they were shushed by their fellow passengers. She could have hugged Toran when he told her that he'd brought spare rations from his ship, but restrained herself to a single nod of thanks.

And nowhere in the hours of work could she managed a spare moment to say anything to Raze. After the meal, she showed the Detyens to their quarters and gave them leave to move around the ship. As she was leaving them to their work, Raze grazed his fingers across her wrist and she shivered, but Toran called him away before she could try to get a word in.

Then she was left to manage the women, explaining the sleeping situation and trying to learn all their names. Tory, Helen, Chi, CJ, Muir, Davy, Nella, Ella, Laurel, Monica, Valerie, and Quinn. Maybe she could get them to wear name tags. According to the mission brief, Muir Henderson was the niece of the senator who had agitated for the mission in the first place. The young woman couldn't have been more than twenty. Her stringy blonde hair could use a good wash and she was so pale that her skin took on a bluish tint under the harsh light of the ship. She had bruises under her eyes and wouldn't say a word, even when asked a direct question. She'd need therapy and lots of it, Sierra was sure. All of the women would. But some seemed to be in better spirits than others.

Quinn, the black woman with short hair who'd spoken up earlier, seemed to have taken up the mantle of leadership. She spoke for the other women and asked Sierra a barrage of questions ranging from who she and her team were, where they'd come from, where they were going, who had captured them, how did the women know they could trust Sierra, who were the aliens on board, and why did they all have to share beds. Every time Sierra answered one question, another three popped up, and by the time she extricated herself from Quinn, her throat hurt and she just wanted to take a nap for the next three days.

Instead, Sierra satisfied herself with a glass of water and hid in her room for five minutes while she scarfed down her own neglected protein bar and took a few seconds to collect herself. When a knock sounded at her door, she stifled the groan and wedged herself up from her bed, crossing the three steps to the door as if she were walking on hot coals. She placed her hand on the latch and took a deep breath, putting her game face back on before swinging the door open.

She couldn't keep the shock off her face when she saw who it was. "Raze?"

Chapter Fifteen

She backed up a step to let him in and closed the door just as quickly, half afraid that he'd flee if she didn't cut off his escape route. With Raze in her quarters, they shrunk to half their usual size, his bulk taking up every spare centimeter. A person's size was never more clear than when they stood on a space ship. Planets had a way of dwarfing a person, distance and space giving a false sense of perspective. But in her little room, where she could touch opposite walls at the same time if she stretched her hands out far enough, there wasn't any disguising Raze's bulk or height, and that sent a not so secret thrill through her.

She'd never paid much attention to the heft of her lovers before. A man could be just as pleasing if he stood a head taller than her or if she had to look down at him. But standing next to Raze right now, she felt safe, protected, like he would stand beside her and fight any battle with her and prevail against any foe.

Had she really only known him two and a half days?

"What are you doing here?" she finally asked, finding her voice. "Is everything alright?" Just because her mind went to a naughty place anytime he got into close proximity to her, didn't mean that he was ready to lay down on the bed right behind her and see exactly what they could make one another feel, how much pleasure they could conjure between them.

She really needed to get her mind out of the gutter, somehow, or the next three days were going to be absolute hell.

"Everything is fine," Raze reassured her. "Toran and Kayde are resting."

Hope fluttered in her belly, but she forced herself not to jump to any conclusions. He wasn't even touching her, even though all he'd have to do was lean forward the tiniest bit and they'd be pressed flush up against one another. "That's good. I'm sure we could all use some sleep." *No*, why did she say that? Raze tried to take a step back and she shot a hand out to keep him from moving. "I mean, *eventually.*"

"Most of the women out there seemed to be settling in. Your pilot switched the lighting over to sleep mode." He ran his fingers lightly over the back of her hand, tapping out an unfamiliar beat.

Sierra glanced at the clock on the wall. "It's late," she agreed.

"I couldn't end the day without seeing you," he confessed, his other hand coming up to rest on her shoulder.

She smiled, "I know the feeling." She stepped forward, wrapping her arms around his waist and laying her head against his chest. Tension loosened in her spine and some of the day's troubles melted away as she absorbed some of his warmth. She never wanted to let go. "Will Toran give you trouble for being here?" she forced herself to ask. As much as she wanted to be near her man, she didn't want to cause strife on his team, not when they were all stuck in such close quarters.

"He didn't forbid it," Raze said, which wasn't exactly an answer.

"Why would he?" Her heart hammered as the comfort of the hug shifted to something deeper, something treacherous and terrifying and full of hope for something she'd never known to dream about.

"I think he suspects something," was all Raze said.

She knew the suspicion had little to do with sex. And so she forced herself to ask the question she was terrified to have him answer. "Is it that I'm your mate?"

***

The pain had come in fits and starts throughout the last few hours. Whenever he saw Sierra, suddenly Raze could breathe again, but when she went away, his lungs filled with sand and his organs twisted into unnatural shapes and squeezed him from the inside out. Touching her now was the first time in hours the pain was completely gone, and that, more than anything, proved to him that she was who he knew she had to be.

He saw the hope and the fear in her eyes and knew it was reflected in his own. They had somehow stolen another three days of togetherness from the hands of fate, but things had become even more uncertain since they'd made plans to meet at Honora Station in a few months' time. But none of that mattered now. They could figure out the future later. He had Sierra in his arms, the soft press of her skin warm against him. There was nowhere else he'd rather be, no matter what it cost him down the line.

"You are my denya," he told her. "It shouldn't be possible, but you are my miracle."

Her tongue darted out to wet her lips and Raze's desire stirred deep in his belly, his cock twitching. "Show me," Sierra said, taking a step backwards towards her bed and pulling him along with her.

Raze captured her mouth with his, crushing her close so that no distance kept their bodies separate. A fire of need flooded his veins and his focus honed in on her and only her. His Sierra. His woman. His mate. She opened under him, her tongue meeting his in an ancient dance of longing. One of her hands came up and dug into his hair as she let out a moan loud enough to nearly echo around the room.

His heart and his body pulsed at him to take her now, quickly, before they were interrupted by any of their responsibilities. But Raze needed to take his time and savor Sierra, to make this right for the both of them.

They both wore too many clothes and their hands tangled as they tried to get at each other and remove jackets and shirts and pants. Sierra pulled back with a gasping laugh and placed her hand on his chest, eyes bright. "Hold on," she said. "Let me watch you." She backed up further until her legs hit her bed before falling backwards and sprawling like a decadent queen viewing her humble supplicant.

Raze wanted to fall to his knees and worship, but her eyes were dark with hunger and she'd asked him for a show. There was no wish he wouldn't grant for his denya. He started with the zippers at his neck and worked his way down, his eyes flicking over to hers every few seconds to see her reaction as he bared himself for her. His outer jacket came off to reveal a thin, long sleeved top, and though his first instinct was to rip it off and throw it away to get naked as fast as he could, he teased her, his hands gripping the bottom hem and pulling it up slowly, revealing his abs before pulling it back down and reaching behind his neck and pulling the top off completely, baring himself from the waist up to his denya.

She moaned again and her chest rose and fell quickly, her cheeks flushed and eyes bright. She could demand anything right then, but all she said was, "More."

***

He was male beauty contained in corded strength and bulging muscles. Every bit of skin he bared for her only made her want more, want to see, to touch, to taste. She'd expected him to be that same green with silver undertones all over, but his chest was a surprise. He was covered in marks from his shoulders down across his chest in a deep vee, the dark, nearly black squares almost like birthmarks or moles. Her fingers ached to feel and she rolled up from her lounging position to get a closer look.

"Do you like my clan markings?" he asked with a grin.

Sierra reached out a tentative hand and flicked her fingers against the dark patch. It was thicker than his normal skin. "It doesn't hurt, does it?" She'd never had sex with an alien before and didn't want her ignorance to cause him any suffering.

"No," Raze promised. "It feels good."

She flattened her hand against his naked chest, but before she could do more than take the smallest feel, he stepped back, pulling a sad mewl of loss out of her throat.

"Uh uh," Raze said in a tone she'd never heard from him before. From anyone else, she'd call it playful. "Your turn." He pointed to her top and suddenly the heat in the room shot up by thirty degrees.

She tore at her jacket, casting it off like it was made of hornets. Raze grinned at her, eyes hungry and devouring. But when she went to unbutton her shirt, she forced herself to slow down. He'd given her a show, and even though she was flushed, wet, and ready for pleasure, she wanted to return the favor. She laid back on the bed, spreading herself out for him like an ancient sacrifice to a terrifying pagan god. His eyes flared red as she flicked the top button on her shirt and bared her throat to his gaze. She could feel the burn of his regard all the way to her toes.

A second button came undone and the top of her breasts was suddenly in sight, on display for her mate. Raze took half a step forward before he seemed to realize what he was doing and Sierra couldn't help but grin up at him. "Do you want to touch?" she teased with a smile and placed a finger on the next button.

The strangled noise that came out of his throat went straight to her sex and she pressed her legs tightly together, her hips rising off the bed as she imagined him between her thighs, pressing into her with the heat of his cock. Instead of showing them both mercy, she let her fingers flit down to the bottom button and undid two, until three buttons in the center of her top were all that covered her undershirt.

Raze stepped forward and fell to his knees beside her bed. His hands found the top and he gripped both sides, ready to rip it open before her eyes flew wide and she placed her own hand on his wrist. "Wait! I don't have anything to mend it." As soon as the words tumbled out, she wanted to call them back. She had this handsome barbarian at her feet and she was worried about her *clothes*. Was she crazy?

Her mate seemed to sense her regret. He met her eyes with those searing red pools of his, his voice gruff and just on this side of control. "Do you really care?" he demanded.

"Not a bit." She grinned. Maybe she should have been terrified, especially when those claws she'd only felt before slid out, and he traced a careful line around each of the buttons until her shirt fell open, leaving only the thin, white undershirt. She wrestled the sleeves of the buttoned top off and Raze placed a clawed finger on her shirt over her sternum.

He met her eyes, black flooding back over the red. "Do you trust me?" he asked, his words heavy with more than sex, more than affection, filled with something she wasn't quite ready to name.

"One hundred percent."

He tore through the thin material of her tank top and the built in bra underneath it, exposing her bare skin to his hands and claws. The claws disappeared between one heartbeat and the next, disappearing into his hands like they'd never been there in the first

122

place. He flattened his hands on her sides and explored her by touch, his calloused palms tough against her sensitive skin. She writhed underneath him and spread her legs, trying to urge him closer.

Raze's head bent down and he trailed his lips up from her belly button to the valley between her breasts, teasing her with gentle nips and playful swipes of his tongue, driving her crazy inch by tortuous inch. She wanted to return the favor, but every time she made a move to touch him, Raze made a sound in the back of his throat that pinned her in place, commanding her to stay still without any words necessary. It was his turn to bring her pleasure, he said with that one syllable, a gift that she had to lay back and take.

But she cataloged every kiss and caress, ever swipe of his tongue and pinch of his fingers, just waiting to drive him to crazed insanity in the same way he was driving her.

When he made his way back down to her waist, she gasped as he undid the clasp of her pants and eased them down over her hips, taking her underwear with. When her boots got in the way, he let out an inarticulate growl and this time Sierra did have to speak out.

"Seriously," she warned, "I need those boots. Don't tear them." He glanced back up at her face with those red eyes and any other teasing words died in her throat at the intensity writ large in his expression. With almost reverent care, he undid the straps and slid first one boot from her foot and then the other, placing them under her bed so they wouldn't get lost or get in his way. Then, he was yanking her pants off again until she was completely naked and laying on the bed, a feast for his eyes.

He ran a hand over his cock, still trapped by layers of fabric that Sierra wished would just spontaneously combust so she could see the goods. She started to lean forward to undress him, but he darted forward and plastered her hands to the bed, covering her with his hot, heavy body, the length of his cock pressing hard against her stomach, the length impressive even through his pants.

"Mine," he growled against her ear, possessive and a bit feral.

A thrill shot through her, even though she'd never gotten off on that shit before. But now the need to claim ran just as hot in her blood. She captured his lips, tugging at his bottom lip with her teeth until he hissed against her and released her hands to cup her head. She held herself in place; no matter how much she wanted to touch him, she wanted his control in a way she'd never known to want before. He conquered her mouth until there was nothing left but the heat and the connection burning like a conflagration between them.

It was too much. It wasn't enough.

She needed more.

***

Any more pleasure and his heart might give out. Any less and he would die. There was no part of Sierra that he didn't need to touch and taste, no ounce of pleasure he couldn't wring out of her. She was bared before him, all her strange, human beauty his for the taking, and the only thing he could do was devour her lips, taking her taste into him with one swipe of his tongue against hers at a time.

She moaned under him and his eyes flicked up to watch her hands reach out until she gripped the edge of the bed to keep them in place, to keep herself from reaching out. If she touched him, he'd come undone, and they'd barely even started. He would let her touch him later, for now this was all about giving her exactly what she needed and taking everything that he wanted.

He slid down her body with a trail of kisses and licks, the salt of her skin sweet against his tongue. He could explore every hidden secret she had, but for now, he had only one goal in mind, the wet heat radiating out of the crux of her thighs. She opened under him, her hips arching up in a silent plea as he kissed over her abdomen and down one thigh. A wordless sound came out strangled as he licked over the soft skin of her thighs and back up over her mound, teasing her without any relief. She arched up again, her hips coming fully off the bed as she searched for his tongue with her body.

"Please!" she finally gasped, the sound echoing in her tiny room.

Raze showed mercy, using his tongue and his fingers to bring her pleasure until she was gasping against him, one leg kicked over his shoulder to give him more access to her core. She let out a string of curses when he hit a particularly sensitive spot, and when he circled his lips around the seat of her pleasure, she cried out and writhed against him, begging him for more.

With a shout, she let go, shuddering around him and breathing hard as he took her over the edge for the first time. Her hands tugged him up and he came willingly, kissing her again as she tried to regain her breath, sweat coating her and the heat between them still as strong as it had ever been, stronger.

"I need inside you," he murmured against her lips, the sound a muffled exchange.

"Now, yes," she panted, reaching down for the clasp of his pants and struggling in her haze of pleasure to get them undone.

Raze's own hands were shaking and he was so hard he knew he wouldn't last long. But he needed her now, today, forever. He pushed his pants down, freeing his erection, and settled himself back between Sierra's thighs. With care, he guided himself to her entrance and met her eyes, knowing his own must be glowing red with how much emotion overpowered him, urged him on.

"Do it," she said, placing her hand over the one he had braced on her hip. "Make me yours." She might not have known all the technicalities of the denya bond, but he could see in her gaze that Sierra understood just how important this was, how much it meant.

She was slick with pleasure and open for him. He forced himself to go slow, easing in to the tortuously pleasurable heat until he was seated all the way in, joined as completely as two souls could ever hope to be. And then he began to move, driving into her, finding his pace and touching her reverently until her own eyes clouded over with pleasure and she let out contented little moans and gasps, begging him for more.

Sensation washed over him, almost painful, and something cracked inside of him, whipping out and reforming him, reaching out for his mate from the depths of the soul he thought he'd lost and tying them together in the most visceral connection of his people.

Sierra shuddered again, her walls rippling around his length and with a roar, Raze came, emptying himself inside of her and sealing the bond between them.

His vision went white and on the heels of the greatest pleasure he'd ever known, pain stabbed through his chest. He gasped, reaching out and trying to stabilize himself as a hurricane of emotion roared into him, tearing him apart from the inside.

As he slumped to his side, everything went black.

Chapter Sixteen

For three seconds, Sierra didn't realize that anything was wrong. But when Raze slumped over with a groan and rolled to his side, completely unconscious, she went from delightfully sated to the edge of panic, the blissful haze of sex wiped away in an agonizing moment. She checked for his pulse, belatedly realizing that a Detyen might not have a heartbeat in exactly the same place. But the steady, if a bit fast, rhythm under her fingers was enough to get the panic to abate for a second.

Next question. Was this a Detyen sex thing? A mating thing? Or something weird and wrong and dangerous? There were only two other people on the ship who might be able to answer that. It hadn't been Sierra's intention to go around announcing what just happened between them, but fear for Raze's life got her ass into gear. It wasn't that she wanted to hide what they had together, but there was a lot of talking they needed to do before they started announcing that they were dating... mated... whatever.

Talking could come later. After medical attention.

Though Raze tearing her clothes off had been just about the hottest thing she'd ever lived through while it was happening, now she cursed as she had to dig through her pack to find an intact shirt. She pulled it over her head and grabbed for her pants. Before she could take her first step towards the door, Raze groaned and rolled to his side. She was torn, but couldn't just leave him there in pain. She sat on the bed beside him and placed her hand on his chest, rubbing it up and down gently, trying to soothe any pain he might be feeling at the moment.

Raze's eyelid cracked open and the sense of relief that pounded through her would have taken her legs out from under her if she'd still been standing. He groaned again and blinked both eyes hard. "What happened?" he asked.

He was asking *her* that? Sierra tried to get her roiling emotions to calm down, but she kept picturing Raze collapsing in pain. "I could ask you the same thing."

He rolled onto his back and tugged her down beside him, but when she lay down, he picked at her shirt, trying to tear it off with unsteady hands.

"Maybe I should go get one of your guys," she said. He still looked pale and she had no idea if he was okay now or if he was about to collapse again. She definitely didn't want to take her clothes off again until she was sure he wasn't about to keel over. "Or at least a med kit."

"No." He tugged harder at her shirt and Sierra relented, pulling it off before shimmying out of her pants and laying down beside him. "I don't need medical attention."

She cuddled into him and his arm came around her. "Was that supposed to happen?"

He pressed a kiss against her forehead. "I can feel it. Can't you?"

Okay, maybe undressing had been a bit premature. But he was a warm, solid presence and the safety of his arms was a soft blanket of strength around her. "Feel what?"

"*Everything.*" His eyes shone, shifting to that demonic red for a second before fading back to black. "I didn't realize how muted it all was until just now. It was like everything that's been suppressed for two years exploded in my chest in a single second. My soul..." he paused for a moment and squeezed her tighter, "I think it's *there.* And our bond..."

She felt something, like a weight anchored just under her heart, and if she concentrated on it, she could sense Raze right there. It was unlike anything she'd ever felt before, less than a physical connection, but more substantial than emotion; she knew it was something that could never be severed. They'd be connected, heart to heart, soul to soul, to the end of their days.

"It's beautiful," she admitted. "And kind of terrifying."

Raze tilted her chin up until they were looking eye to eye. "Why are you scared?" He seemed to savor the word, as if talking about any emotion were a forbidden treat.

"Why aren't you? We live on different planets, this is supposed to be impossible, we're different fucking species!" All of the ways things wouldn't work between them cascaded until Sierra's head was aching and her heart threatened to break. "I have no idea how to make this work," she admitted, "and I think letting you go would

128

kill me." It was heady to feel this way, to know she belonged completely to the hulking warrior lying beside her, and that he was hers. But she was so terrified that she was practically shaking with it. She'd never felt even a tenth of this much for someone, and it had all happened so quickly that she was afraid she'd wake up one morning and find that it had all been a dream made from too many media shows and sleep deprivation. Raze was so solid, so real next to her that she couldn't doubt him in this moment, but soon they'd have to part again, and there was only so much time they could steal until the real world came calling.

He wiped the pad of his thumb across her cheek and it was only then that she realized a tear had escaped. "We will figure this out," he promised. "I won't give you up, no matter what we have to do to make it work."

Her mind reeled, trying to come up with a solution, something that would make them both happy. She couldn't ask Raze to leave his people, not when they were so desperate, but she was loyal to Earth and didn't know what leaving would mean.

Raze kissed her and pulled her close until she was half-draped over him, their legs tangled together. "Leave it for tonight. We will deal with our problems tomorrow."

She checked the clock on the bedside and saw how late it was. It occurred to her that she should check in on the women to make sure they were sleeping okay, but with Raze next to her, she knew that could wait. They couldn't get into that much trouble on a ship this size. He'd have to leave at some point, but she wasn't about to push him away a moment sooner. Not when any moment could be their last.

***

Raze woke to a tidal wave of sensation and the colors of the room assaulted him as his eyes opened. He teetered on the edge of a dozen emotions, his body caught between laughter and tears and lust. The scent of Sierra enveloped him, grounded him, and as he sank into her presence, the overload faded slightly until he could begin to process everything that was happening.

His soul was back. His emotions, *all* of his emotions, were back. He had a mate. And she was looking up at him with wide eyes, full of the same wonder and fear that rattled around his chest.

"You looked a little freaked out there for a second," she said, concern written across her features. Her red hair was a halo around her and her skin gleamed in the dim light of her room.

For the lighting to be this low, it still had to be late, but he wasn't sure what woke him. He didn't want to make his mate worry, but he would not lie to her. "My emotions, my senses, they will take some time to adjust. I lost so much along with my soul and regaining it is... overwhelming."

"Will Toran and Kayde be okay with it? With us?" She cut to the heart of the issue, laying out his biggest concerns with her simple question.

And he didn't want to give her that answer. Change did not come easy to the soulless, nor to anyone in the legion. His relationship with Sierra, his bond, represented the biggest change they'd encountered since the destruction of Detya. "There are strict protocols for soldiers like me and Kayde," he admitted. "Any change in our mindset must be cataloged and reported. If we're deemed to be unstable, the decision is made to put us down so that we do not become a danger to anyone else."

She jolted up, her hair flipping back and eyes wide. "Put down? As in executed? What the fuck?" Her voice got so high that she practically squeaked out the last word.

Raze didn't want to die. The fatalistic acceptance he'd had of that conclusion had blown away the second he claimed Sierra, and he would fight the sentence with everything in him. But he also understood his people's logic. "It's necessary," he explained. "The soulless, soldiers with no emotion, they can easily become violent. In the early days of the legion, rates of murder and suicide among us—them—were astronomically high. Detyens aren't meant to live without their souls. We cheat death to grab a few more years, but the average life expectancy for one of the soulless is thirty-five. The oldest now is forty-two, and the oldest *ever* was forty-seven. My own brother will need to make his decision soon, and even before today I didn't want him to walk the same path as I did."

130

"You have a brother?" Sierra asked, then she shook her head. "Not the important part right now, but we should probably circle back to the details of our lives before long. I *know* you, but there's so much *about* you that I still need to learn."

He leaned in and stole a kiss, unable to resist the siren song of her lips. "We'll make time," he promised, though his mind still hadn't come to a solution there. "But do you understand what I'm saying? Kayde can no longer tell between right and wrong. He can only rely on a strict set of rules and procedures to keep himself from being a threat to others. We should have taken the origin of the soulless as a warning. Even in our desperation, we should not have created monsters."

She reached down to cradle his cheek, her hair falling around her like a veil. "You wouldn't be here with me if your people didn't do that. I don't think I like the alternate universe where you died two years ago and I'd never have any idea who you were."

"The origin is not a pretty story," he insisted, even as he agreed with everything she'd just said. He'd sacrificed everything in becoming soulless, but meeting Sierra made it all worth it.

"Tell me anyway?"

He hesitated for a moment. Everything he'd said since he woke up was forbidden knowledge. Those who weren't members of the legion weren't ever to know. He could be imprisoned or executed for spilling their secrets. But Sierra was his mate, and his duty to her came before all others. And because she was his, that made her a part of the legion so long as he was a member.

"At first, the survivors of the destruction of Detya thought it was a legend," he began. "It happened hundreds, maybe thousands, of years ago. When the planet was still healthy and when we lived in peace, finding a mate was common. There was an entire system in place to pair potential matches and ensure survival. But still, some people were not lucky. Perhaps, like me, their mates weren't Detyen." It hadn't occurred to him before, but it made sense. Even if Detya were still around, he would not have met Sierra there. "So there was a scientist who had several children. One by one, they reached thirty without finding their mates, and they died. The scientist became obsessed with finding a way to save them. His final child, a daughter, was about to turn thirty, and he thought he'd found success. He performed a procedure on her, and she survived her birthday. But then, she killed him, destroyed his laboratory, and killed herself because what had been done to her wasn't worth it. She knew she was a monster and that she shouldn't exist."

Sierra's eyes were wide. "How terrible. Is it true?"

Raze shrugged. "Parts of it must be. Whoever the scientist was, he had sent a copy of his findings to a colleague. Those papers were uploaded to a server somewhere and had been buried deep in a military archive. Someone in the legion discovered them and a vote was taken among the survivors when it was clear that mates were scarce. They decided to experiment and see if they could prolong Detyen lives through the removal of the soul. They succeeded. And here we are today."

Her eyebrows drew down as she thought. "And you're the only one who got your soul back? Or grew it back? However that works."

"As far as I know, yes." He knew it was possible that there had been others before him, but he'd never even heard the hint of a rumor, and gossip spread fast in a group as small as the legion. Someone would have whispered *something* if it had ever happened before.

She traced his cheek and kissed him again. They couldn't seem to stop touching one another. "I could talk to you about this stuff all day," she said. "But if we don't get up soon, everyone will be up before us. And even though you didn't quite say it, I'm taking from everything that you said, that telling Toran and Kayde is off the table until we figure all this out." She didn't sound resentful and Raze kissed her in thanks.

"This *will* work out between us."

Hope and skepticism warred on Sierra's face, and Raze was amazed at how easy emotions were to read now. A week ago, he could barely discern if someone was happy when they smiled from ear to ear.

She ran her fingers through his hair before pulling back and rolling off the bed. "Get dressed. I'll leave first and if the coast is clear, I'll knock once on the door. More than one knock and there are people in the hallway."

They dressed in silence, but it wasn't awkward. Neither he nor Sierra were self-conscious about their nakedness, and they kept stealing looks at one another and grinning when they caught each other. It took the utmost discipline to keep his hands off, but he knew if he touched her, they'd both end up back in the bed, or against the wall, or on the floor, and for the moment, they didn't have time.

She gave him a final kiss and pulled away reluctantly before walking out the door. A moment later, a single knock echoed through the room. Raze slid out behind her and brushed his hand down her arm before heading back towards the kitchen and away from his mate. With every step he took away, the bond tethered him back to her, and he knew that he'd never be alone again.

But the feelings of connectedness and contentment were doused when he walked into the kitchen and found Toran standing there with a curious look on his face. "What are you doing here?" he asked. "And where did you sleep last night?"

Chapter Seventeen

Fewer than half of the women were asleep, but most of them were hanging out in the bunks they'd been assigned to. The ones who'd been talking quietly clammed up when Sierra walked in and she tried not to take it personally, reminding herself just how bad of a situation each of them had been in. She'd shut up around strangers too.

Quinn, the ringleader, was sitting on the floor beside one bunk, a blanket wrapped around her shoulders. "Come to check out the merchandise?" she asked, the edge in her voice undercut by the yawn that escaped as she was talking.

"You're not merchandise," Sierra reminded her. "We're headed back to Earth where you'll be safe."

The sound of disdain Quinn let out wasn't quite a laugh or a snort, but it let Sierra know exactly how much the young woman believed her. She wanted to get defensive, wanted to ask Quinn why no one believed that three human women who all spoke English and claimed to be from Earth would be lying about rescuing them. But she was almost afraid to hear just how bad the things that had happened to the women were.

"There's rations in the kitchen for anyone who's hungry," Sierra said after a moment. "And plenty of water. It's easy to get dehydrated on board, so I hope you're all drinking enough."

"We're not children."

"Clearly."

Two women, one Asian with short brown hair and the other with light brown skin and tangled brown hair, walked up from the back of the hall, talking to each other in serious hushed tones. One of the other survivors cleared her throat and the Asian woman looked up and placed her hand on her companion's arm. They both quieted and watched her, full of distrust. Davy and Monica, Sierra was pretty sure were the names of these two, but she wasn't positive. She smiled and nodded, but Monica glared and Davy turned away without a word.

Clearly the campaign to win the hearts and minds of the survivors was going well.

Another woman, short with unevenly cut, chin length blonde hair came up from the same direction as Monica and Davy, but she didn't look at either of the women or at Sierra when she climbed into one of the bottom bunks and pulled a blanket up over herself. What were the girls doing back there? The bathroom they had access to was in the other direction, so was the kitchen. There was nothing behind them but the cargo hold and the engine room.

Sierra looked down at Quinn, but Quinn had burrowed into her covers and seemed to have fallen asleep, or she'd closed her eyes to more easily ignore Sierra. Whatever. Sierra stepped past the young woman and tried to keep her expression neutral as she walked further into the depths of the ship. She didn't want to accuse the women of hatching some scheme to take over the ship or something like that. But Quinn, as the representative of the survivors, had made their distrust perfectly clear. Twelve determined women could do a lot of damage if they put their minds to it.

But the tension that had gathered between Sierra's shoulders released when she got to the engine room door and saw that it was locked and it didn't look like it had been tampered with. She didn't try to go in. Mindy and Jo might kill her if she touched the innards of their precious ship.

Sierra went a little deeper, back towards the cargo hold, where she found a pile of protein bar wrappers. Had they snuck back there to eat? Maybe they had issues about eating in front of the crew, or maybe they didn't trust that Sierra wouldn't take the food back if they did something she didn't like. If they needed this little rebellion, she'd let them have it. She bent down to scoop up the wrappers, but thought better of it at the last moment. She didn't need to announce that she'd found their little safe corner. Instead, she left the litter there and headed back out.

None of the women said anything to her as she walked through their territory once more, and the short blonde whose name she couldn't remember was still curled up in her bunk, now quietly whimpering, possibly in the throes of a nightmare. Sierra's heart broke and she wanted to help, but there was nothing she could do for them right now except keep them fed and get them home safely. She just hoped that it would be enough.

***

Panic was a new and unwelcome emotion that flashed through him for a second before Raze got it under control. He hadn't realized that it would take effort to put on the mask of the old Raze, and he knew that he didn't school his expression before Toran caught a flash of emotion. But he had endured and survived much more harrowing situations than this one, and today would be no different.

"I didn't realize that you wanted me confined to the room for the night," he said instead of directly answering Toran's question. His soul yelled at him to declare his claim to one and all, to make them know that Sierra was *his*, but until he had the situation under control, his mind knew that it was safer for the both of them to remain quiet. For now.

"This isn't our ship," Toran hissed, voice barely audible above the sound of the air circulators. "Why would you think you can go wandering around like you own it? You aren't acting like yourself."

He was in dangerous territory. One word to their superiors once they were back home and Raze's life would be forfeit. And if he was too out of character before then, Toran might just finish the job.

Before Raze could formulate a response, the door behind them slid open and Sierra came through. Their eyes connected and the spark of their bond flared to life deep within him. He caught himself just in time to keep from smiling, but he couldn't keep his eyes from trailing her as she passed them with a polite nod and continued on to the cockpit. He might have been the one to live without emotions for the last three years, but it seemed that Sierra had a better handle on the concept of discretion.

What exactly *did* she and her team do? They'd never quite gotten around to talking about that.

"Are you fixating?" Toran asked, the words freezing the air around them with their frigidity.

"No." It was a nasty habit that a few of the soulless fell into, obsessing about a single person or place to the point of destruction. The concern had occurred to him when he first met Sierra, but now he knew that it had nothing to do with harm; he'd never hurt her and would do anything to make sure no one else did either.

"Are you sure?" It was obvious Toran didn't believe him. Raze hadn't realized just how difficult conversation had become; now interpreting emotions felt like a superpower, something only a select few—of whom he was one—could do.

"Yes." The soulless didn't bother with long explanations to yes or no questions. And, lucky for him, the habit was so ingrained that he had no trouble keeping it up in this conversation.

Toran leaned back and crossed his arms, not bothering to keep the naked look of worry off his face. Why would he? Raze shouldn't have been able to know what it meant. "I thought Kayde was going to be my problem on this mission," his leader admitted.

Raze didn't respond, though his new emotions had him biting back a question there. The soulless didn't have curiosity.

Either Toran sensed that Raze wanted to know, or he just wanted to talk. "He's been on edge for months, and there's a flag in his file. Seems he's been collecting rocks from every planet he's sent to."

How that was a cause for worry, Raze didn't know, but he still said nothing.

Toran continued. "You gave spot on answers during my evaluation. He's ready to shoot anything that moves. He doesn't have the faintest echo of empathy left, but he was an utter bastard before, so I don't know if that's anything new. I fully expected to need to turn him over for review the moment we got back, but he's executed this mission perfectly. You, though..." Toran shook his head.

When he didn't say anything else, Raze couldn't hold himself back. "What about me?"

"That!" Toran pointed at him. "That's what I'm talking about. You've deviated from parameters. You've asked questions you've never asked before. Your eyes—" he cut himself off before completing the accusation, but Raze knew exactly what he planned to say. His eyes had glowed red, something the soulless lost the capability of. "Do you have any reason that I shouldn't recommend your actions for review when we get home?"

It could be months before they made it back. For security reasons, they hadn't mentioned the coordinates of their home base, and finding a ride would take a good deal of time. And with everything Toran was saying, he didn't think going home would be an option for much longer. Not that he'd ever planned to leave Sierra once they were mated, but he'd wanted the option to take her with him.

Toran looked desperate, like he'd been holding onto a single thread of hope that Raze wasn't too far gone to save. They'd been friends once, many years ago, even though Toran had been an asshole and Raze too nice to tell him to get lost. And in the memory of that friendship, Raze put his faith in hope, for him and for their people.

"Do you remember what you told me about the human denyai?" he asked.

"Of course."

"Would you believe me if I told you that I met mine?" It was supposed to be a joyous confession, but Raze had to keep everything out of his voice. The second he slipped, Toran would do something that couldn't be undone.

"That's impossible," he said. "Whatever it is, you're confusing it with fixation." He didn't glance at the cockpit, but they both knew exactly which of the humans that Raze was talking about.

"I can feel, Toran. My soul isn't dead anymore. And it's all because of her." What if some of those cases of fixation had been the discovery of the bond too late? What if past soldiers had been put down, rather than freed through mating? He hoped he was wrong, but feared the likelihood.

"You—"

The ship jolted around them and Toran fell forward, straight into Raze, who reached out to brace his teammate from crashing to the ground. They glanced at each other and moved towards the cockpit without needing to say anything. The door was still open and they could hear the humans talking.

"What the fuck was that?" Mindy, the navigator, demanded.

138

The pilot, Jo, sounded equally confused. "We just fell out of FTL, one of the engines went down."

"Went down?" That was Sierra. "You did maintenance before we left, how is that possible?"

"Who went in *my* engine room?" Mindy asked, her chair squeaking under her. "Log shows one entrance two hours ago."

"I checked it a few minutes ago, the door was locked," said Sierra.

Jo hissed and he could hear her scramble. She cursed. "The auto lock was set on a twelve hour delay. I forgot to switch it over. That door was unlocked until an hour ago."

There was more jostling and a moment later a blur of colorful hair ran past them, presumably headed for the engine room. Sierra came out a moment later and spotted them. She took a step towards Raze before she realized that Toran was still there and paused. She took a deep breath and gave them a bright, utterly false smile. "Hello, gentlemen. Please take your seats. We just have a momentary issue, everything will be fine in just a minute."

From where they were standing, it was obvious that they'd heard everything said in the cockpit, but neither he nor Toran contradicted her. This was the humans' ship, the humans could fix it.

139

Chapter Eighteen

Everything was *not* fine.

The only bright side, if it could be called that, was that neither Mindy nor Jo had enough time to question whether or not Sierra had been able to snag any alone time with Raze last night. Judging from the expression on Toran's face when she'd burst through the kitchen earlier, Raze hadn't been so lucky. She wanted to find him and make sure he was okay, but at the moment, they were practically stranded in space with limited food supply and a dozen angry, traumatized women who already didn't trust them. She and Raze would need to wait.

Two hours after the initial drop from FTL, they were still stalled. The regular engines worked, but the consultation with their star maps put them too far from any jump gates to get home before their food supply ran out. The only jump gate within range was poorly documented in all of their data, and they had no idea whether it led to a populated system, a barren wasteland, or to the edge of a black hole. Humans hadn't managed to map all of the jump gates, and it was times like these that Sierra really regretted that.

But they hadn't given up hope yet. And her main focus right now was keeping the women calm. Quinn and a few others had caught on that something was wrong, but in a surprising turn of events, she was working with Sierra to keep panic from setting in.

"Can you ask them if anyone went into the engine room? It could have easily happened by accident." Sierra knew the question would go over better coming from Quinn, though Quinn scowled as soon as she made the request.

"What? You think they're too dumb to read the sign on the door? Or do you think someone went in and sabotaged shit?" She crossed her arms, but kept her voice down, shooting a harsh look at the women a little further down the hall, as if a glare would keep them from hearing.

Sierra wanted to throw her hands up in frustration, but that wouldn't get them on the way home any faster. "I said it could have been an accident. And—" she cut herself off and jerked her head to the side, urging Quinn further away from the huddled survivors. "It's not like any of you trust us. So, yeah, maybe someone did something stupid. If we know what they did, we might be able to fix it."

Quinn tapped a finger against her arm and didn't meet Sierra's eyes. After a moment she let out a heavy breath. "There were a couple of girls eying the door, and they got weird when I mentioned that the bathroom was the other way. Let me do the talking, okay? They won't tell you shit."

That startled a laugh out of Sierra. "I got that already."

"And," Quinn added, "I wouldn't sabotage the ship if I were planning something. We need it to get home."

Thoughts of control chips and panicked women danced through Sierra's mind, but she kept them to herself. Quinn was barely an ally right now, and she wasn't about to make this any worse. "Let me know if anything comes up."

"And when they ask when we're going to be moving again?" Quinn demanded.

"We are moving," Sierra responded. "Just not fast enough." She didn't give the survivor's leader a time frame; there was no way she could do that without causing more worry or false hope. Instead, she headed back to the cockpit.

"What's the situation?" Jo asked, her monitors made up of different star maps and projected routes. Mindy sat next to her with a tablet in hand and a stylus in the other.

"As expected," Sierra reported. "They're on the edge of freaking out, but a couple of the women are keeping order. Quinn said a few shifty characters might have eyed the engine room for some reason. She's going to ask around."

"So no one fessed up to sabotage?" Mindy asked, not bothering to look up.

"Shockingly, no," Sierra replied. "How's the path home looking?" And she asked it that way because they *would* get home somehow, even if it took months and they had to stop at twenty space stations and planets along the way.

Mindy cursed and Jo reached out and put a hand on her shoulder in comfort. Sierra's eyes bugged out and her jaw dropped open, but she didn't make a sound and had schooled her expression into something less shocked by the time Jo looked at her. It looked like stress really was bringing out the best in these two. "It's not good," Jo said, her thumb still tracing circles on Mindy's shoulder. "The shortest path I've found would take us seven months and has three stretches that will almost completely exhaust our fuel reserves. Any little problem and we'd be stranded."

"But there's a safer path?" Sierra hoped.

"Not quite," Mindy quashed those dreams. "But there are a couple less dangerous ones. They'd take fifteen months and three years, respectively."

Sierra cursed. It was on the tip of her tongue to apologize for insisting they rescue the women. But she wasn't actually sorry about doing it, just that it had put their ship in danger. And tempers were simmering between all of them, it would only take one spark of irritation to set them alight. She wasn't about to do that to assuage her guilt.

"We need to make a decision soon," Jo warned. "We're burning fuel aimlessly right now, and the longer we do, the fewer options we have."

"How long?" asked Sierra.

"We can try to fix in situ for another day."

Mindy jerked up and looked at the two of them as if just now noticing they were in the room too, even though she'd been working with Jo for a while. "We should ask the aliens."

"What?" Sierra had been doing so well at not thinking about Raze for the last forty-two minutes or so that she nearly jumped out of her skin at the suggestion.

"Down girl," Mindy actually laughed. "We're not trying to steal your boyfriend."

A denial of the label didn't even try to spring to Sierra's lips and Mindy's eyes brightened when she didn't protest.

"Anyway," Mindy continued. "We don't know where they're from, but they might know something we don't."

"That much is obvious," Jo muttered.

Mindy and Sierra ignored her. "Let's do it," Sierra agreed.

The wait between using the speaker to request their presence in the cockpit and when the three men actually showed up felt like an hour, even if it only took a matter of minutes. Sierra kept her eyes glued to Toran, afraid if she wasn't careful, she'd spend the whole time grinning at Raze, whose presence behind his leader was like a burning sun.

Jo explained the situation quickly and laid out their possible survival routes. Toran showed no response to the news that they could be stuck on the ship for months, though Sierra realized that the three men could just as easily jump off at the first space port. That thought almost had her jerking her gaze to Raze, and her jaw ached with the force of keeping her eyes trained on Toran.

"May I see the map?" Toran requested.

Mindy handed over her tablet and they all watched silently as he manipulated the device, looking for something. After a moment, he stopped playing with it and looked back at his men, but said nothing. No, he wasn't looking at his *men*, he was looking at Raze. And if she had to pick an emotion to match to the look in his eyes, she'd say he looked regretful.

He circled a location with his finger and handed the device back to Mindy. "If you go to those coordinates, I can guarantee that your ship will be fixed and restocked."

"That's close." Mindy showed the device to Jo. "What is it? It's not on any of our maps."

"It's the Detyen home base."

***

A million questions buzzed through Raze's mind as they closed the final distance to the Detyen base. Why had Toran given away the base's coordinates? It was a secret held almost as tightly as the existence of the soulless, but he'd told three humans with barely any hesitation. But Toran hadn't said a word since they walked out of the cockpit, and every time Raze opened his mouth, he was hit with a quelling look that meant no questions would be answered. So he kept quiet. Maybe Toran was acting out of gratitude, or duty. Or just the desire to be home when they were so damn close they could taste it.

It didn't matter. But Raze's other concerns were whirling like mad. He thought he'd have days, if not more, to come up with a solution to his and Sierra's distance problem. Now they were practically back on the Detyen base, and reality was about to come crashing down on their heads far worse than he could have imagined.

As they made the edge of the solar system where the home moon lay, Toran made his way to the cockpit at Jo's request. He could hail their communications towers and hopefully make sure the ship was granted permission to land, or at least that it wasn't shot out of the sky. That left Raze and Kayde strapped in next to each other, stewing in silence. Well, Raze stewed, Kayde just sat.

"Our base's location is not meant to be given to outsiders," Kayde observed, nearly shocking Raze out of his seat. "Not even when our lives are at stake. Did Toran reveal his motives to you?"

It was the most Kayde had said to him outside of a mission in years. "No."

"This will be noted when he applies for the extension," Kayde said, as if making stray observations were a totally normal thing.

Had Raze been so wrapped up in his own troubles that he hadn't noticed anything wrong with Kayde? He wanted to gnash his teeth at the standard euphemism, though. 'The extension' was the most bloodless way of describing soullessness, as if sacrificing everything that made a person himself was a matter of paperwork. Not everyone who volunteered for the procedure was accepted, and Kayde had a point. Something as extreme as giving away the coordinates of their base to a team of unknowns could easily disqualify Toran.

"I'm sure he has his reasons," was all Raze could come up with to say before they lapsed into silence once more.

The landing came more quickly than he expected. From the hull of the ship, there was no clue that they'd approached the planet, other than the rocking as they broke through the atmosphere and the popping in his ears as the pressure changed. Chatter from the back of the ship told him that the women were excited to be somewhere, though he was certain that the deviation from the promised path was leading to rumors of more slavers and abduction.

"Welcome home," Kayde said.

Raze didn't respond. His home was sitting up in the cockpit, and this hunk of snowy rock was only a place that he'd lived, a place that had tried to tear away everything he was and had almost succeeded.

"Good morning, passengers," Jo's tinny voice came over the speakers. "It is not long after sunrise on this stopover moon. Because of security concerns, we will be escorted by armed soldiers to our quarters while the ship is fixed." A shout of alarm sounded from the back, shot down by frantic whispering. "Please don't be frightened, no one here wants to hurt you. But you will need to go along with our escort and follow instructions while the ship is under repair, if not, you may be detained. Prepare for boarding. Pilot out."

The speaker cut out, but the whispers didn't. Tension ratcheted up as the sound of a ramp lowering screeched to life, followed by the slow roll of the main door moving to one side. Booted feet pounded up and six masked soldiers, covered from head to toe, stomped into view. One woman screamed, but the rest maintained a terrified silence. This wasn't going to end well, and there was nothing Raze could do about it right now without making things worse.

Toran came back from the cockpit and waved at the soldiers. He gestured for Raze and Kayde to follow and they did, leaving the ship and the women behind. Raze locked his gaze forward, his neck straining to turn back and try and catch a glimpse of Sierra, but he had to hope they'd have time for that later. No, he needed to get through his debriefing and survive whatever evaluation Toran had in store for him.

They'd landed in a hangar with a retractable roof, rather than in the airfield outside. It would make repairing the ship easier, and also make it more difficult for any passenger to get a report of where they were.

"Kayde, you are scheduled for debrief and evaluation in three hours. Go to your quarters and get cleaned up before then." The man nodded and trotted off down one of the hallways splitting off from the main corridor. They were far from the central hub of the base, but everything was still close enough to walk to. There weren't enough Detyens in the legion to need a city-like structure.

Toran turned to him, his face taking on a gray tinge. "You've been scheduled for immediate evaluation. Is there any objection?"

At least his leader didn't *quite* have his hand on his blaster. Objecting now would only see Raze stunned or worse, and would surely lead to a swift execution. "No objection," Raze said.

"I'm sorry."

Raze stared at him for several seconds before shaking his head. "Did you give them the coordinates to expedite my execution or because you wanted them to survive?"

Toran didn't answer, and Raze had no idea what he was thinking. They walked down the central hallway to the examination cells, every step taking him further away from the hope of a future and his mate's arms.

***

Sierra really didn't like this place. There was something weird about it. Not that she or any of the group of humans they'd ushered here had actually seen anything other than the small suite of rooms they'd been assigned. If Toran hadn't said anything, she wouldn't have even known that they were in Detyen territory. All of the guards were covered from head to toe and all of the signs on the walls were written in IC. They could have been anywhere.

Confined to stark gray rooms, all of the women had their own beds, and they'd been given plenty of food. After a restless night's sleep, Jo and Mindy had been escorted back to their ship at the break of dawn to begin the necessary repairs, leaving Sierra to manage the women. Quinn wasn't speaking to her now that they were under armed guard, and only about half of the women would even meet her eyes. One of them, whose name she still didn't know, a short blonde, had squeaked and run away when Sierra came within a meter of her.

They were all on edge and ready to burst with anxiety. And on top of all that, in the depths of Sierra's heart, she knew something was wrong with Raze.

She'd seen no sign of him nor his men since they'd exited the ship. And for the first few hours, that hadn't seemed strange. He was a soldier, he had a mission and orders that had to take precedence. But she'd expected at least a message from him by nightfall. And she'd *hoped* for an invitation to his quarters, even if her responsibilities to her people would have forced her to turn him down. But an entire day with no contact? That didn't seem right. Especially when she concentrated on that bond seated right below her heart and felt a churn of anxiety and sorrow.

She had the anxiety in spades, but nothing about this situation should have been bringing up sorrow. Which made her think that wasn't her emotion, it was Raze's. And because of the magic—or whatever—of the denya bond, she could feel him.

"Hey! Where'd you get that?" Sierra heard one of the women yell and let her head fall to her hand for all of three seconds before pushing herself up from the table she'd claimed as her own and marching over to a cluster of yelling women.

Yelling was better than crying, she supposed.

"What's going on?" she demanded. The petite blonde was clutching something close to her chest while Davy tried to pry her arms open and get at whatever it was. "No fighting, come on." She felt like a teacher on the schoolyard, but Davy looked ready to use her nails to gouge deep cuts into the blonde if she didn't let go.

"Laurel stole something," one of the women snitched.

So the blonde was Laurel. Okay. Sierra put a hand on Davy's shoulder and was almost shocked when the woman actually pulled back. Laurel had curled onto one side and the metallic edges of something peeked out from under her arms. Sierra held out her hand. "Give it here."

"I didn't steal it," she said in a pathetic whisper of a voice.

Sierra didn't even care that she was lying. She was working on too little sleep and the stress of wondering if they were going to get out of this place, and uncertain of whether her mate was in trouble or if she just had indigestion. "You're not in trouble," Sierra grit out. "Just give it to me."

Laurel cast her eyes down and swiped her palm against the screen as she handed it over. Sierra clicked around and saw an open media game. She noticed that the device had somehow connected into the station wireless network, but it must have been an automatic setting, since the game was in offline mode. She tucked the tablet into her pocket. "Where did you get it?" she asked.

"I found it," Laurel mumbled.

None of the women had come to the ship with tablets, which meant Laurel had 'found' it in Sierra's, Mindy's, or Jo's bags. Awesome. "There's a media station in the central room. If you want entertainment, go there. No more finding shit." She left it at that; she wasn't going to punish someone for using a tablet without permission, and they were stuck together long enough that she didn't need this drama now.

A few minutes later, Mindy and Jo came back and the tension in the room was thick enough to taste. They each shot Sierra a look, but she shook her head, not wanting to add to their pressure. Her colleagues sat at the table beside her after grabbing drinks and some food from the processor they'd been given access to.

"How's it look?" she asked.

"A few burned out wires and a missing compressor. We're lucky we didn't explode when we fell out of FTL," Mindy said around bites of her stew. "They need to manufacture the compressor in one of their machining printers, and they said they'll have it for us tomorrow. Then we should be cleared to go."

"Armed guard escorted you here?" Sierra asked. She hadn't left the suite since they'd been put there.

"Yup," Jo said, her lips popping on the p.

None of them mentioned the possibility that the Detyens might not let them leave. Besides, why would they let them repair their ship if they were just going to be stuck here?

"You said a compressor is *missing*?" Sierra asked, circling back to the issue at hand. "How the hell did that happen?"

Mindy glanced at the survivors and then back. "Someone had to remove it. Someone with a bit of skill. Or instruction." Her voice had dropped low and Sierra could barely make it out.

"Like, say if one of the girls had a control chip and was instructed to stall the ship so someone could come collect them?" Sierra was equally quiet.

Mindy nodded.

"Or the aliens lured us here." Jo threw that bomb out like it was nothing.

Sierra had to choke on her denial. Raze wouldn't. But Toran sure had been quick to give out the coordinates. Still, it didn't make sense. "Why?" she asked.

"Fifteen ladies to encourage their recruits? I don't know, people are fucked up." Jo shrugged, and even she didn't seem convinced by her theory.

"From what I've heard, it doesn't work like that here," was Sierra's response.

"And you trust what you've heard?" Jo asked.

"Maybe we can get their medics to check for control or tracking chips," Mindy broke in, making peace. "Or they can lend us a scanner. It won't be perfect, but it will give us some answers."

Sierra didn't want to turn that kind of suspicion on the women, but there were only so many options for who had done the deed. Raze had been with her the entire time, and neither Mindy nor Jo had motive. That left the twelve survivors and two Detyen warriors.

The door to their quarters opened and for a moment, Sierra's heart lifted. Though at first glance Toran looked a bit like Raze, he was too green and a little shorter than her mate. His eyes met hers and he jerked his head towards the door. Sierra excused herself from the table and went with the Detyen. Finally she could get some answers about Raze.

And she didn't even have to ask.

"What is Raze to you?" he asked. The guards that had been posted to their door were nowhere to be seen, and the nondescript gray hallway could have belonged in any building on any planet that Sierra had ever been to.

They were really doing this now? Thoughts of secrecy vanished as the anxiety in her stomach spiked into outright fear. "He's my mate and if you've done anything to hurt him, I will end you. Where the fuck is he?" Something was really wrong, and she needed to fix it. Now.

"I'm not the one who wants to hurt him," Toran insisted. He placed a hand on her arm and tried to drag her further down the hall.

Alarm bells went off in Sierra's head and she jerked her arm away. "Don't touch me."

He raised his hands in peace. "Please, if there's any hope of saving him, you hold the key."

Saving him? "They're going to kill him?" Her knees threatened to give out, but she locked them and forced herself upright. She wouldn't show weakness in front of this man. "Tell me what I need to do."

Chapter Nineteen

It wasn't a cell. Soulless warriors slated for retirement weren't kept in cells. No, they were confined to locked rooms with a comfortable cot and plenty of food. There was even a window that looked out onto the wintry expanse that was their home moon.

To say his examination had gone poorly would be an understatement. The moment he'd mentioned a denya, he'd been labeled delusional and fixated. No one even suggested speaking with Sierra, even though he'd practically yelled at them that talking to her would explain everything.

But no, he was soulless, and therefore he could not have a mate. He could not feel anything. Despite all evidence to the contrary. The decision to execute him had taken less than half an hour. He'd be given his Final Night, as was custom, and removed at dawn the following day. He would not be permitted to say his goodbyes, and Sierra would never hear of what happened.

Until the door had locked behind him and Raze realized that there was absolutely no way of getting out, he hadn't known what it meant to feel hopeless. Until this moment, every impossible scenario had ended with him finding a way out. When his thirtieth birthday approached with no mate in sight, he'd applied to become a soulless warrior and cheated death. When his men were captured by pirates and under threat of death, he'd found a way to save them. When their ship was floating dead in space, another had been right there to take them home.

But there would be no rescue ship tonight. Nothing but darkness and a scalpel taking him from his mate and the galaxy.

His eyes misted and he blinked hard, holding back tears. He had nothing left but his pride, and he would not give that up, not so soon after he'd found it again.

The final torture was the bond that pulsed bright in his chest. He could feel Sierra's frustration and the anxiety that being grounded in an unfamiliar place brought out in her. She feared that she couldn't protect the women she'd rescued, and a glowing pulse of affection and desire beat strong in both of their hearts, binding them tightly to one another.

Would she feel him die? When the bond snapped, would she know? If any of the gods were real, he prayed that she wouldn't. If he could spare her that one sorrow, he'd sacrifice his soul all over again.

With nothing else to do, Raze stared out the window at the blinding white snow.

A sharp spike of fear traveled down their bond, followed quickly by fierce determination. Raze jumped up from the bed and began to pace. Something was wrong. Sierra needed help, and he was confined to this cursed room with no reprieve.

The lock disengaged and Raze held himself back from tackling the guard that stepped in. He could escape the room, but there was no way off the planet. Buying a few hours would mean nothing but a swift death the moment he was caught.

The guard studied him for a moment. He was a younger man, maybe twenty-five, and Raze couldn't remember his name. "You've been summoned," he said.

"It isn't dawn, it isn't time." He'd still been counting on a miracle, and that miracle was supposed to have at least twelve hours to arrive.

"You've been summoned," the guard repeated.

If he was going to his death, he'd at least do it with honor. They walked down dim gray halls and to the judgment room. Raze stood with his hands behind his back and looked at the three judges who'd sent him to death without waiting for an explanation. "There has been a development, NaFeen," Sandon said. Neither of the other two judges acknowledged his presence.

A development?

The door behind him burst open and Raze didn't need to turn around to know who was there. But how had she known? And why were they speaking with her?

Sierra stepped up and placed a hand on his shoulder. Raze released all the tension he hadn't realized he'd built up. "This man is my mate," she said. "And if you're about to kill him because he's crazy or unstable, you're wrong, and you can't." It all came out in a rush and she thrummed with energy. Raze was worried she was about to launch herself at the judges, but she held back.

Sandon leaned forward, hands clasped together. "You are a human," he pointed out. "And even if what you claim were possible in general, it isn't possible with him." One of the other judges nodded, while the third remained still, shrouded in shadow. All tribunals like this consisted of a mated warrior, a warrior who still had his soul, and one of the soulless. The still one must be soulless.

"Since I'm standing here with him, it clearly is. Look," she drew herself up, "I don't know if there's some sort of test you can do, or some way we can prove this is true, but it is. And if you refuse to acknowledge it, then I must insist that you hand him over as a citizen of Earth."

The room went utterly silent as everyone looked at Sierra as if she'd grown a second head.

"Earth has no jurisdiction here," Sandon pointed out. "And even if it did, Raze is no citizen."

Raze remained silent, even as his mind tried to catch up to the game that Sierra was playing.

"He *is* a citizen, as my mate," she insisted. "The Alien Recognition Treaty of 2167 acknowledges that all marriages or equivalent ceremonies between an Earth citizen and a non-Earth citizen bestow Earth rights upon the spouse. In light of that, you are holding my mate, my *spouse*, in contradiction of that treaty. He is mine, and you can't have him. I will not let you execute him."

She was brave, and a little crazy, and Raze couldn't love her more.

The judges leaned in close and Sierra's hand dropped down beside her thigh and reached out to brush his. Raze gripped her hand tight, hoping her plan somehow worked. The judges kept speaking in low voices and seemed to pay no attention to them, though Raze didn't for a moment believe that was the case. Several more minutes passed by and when Sandon leaned forward again, Raze's anticipation skyrocketed.

"This is a previously unknown and unanticipated turn of events," he said evenly. "It has always been the goal of our force to preserve Detyen life and keep our culture alive. In protecting our people, the judgments we must make are often harsh. But we cannot survive by inflexibility. The judgment on the status of Raze NaFeen is hereby reversed, and his mating acknowledged."

Sierra bit off an excited sound and Raze's eyes widened. That was it? He was saved? She was his?

"However," Sandon continued. "In light of this new information, you will both be required to undergo a series of tests to determine if this was a freak accident, or if more such matings can be expected. Report to the med bay tomorrow."

Raze squeezed Sierra's hand, as if that could stop her from protesting, but she stayed quiet. The judges filed out of the room through a back door, and he and Sierra left through the main entrance. In the hall, they remained quiet and shocked for all of ten seconds before she let out an excited whoop and jumped into his arms. He held her close and she wrapped her legs around his waist, giving him all of her weight.

"Holy shit," she breathed into his ear. "I can't believe that fucking worked."

Her heart beat out a steady rhythm against him and her hands were practically vibrating where she was touching him. "You're amazing," he said, unable to stop grinning.

"You got a place more private where you can show me that?"

And then they were rushing down the hallway, uncaring of who saw them. They were here, alive, and together. And whatever the next day brought, nothing was going to change that.

   ***

There really was no luxury on this base. Already, all the drab walls were kind of getting to her, and Raze's room was just kind of sad. Or, it would have been, if her mate wasn't already half-naked and panting, red eyes devouring her like she was the tastiest dessert on the tray.

"So I'm a citizen of Earth now?" he asked.

"Um," Sierra let out a nervous breath. "To be honest, we barely covered that treaty in school and there might have been some shit I

154

made up right then. But they bought it, and that's what counts, right?" She'd been clinging to the edge of panic the entire time they stood there, ready to scream or do something truly crazy if she couldn't get them to listen. Raze was perfectly healthy. Who were those assholes to tell her that he needed to be put down like a sick pet because he was acting differently than they expected?

Raze tilted his head back and laughed, the warm sound wrapping around her as tightly as a hug. "You bluffed!"

She blushed and ducked her head. "That was the least of what I would do to get you out of there." The strength of her fear—and other emotions—scared her, but not enough to make her hesitate. "And," she conceded, "they could have been less reasonable. I *highly* doubt that would have worked on Earth." What if her father had been sitting on a panel like that? A cry of *Daddy, I love him* would not have been enough to save any man's life.

"Then we count ourselves lucky." He reached out and grabbed her wrist, gently pulling her towards him. Sierra's hands wrapped around his waist like they belonged there and she placed her cheek against his naked chest, the beat of his heart steadying her.

She traced over the clan markings on his chest, her fingers drawing little lines against the slightly raised, dark skin that dotted his chest and down his arm. Raze shivered under her touch. "Are they sensitive?" she asked, not letting up.

"A little." He held still, letting her explore.

Her tongue darted out to trace along the edge of one mark on his pec and Raze sucked in a harsh breath. *A little*, sure. She could feel the thick length of his cock pressing against her and just his presence meant she was practically ready to explode. She didn't want to waste time with a striptease today, not when she'd almost lost her mate just after finding him. No, today she needed something else. Desperately. "Get your clothes off," she ordered, pulling back.

Raze grinned. "You're commanding today."

"And you're not getting rid of me, so get used to it." It could have come out harsh, but her voice was shaky with desire. Half-naked, he was the most handsome man she'd ever seen. Nude? He was a work of art.

He dipped his head and captured her lips and somehow Sierra ended up plastered against his body, one leg slung over his still clothed form. He pulled back and they both gasped, chests heaving. "Don't want to get rid of you," he said, those eyes flashing between red and black again. God, that was sexy.

"Good." She traced her hand over his cheek, fingers finding a ridge there, like there was cartilage giving his cheekbones a sharp edge. She kissed him there too, learning his every secret with her fingers and her lips. "Pants off," she whispered in his ear.

Her playful mate placed his hands on her waist and start to guide *her* pants down, exposing her to the cool air of the room. She pulled her top off while he worked and stepped out of her pants once they fell all the way to the floor. Raze stepped back and devoured her with his gaze, licking his lips in a way that made her shiver and caught a moan in the back of her throat. All that intensity, that strength, it was all hers.

Raze made quick work of his pants, casting them off and standing proud and naked before her, his cock hard and right *there*, all for her. She licked her own lips and imagined the taste of him, but her own sex was hot and wet and she needed him inside of her right now. Their first time together it had been a little strange, good—*great*, actually—but strange. There were some sort of ridges on his dick that hit her just right, giving her sensations she'd never before felt. And right now she wanted to feel them again.

They fell onto his bed together, scrambling a bit to find the right position on the small cot. His room hadn't been made to accommodate two people, it barely fit him. But with hot skin pressed against skin, they made it work in a writhing mess of moans and pleasure, slick with sweat and the evidence of their mutual arousal.

He found his way to her entrance and Sierra gasped as he slid in, slid home, and seated himself deep inside her. Her head fell back and his lips were there, kissing along the column of her throat as he thrust in and out, whispering words of devotion she'd never before wanted to hear but now couldn't live without. This man, this alien, was the one person in the entire universe meant for her, and it couldn't have been clearer as they tangled together on scratchy sheets and spelled out their devotion with their bodies.

Pleasure crested in a wave and Sierra called out, clutching Raze close as he emptied himself into her, his lips never ceasing to taste as he marked her as his with his lips and his tongue and his cock.

Time floated around them as they came back down, and before long Sierra was draped over half of Raze's body, clinging to him close as the haziness of sleep tried to capture them.

"I didn't think it was possible," she mumbled, her lips brushing against his chest with every word.

Raze's fingers tangled in her hair, playing with it gently. "What?"

"To fall for someone this quickly. This completely. But I love you, you got that, right?" She'd thought the words would be hard to say, or that she'd be too afraid to speak it out, but with Raze there was only comfort and the certainty of her place in his life.

"I love you too," he told her.

"We've still got shit to figure out." They might have figured out one obstacle, but too many remained.

"We will," Raze promised.

And for the first time, Sierra fell asleep full of hope.

Chapter Twenty

A part of Raze had been worried that Sierra would be gone in the morning and he'd wake up back in that holding room, awaiting execution. But his mate was beside him, safe in his arms and still caught in the peace of sleep when his schedule chimed that it was time for him to wake up. He tried to extricate himself from her arms without waking her, but the cot was too small and he was too large to move without causing a disturbance, and Sierra grunted and moaned, cracking her eyes open as he slid out of bed.

"What time is it?" she asked, voice full of sleep.

"Early," he assured her. "You can go back to bed." He liked her here, in his quarters, in his bed. He hadn't noticed the drab colors or the harsh light before, but she brought a softness and beauty to the place that he hadn't realized it lacked.

Sierra wiped at her eyes and sat up, scooting back until her back was against the wall. "I should get back to where they're keeping the humans. I kind of left yesterday without a word. They might be worried. Or pissed."

"How did you know where to find me?" They hadn't spoken much of what had happened yesterday, and now that some of the panic and relief was starting to subside Raze began to wonder.

"Toran found me." Sierra played with the edge of the blanket and pulled it up so that it covered her shoulders. "He said you were in trouble."

"Toran?" The same man who had turned him over for immediate evaluation without a regret?

Sierra nodded. "He looked torn up. I was kind of shocked when he showed up. Honestly? That guy is..." she trailed off and glanced away, as if she didn't want to say anything bad about the people he knew.

"Ruthless?" Raze suggested.

She grinned and rolled her head over to meet his eyes, "I was going to call him a dick, but that works too." She leaned forward and kissed him. "Good morning."

"Good morning." He couldn't help the matching grin that spread across his face or the lightness in his heart. His mate had awoken in his bed. His sheets smelled of her, and she was still naked, even if she'd covered herself up due to the chill in the room.

His tablet beeped and Raze groaned, reaching for it off the bedside table. He flipped open the message and his brows drew down in concentration.

"Duty calls?" Sierra asked, tugging him back down to bed until he was seated next to her, still reading.

Raze looked up and nodded at the message. "Kayde was able to analyze some of the data from our mission."

She didn't ask, but her brows shot up and her face was a mask of curiosity.

He slung an arm around her shoulders and she snuggled in. The data Kayde had sent was more than a hundred years old, and none of it looked secret. Besides, Sierra was his mate. If he couldn't trust her, who could he trust? "It looks like it's a passenger manifest from the *Lyrden,* a ship that was near Detya on the day of its destruction. He flagged one of the names as a person who's come up before."

"Yeah?" She leaned forward, her eyes scanning over the report quickly, as if Raze would come to his senses and close out of it before she could get to the end.

"Yormas of Wreet," Raze read. He scanned down a little further. "Looks like we have a picture. Oooh, he is *not* pretty." Bright yellow skin practically glowed, with a sickly greenish undertone. But it was his teeth that put Raze on alert; they were all sharp and huge and ready to take a bite of something. A carnivore's teeth, those were, and something that could rend flesh from bone with little difficulty.

Sierra stiffened. "You think he had something to do with the destruction of Detya?" Her voice had gone quiet, intense.

"It's too early to tell, but this is more information than we've ever had." A second report came in and Raze clicked through. "And the evidence might be stacking up." He'd expected to feel anger, but all that surged through his veins was a sense of determination. "The

Lyrden sent a message that day. Most of it was corrupted, but Kayde has unscrambled some of it. 'Talks have failed, destroy them.' No note of who said it or who it was sent to, but that's something."

Beside him, Sierra practically vibrated with tension. "Can I take a closer look at that picture?" Raze handed over the tablet and watched as Sierra pulled it close and expanded the view. "I've seen this guy before," she said. Her brows furrowed and her head snapped up, eyes wide. "He's an ambassador now, on Earth. Is that possible? What's the lifespan of his species? Or maybe they clone each other?" She shook her head and handed the device back to him. "My dad has an event with him coming up. He asked me to go with. He definitely said Ambassador Yormas of Wreet. Shit, what if they're planning on hitting us?"

She tried to sit up, but Raze placed a hand on her shoulder to keep her next to him. "Deep breaths," he suggested. "Just slow down for a second."

"Slow down?" she yelled. "Your planet was destroyed and this guy might have done it! Now he's on my planet and I have no idea what his motives are. I need to get home, warn someone. Do *something*. What if they've been sitting on whatever they used on you guys? I can't just sit here." This time she did pull completely away from him and stand up, finding her strewn clothes and jerking them on.

"We don't know enough." Raze tried to keep his calm, but emotions were still new to him and with Sierra's stress beating inside his chest, his own started to mount. "He might have just been there. Or the person on Earth might just happen to have the same name. Do you know how many Detyens named Raze there are? How many humans named Sierra?"

"I've seen his picture!" Sierra struggled against her shirt and let out a frustrated growl before finally popping her head through the right hole. "He's there right now and by the time I get back, he might have made his move. Earth needs to be warned!"

Before he could say anything to that, red lights began to flash and a moment later, a siren went off.

Raze jumped out of bed and began throwing his own clothes on as fast as he could.

"What's that?" Sierra asked.

"Attack."

***

Sierra raced down the hall, trying to find her way back to the humans while Raze took off for his own people. She didn't want to leave them. If the base was under attack, he could be running into danger, and she'd just got him back. He didn't get to go risk his life now that they'd finally found one another. But it was only knowing that he must be feeling just the same about her that kept her running in the opposite direction.

They wouldn't be the people they were if they didn't need to protect their people.

She made it to their suite and burst in to find chaos. Half of the women had cornered Laurel, the blonde with the stolen tablet, while Jo, Mindy, Quinn, and a few others were trying to hold them back. They were yelling and grabbing and hitting and seemed oblivious to the flashing lights around them. The sirens, thankfully, weren't constant, or Sierra might have gone deaf.

Tension rode everyone hard. There was some sort of threat coming from space, but so far the sky was clear and there was nothing but a blue, wintry morning outside.

"Hey!" She tried to get some attention, but the mass of bodies was too focused on themselves to stop the pile on. Sierra looked around, seeing if anything in the room could be twisted to her advantage. And right there was the metal table she and her crew had sat at yesterday, mostly empty. She got a good grip on it and flipped it, sending it crashing to the ground with a deafening clatter.

That froze everyone in place. Sierra stalked over and the mob parted before her. She stood in front of Mindy and Jo, who she trusted no matter what was going on, and crossed her arms. "What the fuck is happening here?" she demanded.

"She used the tablet to send out our coordinates. She wants to be their fucking slave!" one of the women in the crowd yelled and a chorus of angry agreement backed her up.

"I didn't," Laurel whimpered, cringing in on herself. "I don't remember. I don't—" Her denials choked off as she blubbered out tears.

Sierra looked at Mindy, eyebrow raised.

"There was a message sent from that tablet you took off her," she confirmed. "And there's a splotch of oil on her pants that could have come from the engine room."

Sierra held her hands up and pushed at the air like she could somehow summon magical powers and push the angry survivors back. "Mindy, Jo, and I will deal with Laurel," she promised them. "But right now shit's about to get real and you need to get your stuff and be ready. I don't know the procedures here, but we might need to make a run for it."

"I'm not running with *her*," another one of the women said. All the ones that were talking seemed to be hiding in the middle of the group, as if they couldn't speak up if they showed their faces.

Quinn had disappeared when Sierra showed up, but she came back with strips of cloth that looked like they might have once been a shirt. "If we tie her up and guard her, she can't fuck with us anymore."

Laurel let out an even worse cry, her pale skin now blotchy and red.

Sierra didn't let pity into her heart. Maybe Laurel had done something, maybe not, but if they didn't show the women action right now, Laurel would end up dead before they could get to the bottom of this. "Do it," Sierra told her. "Just to restrain, not to hurt," she warned. Quinn didn't seem like the overly violent type, but she wasn't taking any chances.

Quinn went to work, tying incredibly competent knots that Sierra knew she couldn't have gotten out of without a knife. If they had time, she might have asked where Quinn learned something like that, but everyone was in motion, packing up the few belongings they'd gathered and now talking quietly in the little factions that had formed among the survivors.

Mindy and Jo found her and neither wasted time asking where she'd been, not when things were in the middle of going to hell. "We think it's a control chip," said Jo. "No way to get it out without turning her over to the aliens. And we don't know how much she sent. The message was coded."

"Shit. Is our ship ready to fly?" She did not want to hear that Laurel had managed to leave any more surprises while she was free to wreak havoc.

"Not quite, I would have finished today if it weren't for that." Mindy jerked her finger up at the flashing lights.

"We need to keep them safe. And we need to tell someone what we sent them." Most of Sierra protested against giving strangers information, but these strangers were the only thing standing between them and certain death or slavery. Plus, her mate was one of them. That had to count for something. "As far as I can tell, they're surprisingly flexible when it comes to new information."

Neither Mindy nor Jo looked convinced by that, and Sierra couldn't blame them. "If she did this because there's a control chip in her head, I can't justify potentially handing her over for execution," Mindy whispered, leaning in close so the other women wouldn't hear.

"No one said anything about execution," though Sierra knew first-hand just how death happy the Detyens could be.

The sirens blared again and the pulse of the flashing lights changed. The three humans looked up, as if flashing lights might give them some insight into what was to come. The ground beneath their feet shook and Sierra reached out and placed a hand on the wall to steady herself. They silently met each other's eyes, knowledge of danger hanging heavy between them.

The battle had begun.

***

Toran and Kayde were suiting up when Raze found them. Toran looked at him like nothing had changed between them and it was Kayde who did a double take. "Your evaluation was satisfactory?" he asked, betraying with the question, if not his tone, that he wasn't as neutral as he was supposed to be.

Even with the world crashing down around him, Raze wanted to smile. He'd survived and he had his mate. A little battle couldn't quell that joy. And, remembering that his new status as a mated man was known, he let his lips pull into a grin. "Eventually," he answered.

Kayde stared at him like he'd grown a second head.

"Didn't you realize everything was fine when you sent that report?" Raze asked. He didn't want to talk about his newfound expressions and emotions right now. They could deal with that when they survived.

"I sent it to the team," Kayde confirmed. "There was no notification to keep anything from you."

"We need to move," Toran broke in. He looked at Raze, who wasn't bothering to school his features into a blank mask any more. As Kayde took a blast rifle and jogged away, Toran stepped into Raze's space and spoke quietly. "You may not believe me, but I'm glad you got your miracle."

"I believe you." He understood why Toran had turned him in, but that didn't mean he was ready to joyfully accept the hand of friendship, if that was what Toran was offering.

Toran nodded. "Good."

They both ran to catch up with Kayde, who was standing by Sandon awaiting instructions. Sandon nodded to both of them as they approached. "You and Druath's team will go and guard the humans. We can't risk them getting in the middle of this mess."

"Shouldn't they be safe where they are in the complex?" Toran asked.

Another team of three warriors, this one led by Druath, a tall man whose skin was almost as purple as an Oscavian's. Raze's brother, Dryce, stood next to the man and a third warrior, the soulless Nokta, stared at them all, her eyes blank.

"Someone revealed our location to that ship," Sandon replied. "And it's best if they don't do anything else." His eyes shot over to Raze. "Is that going to be a problem?"

"No." Raze didn't know how any message had made it to the Oscavian warship, but he knew Sierra didn't send it, and she wouldn't have let it be sent. If one of the women with her somehow did it, she would be dealt with.

Dryce was looking at him and Raze realized his brother had no idea what had happened. They hadn't seen each other in weeks, or perhaps longer. Ever since Raze had become soulless, meetings between the two of them had lessened to the point of near nonexistence. As the two groups tore away to head to the heart of the compound where the women waited, Raze stepped back to run beside his brother.

"A lot has happened. We need to speak when this is done. There's someone I want you to meet." It was more than he'd said to Dryce in three years.

From the widening of his brother's eyes, he realized it. "Who *are* you? Something's wrong."

A laugh caught in his throat and Raze couldn't stop the smile. "I promise, brother, there is nothing wrong at all. I've met my denya." Toran cast a glance back at him and Raze nodded. "We'll talk soon." He left his brother gaping there and caught up to his team.

"Your good news will make its way around the base by the end of the day if you keep acting like this," Toran warned, giving him a strange look.

"Is there a reason I should be wary of that?" They passed dozens of warriors running in the opposite direction. Most of the defense would be done by drones, fighters, and anti-ship gunners and they had no reason to hunker down in the middle of the base.

"Change is not an easy thing to adjust to. Especially not for us." Whatever warning Toran was trying to give, Raze didn't care.

"This isn't something to keep secret. And now that I'm not about to be executed for *having* feelings, I have no reason to hide them. She's my mate. I'd sing it from the rooftops if they weren't

165

covered in two meters of snow." Even before he'd given up his soul he hadn't been this demonstrative. But Sierra was his, and he could do nothing less than proudly claim her.

"I worry," was all that Toran responded with.

"About?" Now was really not the time for this conversation, and they were getting closer to the women's quarters, but Raze's curiosity was piqued and he found he didn't have as much control over his emotions as he should. He wanted to know what Toran thought and he wanted to know *now*.

"Some among us are not so eager to lose their souls." He'd dropped his voice until it was barely more than a whisper and Raze had to struggle to hear over the echoing halls and pounding feet. "They may look to those defenseless women as a way to salvation."

He understood the implication, and it made him sick. "You can't force the denya bond."

"That doesn't mean someone wouldn't try."

Raze was saved from answering by their arrival at the women's suite. Just as they were getting into position, the ground around them shuddered. Raze widened his stance to steady himself and pulled up a feed on his tablet. "They've breached atmo," he told those gathered around them.

"Our brothers and sisters will do their jobs," Druath assured them, though among the six of them there was no doubt. "We'll take the hall," he told Toran. "Will you stay inside?" He nodded to the door.

"Got it." Toran opened the door and Raze immediately knew that something was wrong.

***

Panic set in and Laurel started to wail. Whether it was because of the chip Sierra was almost certain was in her head or the glares from her fellow survivors was unclear, but Sierra was reminded that she wasn't among a group of battle-hardened women who spat in the face of danger. No, this was a group of traumatized survivors who were doing as well as they could, given the circumstances.

Most of the women had split off and huddled among themselves, far away from Laurel, but Quinn and Davy sat next to her and spoke quietly, trying to calm her down.

The door to the room opened and Sierra reached for her blaster before she remembered that she wasn't armed. Her eyes darted around for a weapon, and she relaxed slightly when she saw Toran enter. Raze followed closely behind him and she shot him a smile and a nod, taking him in from head to toe. He wore all black, and looked ready to fight a dragon, from his tactical gear to the large rifle slung across his back. Toran and Kayde were dressed the same, but her money was on Raze for martial prowess.

"What's your boyfriend doing here?" Jo asked, some of her old sneer leaking back into her voice with all the pressure around them.

"Mate," Sierra corrected.

Both of her teammates stared at her, mouths agape. Jo recovered first, snapping her jaw shut before speaking. "Come again?"

"Later." Sierra couldn't have stopped the joke if she wanted to, but neither Mindy nor Jo were laughing. She rolled her eyes. "He's my mate. It's a thing. Let's not make a big deal about it right now."

"Mate?" Mindy's voice got comically high pitched for how quietly she was trying to speak.

"The technical term is denya. It's all new to me, but I really need you two not to freak out now. You know, big giant alien ship attacking?" She pointed up at the flashing lights as if that would shut down the conversation.

Jo grabbed her arm, but she didn't try to move it. "Have you gone fucking crazy? He's not human, he doesn't even live on Earth, and your job is not exactly conducive to relationships."

Sierra took a deep breath and tugged her arm back. "Thank you, Mom." She rolled her eyes. "None of your business, and I already know this shit. So can we get back to the imminent threat to our safety?" The Detyen warriors were walking towards them and this was *not* a conversation they needed to overhear.

Jo seemed to get the point, but Sierra could see that she didn't plan to let this go. Too bad. Jo wasn't her commander, wasn't her family, and they were barely friends. So what if being mated to Raze was complicated? That was her shit to deal with and damn anyone who said otherwise.

A warm hand brushed against her back and Sierra leaned back into Raze's touch as Toran and Kayde stepped up next to him. She wanted to give him a kiss, but now was *really* not the time for that. She let her hand fall and brushed it against his outer thigh, grounding herself in his presence.

"We're your guards," Toran told them. "A secondary team is outside to ensure the safety of your people."

She, Mindy, and Jo exchanged looks and the conversation from before played out in their eyes. Sierra glanced down to the large pocket in Mindy's pants where the tablet was sitting; she raised an eyebrow. Mindy gave her a small nod and pulled the device out.

"We think one of the girls has a control chip installed," she spoke quietly so none of the women could hear the accusation, even if much worse was already floating out among the group. "She stole my tablet and sent out a message after somehow connecting it to your wireless system. The message was encrypted, so we don't know what it said, but," the building rocked again and the sirens quieted. "But," Mindy repeated, "given the current situation, we're pretty sure she sent out the coordinates."

"And she might have disabled our ship," Jo added. "She says she didn't do it, so either she's lying, she doesn't remember... or she didn't do it. We have her contained for the moment and will deal with her once this is settled."

Kayde took the tablet and started it up, his fingers flying against the screen. Toran and Jo stared one another down and Sierra knew that if he demanded they hand Laurel over, this whole situation was going to go to hell. They couldn't hand her over, no matter what she'd done.

"Intel will need to look at this," Kayde said, after several moments. "I can't decrypt it."

168

Toran and Sierra stared one another down and she waited for him to make the next move. Raze's warm presence at her back was the only thing keeping her from saying something she'd regret and giving the other Detyen time to make his move.

He broke their stare down to talk to his man. "Give it to Nokta and have her run it to central command. If Dru has a problem with that, go in her place."

Kayde nodded and made for the door, leaving the five of them standing there, waiting for something worse to happen.

"This doesn't have to end poorly," said Toran, he glanced over at the cluster of women and quickly looked away. It almost looked like he was trying *not* to see them.

"Yeah, that's up to you," Jo responded.

"She's your problem," Toran finally said. "Unless we find something more than our coordinates on that tablet."

They settled into an unsteady agreement after Kayde came back. The soldiers kept watch near the door and observed the women as unobtrusively as possible. Sierra, Jo, and Mindy did their best to keep the peace. Thirty minutes or so into the battle, the building was near constantly shaking and several of the women were no longer able to muffle their terrified sobs.

Quinn came up to Sierra and leaned against the wall. "Is there some sort of escape plan we should be making if this whole building crashes down around us? Or are we officially prisoners again?" She cast a glance at the Detyens and seemed to get caught on Kayde for a moment before snapping her gaze away.

"We're not prisoners," Sierra assured her, even if her mate was really starting to look like a prison guard. "They just don't want us getting in the way."

"You sure about that?" The woman wouldn't quit.

"Do you really want to run out onto the battlefield right now? Cause I'm not complaining about the dudes with guns standing between us and the enemy that wanted to make you all—" she cut herself off and took a deep breath. "It will be fine, I promise."

A few minutes later the building shook more than it had and a tile in the ceiling crashed to the floor, almost hitting one of the women, who didn't stop screaming until another gathered her into her arms and rocked her tight. Sierra tore the med kit down from the wall and went to check for any wounds. Once that was done, she looked up, trying to spot her mate in the mess, but Raze and Kayde were gone.

Chapter Twenty-One

"They should have told us before leaving their post," Raze said as he and Kayde walked down the barren hallway in search of Dru and his people. That last blast had set Toran on edge and he didn't like that there'd been no communication for a quarter hour. When they saw Dru and Dryce gone without a word, he and Kayde were instructed to quickly investigate.

"I can't get them on my comm," Kayde confirmed, tapping at a button on his forearm where the comm commands were located.

There was no sign of a struggle, but if they'd moved on for any other reason, they should have said anything. Raze pushed worries about his brother aside as scenarios played out in his mind. Clearly, something had gone wrong, and they must have had a reason for not telling them. It could be as simple as Sandon calling them away.

Wind ruffled the back of his neck and Raze shivered from the cold. He snapped his head back, looking for the source. "What's the temperature in here?" he asked.

Kayde took the reading and did it a second time without telling him the result. After a third check, he finally spoke. "Well below standard range. The heat regulators might have been hit by blaster fire."

Or there was a breach.

He and Kayde picked up the pace, looking for anything that could answer that question. They got their answer when they found Dryce huddled next to a bleeding Dru, his hands covered in green blood as he tried to stanch a wound on his leader's stomach. Nokta was nowhere to be seen.

Raze ran back the way they'd come until he found the medkit he'd spotted on the wall earlier. By the time he was back, Kayde and Dryce were speaking in low voices and Dru's eyes had slid shut. He threw the kit down and opened it, reaching for regen gel and a wound sealer.

"We didn't even see them coming," Dryce was saying. His fingers shook when he pulled them away from Dru's wound. "Nokta called for backup while she was coming back from intel. By the time we got here, she was gone. They were like fucking ghosts!"

Raze slathered gel on the wound and sealed it. Dru had lost a lot of blood, but he was breathing evenly. A shot of painkiller and a stimulant had his eyes snapping open. He shot up from his position and winced, cursing out an impressive streak of swears. "Nokta reported a breach," were the first coherent words out of his mouth.

"Can you move?" Kayde asked.

Dru took a minute, but he nodded. It took all three of them to get him up, but he could move with only Dryce's support once he was on his feet. Kayde took the rear, his rifle at the ready, while Raze led the way, alert for the enemy. He tried to signal Toran on the comm, but something was blocking the signal, probably whatever had kept Dru from calling them.

Wherever the enemy was hiding, they weren't in the hallway on the way to the women's suite. The four of them shuffled in and locked the door behind them, settling Dru down onto a chair. Sierra came up with a bottle of water and offered them towels that she must have procured from somewhere. Her teammates came up behind her along with another woman who Raze didn't know.

"What's going on?" asked Mindy. The four women had formed a wall around Dru, blocking him from view of the other survivors. Of course, they didn't want to cause a panic. They weren't going to like the news.

"There's been a breach and our comms are malfunctioning. Dru was injured and Nokta is missing. We saw no one in the hallway, but we suspect some of the Oscavians are inside." The sentences came out choppy, but he reported the information as quickly as he could.

"How the fuck do they keep screwing with the comms?" Mindy demanded. "I chalked that shit up to the atmosphere on Fenryr, but now comms aren't working here too?"

Jo made a slashing motion with her hand and shook her head. "Worry later."

Sierra looked between all of them, her face pale but determined. "So we have twelve civilians, one of whom is restrained, an injured soldier, and few weapons with an unknown amount of hostiles. What's the plan?"

***

At some point in the discussion, Sierra had migrated to stand next to Raze. She didn't even realize that she'd laced their fingers together until her palm started to sweat, but she left it where it was. She hadn't known that she could hate those damn slavers any more, but now that they—or their client—had followed the ship to this base and compromised its location and attacked Raze's people, she wanted to do something rash and destructive.

Instead she was stuck babysitting while an unknown number of hostiles had broken into the facility and might be intent on retrieving the women in her care. Raze's hand wasn't enough. She gave herself five seconds and leaned her head against his shoulder. He leaned into her touch, but before anyone but the uninjured Detyen that she hadn't been introduced to could give them a weird look, she straightened and waited.

"Where's the hard line in this room?" Toran asked. His eyes skated over the walls, jumping past the cluster of survivors and completely missing the panel embedded in the wall behind them.

Sierra pointed straight at the mass of women. "It's locked down," she warned. "We were only given access to the media player. I wish it had been enough." She muttered the last part, but it was still loud enough for them to hear her.

Toran just nodded. His jaw set and he steeled his shoulders before marching towards the panel and moving around the women like they were a giant boulder in the road.

"What's his problem?" Sierra whispered to Raze. This wasn't the first time Toran had glared at her people. At first she'd chalked it up to the complications she'd caused in their life, but he looked at *her* just fine. It was only when he had to interact with the women they'd rescued that he got strange.

"Problem?" Raze looked past her to where Toran was now speaking into a wired communicator. "I haven't noticed anything."

"Seriously? I've known the guy for a week and can tell he's acting squirrelly. He doesn't like the survivors." Out of the corner of her eye she caught the Detyen stranger staring at them again. She flicked her eyes over to him and stared. "Hello, can I help you?"

His eyes widened when she addressed him, making it more than clear that he wasn't one of the soulless Detyens wandering around. He glanced at Raze and his mouth gaped. Raze squeezed her hand and turned toward the man. "Dryce, this is Sierra, my denya. Sierra, this is my brother."

Right, the brother. He'd mentioned him before. Sierra nodded at the other man and now that she was looking, she could see the resemblance. The set of their eyes and the strong lines of their noses, the golden green tone of their skin, even the disbelieving expression that momentarily coasted over the Detyen's face matched what she'd seen of her mate. Dryce recovered quickly, though he still glanced at Raze every so often as if he thought the man would disappear in a puff of smoke. "I am glad to meet you," he said.

They didn't have time for more conversation before Toran came rushing back. "Comms are glitching all over the base. The enemy has taken out a terraforming station and already the casualties are mounting. The Oscavian leader has chosen not to identify himself, but he's made it clear that he and his men will retreat if we give over the women that were stolen and those who did the stealing." Toran glanced over at her and then to Mindy and Jo.

That declaration hung out there for several seconds before anyone spoke. "And?" Jo finally prompted.

"And Sandon isn't the type to turn civilians over to slavers, but he's meeting with a representative and an hour-long ceasefire has been called."

"You really think they're just going to forget this place if you give us to them?" Mindy demanded.

Sierra watched as Toran flinched. "It's not Toran's decision," she found herself saying. "And he's not going to give us over." Where the defense of the man came from, she wasn't sure. But he hadn't let Raze be executed and even in his discomfort, he'd defended the women in this room.

Toran nodded at her. "Sandon is buying time, both to mount a defense and to get us out."

174

"Our ship isn't ready."

"Us?"

She and Mindy spoke over one another but Toran just nodded as if a nod answered either of those questions. "We're not taking your ship. And the defense is yours, if you want it." He flicked his eyes to Raze for a moment and then back to the rest of the group. "They might have short range tracking chips in the survivors, or another control chip. Earth is a long way away, and that journey isn't easy. But if you wish to leave the four of us behind," again with a glance to Raze, "that is ultimately your choice."

Mindy and Jo visibly re-counted the Detyens in the room, confirming that there were five, not the four Toran mentioned. Then they looked at how close Raze and Sierra were standing and neither needed to announce that Raze was coming with no matter what.

"We could use the muscle." There wasn't time for any more discussion or debate. Toran gave a rundown of the path they'd be taking and the potential dangers. Piloting off the planet in stealth mode while an Oscavian warship hovered overhead was the biggest risk, barely dwarfing the fact that they could run into Oscavian warriors bent on abduction and death at any moment.

Sierra found Quinn and they got the women into order, and a wave of relief washed through the room as they learned they were about to go home, even with the threat of blaster fire all around them. And in less time than expected, they were lined up and ready to go. Kayde handed out blasters that he'd retrieved from a nearby locker to Sierra, Mindy, Jo, and a deputized Quinn. Quinn took the lead with the Detyens while two of the survivors stayed near Dru to help him if he stumbled. Raze dropped to the back of the pack with her, Mindy, and Jo to help cover the rear.

And like that, the merry band of survivors and warriors was running blindly through a besieged fort, trying to beat the enemy to safety.

***

The first sign of trouble started halfway to the hangar. The women had kept up well, even if Toran and Dryce set only a

175

moderate pace for them to move. Dru couldn't run with his still healing wound and most of the women didn't have the endurance to do more than walk briskly. But with a group as large as they were, they made good time. The halls were deserted and with the ceasefire underway, everything had taken on an eerie silence, every move they made echoing down long hallways until he was sure they could be heard all the way outside.

A Detyen warrior lay unmoving on the ground as they turned a corner and one of the women let out a gasp while another began to scream before she was cut off by someone else. Raze hung at the rear of the pack while they paused to check the warrior's vitals. Dryce met his eyes and shook his head; there was nothing they could do to help him but wish him well on his journey to the afterlife.

They continued on, now even more cautious. The hangar door was just out of reach, down one more hallway, when a giant purple warrior covered in silver armor stepped into the hallway, blasters in each hand.

"Down!" Toran called, and to the women's credit, they all dropped except for the bound blonde who had to be pulled to the ground by two others. The women scrambled back around the corner, taking cover as they'd been instructed to do before they left their quarters. Raze's blast rifle was heavy in his hands as he heard every shot let out from where he sat. He shuffled over, watching as Mindy, Jo, and Sierra kept their eyes trained behind them to make sure no one came up behind them and caught them unaware. Raze peeked around the corner and saw that his team and Quinn had taken cover, but the armored Oscavian still hadn't been hit. His armor seemed impenetrable, but he wore no helmet.

Raze steadied his rifle and aimed. He'd only have one shot, but even if he didn't hit, he hoped the distraction would be enough to let the others get their hits in. He let out his breath and fired, the stream of red shooting too quickly for his eyes to follow before the Oscavian collapsed. Blaster fire wasn't usually deadly, but a hit to the face from a blast rifle could end a person.

They stayed under cover for several more seconds before checking for more hostiles. Once it became clear that the armored

Oscavian was the only threat at the moment, everyone got moving again.

The blast doors to the hangar slid open under Toran's command and the cold air inside froze Raze to the bone. The heating system was busted here and there could be a breach in the walls. He looked for a sign of danger, a sign that this was where the Oscavian had come from. Tools were strewn on the floor and a patch of sticky liquid caught in shadow might have been blood, but he couldn't tell.

Their ride sat on the far side of the room, a long-range freighter that had been retrofitted with stealth capabilities and one defensive gun. Its shield was meant to guard it from space debris, but it was the best ship available to them right now. The women ran for the door, entering through the ramp at the back while Raze's senses went into overdrive trying to see if they were really in immediate danger or if he was just paranoid.

The last of the women boarded and he followed Sierra while his people and Quinn took up the rear. In under a minute, they were on board with the ramp raised. The women had found the seats and he followed the warriors and soldiers into the cockpit.

Kayde and Jo had taken the pilot and co-pilot seats while Mindy sat in the navigator position.

"Where's the exit?" Jo asked. Sierra stood behind her chair, hands on the headrest.

"The roof retracts," Kayde informed them.

"And is that going to be obvious to the giant warship squatting in the sky?" Mindy sniped. Tempers were running high, for those in their group who had them, and they needed to get away quickly.

"Probably not," was Kayde's less than reassuring reply. "We're on the far side of the base and this ship is small, we don't need it open all the way. We can close it remotely once we're out."

"The stealth engine on this ship will see us away safely," Toran assured them. "Let's take our seats and get out of here."

It took several minutes to power up the ship. Raze sat next to Sierra at the back of the large cockpit with Dryce in the row of seats behind them. No one said anything, as if the sound of their voices could be enough to alert the Oscavians to where they were. The lights came on and the whir of an engine whistled around them. Raze gripped Sierra's hand, needing to do *something* when it was now all in their pilots' hands.

Another several minutes passed and even Raze, who knew very little about ships, was beginning to think that something was wrong. "Shouldn't we be gone by now?" he finally asked.

"The door isn't opening," Kayde said, even and soulless as always.

"What?" Sierra leaned forward to get a better look at the view screen. "Why not?"

"Maybe it's whatever is fucking with the comms," Mindy suggested. "Whatever it is, we're stuck until we get it to work."

"Or someone goes out and opens it manually. The controls are on the far wall," Kayde pointed towards where he meant. "It should be one of us." He meant the Detyens. "They'll need to close the door behind us. I would do it, but they need the extra pilot." Raze expected Jo or Mindy to protest, but apparently his claim was true.

"I'll—" Dryce was cut off before he could volunteer.

"You should have left me in the first place," said Dru. "I can open a door. Fly well." He grabbed his blaster and exited the ship through the rear ramp without further argument. The ramp closed up behind him, sealing them back in the ship.

Raze leaned forward, trying to get a look at Dru's progress, but he was too small on the screen and Raze was too far back to get a good look. Minutes passed, but then he heard a screech outside as the door above them began to retract.

"Everyone buckle up," Jo warned over the intercom. "We're going for a ride."

Chapter Twenty-Two

They made it through the door and the Oscavians didn't see them. They flew along a steady route away from the base and the Oscavians still didn't see them. They broke atmo and nothing shot after them. But Sierra didn't fully let out her breath until they were several thousand kilometers away from the base and speeding their way towards the right jump gate, still wrapped up in the ship's powerful stealth engine.

"Our path is mapped," Mindy told them. "We should reach Earth in a week."

After they were through the jump gate, Sierra got up and went to tend to the women. She did a head count and checked it again when she only came up with eleven survivors, a certain blonde conspicuously absent. Rather than level an accusation at the group, she crouched near Quinn's chair. "Please tell me Laurel is locked in a room somewhere on this ship."

Quinn's head whipped around and she did the same count that Sierra had just done, eyes wide. "I could have sworn she was with us. I saw her all the way to the hangar, I'm sure of it."

Sierra nodded and stood. She surveyed the women again and saw a few wouldn't meet her eyes. "Has anyone seen Laurel?" she asked, trying to keep her voice steady.

A few looked away from her, but one, Valerie, smirked. "I guess she missed the bus."

Rage flashed through Sierra and she took a step towards the woman before she felt Quinn's hand on her leg. Footsteps down the corridor let her know Raze was on his way, her emotions flashing in his mind. "You left her *behind*?" she yelled. "It was the middle of a battle!"

"One that she called down on us," Valerie crossed her arms and sneered. "We couldn't trust that traitor not to sell us out as soon as we made it somewhere else. She made her choice."

"She didn't have a choice!" Even though she knew she should keep her voice down, Sierra didn't care. "It could have been any of you who go stuck with a control chip and forced to do that shit. You are all—"

Raze placed a hand on her shoulder. She looked back to see him shake his head slightly. Even if a distant part of her understood what some of the women had done, she wanted to tear into them. No matter what Laurel had done, it wasn't okay to leave her on the battlefield where she was vulnerable to attack and capture.

"There are three rooms just down the hall." She forced false evenness into her voice. "Choose your quarters. We'll be home in a week."

She grabbed Raze's hand and tugged him through the sea of women to the room she'd claimed for them. She'd managed to rescue her bag full of a few changes of clothes, and luckily the ship was stocked with enough soap to keep them all clean for the next few days. Raze had nothing but the clothes on his back. And her.

"They left her there to die," she said against his chest as he pulled her close.

Raze brushed his lips against her forehead. "If any of my people find her, they'll keep her safe and remove whatever is in her brain making her do this." Neither of them mentioned what would happen if the Oscavians found her first.

Crashing behind the weight of Laurel's disappearance was another realization. "Are you okay with leaving like this?" Her head snapped up to see calm dark eyes. "We never got around to *this* conversation and I know how much your—"

His finger covered her lips as she started to speed up and spiral into panic. After a second, he replaced it with his mouth, capturing a quick kiss. "My home is at your side, denya. Don't make this one of your burdens." He tugged her forward until they were both laying down on the narrow cot and he held her close, his arms around her.

Sierra played with the green fingers in front of her and smiled when her hands roamed over his knuckles, remembering the dangerous secret he kept hidden there. After a moment, a laugh burst out of her and she couldn't stop it, rocking against Raze as a realization crashed down. He didn't say anything, just held her as hysteria swept through and left her a mess, almost like she'd been crying. Several minutes later, she calmed down enough to breathe evenly again. "My dad is going to freak the fuck out when he meets you."

Raze tightened his hold. "He'll object? Can he? I am not familiar with Earth mating customs."

That sent her off laughing again and she vaguely realized that it was the stress of the battle and the loss of Laurel that had her off this cliff. It was laugh or cry, and Sierra hated crying. "Sorry." She lifted her mate's hand up and kissed it. "No, he can't object. I mean, he can say shit, but he has no hold over me like that. I'm an adult. He's just..." Was there a good word to describe her dad? "He adopted me when I was little out of a very bad situation, and I think that makes him more protective than a lot of parents. He's always wished I were a soldier rather than in intelligence, and he doesn't understand the choices I've made. He might think you're a rebellion."

Raze didn't react to her roundabout confession to being a spy, which she hoped was a good thing. Sol Intelligence and Defense were going to have a lot to say about everything that just happened, but they'd never objected to aliens on principle before. There might even be a place there for her mate, if he wanted it. But she'd save those suggestions for later, when they weren't riding a survival high and still in the process of escape.

Raze kissed her cheek. "A rebellion?"

"You're not," she felt the need to reassure him, and then it was Raze's turn to laugh. She flipped over so they were face to face and knew she'd never get tired of looking at her mate. He was still so new to her, but he'd become vital, and she'd spend her life memorizing every piece of him until there was no way she didn't know him. "I can't promise you that it's going to be easy," she warned.

"I don't need easy," he said. "Just you."

They lay there together as the ship rumbled closer to home, closer to an entirely different set of problems. Was the ambassador she'd seen in that picture a threat? Would her father have a problem with her mate? Would the survivors be okay once they were back on Earth? None of it was easy, and she couldn't guarantee success. But lying next to Raze, it didn't seem impossible. If Earth was under threat, they'd face it. They'd find a way to help the survivors, despite what had happened to Laurel, and *somehow* she'd bring her father around to suddenly having a giant green son in law that she was crazy about.

"I can't wait to figure this all out," she said, and kissed him. That part came as easy as breathing.

***

Ruthless: Detyen Warriors

By

Kate Rudolph

and

Starr Huntress

Published by Starr Huntress & Kate Rudolph.

www.starrhuntress.com
www.katerudolph.net

Chapter One

Iris could just barely make out the Potomac from the window of the office where she was standing. They were nestled in an unimpressive building in northern Virginia that had stood mostly unnoticed for more than 300 years. Outside, it was all unassuming brick and chipped paint, but inside, the walls were a sleek gray and the technology embedded everywhere was the highest quality. The Sol Defense Agency wouldn't accept any less.

Not that Iris worked for them, not directly. She'd never been a soldier, and she didn't want to be. But when the agency had questions, they called her, and she did her best to answer them. That was the role of the consultant. And they usually didn't make her wait. But something was up. Something had been up for the past several days, and she hoped she was about to find out what was going on. Media reports were whispering about a secret mission and recovered abductees, but there was no official report, not even a statement.

If this ended up being about something unrelated, Iris was going to scream. She didn't consider herself very curious, but anyone who knew her would say otherwise. After all, she'd been on a first name basis with the security guard at her high school, who kept catching her breaking in to areas where she didn't belong.

The sun was setting and the city was lit up by the red lights of cars darting around, both on the road and in the sky. It was a dizzying mix of movement and speed, and Iris's eyes crossed as she tried to follow one vehicle on its path. Before she could give herself a headache, the door to the office opened and a woman in her mid-forties with straight blonde hair and a serious expression walked in, her back ramrod straight. That serious expression resolved into a smile when she spotted Iris.

"Have you been waiting long?" Selma Daniels asked. She'd been Iris's contact at the agency for more than five years. In that time, they'd gotten to know each other fairly well, and Iris had even attended Selma's daughter's last birthday party.

"Only a few minutes," Iris replied. "Your assistant let me in. I didn't catch this one's name."

Selma barked out a laugh and placed her hand on her chest. "I haven't either. Oh no, that can't be a good sign." She was a tough woman, and notoriously hard on her staff. Those who survived were the best in the agency, and Selma would do anything for them. But because of her standards, every time Iris started a new assignment, Selma seem to have a new assistant.

"I thought you liked the last one."

"I did!" Selma smiled as she took a seat, and gestured for Iris to do the same. "That's why she got promoted."

"Good for her." Iris sat down, and rested her hands on the arms of the chair. "So what's going on?" Neither of them had time to gossip all day.

Selma's smile flattened back into her serious expression. She pulled out a thin disk with an etched code in it and slid it towards Iris. "You've been watching the news?"

Iris bit the inside of her cheek to keep her expression bland, but one of her hands curled into a fist of victory. "I have."

Selma stared at her for a bit too long, a knowing look in her eyes. "The details are on the disk. You can scan it when you're at your secured station. If you take the job, of course. But the basics are this: four days ago, an alien ship entered the solar system carrying eleven women who'd been abducted from Earth over the past three years. One of those women is the niece of a United States senator. With them were three operatives from the Sol Intelligence Agency and four alien men. The aliens are Detyens, a race with whom we've had minor contact. They do not have a large presence on this planet, but some have settled here."

"Detyens?" Iris wracked her brain trying to think of what she knew of the species. They were a mystery. "Where are they from? I've never heard of them."

"We don't have much data. It seems they stopped being active before humanity began its period of space exploration. Our records are sparse. I put in a request with the Oscavian Interstellar Library for more history, but you know how long those requests can take." Selma leaned back and flattened her palms against the dark wood of her desk. "In their initial interviews, the Detyens claim they want to help. That they're friendly."

"You have your doubts?" Iris asked. Earth was not a hub of alien activity; it was too far out of the way from the main shipping lanes and the giant empires to get much attention. The aliens who moved here normally came seeking a better life, or the excitement of a planet fascinated with new intelligent species.

"I don't know enough yet," said Selma. "But there is something weird about their story."

"What?" Iris had to concentrate hard to keep from leaning forward as excitement for the information thrummed through her.

Selma tapped the disk. "The human operatives were sent to retrieve information about twelve women who'd been abducted. They came home with eleven. There's something off with the story they've given us. Something off with the entire thing. They can't give the coordinates or much information about where they got the alien ship. And they claim that the SIA ship was inoperable when they were forced to leave whatever mysterious place they were in. Toran is the one who speaks for the aliens. Find out what he's hiding, find out if he's a threat. Find out if we can let him go home."

Iris's palms began to sweat and her heartbeat picked up. This job was bigger than anything she'd done before. It was fate of the world stuff. The big leagues. Selma was trusting her to determine if someone posed a threat to humanity. If Iris got this wrong, people would die. That should've terrified her. But she reached towards the desk and palmed the disk. "I'll see what I can find out."

Selma smiled. "I knew I could count on you. Now get out of here, I have an assistant to fire."

Iris huffed out an unexpected laugh and stood, placing the disk in a secure pouch in her bag. She reached out and shook Selma's hand before bidding her farewell and leaving the office. The disk seemed to weigh a hundred kilos and she couldn't wait to get home and read the file from her secured station.

Toran. She rolled the name around in her mind, batting it from side to side. *I'm going to get you*, she thought. *You're mine.*

***

Seven days. They'd been stuck on this backwards planet for seven damn days. Fourteen days since they'd left Detyen HQ in the midst of a battle, and Toran burned to know how that had all turned out. An Oscavian warship was no laughing matter. The legion was prepared to defend itself, but with no way to communicate with them, Toran feared the worst.

At least they weren't prisoners. Not quite. He, Kayde, and Dryce had been given a suite of rooms near the headquarters of the Sol Defense Agency, and they'd been invited to explore the city of Washington, DC as much as they wished. Raze, as a newly mated man, had moved into Sierra's quarters and Toran had barely seen him since. He could not blame the man. After years of an emotionless, hopeless existence, he'd been granted a miracle. No, in these uncertain times a denya was always a miracle. Raze had been granted ten miracles on top of one another.

"If you keep that up much longer, the floor is going to collapse," Dryce teased from where he sat on the sofa. Kayde merely looked at him silently.

Toran stopped and turned on his heels to face his men. He was used to long missions in cramped quarters, but this was different. Frustration replaced the blood in his veins and the need to move beat at him at all hours. If the walls were any higher, he'd be climbing them. But as it was, he could brush the ceiling with his fingertips without needing to strain.

"You seem relaxed," he observed. Dryce was a bit younger than him and seemed to be taking this unexpected delay on Earth like it

188

was some kind of vacation. Detyen warriors did not get vacation; they couldn't be spared. Not with only a few hundred of them left.

Dryce clasped his hands behind his head and grinned. "I've been getting my exercise, and it's been much more enjoyable than pacing."

Sex. He'd seen human women eying the younger warrior, taking in his green skin and dark clan markings and the muscular frame underneath. Detyens and humans looked enough alike, were built enough alike, that sexual compatibility was not in question. And the women of this city were adventurous. Dryce had made it clear he was more than up for the challenge.

Toran would leave it to him. He didn't have time to take a lover. Not even for a single night. If he'd been on this mission in the early days of his soldiering, he might see things the same as Dryce. They were trapped on a new world for the time being, and the locals were friendly and eager. But the shine had worn off, and Toran wanted to go home.

A traitorous part of him, the one that forgot his duty, whispered that Earth was his best chance. His denya wasn't hiding among the women of the legion and he was getting close to his thirtieth birthday. He quickly glanced at Kayde but looked away before he could get caught. His fellow Detyen had dark, dead eyes and a flat expression that had nothing to give away.

Kayde was one of the soulless. One of the Detyen warriors who'd sacrificed his emotions to steal a few years and escape the denya price. Without a mate, Detyens died at the age of thirty. It was an evolutionary quirk that would doom their race to extinction. If their home planet of Detya hadn't been destroyed, it wouldn't be a problem. But he couldn't change the past, especially not a tragedy that had happened over a hundred years ago.

"I don't think thrusting will serve as an adequate defense against an Oscavian blaster. Let's get some gym time in." Dryce didn't complain about Toran's jab, but he rolled his eyes. Kayde merely stood and ducked into his room to change into something appropriate.

In the long-term, the equipment in their building would not be sufficient for the workouts that the Detyen warriors needed to stay in prime condition. But they could make it work for now. They worked silently on the weights for several minutes before Dryce let a barbell drop with a loud clang.

Toran's gaze snapped over to him, ready for a threat. But Dryce was merely taking a sip of water. "You think they're ever going to let us leave?" he asked, giving lie to his laid-back attitude. Dryce might be enjoying all that Earth had to offer, but that didn't make it his home.

Kayde gently set down his own weights and wiped sweat from his brow with the towel. "We are not a threat to them. We have been nothing but helpful. They have no reason to keep us here."

That was optimistic. But maybe Kayde had lost the ability to see the different angles of the situation. He didn't have emotions, and he couldn't process the way the humans were acting. "They still haven't secured their place in the intergalactic hierarchy," Toran countered. "We are too far from the Oscavian Empire for it to be much of a threat. But that doesn't mean that the humans aren't afraid of some superior force coming in and trampling them. For all they know, we're the advance team."

Dryce sputtered. "Detyens wouldn't do that. Not even—"

"It doesn't matter," Toran interrupted. He didn't want to speak about the destruction of their home world. That generational wound tore at him and reminded him of more recent wounds that he also couldn't fix. "We have to be on our best behavior. We have to make them believe we are not a threat."

"Or we could just steal a space ship and go home," Dryce suggested with a shrug. He leaned back against a wall and crossed his arms, a model of nonchalance.

Toran bit back a smile at the ludicrous suggestion. Yes, he wanted to say, the best way to prove they weren't a threat was to abscond with human technology and return to their people as quickly as possible. But he kept it to himself. "We need to make the most of our time here."

Both Dryce and Kayde straightened at that suggestion. There was one thing Earth had that they didn't have at Detyen HQ. Yormas of Wreet.

The Detyen Legion had one primary objective: discover who destroyed Detya one hundred and three years ago, and exact justice for their people. The destruction of the planet had come as a complete surprise, and only those who were already off planet or had access to a ship survived. The Detyen Legion represented the survivors of the only military ship in orbit that day. They took their mandate seriously and most of their missions dealt with gathering information about what had happened in their system that day.

Toran and his men had been assigned to retrieve data from a ship wrecked on a planet hundreds of light-years away from Earth. They'd only run into the human women by coincidence, and a lucky shot had seen their original ship destroyed. But for the first time in a century, they had a real lead on what had happened that fateful day when their planet was destroyed.

A message had been sent stating that talks had broken down and called for their destruction. The man who'd sent that message was called Yormas of Wreet. Toran had never heard of Wreet, and the man was a stranger to him. But Sierra Alvarez, Raze's human denya, recognized the name. He was now an ambassador on Earth, but whether he was a threat, or even the same man from the recording, was unknown.

"We have an opportunity that we may never again have," said Toran. "If Sandon or any of the other members of the leadership could speak to us, they would instruct us to gather more information and report home. So that's what we're going to do."

"And do you have any ideas about how were going to go about that?" Dryce asked. "It's not like we can kidnap the guy. That will not help our reputation here. And if he wants to pull the same trick again, we don't want to tip him off."

The younger man had a point. No one was quite sure what the weapon was that had destroyed Detya. It had never been used again. And no planet had taken credit. But if Wreet was the perpetrator, he might still have access to whatever tools they'd used back then. And Toran did not want another planet to suffer the way his own had. Not if he could stop it.

"Talk to your brother," he said, referring to Raze. "He and his denya may have access that we don't. If not, then her father might." Sierra's father was a famous human general, a hero to his people.

Dryce nodded.

Toran turned to Kayde. His role was a bit tricky. The existence of the soulless was the Detyen Legion's best-kept secret. No one could know about it. They wouldn't understand. They might think the Detyens were monsters, beasts who would sacrifice everything for just a few extra years. No one but a Detyen could understand the toll the denya price took on them.

"Keep your ears open," he told Kayde. "We can follow any leads you find."

Kayde nodded, seemingly not bothered that he was forced to take a passive role in the investigation.

"And," Toran added with a smile, looking at Dryce, "if we have nothing by the time the month is out, we can steal that ship."

Dryce laughed, and scooped up his water bottle and towel. "It's a good idea, you'll see."

He and Kayde left Toran in the gym and Toran heard the door shut behind them. When it opened and closed again, he thought Dryce must be coming back for a parting shot. "I'm not letting you steal anything else either. Go find another woman to sleep with."

A floral scent tickled his nose and he was already turning before a woman—not Dryce—spoke. "Do you normally approve of theft?" she asked, in a voice like honey that covered him in its sticky sweetness.

192

Toran got a glance at her and recognition tore him apart, punching him in the chest and squeezing his heart to pieces.

Denya.

Chapter Two

Oh God, he was even hotter in person.

The first thing Iris had done after receiving her assignment from Selma was read through the transcripts of the initial entry interviews of the aliens she was meant to analyze. And it was a good thing, because the moment she caught sight of Toran NaLosen her mind went straight to the gutter, and she imagined all the dirty things he could do to her if he had her alone in his bed. All those fantasies popped up just from his voice and his picture.

The picture in his file didn't do him justice.

It was a full body shot, and the outline of his muscles had been clear, even under the thin shirt he'd been wearing. His skin had appeared golden, but not that far off from the tones she saw in some humans. In person, he was a work of art, and there was no mistaking him for someone from Earth. He gleamed. Dark splotches and triangles dotted his arms, and she was reminded of a stalking jungle cat who waited in the trees and dealt death with a single blow. He was looking at her now with a predator's gaze, frozen in place and ready to pounce.

Her fingers ached to touch him. She took a step closer before she realized what she was doing, and when they were barely more than an arm's-length apart she made herself stop and planted her feet like she was standing in wet concrete. He didn't answer her question, and so she tried another.

"What about sexual partners? Do you approve them for your men as well? Or is it merely the act that you order?" What had come over her? This was beyond inappropriate. But she was heated to the core, and she was afraid if she gave another inch she'd launch herself at him and capture his full lips with her own. What did an alien taste like? What did *this* alien taste like? She'd never wondered before—she must've been waiting for this man. And he was the one she couldn't have.

That thought was a cold wave of reality, and it couldn't have come a moment too soon. She was here to see if Toran was somehow responsible for the disappearance of a victimized woman. If he'd killed a human or perhaps sold her into slavery, she couldn't afford to lust after him. She couldn't afford for her judgment to be called into question. Her entire job, her reputation, depended on it. If Selma caught wind of the fact that she was making eyes at one of the aliens she was supposed to be evaluating, she wouldn't just ruin this assignment, she'd never be hired by the SDA again.

He smelled so damn good. Masculine, earthy, and with a hint of something she couldn't define, something she wanted to smell in her sheets. His scent imprinted on her nose and tickled its way into her brain, and she knew if she ever caught a hint of it outside she'd be thinking of him for the rest of the day. This was crazy. She'd never had such a visceral reaction to any man, or alien, before.

And Toran was just as fascinated. But his feet weren't stuck in metaphorical concrete. His eyes were supposed to be black; she'd spent enough time staring at his photo to know that. And she was almost sure that they had been black when she walked into the room. But now they flashed red, like he was some kind of demon sent to drag her down to hell and show her all of the perverse pleasures that the dark side had to offer. And she was ensorcelled enough to want to go with him.

He stepped forward, and suddenly that small distance between them disappeared. His fingers found her wrist and gently scraped against the sensitive flesh. A shiver raced up her arm and then down her spine, and then through the rest of her body, loosening the roots she planted in the floor. All she had to do was take half a step closer and she'd be pressed up against him. But she had just enough self-control to stay in place.

Toran's eyes, his fiery red eyes, met hers and singed her to the core. It was like looking into the heart of a volcano. "It isn't my teammates' sexual partners that I care about." His voice sent another shiver through her, as she imagined what he could do with that mouth of his. They'd barely said anything, but that just made her more fascinated. Was he saying that he cared about *her* sexual partners? Did he care if she was seeing anybody? Or would he throw her down against that weight bench there and take her to the heights of release no matter who existed for her outside of this room? Because inside this room it was just the two of them. The rest of the world had ceased to exist.

His gaze raked down her from head to toe, something proprietary that told her they would have sex, lots of the sweaty kind, and she would love it. She normally hated when guys looked at her like that. But she never wanted Toran to stop. He still had a hold of her wrist, and never breaking eye contact, he raised it to his lips and kissed her fluttering pulse, flicking his tongue out as he pulled away.

She leaned in, her body instinctually closing the distance between them.

Somewhere down the hall outside a door banged shut, the sound loud enough to reverberate off the walls. Iris jumped back, the spell cracked, but not broken. She cleared as much of the room as she could while her mind reeled, and wasn't satisfied by the distance until she had two weight benches between them. It wouldn't be enough, not if he was determined, but Toran just breathed heavily and stared at her, as if he could force her to move back with just his eyes. And if she let him stare at her for too long, he might just be able to.

Were all Detyens like this? Nothing in the file had suggested this level of sexual magnetism, so Iris wasn't sure. But she made a note to add a warning about crazy alien sex pheromones. Because that was what this had to be. Otherwise she didn't know how she was going to get through this assignment. Not without being debauched by the demonic alien with his golden skin and sexy red eyes. She was so screwed.

***

In a single blinding moment, everything Raze had done over the last few weeks made sense to Toran. The man had risked his life and his place in the Detyen Legion for a woman he'd known for a few hours.

Of course he had, she was his denya.

She was worth risking everything. Some small part of him had thought that there was something wrong with Raze, that he wasn't as soulless as he'd claimed to begin with. How could the denya bond overcome something like that? Now he knew. Toran wasn't soulless, he hadn't had to make that decision yet. But he burned for the woman in front of him, and the need to claim her overrode everything else. Yes, this could override soullessness. Easily.

The first thing he noticed, once he could start noticing details, were her big brown eyes. They were wide and the color deep, and if he stared too long he was going to fall into them and drown in their depths. In them he saw a core of inner strength and determination wrapped up with a hint of fear and a longing for understanding. Maybe it was the bond telling him these things; he'd never before been able to read strength and grit and hope and terror in a single glance. But it was all there for him to see. Her long brown hair was braided close to her head and made her pale skin seem even paler. She was tall too, but not quite as tall as him. Human women were shorter than Detyens, and he found he liked that. He liked everything about the woman in front of him, even if he didn't know her name or anything else about her. But merely brushing his fingers against her wrist was more satisfying than any sexual experience he'd ever had, and at that moment he couldn't recall any of those meaningless encounters.

When his denya pulled back from him and practically flipped over several pieces of gym equipment, he forced himself to stay in place. Her cheeks were flushed, and she was breathing deep, just as affected by the bond as he was. But she was human, and she had no idea what was going on. If he pressed his advantage, he might sneak a taste of her. But he didn't want her only for a moment, no, she was his to keep.

With a little space between them, he was starting to get a hold of the bond and could think. Could question. Why was she there? The building he, Kayde, and Dryce were staying in was owned by the SDA. Only SDA personnel were allowed inside. So did she work for them? Was she here to tell him that they could go home? Could he take her with them? They'd have to work that out, because there was no way he was leaving her behind.

"Who are you?" It came out gruff, demanding, and his denya stiffened at his tone. He had to get control of himself, he couldn't scare her away.

"My name is Iris Mason." Her voice trembled a little, but the set of her shoulders was determined. "I have a few questions for you. Maybe I should come back later." The heat was still there in the way her body was canted towards him, leaning forward despite the space between them. And the flames in her eyes could start a fire. But you wouldn't know it from the tone of her voice. Now she was all business, though he didn't know whose business she was.

"Stay," he demanded. He wanted to curse himself. He'd been leading his men for the better part of a decade, and he'd never relied on this high-handed bullshit before. But put his mate in front of him and he turned into a barbarian who couldn't control himself.

She stiffened even further, and her jaw set. "I should've called first." She took half a step back, but didn't turn away from him.

Toran took a deep breath before he spoke and made sure that his tone was even and inviting. "It's no trouble," he insisted. He picked up one of the light weights from the rack beside him and moved it from hand to hand, just to do something to keep from crossing the room and boxing her in. "What do you want?" He wanted her, anything else was up for debate.

His new tone seemed to put her at ease, and her eyes were drawn to the bright green weight he was moving from hand to hand. "As I said, I need to ask you some questions." She stuck her hand into a messenger bag he hadn't noticed before and pulled out a small tablet, her hand shaking as she scrolled.

Toran was more flustered than he realized, if he hadn't noticed the giant bag hanging over her shoulder. She could have had a weapon, she could have taken him out in a second, and he wouldn't have seen it coming. "About what? Who sent you?" Sanity and his duty were starting to war with the bond, and he knew he shouldn't trust her. Who was Iris Mason? Who did she work for? Who was she, other than his mate?

"I work with the SDA," she said, though that didn't answer much. "There are just a few things they want me to go over concerning your visit to Earth." She held her tablet like a talisman, like it was something that could ward him off and protect her from their fate.

"We just want to go home." That was what he would have said an hour ago, before she walked into the room. Now going home wasn't the only thing he wanted. Not when his mate was standing on the other side of the room. Not when he needed to taste her, not when he needed her under him. But she wasn't ready for that yet. And unless she was about to lead him to a ship, he had time to get her there. They could sort out the rest later.

Iris was oblivious to those thoughts, and nodded at what he said. "I'm here to make that happen." Her tone was bright, but she was holding something back. He and his men had answered dozens, probably hundreds, of questions from the SDA. They'd given them almost everything they wanted, except for the location of the Detyen HQ. So why was Iris being sent in now?

"Ask your questions." He was going to find out just why she was here. He was going to find out what the SDA wanted. And he was going to claim his mate, and find a way to keep her by his side. Because one thing was clear. His time on Earth had just become a lot more interesting.

Chapter Three

Whatever spell had captured them seemed to release them just as quickly. After challenging her to ask him questions, Toran was all business. But he was practically hypnotizing her with the way he was moving the small hand weight, tossing it from side to side like it weighed nothing. Well, it only weighed a couple kilos, and to someone as big as him it must have been like moving air.

"Do you mind if I record this?" She technically didn't need his permission, but she liked to ask. It usually made her subjects think that she respected them.

"That's fine." Toran set the weight back on the rack and leaned against the wall, arms crossed.

Iris took a breath and engaged the recorder. Her hands were still shaking and she wished she could shove them into her pockets to hide that. She only hoped that Toran didn't notice, or if he did, that he didn't realize it was because of him. "What is your purpose on Earth?" The question sounded philosophical to a human, but Toran didn't take it that way.

"We're here to deliver the women we recovered from Fenryr 1." That was the same answer he'd given three times before. She was inclined to believe it. Though she doubted that it was the whole truth.

"How long do you want to stay here?" Another standard question, and she expected a standard answer.

He didn't disappoint. "We have no intention of staying longer than you keep us here." Similar to what he'd said before, she noted.

"Do you hold any ill will towards Earth?" She didn't expect him to admit it, but she liked to have the answer on the record.

"No." At least he didn't seem insulted to be asked.

With those baseline questions out of the way, she could get to the meat of the interview. "What is the nature of the relationship between Sierra Alvarez and Raze NaFeen?" She'd read the files, but everything she inferred about them came from reading between the lines. Technically, Raze was supposed to be living in the same quarters as Toran, Kayde NaDetya, and Dryce NaFeen. But entrance and exit logs indicated that he hadn't spent a single night there.

Toran's eyes narrowed, and she noticed that the red had faded. Now they were dark, and should have been impossible to read. "Is that relevant?"

"Yes." Why else would she ask it? She kept that thought to herself.

He waited a beat to answer, as if he hoped she would withdraw the question. "They are romantically involved," he conceded.

She had guessed that much, though right now she didn't want to think about what it meant to be involved romantically with a Detyen. "And does Raze plan to leave with you?" *And what would you do if something happened between us?* Woah! What the hell was that? Ten minutes with the guy and she was already imagining wedding bells. Alien sex pheromones. That had to explain it.

Thankfully, he couldn't read her mind. "You will have to ask him," Toran said evenly.

She had more questions, but that line of inquiry was making her uncomfortable. Right now, she really didn't want to think about what it would take to romance a Detyen. So she scrolled down further and found her next question. "How many women did you recover from Fenryr 1?" Sometimes the best way to get to the bottom of the problem was to ask.

"Eleven."

"Eleven?"

"Eleven were returned to Earth," Toran confirmed.

She knew that much, and he knew that she knew that much. She wasn't here to play games. "So there were only eleven women being held on the planet?"

"No." Had he been coached to give single word answers? Did he know that it was wise not to expand on what he told her? Or was this merely how Detyens spoke naturally? No wonder the SDA was frustrated. It was like she was questioning a particularly cagey rock.

"How many?"

She saw a tic as his jaw tightened. "Twelve."

He was honest, she'd give him that. "And what happened to the twelfth?"

"I don't know." His hand flicked down and rested on the rack of weights, but he didn't pick any of them up. In other circumstances, she might have been worried that he would use them as a weapon. But even though he didn't seem happy answering these questions, she wasn't concerned for her safety. Alien sex pheromones, she reminded herself. She needed to be on guard.

"Was she recovered by her abductors?" It took more effort than usual to keep her mind on the questions and not let her emotions show.

"I don't know," Toran repeated, his tone the same. Frustrated, but not hiding anything.

"Was she killed?" So many bad things could've happened to Laurel, the vanished woman, and it made Iris sick to name them all, but she kept her face a mask of cool disinterest.

"I don't know," Toran repeated again, this time more emphatic.

Pushing him wouldn't get her anywhere. If he didn't know, he didn't know. And if he did, he clearly wasn't ready to tell her. She changed her tactic. "Why don't you know?"

He let out a sound somewhere between a groan and a growl. "Because we were busy trying not to be killed by slave traders when she disappeared!" He gave the weight rack a light shove and one of the precariously balanced weights toppled off, echoing in the room.

That was something. "And where was this?" The point of questioning a subject so ruthlessly was to rattle him. And it was taking more effort than usual to keep her voice even, like she didn't care what happened to the woman, like she didn't hope Toran hadn't done anything unforgivable.

"No comment." His face shuttered, emotion draining.

Now she had to be careful, because if he shut down she didn't know if she could get him to open back up. "I'm here to help you. You want to be cleared to leave, and I want to clear you. But you need to answer my questions."

Toran stared at her with black eyes, not red, and it had nothing to do with whatever had overtaken them when they first caught sight of one another. He didn't want to be here, not on Earth, not on this room, and certainly not with her. Why that hurt a little, Iris couldn't say. But she wanted the truth, she needed it. And that meant she needed to get to the bottom of this. But before she could start a new line of questions, the door to the gym opened and one of the other Detyens stuck his head inside.

This one was kind of a bluish-green, and a bright smile lit up his face when he saw her. She knew the type—players were the same no matter what planet you were on, no matter what species they came from. Been there, done that, had the stolen car and broken heart to show for it, along with the scars no one could see. But this guy couldn't see that she was already on the verge of telling him off from one little grin.

"Hello," he said, all smiles, stepping further into the room, now closer to her than Toran.

And then things got a little weird. Toran growled, actually literally freaking *growled*. Had she thought he was some kind of cat before? No, he was a wolf. And he pushed himself off the wall with the same fluid grace, and bounded across the room until he placed himself between her and the other Detyen, like he was trying to protect her from the playboy.

Were those claws? She eyed his hands and saw the sharp, deadly tips of claws shoot out from where his knuckles used to be. That sure as hell wasn't in the file. His back was to her, and the smart thing to do would be to step away. So why did she want to touch him? Why did she want to step closer? Maybe it was just because he was the devil she knew.

The playboy gave Toran a questioning look. "Are you ready for lunch?" he asked.

The tension drained out of her alien. Her alien? She mentally shook her head. No, the alien that she knew a little better, that was better. "Yes, we're done here."

That wasn't exactly true, but Iris needed a break. "I'll call you if I have more questions."

Toran turned fully to face her, and stepped close so the heat between them was hot enough to sizzle. He placed his fingers, claws gone, on her wrist and slid them back so he shook her hand with the motion of a caress. "I look forward to it." He followed his fellow Detyen out the door, leaving Iris alone in the gym. She had a lot to think about, but she was pretty sure this alien wasn't a threat. Not to Earth, at least. Maybe to her. One thing was certain, he wanted her, and she wasn't sure how she was going to resist.

***

The next two days stretched longer than the last seven, and with every hour that passed Toran was half convinced that Iris was a dream born of exertion and frustration. When he first began to doubt that she was real, he consulted the information console in their suite and ran a cursory search. There were fifteen women by the name of Iris Mason within a hundred kilometers of him. But when he looked at their pictures it became clear that none of them was his denya. Every time he closed his eyes he felt the overwhelming sensation of that first instant of recognition, and there was no way that he'd imagined it. When he slept, Iris was there beside him in his dreams, and more than once he woke up aching for a release that couldn't be satisfied without her.

Iris Mason was a mystery, one that he would solve.

But he was thankful at the moment that Kayde and Dryce weren't there to see him. He'd never been one to pace, no matter what Dryce must think. His time on Earth was making him develop all sorts of bad habits. The lock on the door disengaged and Toran froze in place. But when it opened, it wasn't a Detyen warrior standing in the threshold. No, it was the woman who'd gotten them into this mess in the first place. Sierra Alvarez, Raze's mate.

She wasn't as tall as Iris, but she was paler. Her hair was long and red and held back in a similar fashion to Iris's. They both had that tough, competent look to them, but other than that they looked nothing alike. Toran peered at her and tried to determine if she looked any different to him now that he had his own denya. Did she repel him? No, but he didn't need to get any closer.

Sierra closed the door behind her and engaged the lock before turning back around and crossing her arms. "What?" she asked, her voice a whip of demand.

Toran stepped back and sank down onto one of the comfortable chairs, keeping his posture friendly. "Nothing." They hadn't started on the best of terms. When they first met, Toran had tied Sierra up and thrown a bag over her head before dragging her in front of the rest of his team. At the time, he hadn't known who she was to Raze. He hadn't known that Raze could have a mate. She hadn't held that part against him, but their time on the ship between Detyen HQ and Earth had been all awkward silences and avoidance techniques.

"You're staring," she accused, coming further into the room and taking a seat opposite him. "I thought we were past that."

He might've stared at her a few times on the ship, trying to determine what Raze saw in her, what made her denya material. He'd had no fucking clue. So Toran just offered her a smile and continued to sit silently.

Sierra's eyes widened and she rocked back, tilting the chair with her. "Holy shit, have you been possessed?"

"Why?" he asked. Human logic could be strange, and their humor stranger, but he was fairly certain she didn't think he was actually possessed by some demonic spirit. Pretty sure.

"I don't think I've ever seen you smile," she said, cautiously leaning forward and studying him with narrowed eyes.

"We haven't known each other for long." He'd never been one to hold his smiles in reserve, but he wouldn't show emotions he didn't feel. It felt like a betrayal of those who'd sacrificed their souls for the cause.

"Dryce has been all smiles since the day we met," Sierra informed him. And that reminded Toran of why she was here. Dryce and Raze had gone to lunch together, and Sierra was meant to meet her mate once they got back. It must've been that time already.

"He's Dryce," said Toran, as if that explained everything. The young Detyen chased after every experience and lived his life to the edge of his emotions. It must've been difficult for the man to see his older brother lose his soul and that relationship.

Sierra cracked a smile. "Good point," she conceded.

They fell into a companionable silence, a first for them, as the minutes ticked by and they waited for Raze and Dryce to get back. While she sat there, Toran realized that Sierra could help him in ways he hadn't thought. She was a spy, and knew how to extract information that other people didn't have access to or weren't supposed to know about. And she was the human mate of a Detyen warrior. She knew what it meant to be bonded, what it meant to come from two disparate cultures and forge a life together.

"Do you ever wish that your mating was easier?" he asked.

"Wh-what?" she sputtered, her cheeks as red as her hair.

He held up a hand to ward off anything she might say. "Not the act, please tell me nothing of that." He had no desire to know what Raze was like in bed. "I speak of the bond."

Sierra studied him for a long moment, the red gradually draining from her face. "That's kind of personal," she pointed out.

"You turned my life completely upside down." If they'd never met, he would be back at Detyen HQ analyzing the data they'd grabbed from Fenryr 1, and that much closer to finding out who had destroyed Detya. "I think I'm entitled to a few personal questions."

"How many?" she asked with crossed arms.

Why did humans have to be so difficult? He just wanted to have a conversation and she wanted to play a game. But he needed information, so he played along. "Three." That seemed like a good number.

She sighed and uncrossed her arms, mirroring his open position on her chair. "Fine, but I might not answer."

He would take any information he could get. "So?"

"It's been... messy." It took her a moment to settle on the word, but she continued unprompted. "You heard that I got suspended from the SIA? Yeah, not cool." Sierra worked for the Sol Intelligence Agency, a counterpart to the Defense Agency currently keeping them under supervision. "But if some genie or something appeared in front of me and offered to make things normal again, I'd tell him to get lost. I wouldn't give Raze up for anything." It came out vehement, like she'd been practicing the speech and waiting for the opportunity to give it.

Toran was glad that Raze had such a dedicated mate. His fellow warrior deserved it. "And what if he has to leave Earth?" The four Detyens could be sent away at any moment if the human government decided that was the best option.

"You think we don't talk about the what ifs?" she challenged him.

Toran shrugged; he didn't know what mates talked about. His own parents had died when he was young, and he couldn't remember their conversations.

She was staring at him again. "You're curious all of a—holy shit! You've met her." It wasn't a question; now Sierra was leaning forward, hands on her knees and eyes bright with excitement. "Who is she? Do I know her? Does she know?" The words came out rapid-fire, like she was using her blaster to keep the enemy at bay.

He hadn't told anyone about Iris, as if saying it out loud would make her disappear. But if he wanted information he'd have to open up to someone. And who better than a spy to find out what he needed to know? "Her name is Iris Mason and she somehow works for the SDA. You know how to get information, can you find some for me?"

Now Sierra was grinning and practically bouncing in her seat. "You want me to spy on your girlfriend?"

Toran couldn't see what was funny about this situation. "My mate," he corrected, "but yes." It might have been a little underhanded, but he needed to see her again, to find out more about her.

Sierra tipped her head back and laughed before settling down with a deep breath. She let out a whoosh of air as she calmed. "It's not like they can double suspend me." They both looked over as the door opened and Raze entered, Dryce nowhere to be seen. Sierra continued talking, as she held out her hand to her mate and beckoned him closer. "Give me a few hours and I'll send you what I find."

Raze looked between the two of them, clearly confused by their newfound camaraderie. "What's this about?" he asked with a laugh. "She's my denya, find your own." Toran was still getting used to the easy emotion and open love that Raze displayed. It made him joyous to see it, but until two days ago, it also made him a little sad. And now he was envious, and he'd continue to be so until he could find his mate once more and claim her.

That sent Sierra into another fit of laughter and she tugged on Raze's arm until he bent down and swiped his lips against hers. When he pulled back, she was still grinning. "He did! Come on, I'll tell you on the way home."

Raze shot him a questioning look, but followed his mate silently out the door, correctly assuming that she would give him more information than Toran would. Things were about to get a whole lot more complicated, but Toran had hope that by the end of the day he'd be on his way to finding Iris Mason.

Chapter Four

When Iris finally crawled out of her bed on the third morning of her investigation, she could barely crack her eyes open as she stumbled her way into the kitchen and engaged the coffee pot in the food processor. Sunlight streamed in through one of the windows as if to remind her that the morning was bright, and that she should be happy about it. But, at best, she was running on four hours of sleep and she could barely string two thoughts together. The sun could explode for all she cared. As long as she could down two liters of coffee in the next quarter hour, she might start to feel human again.

She'd always had this problem, case-related insomnia. Her mind got hooked on the question that she had to ask, that she needed answered, and it refused to release her even when she was barely coherent with sleepiness.

Who are you, Toran NaLosen?

She should've been studying the data, collating and collecting information and making it all nice and orderly for her report to Selma. She'd been studying alright, studying the curve of Toran's muscles on every picture she could find of him, four in total. She'd been imagining what he would feel like looming over her, pressing her into her soft mattress. She'd been hoping that Detyens were just a sexual as humans. And she'd been waking from those precious minutes of sleep desperate to feel something, to feel him, between her thighs. Her fingers just weren't doing it. Sure, she got off, but it wasn't enough.

The processor beeped and Iris's first cup of coffee was ready. She lifted the mug to her lips and winced as the bitter concoction scalded her tongue. It didn't matter, she was practically dead on her feet and needed caffeine more than she needed taste buds.

Her brain was stuck on Toran. Even when she was supposed to be studying him and his crew, all she could focus on was the golden alien who looked at her like she was good enough to eat. The golden alien with the color shifting eyes and the predatory spots. None of that belonged in her report, and if even a hint of it leaked, Selma would send her packing before she could concoct an excuse. Iris should have been more concerned about that, but she blamed her apathy on the coffee, not the horniness. Because she definitely wasn't stupid enough to risk her career to get laid.

She was a tight ball of frustration. In three days she hadn't uncovered anything that the SDA didn't already suspect. Maybe that was a good thing. After all, if there was nothing shady about Toran, then it meant that he and his men could be sent on their way safely. It meant that Earth wasn't facing a significant threat.

It meant she wasn't wrong to lust after him.

She'd almost given him a call yesterday, almost made up more questions to ask him. She could invite him over to her place, conduct the interview in private and answer the questions she was too afraid to ask. But she wasn't about to invite him to a private location with easy access to a bed. Her self-control only went so far.

Was this some weird mix of his alien sex pheromones—the ones that she was certain existed even if she couldn't confirm it—and the fact that she hadn't had sex in more than six months? If she went out to some seedy bar and picked up a random stranger to scratch her itch, would some of this crazy obsession dissolve?

Her entire body shuddered at the thought. Someone other than Toran put his hands on her? No, it made her sick just to think about it. Could pheromones do that? Besides, even if she could stand the thought, it was way too early for a hookup.

She glanced at her communicator and tried really hard not to think about the fact that she could be connected to Toran with the click of a few buttons. As if the device could read her mind, the alert engaged and notified her that she had an incoming call. She checked the ID and tried not to be disappointed when it wasn't the alien who dominated her every last thought.

She engaged the call, and a young police detective that she'd been working with on another matter appeared as a hologram above the device. "Miss Mason," Detective Charles said. She might've been younger than Iris, but her dark eyes were hard and evidenced that she had seen some shit. "We have news on the theft case."

"Which one?" Six months ago, she'd filed report after report after coming home to a nearly bare apartment.

Charles appeared to shuffle through a stack of files. "This is about your vehicle."

"What's the news?" The car hadn't been flashy or expensive, but it had been hers. The first one she'd ever been able to buy for herself. Sure, insurance had seen it replaced relatively quickly, but nothing could ever beat her first.

Charles didn't know that and she didn't care. She spoke matter-of-factly, her emotions disengaged from the case. That made her a good cop, but that didn't mean Iris was happy about it. "It was found in a small town in Oklahoma. Unfortunately, by the time authorities were able to get there, it had been destroyed."

That should have hurt. Her first big purchase destroyed by her first love, but she had time to get over it and now all she felt was a hollow sense of closure. "Of course it was. Is there any evidence that might implicate Dan?" His name curdled on her tongue and she wanted to spit it out. Instead she took another sip of coffee, a bitter brew to wash down bitter times.

"No, not at this time. He's still in the wind." At least Charles didn't seem happy about that. That was something. "What would you like us to do with the car?"

Iris sighed, her brain still struggling to catch up to everything that was going on this morning. "I'll contact my insurance. Thanks for the update." They disengaged the call and Iris made a note about it in her planner. She slumped down on the single chair at her rickety kitchen table and glanced over at the wall opposite where her media station used to be. She'd managed to replace it with a used model, but the old one had been top of the line. The apartment used to be nice, used to be a home. Now she could see the faint outline where artwork and family pictures used to hang. An old dog toy sat on the edge of the counter, one end of the bone chewed clear through with excited teeth marks from a young puppy. He even took the damn dog. Cheater, thief, dog stealer. She really knew how to pick them.

If Dan had ever been good for his half of the rent, she might've had to move. Maybe that had been a warning sign, but now she was glad that she could afford this place by herself. He hadn't stolen that one last thing from her. And she probably had to send Detective Charles a thank you note. Thoughts of taking Toran to bed were washed away by the jagged memories of just how wrong a relationship could go.

Residual lust had nothing on the memory of what it felt like to have her heart ripped out and stomped on by a guy who couldn't even be bothered to leave a farewell note. Then again, if he had left a note, she would have had enough evidence to see him rotting in jail.

Iris drank down the last dregs of her coffee and winced at its harshness. But she needed harsh right now, needed to keep reminding herself that there were no happy endings, and that it wasn't worth it to risk anything for a guy. Especially not a shady one, especially not one who was suspected of being a threat to Earth. No one had suspected Dan of shit like that, and look at what he'd done. Toran might want to destroy the planet. And given her track record, he probably did. If the last guy she'd wanted was bad news, why should she think this one was any different?

She had to get control of her libido, learn how to ignore the alien sex pheromones. She'd put in a request to see the Detyen file that the Sol Intelligence Agency kept. They had much more information than the SDA, and could probably confirm that pheromone thing. But one thing was certain—she had to get this job done and judge Toran as a potential hostile, not a potential lover. She couldn't sacrifice her future, or even risk it, for a man who might be a threat to the planet. Because even if he wasn't, he wouldn't be here for long, and she didn't think she could deal with another heartbreak.

***

Sierra had been as good as her word. In a matter of hours. she got ahold of Iris's communication code, her address, and a basic work history. Interestingly enough, that work history hadn't been updated in five years, and according to it she had nothing to do with the Sol Defense Agency. But before Toran could begin to untangle that knot, he was forced back to his original mission. Find out more about Yormas of Wreet.

It couldn't be avoided, not when a perfect opportunity presented itself. Before she'd left earth, Sierra informed them, her father, General Remington Alvarez, had invited her to attend a soirée in honor of the ambassador. At the time she hadn't known who he was, but as soon as Raze had told her about the information recovered from the *Lyrden* on Fenryr 1, she had explained the connection. And now she, Raze, and Toran were entering the grand hallway outside the ballroom where the fete was being held.

For obvious reasons, Kayde had stayed home, and Dryce couldn't get an invitation. He'd wanted to use the time to take advantage of Yormas's absence and find any necessary information that lived in the man's office. But Toran told him no. If he and his men were being investigated, if someone thought they were a threat, they couldn't afford to get into trouble. Besides, the chances of something incriminating being left in a semi-public office were slim to none, and it wasn't worth the risk.

The ballroom showed all the opulence of old Earth. Bright yellow lights hung from the ceiling, sparkling off crystal chandeliers and casting the room in a hazy, dreamlike glow. Sleek androids with convincing human frames walked among the attendees offering drinks and canapés to any who wanted them. The androids were skinned in gold and silver and the light from the chandeliers winked off crystals that were embedded on their faces. But compared to the guests, the androids were dowdy.

It was an explosion of color from all quarters, and Toran felt underdressed in his black wraparound suit and blue pants. The dress of a woman who stood near him shimmered from color to color, red to orange to yellow to green to blue, before swirling around and reforming in new patterns. The fabric was a strange camouflage in a way; he could not describe her if someone

214

threatened to shoot him with las fire. And it wasn't just the dresses and suits that caught the eye, many attendees wore tall hats in stark black or white, the decoration dependent on the cut of the fabric.

But that was the humans. The aliens were a more sedate bunch, wearing simple suits like he and Raze, or dresses featuring no more than three colors, and none of those fancy color-shifting patterns.

Sierra and Raze had broken off from him to go and greet Sierra's father, but it wasn't difficult to keep them in his sights. All he had to do was follow the gaze of the crowd. Though there were plenty of aliens in attendance, few had come with human escorts. He didn't see censure in those who looked at Sierra and Raze, but there was enough curiosity to make him uncomfortable. Sierra might have felt the same. Her face was a pleasant mask of indifference except for when she smiled up at her mate, but Toran had gotten to know her enough to know that she was ready to punch someone or run away if anyone said anything bad about her mate. Not that she would, she was too good of a spy for that. But that didn't mean that she didn't want to.

Awareness tickled the back of his neck and Toran knew exactly who he would find the moment he turned around. Iris stood in the doorway, her hair haloed by the yellow light that glinted off her strikingly simple blue dress. Time stopped and their eyes met, gazes locking and rooting each of them in place. The rest of the crowd must've disappeared because Toran sure as all the Hells couldn't tell where they were. It was only Iris. The days apart had been torture and he needed to touch her as soon as he could.

But something flashed in her eyes, and even though he was too far away to physically see it, he knew it was panic. She wrenched her head to the side, like she was breaking a physical connection between them, and turned away from him. Toran took a step towards her, but the crowd came back in full force and before he could dodge around anyone, she was gone.

He didn't growl, but it was a close thing. His claws itched under his skin, and when he caught a hint of a blue dress next to a tall human man he wanted to reach out and deal violence, to drag his mate by his side and show her who he could be to her. But tonight he was here to be civilized and to do the duty he owed to his people as one of the last surviving members of the Detyen race.

Still, he might have given that all up if the man of the hour hadn't spotted him at just that moment. Yormas of Wreet was a short man, his head stopping lower than Toran's shoulder. But he held himself like he was ten meters tall, and had all the confidence of a man secure in his position. His skin was a neon yellow that could have competed to be eye-catching with some of the outfits, and he had the teeth of a predator, sharp and ready to tear into flesh. When he smiled, Toran was certain it was a threat, but he doubted that many of the humans realized it. Was this the man who'd ordered the destruction of Detya? He didn't look like he was more than a hundred years old, but he was an alien, neither Detyen nor human, and Toran had no idea how long Wreetans lived or what their elderly looked like.

"I've heard this party should be held in your honor and not mine," Yormas said with that predatory smile. His voice was smooth, like he was used to soothing the egos of the less secure. But even speaking to him made Toran's stomach clench, and he was regretting the one canapé that he'd eaten.

"Is that so?" He had to say something to keep this conversation going; any opportunity to talk to the man would give them more information about his potential culpability.

"You're the big hero." He didn't say it like he was trying to stroke Toran's ego, but something in his tone put Toran on edge.

"Where did you hear that?" The Detyens may have been involved in the recovery of those women from Fenryr 1, but the SDA was trying to keep that quiet.

Yormas laughed like they were old friends. "A man has his sources. I don't believe we've officially met. I am Yormas."

"Toran." He needed to say more than that, needed to keep talking. But holding a civil conversation with the man who might have been responsible for the genocide of his people was more difficult than he expected. Though, thinking about it, Toran wasn't sure why he thought this would've been easy. "This is quite the party they have, are things like this back on Wreet?" There, that was a completely civil question.

Yormas smiled and shook his head slightly. "Not quite, but we do know how to celebrate. Though I haven't been home in decades, maybe longer."

"No?" Toran filed away that bit of information. Yormas was older than he looked, but they'd already suspected that.

"The universe is a vast place, and it has so many secrets to surrender. One planet could never satisfy me." He smiled again, and this time Toran was certain of the threat. But before they could finish their conversation another guest stepped in to greet the ambassador, and their moment was over. Had that been a confession of some type? Or a threat? If Toran wanted to read into it, he could think that Yormas had confirmed that he'd destroyed Detya and that he had designs on Earth. But Toran forced himself not to jump to that conclusion. The man seemed a bit slimy, and he liked to talk, liked to be cryptic. But one cryptic conversation wasn't enough to convict him for such a heinous crime.

He'd think on it more when he discussed the party with Sierra and Raze, and they all shared their conclusions. But now he had discharged his duty for the night, and he had a woman to find. A flash of blue in the corner of his eye caught his attention, but when he looked over it wasn't Iris, but another woman in a blue dress. He wasn't discouraged, because he could feel in his chest that she was still there. And he wasn't about to let her go without a confrontation. Not tonight.

Chapter Five

When Toran was added to the guest list at the last moment, Iris knew that she had to attend this party. It was a chance to see the Detyens interact with other people while they didn't realize they were being studied. And since only Toran and Raze were invited, she'd called in a favor to make sure that Kayde and Dryce were being monitored while the party was going on. Not that she expected them to do anything interesting, but parties like this had been used as cover for nefarious actions before, and she wasn't going to be negligent just because something was unlikely.

Every single one of her plans went up in smoke the moment she stepped through the door to the ballroom. She was drawn to Toran like a magnet and their eyes met and locked three seconds after she entered. She panicked, and then she panicked even more because she was panicking. Iris wasn't like this, not usually. She kept a tight control on her emotions and her reactions and did her job as assigned. Except for when it came to this one Detyen. When she saw him, her Earth tilted on its axis and everything tried to realign until it was just her and him and the rightness of their connection. But that was just the lust talking, they didn't have a connection. They didn't know each other. And she had to wrench herself away, practically throw herself out of his path to stop from doing something stupid like approaching him and asking him to dance, or kissing him. If she got within two meters of him she was going to kiss him, and that wouldn't be good for anyone, not in the long run.

It was easier to observe him when he wasn't looking at her, and she got a little thrill from watching him. Could he feel her eyes on him? Or was he completely oblivious? He was speaking to the guest of honor, Yormas of Wreet, and seemed to be giving the conversation his full attention. His gaze was intense, but not that red intensity he'd given her the first time they'd met. But now she was imagining what it would be like to be the sole focus of his entire being and her heart rate kicked up at the thought. If he focused on her like that, he could destroy her, so she had to make sure that didn't happen.

Had he simply come to the party because he wanted to meet the ambassador? She didn't know much about Wreet or the man who represented it, but it was possible that Toran's people did. This meeting could be completely friendly, though the look on Toran's face suggested otherwise. She got the feeling that he did not like speaking to Yormas, and that he wished he was anywhere else. Maybe even with her.

No, she wasn't letting herself have thoughts like that.

With Toran firmly rooted in place speaking to the ambassador, Iris used the opportunity to go find Raze and Sierra and see what was going on with them. She was fairly certain that those two didn't know she was here, and since she'd never spoken to them they wouldn't recognize her. But when they came into sight, Iris almost tripped over the hem of her skirt. It had nothing to do with the alien or the woman beside him, and everything to do with the older human man they were speaking with. General Remington Alvarez, the Savior of Mumbai, and her childhood hero.

She'd known that she might meet him on this assignment. After all, he was Sierra's father. But knowing that in her mind, and knowing it in her gut were completely different things. Iris didn't know if she wanted to approach them and shake the man's hand, or if she wanted to find a place to hide and privately freak out about coming into contact with a man she'd looked up to since she was five years old. He'd defended Mumbai from an alien attack that no one saw coming, and turned what would've been a massacre into a minor battle. She'd followed his career in the SDA and had almost followed in his footsteps before realizing that military life wasn't for her. But fighting wasn't the reason that she looked up to Alvarez, no, it was defending Earth, and she was still doing that, just in a different way.

In other circumstances she might have approached him and told him what an inspiration he was. But she couldn't exactly do that while she was busy investigating his daughter's lover and associates.

The skin on the back of her neck prickled, and Sierra glanced back to where Toran had been speaking with Yormas to find that he'd disappeared. Her stomach dropped and she knew that he was coming for her. Why was he so obsessed? He could have anyone he wanted with that golden skin and those muscles that she wanted to run her tongue over. Sure she knew she looked all right, but she was no prize. Did alien sex pheromones go both ways? Since the SIA hadn't gotten back to her with information about Detyens, she still didn't have confirmation about the pheromone thing, but her certainty in their existence had not wavered.

She ducked out of the main ballroom and insisted to her protesting mind that she wasn't hiding, she was just finding a quiet place to take some notes. A small room with a window that looked over the back garden and was warmed by an old fireplace was perfect. The lights were set to low, but when she entered, she triggered the motion sensor and they brightened to a level that let her see clearly. She didn't know what function this room served; it wasn't big enough to hold more than ten people, but maybe it could work as a private dining room or something like that. It didn't matter; for the moment it was hers and it gave her a bit of privacy.

She hadn't tried to lock the door. She wasn't even sure if it did lock. But she regretted not finding out when it opened, and that sexy alien she was trying to avoid stepped inside and closed the door behind him as if he had every right, as if they'd planned an assignation. She stared at him, her throat frozen. She couldn't speak, and her brain seem to be stuttering since it was commanding her to close the distance between them and finally find out just what he tasted like. Luckily, the rest of her body seem to be just as frozen as her throat and she was rooted in place like an ancient tree.

Toran stared at her for several seconds, his eyes flicking from her head to toes as he took in the way her dress fit around her curves. She'd bought the dress for an event a few years ago, and though it was pretty, it didn't stand out among the colors and sparkles of the high society crowd. But the way Toran was looking at her made her feel like a work of art. He cleared his throat and offered her a grin that made her stomach flip. "I expected you to have more questions."

"You did?" It came out high-pitched, but she didn't squeak, so she was calling that victory. She needed to get herself under control; she couldn't act like a schoolgirl with a crush around the central object of her investigation.

"I wanted to see you again."

And then he had to go and say something like that. Didn't Detyens know that they were supposed to play it cool? You weren't supposed to just go around and admit what you were feeling like that. Discomfort nipped at her toes and unease at her heels. Dan had been open about his emotions, or what he'd said were his emotions, at the beginning. He'd said he wasn't holding anything back, and that he could never wait to see her again. That he'd never felt like that before. And look at where that had got her. "You want me to investigate you more closely?" She needed there to be a wall between them, an emotional barrier if she couldn't have a physical one.

But Toran smiled and her unease and discomfort dissolved like it had never been there in the first place. How was he doing that? She was suspicious by nature, it was her job. So why did Toran make her want to trust?

"I think you've misunderstood the nature of our relationship, Mr. NaLosen." She tried to put a reprimand in her voice, but it came out a little husky.

He stepped closer, until he could practically wrap his arms around her waist, but he didn't try. Why wasn't he trying? Iris wanted to lean in and close that distance, her body yearned for it, but she kept herself rooted in place. "I don't think I have," he said, and again his eyes flared red.

Had she thought her heart was beating fast before? It had nothing on what it was doing now, as she stood there with the utter certainty that he was about to kiss her. She could feel the heat of his body in the small space between them and she wanted to reach out, wrap her fingers around the collar of his top, and yank him close to get the damn thing over with. She was lying to herself if she believed that she was going to get out of this party without acquainting her lips with Toran's.

So why was he standing still? Everything in her yearned to lean forward and taste him, and his eyes had shifted to red, which she suspected meant that he was feeling the same thing. One of them had to move either forward or back or they would be stuck here like two statues until someone found them and broke the spell. But Iris didn't move. She was caught between longing and the unwillingness to surrender to the connection between them, a connection she couldn't understand but didn't know how to reject.

"What are you doing?" she asked, even though he hadn't moved a centimeter.

"Do you think I'm doing something?" he challenged, his lips pulling into that heart flipping grin.

Why couldn't he just be a normal human? Or an alien who wasn't suspected of crimes against the planet? Why couldn't she just be a tiny bit less responsible? But he wasn't, and he was, and she was, which meant they couldn't do anything.

"I don't know," she answered. She was unwilling to break their connection with an unfounded accusation, and for some reason she didn't want to see the hurt that that would bring to his eyes. "This isn't..."

"It is." And with those two words, he answered a question she hadn't realized that her heart had been asking. Is this real? Yes.

He took her hand in his and she was ready to be tugged forward, but he didn't put any pressure on it, instead raising it to his lips and brushing a featherlight kiss to her palm. Lightning zinged across her nerves and she almost jumped, but before she could react, he was already pulling away and dropping her hand.

"Until next time, denya." He was out of the room before she could ask him what that word meant.

***

Sierra, Kayde, Toran, and Quinn were gathered in his quarters and studying more of the intel that had been gathered on Yormas. Quinn was a new addition to their team, and she had no experience with soldiering or spy work. But as one of the women rescued from Fenryr 1, she was going out of her mind with the need to get justice for what had been done to her.

222

Justice was a long time coming. The pirates who had captured her were hundreds of light years away, and none of them knew how the battle at Detyen HQ had turned out. The Oscavian warlord who'd tried to purchase her could still be alive, but none of them even knew his name. So, she told them, if she couldn't get justice for herself, she was happy to get vengeance for the Detyens who had saved her. Raze and Dryce had been sent out to keep eyes on the ambassador while posing as tourists and exploring the old city.

Toran knew that he should be listening closely to everything that Sierra laid out; instead, his eyes were focused on a file on his private tablet. It contained a more in-depth background of Iris Mason and could tell him everything he needed to know to win her affections. He'd read through her basic biographical data, but this was the good stuff. Family, lovers, enemies, and anything else that might be gathered about a person.

Sierra hadn't mentioned the contents to him, instead opting to send it directly to his tablet without a conversation. He didn't know what that meant, and he was a little apprehensive of asking. But he was even more apprehensive of opening the file. Iris wouldn't like it—whatever secrets she held close, she would want to be free to tell them to him in her own time. And perhaps that was for the best. He couldn't imagine that there was anything in the record that would make him want her less, but that did not mean that he had the right to steal her secrets from her.

"Jesus, are you even listening?" Quinn snapped at him, waving her dark fingers in front of his face. He noticed that she'd applied some type of bright pink paint to her nails and the color practically blinded him. No one else in the room would have put the question quite like that, but Quinn didn't have a soldier's discipline to fall back on.

Toran leveled his gaze at her. "Yormas has been ambassador here for two years. Before that, he was in the Oscavian Empire for some time, though not the capital. Wreet is a planet rich in iron and some other exports, but it is not a wealthy place. They've engaged in warfare, but aren't particularly bloodthirsty, and when Detya existed there was trade between the two systems. Anything else?" Most of his attention might have been on the moral quandary that

Iris's data presented, but that didn't mean that he wasn't paying attention.

Quinn gave him a nod and a shrug, mollified. Out of the corner of his eye, Toran saw Kayde staring at the human, but he looked away after a moment. He needed to talk to Kayde; the soulless Detyen seemed to be functioning normally despite the unpredictable situation. But between Toran's discovery of Iris, and the investigation into Yormas, Toran was worried that he'd been neglectful in his duties to Kayde. A unstable soulless Detyen was one of the most dangerous beings in the universe. While on their mission to Fenryr 1, Toran had been concerned that Kayde was getting close to the edge, but all of the excitement with the change in Raze had diverted his attention. Not again, he decided. He would keep his eyes on Kayde and make sure that everything remained within acceptable parameters.

"There's nothing questionable in his records, but that doesn't mean much," Sierra said. "He's—" A knock at the door interrupted her.

Awareness lit through Toran, and he was certain of who was standing in the hallway even before Kayde crossed the room and opened it. Iris stood there, one hand clenched on the strap of her bag and her shoulders set in determination. She gave Kayde a passing glance before taking in the rest of the room and noting Sierra and Quinn. Her eyes found his and the nascent bond between them snapped even tighter. She had to feel it; her questions from the party the night before suggested that she did. But if she didn't know any Detyens, she couldn't know what it was. He'd wanted to kiss her then, and everything in her expression and the way that her taut body had leaned into him had told him that she would take his kiss. But there had also been fear there, and he was not ready to make his next move until he was certain that she wouldn't run away from him.

"Is this a bad time?" She glanced back over his shoulder and Toran followed her gaze to see Sierra casually storing the portable holo player that they'd been using to view their information about Yormas. When she looked back at Toran, there was a knowing expression in her gaze, and lust punched him in the gut. She knew something was going on, and her easy competence was fuel to the fire already raging within him.

"Not for you," he replied.

Her eyebrows quirked up and she shot him a questioning look, like she didn't know what he meant, or she was afraid to know. He needed to find some way to bridge this gap between them, to show her that they were on the same side and that nothing would make him a threat to her.

The excitement in the air behind him was palpable, and he could practically feel Sierra vibrating in her chair as she realized exactly who was standing in the door, but by some miracle she kept quiet.

Iris ignored the people behind him. "I had a few more questions."

Toran nodded. "Of course."

"Is this something we can do now? What are you—" she cut herself off.

And just like that, Toran knew what he had to do, knew how to show her that he could be trusted, and that he could protect her. He took a deep breath, and didn't look at the people behind him. If they knew what he was about to say, they'd tackle him to the floor and cover his mouth until he was safely silent. "We're investigating Ambassador Yormas of Wreet. We think he's partially responsible for destroying our planet a hundred years ago, and we're concerned that he's going to do the same thing here on Earth."

Iris blinked several times before narrowing her eyes and leaning in close, as if she hadn't heard him over the small distance that separated them. "...What?"

Chapter Six

Her plan to question Toran again had really just been an excuse to see him, but now Iris definitely had some questions. What the hell? And seriously?—being at the top of her list. And judging by the noises being made by the two women on the couch, Iris wasn't the only person bowled over in surprise. Was that why he'd gone to the party? She hadn't suspected him of anything, not for a moment.

She stepped further into the room and let the door close behind her, the click as the automatic lock engaged loud enough to echo in her ears. She wasn't questioning Toran's motive; she believed that if he told her someone was bad news that he was probably right. And that told her just how far gone she was.

"I'm going to need you to back up," she said, holding up a hand. "Detya, it was destroyed?" Had that been in her file? Her mind still reeled, and she was going to have to yell at someone back at the SDA about the adequacy of their records.

Toran nodded. "Yes, one hundred and three years ago. Someone used an unknown weapon to destroy it with a single shot." He said it with the detached dispassion of someone reciting a history text, with no hint that he was recalling the greatest harm ever done to his people. He nodded back towards the couch and led her further into the room, where she took a seat in one of the chairs. He sat on the arm, keeping close, as if his nearness was a shield.

"That sounds..." It sounded impossible, but she didn't want to accuse them of lying. She didn't think they were. But she'd never heard of a weapon that could destroy an entire planet like that.

"It's true," the robotic Kayde confirmed. There was something off about him, something not right. He didn't act like the other Detyens, but she couldn't get to the bottom of his mystery while she was trying to make sense of what she was being told.

"Okay." She put the questions of logistics aside for the moment. Detya was gone, and the exact how of the matter wasn't important immediately. "What makes you think it's this Yormas guy?" She'd never even heard of the ambassador before the party, neither for good nor ill. And if she had ever been called upon to find someone on the planet capable of destroying it, she knew that he wouldn't have made her list.

They laid it out for her. The evidence they had wasn't much, but it wasn't nothing. A recording of his voice, potentially ordering the destruction of Detya. An identical photo from more than a hundred years ago that showed a man who looked just like Yormas. And they went through all of the boring information about his day-to-day life, who he met, who he seemed to like, and what he was trying to do to improve the relations between his planet and Earth.

Iris couldn't help but look at Toran and be impressed. He had almost as much information on Yormas as she had on him, and he had nowhere near her resources. She wasn't sure how he'd managed to pull that altogether, but she spared another glance for the other people in the room. Sierra Alvarez was the key. Though most paperwork listed her as some sort of analyst for the Sol Intelligence Agency, Iris suspected that she was actually an operative, a spy. And since she was currently suspended from her normal role, she had plenty of time to gather this data.

The door burst open and all eyes turned to the two Detyens who walked through and slammed it behind them. Raze and Dryce NaFeen, the brothers. Dryce's expression was gleeful, and he was bouncing on his heels. "We finally got a lucky break—" He realized that Iris was in the room and cut himself off before trying to recover. "On that... thing that I was... What is she doing here?" He gave up his recovery and stared at her.

"I told her," Toran said simply.

Raze's eyes widened as he looked from Toran to Iris, and there was something in his expression that told her this went deeper than the investigation into Yormas.

Dryce still couldn't keep quiet. His shoulders sagged and he stared at Toran like he was looking at a stranger. "Do you have to tell your denya everything? Even when she's—"

"Dryce." Toran cut him off with a single word.

There was that word again. Denya. After the party, Iris had managed to convince herself that it meant nothing, that it was perhaps a casual endearment. She had a translator, but the word must've been in a language that it wasn't programed to handle, or there wasn't a simple translation of what it meant. Why was some strange alien using that word to refer to her? And why was he specifically using it in reference to Toran?

"I should be reporting this immediately," she said, trying to regain some control over this uncontrollable situation. "You're stalking a political official and might have the intent to harm." This was exactly what she was supposed to be on the lookout for, exactly what could see Toran and his men detained indefinitely.

Sierra grinned at her. "But you aren't going to," she said with surprising confidence. She leaned in and her grin turned conspiratorial. "These guys can make you crazy, believe me I understand. Welcome to the club."

Club? What club? This whole thing was screwed up, and she didn't like how easily Sierra had read her. But, she supposed, that was the spy's job.

"I..."

Toran placed a hand on her arm and she stopped talking, as the warm weight of his fingers grounded her with the comfort she couldn't understand. Confusion roiled around inside her.

He looked back to the two new arrivals, but didn't lift his hand. "What did you find?" he asked them.

Dryce gave her another look, but didn't argue about keeping information from her. "Seems the ambassador is taking a vacation," he said with a grin. He was always grinning, always ready to have fun. "He's spending the next week on that pleasure base on the moon that we keep seeing ads for. I was thinking you could send me up there to keep an eye on him." He kept his tone casual, but his excitement was evident.

Toran stared at him for several silent seconds.

"What?" Dryce asked, all innocence.

Sierra was the one to finally let out a laugh. "I'm sure your eyes would be open wide to the vacationing humans who want a taste of the exotic."

Dryce placed a hand on his chest and staggered back playfully. "I'm wounded, sister mine."

Sister? Records indicated, along with Toran's testimony, that Raze and Sierra were dating. But was it more than that? Or was this another Detyen thing? If she were still investigating these guys seriously, it was something she would have to look into.

And with that, she realized where she stood. Whatever club this was, it looked like she was a member. She placed her other hand on top of Toran's, and squeezed. "If any of you leave the planet alone, you'll be flagged and detained immediately," she informed them. Sierra seemed on the verge of saying something, but Iris kept talking, since she was clearly possessed by something insane. "So that means I should go with Toran. To the moon."

***

There wasn't enough time to argue after Iris dropped that bomb. Not that Toran would have. A week with his denya in a compound created for relaxation and pleasure? There was no better place in the galaxy to convince her to bond with him. And he was more hopeful now than ever, given her reaction to what they were doing to Yormas of Wreet. Maybe she didn't understand it all, but she was with them, with him, and it was more than he could have hoped for.

While he and Iris were off planet, Sierra and Raze planned to lead the charge to find more information about Yormas. With the man gone, now it was worth it to take a look at his office and his quarters, and see if he was hiding anything there. Toran and Iris would be doing their best to keep tabs on the man while he enjoyed his vacation, and they would be paying attention to see if his only reason for being on the moon was a holiday. After all, Sierra had pointed out, the moon would be a great place to meet someone without word getting back to Earth.

Toran met Iris outside when she came to pick him up in a self-driving taxi. He placed his bag in the trunk of the car and slid into the seat beside her. Once his door closed they were off, heading towards the port that would send them hurtling off planet.

For several moments, silence swirled around them, a living being that seemed to sense every doubt and question and hope that lived inside them. The taxi was too small, though it was built to accommodate at least four people. Still, Toran could smell the scent of Iris's soap and if he barely stretched his arm he'd be able to touch her. But he kept his arms close and kept his distance as best he could.

Iris was the one to break the silence, falling back on business to keep them on track. "Everything is settled on my end. Did you make the arrangements?"

"Yes, our quarters are booked." He could still remember Sierra's grimace as she did that dirty work.

Something like amazement tinged Iris's face. "How did you manage that at the last minute?"

"Sierra's father called in a few favors." It was good to know someone as well-connected as General Alvarez, even if they risked exposure with every new request they made of him.

"The general is involved too?" Iris crossed her arms and stared at him, disbelieving.

"No, not exactly." The details of his involvement weren't Toran's secret to tell, and the story that had been fed to him to get him to agree might send Iris running once more.

But she could tell he was holding back. "What aren't you saying?" she asked.

Even if he could have come up with a convincing lie, he wouldn't say it to his denya. He took a moment to figure out the most diplomatic way to explain the situation. "She may have implied this was meant to be a... romantic gift." He was strung as tight as a wire waiting for her response.

Iris's arms dropped and she looked at him for a long moment. "Are you involved with them? Romantically?"

There was something in her tone that he couldn't decipher, but his denial was immediate and emphatic. "No!"

Iris held up a calming hand, but she didn't reach out to touch him. "It was just a question," she said, and this time he was certain that he heard relief.

Toran met her eyes, and held her stare. "My interests do not lie with the two of them." She didn't respond, but the heat between them was there as it always was, ready to roar to life with the tiniest spark of flame.

After several seconds, Iris tore her gaze away and stared out the window beside her. "This is a big job for two people," she said, again reverting to the assignment.

If she was going to keep doing this, Toran was glad that they were now on the same side and working together. At least they had this reason to talk to each other when she was too skittish to contemplate anything else. "Sierra gave me some tools that will help. I'll show you them once we've settled in." Even if they weren't in his bag in the trunk, Toran would not want to risk disturbing them before they left the planet.

Iris nodded, and kept looking out the window. "You seem close to her."

The observation caught him by surprise, and Toran almost asked her to repeat herself. He huffed out a laugh as he recalled the clashes of the last several weeks. "When we met, neither of us liked the other, but we have settled our differences. She is my friend's den—lover. It's easier for all of us if I get used to her." And everything she represented, but he did not say that part out loud. It was too early for Iris to understand everything that Sierra represented to the Detyen Legion. She was a hope that they hadn't known to wish for.

Iris finally looked at him and she seemed sad. "Well the relationship still seems really new. Maybe they'll break up and things will go back to normal."

Toran shook his head. "Everything has changed, I cannot remember what normal is anymore." It certainly wasn't riding in a taxi with a human woman who didn't know that she was his mate. It wasn't being stranded on a planet light years from home, uncertain if he would ever be allowed to return. Uncertain if he even wanted to return anymore.

He thought that Iris would be silent for the rest of the short trip, but she kept sneaking glances at him and when her shoulders drew back like she was ready to strike, he was ready for some kind of question. But not the one she asked.

"What's a denya?"

**

Iris knew that Toran wasn't telling her everything. She could respect that; they'd known each other for a week and had only been allies for a matter of hours. But she couldn't continue like this without knowing what that damn word meant. It kept coming up. And when he'd used it to refer to Sierra, she knew that it was more than a casual endearment. She'd known that for a while, but the evidence kept stacking up, and she couldn't keep ignoring it.

Toran's gaze was an inferno; even if his eyes hadn't shifted to red, he looked at her like he wanted to devour her. And the longer he looked, the more willing she found herself to let him. This had been a bad idea since the moment she suggested it, and there was no way she was going to get out of it without making potentially terrible decisions. Her job was already on the line, and if people looked too closely at the paperwork she'd filed, she might be risking more than her employment. But when it came to Toran, that didn't seem to matter. Helping him was more important, and that terrified her. He was just supposed to be a guy, one that meant nothing but a job. And instead she was risking it all for a man she hadn't even kissed.

"Why do you want to know?" he asked, stalling as if he believed he could put her off.

"Are we really going to do this? Play this game?" Maybe she should just lean in and close the distance between them, let the taste of his lips answer in a way he couldn't deny or withhold. But the heat between them wasn't in question. What she needed to know now was if it ran deeper.

"My race is peculiar," Toran began, his voice quiet and somber. "All species have quirks, of course, but ours is deadly. We are cursed to die at the age of thirty if we do not find our mates and bond with them. The Detyen word is denya." He was staring at her warily, as if he expected her to force open the door and flip out of the moving car.

But Iris was rooted in place and barely surprised even as her blood rushed in her ears and sweat coated her palms. "I'm not Detyen, I can't be a mate." Though if she were, that might explain the pull between them, might explain why she couldn't stop thinking about him no matter how many times she resolved to do so. "How do you even know?"

"I just do, the recognition is instinctual. You felt it too." He was holding himself so still that he practically vibrated with it, and if Iris reached out she feared that he would snap.

Her mind raced as she tried to recall every detail that she'd learned about the Detyen men since being given her assignment. "Your initial paperwork listed all of your ages," she remembered. "Only you and Dryce are under thirty." Kayde was the oldest among them at thirty-three, and Raze was thirty-two. "Did you lie about that? Why?" She couldn't see a reason, but she didn't for one second think that Toran was lying to her now.

He flinched back as she asked the question, and his eyes flashed red as he grimaced. "Please don't asked me about that," he said, on the edge of begging. "It's not my secret to share."

"Secret?" She found herself leaning closer, closing the distance between them, and she didn't realize that she'd reached for him until her fingers met the soft material of his pants over his thigh.

"Yes, Raze and Kayde are older than thirty. And yes, Raze did not meet his mate until a few weeks ago. But I cannot explain why that is. In fact, until Raze and Sierra met, we thought it impossible. Please don't add this to your report, I'll tell you everything when we have a bit more privacy, but I need your word." He placed his hand over hers and laced their fingers together. Though the taxi was self-driving, they couldn't guarantee that nothing was recording them, and Iris understood the concern.

It hadn't occurred to Iris to put the information in his file. "I don't think I can use anything I learn against you." She tried to remind herself of the things that Dan had said and did, of the ways that he'd hurt her and the promises he'd extracted to benefit himself at her expense. But right now Dan was barely a distant memory, an unpleasant time in her life that had no bearing on the present. "What do you want from me?"

His thigh clenched and his hand twitched, holding her even tighter. "I would never take from you anything that you do not want to give," he vowed. He looked at her with the intensity of a burning star, and under the weight of his regard, her doubts dissolved before they could fully form.

She looked forward, and saw that they were coming up on the port. She had a million questions, but it was impossible to grab hold of just one and spit it out before the taxi ride was over. The car dropped them off and in a matter of minutes they'd collected their bags and entered the squat building outside of the port. The place wasn't designed to hold anyone for long, and it was controlled by the same company that owned the moon base. They found themselves herded towards the terminal and seated on the next shuttle scheduled to depart.

And during the entire time, except for the brief security scans, Iris didn't let go of Toran's hand. She had no idea where this was going, and feared that it would end in heartbreak for the both of them. But she couldn't make herself step away, not now that she knew it was more than just chemistry. She didn't know if she could trust fate, but maybe it was time to try.

Chapter Seven

Moon Base Gamma had a much more complicated name, but no one used it. Instead, pleasure seekers and vacationers throughout the system knew that Gamma was the place to go for an escape from responsibilities. It had been built when Iris was a child and she could remember all the ads extolling its virtues. Real life was even better than the promise of the media shots she'd seen for decades.

The shuttle taxied on a specially built runway and entered the base through an airlock. They were dropped off in a glass encased room, where tropical plants grew from floor to ceiling and Iris couldn't tell if the bird calls she was hearing were real or fake. She couldn't imagine how much it cost to maintain the humid environment and the flora all around them, but as they were led down another immaculate hall she saw that there was no place on Gamma where expense had been spared.

No wonder this was a playground for the wealthy and well-connected.

The shuttle had ferried about a hundred passengers in luxurious comfort on the several-hour flight from Earth to the moon. Those passengers were now gathered onto platforms that levitated slightly off the ground. Android attendants monitored each platform, and once they were full they took off towards the heart of Gamma.

Iris and Toran scanned their tickets at one of the stations, but instead of being directed to a platform, an android almost realistic enough to look human greeted them with a false smile on its face. Perhaps it was unfair to criticize the emotions of a robot, but they'd always made Iris uncomfortable. They were just *off* in a way that she couldn't quite explain, and they put her on edge.

"Welcome to Gamma Base," said the android. "We are so glad that you could join us. Please follow me as I direct you to your quarters while you begin your stay with us." Whatever strings the general had pulled, the favor must have been great. It made Iris a little nervous to think that he might have put himself at risk or indebted himself for a mission he knew very little about.

She and Toran followed the android to a private platform that was much smaller than what the other passengers were directed to. Once they were secured, they took off, and her hair whipped back from the wind their speed generated. They were moving too fast for Iris to get a good look at everything, but she was overwhelmed by the size of the place. The moon could not sustain human life, but you would never know it from looking at Gamma. The ceiling soared high in the air as if daring space debris to hit them. There must have been a force field of some kind, but it wasn't visible to her eye.

Several minutes later, the android deposited Iris and Toran in front of a room with a red metallic door. It keyed the lock to their palms and left them alone when they indicated that they did not need any more help. Iris walked inside and couldn't help but gape. A large window took up most of one wall, and it perfectly framed Earth, that blue dot that had always been her home.

"It looks so small." She tried to set her hand on the window but when her fingers got too close, energy sparked and the invisible force field kept her back. "I've seen photos and vids, but nothing compares to seeing it in person." Her cheeks flamed as she realized what that must sound like to Toran. He had traveled the galaxy, had seen dozens, perhaps hundreds, of planets. And here she was gaping at the one she'd been born on.

But he didn't seem to realize her embarrassment. Toran stepped close and placed his palm on the small of her back. Iris leaned into him unconsciously. "Is this your first time off planet?" he asked with no judgment.

"Yes." She meant to leave it at that, but words tumbled out. "Our honeymoon was supposed to be on Mars, that's what we always talked about. That, or a cruise around the system. But we never quite got to the engagement, and—" Iris stopped talking. Toran didn't need to know all about her heartbreak, about all the dumb shit that she'd believed and the dreams that had been crushed.

He stiffened. "Honeymoon? As in marriage?" He looked down at her, and for a moment she was afraid he would push her away, despite what he'd revealed in the taxi. Was he one of those guys who thought it was wrong or dirty for woman to have a life before she met the man she was supposed to spend forever with?

Not that she was ready to say she was going to spend forever with Toran. Her mind was still reeling with the whole mate thing.

But she had brought the topic up, and she supposed that meant he was owed some sort of explanation. "I had this ex." She grimaced as she thought of him. "I thought it was serious, he said it was serious, but he was a cheater and a thief and I'm better off without him."

"Of course you are, you have me." He said it with such confidence that the laugh burst out of Iris before she could think better of it.

"I was better off without him even before I met you." She rubbed her head once against his shoulder before pulling away to grab her bag and find a place to unpack. The room was large, and the embellishments in red and pink and gold made it obvious it was meant for romance. There was only one bed, but it looked like he could easily fit six people as big as Toran with room to spare. Still, she was relieved when she saw the small couch opposite the media station. She didn't know if she trusted herself to sleep in the same bed with Toran without anything happening between them.

Opposite the wall with the window, there was a kitchen station with a fully stocked food processor ready for their use. The meals were basic, she noted as she scanned through the menu, but there were plenty of restaurants on the base that would offer finer fare.

Toran didn't seem as intimidated by the bed. He lifted his bag and placed it on one side, opening it to reveal carefully packed luggage. He dug through his clothes and left them on a pile to one side of his case and picked up a thick foam package that looked like it should be used to transport precious gems.

"Is that what Sierra gave you?" Iris stepped closer, apprehension tempered by curiosity.

Toran nodded and removed the top half of the foam case to reveal a series of discs packed tightly together. They looked like nothing special, but Iris knew that whatever they were they had to be top-of-the-line. "We will need to drop them at intervals around the station, but I've keyed one to the ambassador. Once it locks onto him it will keep him in its sights until it runs out of power or I disengage it remotely."

"When will it run out a power?" Iris was out of her depth. She was a researcher, not a spy.

"Probably around the time that Sierra and Raze are welcoming their first grandchild into the world."

Of course he was joking, though she understood that he meant that they wouldn't need to worry about the battery on the surveillance devices dying. But speaking of the future like that made her think about what he'd told her in the taxi. Dead by thirty without a mate? That had to give a guy issues. She was already coming up on that birthday and there was enough mental crap associated with it to give her a complex. But if she knew she was going to die? She sure as hell wouldn't be on this mission. Then again, maybe Toran didn't have to die. Maybe he would become like Kayde, with some essential piece ripped from him until he was barely a person anymore. She didn't need the finer details explained—it was clear the Detyen was broken in some way.

She kept waiting for something to change between them. He'd said that she was his mate, the woman who could save his life, but now he was all business. She wasn't quite sure how to take that. Was it respect? Or had he decided that whatever fate awaited him was better than a life with her? No, that was her own issues talking. Iris knew she wasn't perfect, but she was pretty sure that if the choice was between mating with her, whatever that meant, or death, a guy would choose to live. Not that she was about to lay back on that bed and invite Toran to go for a ride.

They had work to do.

She vaguely paid attention as Toran went over the instructions for the surveillance devices. It was pretty simple: press a button, put the thing on the ground, and let it be. The devices could move by themselves, but they would be more effective if she and Toran placed them deliberately around the base.

Iris couldn't help but stare as Toran set the devices into two separate piles with those long fingers of his. She wanted him to touch her, wanted to know what it would feel like between them. All she had to do was step close and lay her hands on him. But she couldn't make herself do it. Fear of rejection mixed with all the dangerous memories left by Dan, and she was unable to move forward.

"Iris." The sound of her name on his lips snapped her out of her funk. She liked the way he said it, like it was a little secret she'd shared with him.

Her lips stuck together and she darted her tongue out to moisten them. "What?" She didn't normally space out like that, but it had been an eventful few days.

Toran stared at her, and she could see the shift on his face when he decided not to say whatever he'd been thinking. He handed a stack of the trackers to her, their fingers brushing as she took them. "You can take the north and east, I'll take the south and west," he said, referring to the wings of the station. "I'll meet you back here in two hours. We have a dinner reservation."

"This isn't a vacation." Gamma Base may have been designed for entertainment, but they had a job to do.

"We still need to eat."

He was right. Obviously, already her stomach was starting to growl. "Okay, I'll see you then." They looked at each other for a long moment, each leaning in by centimeters before pulling back and turning away. Did they kiss? Should they? Iris was on uneven footing, unsure of where partnership ended and mateship began. But they would be on base for a while, and that would give them time to figure it out.

She left the room quickly and tried to convince herself she wasn't fleeing something that terrified her.

The base was huge, and she and Toran's room was centrally located, so she needed to take one of those floating platforms to find the north wing of the station. She tried not to gape at all the bright colors and interesting people she saw. And she had to turn away quickly when she spied one of her favorite actors from a popular media show. The platform made stops in front of dozens of shops and at stations that led to other residential wings. By the time she got to the end of the north wing, Iris was the last person on the platform, and it felt like she was in a completely different station than the one they landed at an hour ago.

Though there were no signs forbidding guests from entering, it looked like this part of the station was mainly used for storage. Pipes ran along the walls, and when her hand got too close, she felt just how hot they were. It probably had something to do with the heating and cooling system, if she had to guess. It felt like a waste to drop one of the trackers here when it looked like no one would bother coming to this corner, but, she reasoned, that would make it a great place for a secret meeting. She bent down and placed a tracker on the floor and had to blink when the dark disk seemed to dissolve on the gray tile. She knelt down and placed her fingers over where she knew the tracker was sitting, and though she could feel it, she couldn't see it. That was convenient, and a little scary. These things would make her job so much easier back on Earth, but she shuddered to think what would happen if they fell into the wrong hands.

She worked her way back to the central part of the station slowly, pausing every so often to drop a tracker. As she was heading back from her trip out to the east wing, she heard a familiar voice and caught a flash of that neon yellow skin. Ambassador Yormas.

What would a spy do? She and Toran hadn't discussed what to do if they ran into the ambassador. She was pretty sure they didn't want him to know that they were on the base, though she doubted he'd recognize her. Toran, on the other hand, stood out and was acquainted with the man.

Yormas walked into a small shop that sold mementos and snacks and Iris followed him and pretended to look at a shelf full of statuettes while he shopped. He didn't seem to be doing anything suspicious, certainly nothing that a hundred other guests weren't already doing. A few minutes later he walked out empty-handed and Iris trailed behind, trying to keep a buffer of distance between them.

That buffer was nearly her undoing, as she barely caught sight of him turning down a side hallway. She walked quickly to catch up and was grateful that the path he'd chosen was densely packed with other tourists. A babbling river ran through the center of the hallway, with floating bridges at intervals allowing passage over the gentle stream. Yormas paused in an area of fake greenery. Grass and a few small trees had been set up to look like a small meadow in the middle of the hallway, and benches encouraged guests to use the area to rest and congregate. Yormas took a seat, and Iris stood near a group of giggling youths standing on one of the bridges and stayed there to study him.

Her patience paid off, and a few minutes later a tall man with the distinctive purple coloring of an Oscavian took a seat on the bench next to him. She was too far away to hear what they were saying so she dropped one of the trackers to the ground and hoped that it could crawl close enough to them to pick up the scant details of their conversation. She doubted that two men would be discussing planetary destruction out in the open, and she had no reason to believe that the Oscavian had done anything wrong other than speak with Ambassador Yormas. But something about them nipped at her senses and she couldn't help but want to hear more.

They spoke for several minutes and the group of girls beside Iris eventually drifted away, leaving her standing alone on the bridge. She tried not to stare at the objects of her observation, but her eyes darted back to them every few minutes. The last time she spared a look, her heart leapt to her throat. Yormas was looking right at her, like he could see through her and knew exactly what she was doing. Their gazes locked for several seconds and the grin he shot her could only be described as evil. But then his Oscavian companion said something and the ambassador looked away. Iris took that as her cue to escape.

Now, more than ever, she was certain that Yormas was up to no good.

Chapter Eight

When Iris made it back to their room she seemed shaken, but insisted that she would be fine after a shower and dinner. Though it may have been wiser to keep all discussion of their mission confined to the room, Toran was eager to take her out and never once considered changing their reservation time. True to her word, by the time she'd cleaned and changed Iris seemed more in control of herself, so Toran suspected that whatever had happened, it hadn't been serious.

There were dozens of restaurants on Gamma Station, and though part of him wanted to show off and take Iris to the finest establishment in the place, he'd booked them a table at one of the more casual venues. When they walked in the door, something in Iris's posture relaxed and Toran knew that he'd chosen correctly.

The place wasn't packed, and the booth that the android attendant led them to was tucked away in the back of the restaurant, giving them an intimate sense of privacy.

Once the android was gone, Iris shot him a look. "Did you bribe one of the androids for the seats?" she asked with a grin.

"Have you ever tried to bribe an android?" He smiled back, and for a moment, let himself pretend that they were only two people, two mates, sitting down to enjoy a simple meal together.

"I don't know, maybe there's a Detyen trick to it. What are the androids like back on your planet?" Her grin slipped as she realized what she asked. "I'm sorry, that probably sounded terrible."

"We don't have androids back home. It's not the kind of place that needs them." Maybe Detya had been staffed by those kind of robots, but Detyen HQ was far too utilitarian. The familiar pang of longing squeezed Toran's heart, but this time it was mitigated by the presence of his denya. He could never hope to recapture the past, but the woman in front of him could give him a future he'd never dared to hope for.

"I saw... you know who while I was out," Iris said casually. She bit her lip and glanced around, as if to make sure that they were still the only two people in their section of the restaurant. "He was talking to an Oscavian, but I couldn't hear what they were saying. He..." She trailed off with a shake of her head.

"He what?" Had she put herself in danger? He would not let Yormas touch her, no matter if it put the mission at risk.

"He looked at me," she said, shuddering. "He's creepy, I don't like him. And I didn't like the way he looked at me, but there's no way he knew. I doubt he's ever seen me before."

"You were at his party," Toran pointed out. They'd both been there, that encounter more memorable than anything else.

"We never spoke," she said. "But I'll be more careful next time."

They were sitting beside one another and Toran reached over to lace their fingers together. They hadn't figured out anything else in their relationship, but this simple contact made sense, and Iris seemed to feel the same. She gave him a small squeeze in reply and her lips flirted with a smile.

"I have questions," she said. She darted a glance his way before staring forward once again and tipping her head down to read the menu on the table.

"Whatever answers I have to give, they are yours." He couldn't bring himself to reveal the truth of the soulless, not now, maybe not ever. But anything short of that was hers for the asking.

"Were you ever going to tell me about the denya thing?" She untangled their fingers and pulled her hand away, and though there was only a hand span of space between their bodies, Toran felt cold for the distance.

"It took me by surprise. I like to think that I would have said something before we bond..." He trailed off, still keenly aware of how misspoken words could push her away. But he'd promised her answers, and he could not back out now. "Before we bonded."

"Bonded? That sounds kind of complicated, and permanent." Her finger traced the edge of the paper that the menu was printed on, flicking it back and forth like she needed something to do with her hands.

"The bond is sealed with sex. It's common, or it was back on Detya, for mates to bond upon first meeting. Most choose to stay together, but even if they don't, having a sealed bond ensures survival." He'd heard of mates who abandoned one another; his uncle's own mate had left him and the legion before Toran was born. But having met Iris, he couldn't understand it. He wasn't sure that he could ever leave her.

"So it's not like a magical love thing? It's just survival sex." Her tone gave nothing away as she made the statement.

"It's not *just* anything." Even he could hear how defensive he sounded, but the look Iris shot him was more amused than angry.

"If sleeping together would save your life, I'm not exactly opposed." Even in the dim light of the restaurant, he could see the blush painted across her cheeks, and she was studiously looking back at the table again. "It wouldn't be a hardship."

"And if it were more than merely sex?" Dryce would probably punch him for pushing like this and potentially losing out on a night with his mate. But Toran wasn't Dryce, and he didn't know if he could pull back.

Iris finally managed to look at him, and she was no longer blushing. Something unreadable sparkled in her eyes and Toran wanted to kiss her. "That might take a bit more discussion."

When the android attendant returned to them, they placed their orders and their conversation shifted to more casual matters. Iris told him the story of her first vacation with her parents. They'd taken her to view a famous waterfall, and she'd tried to slip their supervision and climb onto one of the hovering docks that let visitors stand over the falls and get a close look at the drop.

"People used to go over those falls in wooden barrels," she laughed. "I can't imagine it, but if it weren't so suicidal I think it might've been fun."

And in return Toran found himself speaking of his own parents, even though they'd been dead since he was a child. Before they passed, before the tragedy of that explosion, they'd been close. They'd wanted to show him the universe, and though they were members of the legion, neither of them had been willing to sacrifice family for their people.

"Something happened to them, didn't it?" Iris sensed his melancholy and placed her hand on his arm.

Toran savored the touch and nodded. "We were on a supply run, I was just a child. Probably too young to have been with them, but my parents hated to leave me behind on easy missions. It should have been safe, they'd made the same trip a dozen times before. But they fell into the path of a pirate ship. My father was wounded in the initial blast. My mother put me in the escape pod and programmed it to find the legion vessel that trailed not far behind. I thought she would be in the pod behind me. But only moments after I cleared the ship, the pirates struck it with something powerful and it blew up. We couldn't afford the time to try and recover their bodies. Likely there would've been little left of them. After that, my uncle raised me. He loved me, of course. He treated me well, but they were my parents." He could still see the blast of the explosion when he closed his eyes, and he could almost imagine feeling the heat, even though he hadn't. For years he'd had nightmares about that day.

Iris's arm slid around his shoulders and she held him close as he recounted that trauma from his childhood. Most of the time he kept the memory locked away, he forgot about the years where he would wake up in the middle of the night screaming out for parents who would never find him. He didn't cry. His tears had been shed long ago, but he welcomed the comfort of Iris's touch and leaned into her warmth.

"My folks split up when I was a kid," she said after a moment. "Mom got sick after college and passed about four years ago. My father is still alive, but I can't remember the last time I saw him. We weren't close. Aren't close. I can't imagine what happened to you. It sounds terrible." She leaned her head against his shoulder, as if her presence could give him the comfort that her words could not.

"Let us speak of happier things," he suggested, unwilling to sacrifice the night to sadness and regret. Not on this first night with his denya. "Are you finished with your meal? If so, I would love to take a walk. The station is supposed to be beautiful at night."

***

Toran was right, the place was gorgeous at night. They walked side-by-side down the same hallways that she'd traversed earlier in the day, but with the lights dim and faint music playing in the background, the place was transformed into a magical oasis. Iris didn't have any destination in mind, and when Toran led them down certain pathways he seemed to be choosing at random. Their talk turned from the deep and painful conversation at the end of dinner to the light banter of people watching.

There were all sorts of people at Gamma Station, and most of them seem to see style as the most important thing. Iris chose her own clothing for function and affordability, but the outrageous patterns and complex construction of the materials they saw the men and women wearing on the station were anything but comfortable or affordable.

In the distance there was a pulsing thread of music echoing down one of the halls. Iris tugged Toran in that direction, their fingers laced together once more. She seemed to keep holding his hand, and the more she did it the more natural it felt. But he didn't mind, and she found that she liked the warm press of his palm against hers.

She expected to encounter people in the hallway as they got closer to what sounded like an exciting party, but they must have chosen a less traveled path since they were the only two people there. As they got close enough to see the door with flashing lights faintly lighting up the windows, a sensor in the ceiling beeped and the light above them flashed green, as if their identities had just been confirmed and approved to go further.

"What's that?" she asked, eyes rolling up to glance at the ceiling.

"Some areas are age restricted at night," Toran replied.

Neither of them suggested turning back; they were both adults and there was no reason to fear an age restricted party. Besides, Iris wasn't sure that she was ready to go back to the room. Not after that talk about mating or whatever. Sex would change everything, would complicate everything. And things were already complicated enough. Toran would literally die if she didn't go to bed with him. That was a line she would have never thought that she would believe. But the story was too outlandish to be anything but true. Even so, it wasn't like he was going to die tomorrow, and though he'd spoken openly, nothing he said made her feel pressured by him.

She put thoughts of mating to the back of her mind, she'd deal with that later. Tonight they were getting to know one another and they could deal with the deeper relationship complications later. As long as she didn't think about sex everything would be fine.

They made it to the doors which slid open to reveal a mass of dancing, sweaty bodies. The place smelled of writhing humanity and some kind of perfume that Iris couldn't identify. As she and Toran stepped into the room, the doors slid shut behind them. And as her eyes adjusted to the dim light, intermittently interrupted by strobe lights, she bit back and ironic laugh and buried her face in one of her hands.

The universe had it out for her. They'd just walked in to an orgy.

It wasn't all sex, that was the only thing that kept her from turning around and bolting. But in the darker corners of the room she could see the entangled limbs and flashes of flesh that people normally kept covered. She looked at Toran out of the corner of her eye, and he seemed just as dumbfounded as her.

"We can go somewhere else," he offered as soon as he tore his eyes away from the entangled couple nearest them.

The beat pulsed in Iris's blood, and the overwhelming scent of the place made her head spin in a good way. She would have never gone to a place like this on Earth, not knowingly. And given the choice, she would have never stuck around. But she wasn't on Earth right now, and she didn't need to be the girl who ran away when things got a little uncomfortable. She was on the moon, on a base designed to cater to all the hedonistic pleasures of life. She was with an alien who said they were fated to be together. It was time to live a little.

"Let's dance." It was a challenge, both to him and to herself. By staying in this room, she wouldn't be able to keep sex off her mind, but the longer she spent in Toran's company, the less she cared about that. He was the hottest guy she'd ever seen, human or alien, and he said he wanted her. That mate stuff made it complicated, but it didn't need to be. Not tonight. Tonight they could just dance and see where the evening took them. And if it ended up with her pressed up against one of those walls, his lips on her neck as he pushed himself into her, maybe that was meant to be.

A thrill of arousal shot through her at the thought. She'd never been an exhibitionist before, never wanted to share the intimate details of her love life with anyone in that way. But to be claimed so publicly by Toran? To show everyone on this base that he was hers and that they couldn't have him? Yes, she found herself warming up to the idea.

He didn't move a muscle until she tugged on his hand again and they dove into the mass of people. His arms went around her and he fit her tight against his body as if that was where she belonged. The bass thumped a fast beat, but she and Toran swayed together slowly, learning each other's rhythms before attempting anything else.

Time melted away, and though she was aware of the people around them, no one mattered but Toran. The beat turned sensual and Iris ground her hips against his, moaning at the feel of his hard length pressing against her. She wanted that, wanted him. Whatever the complications, he would be worth it.

She kissed Toran's neck and he groaned. He pulled her even closer, something she hadn't realized they had the space to do, and if he had felt close before now there was not room for a molecule of air to pass between them. Her kisses traveled up, tracing a line of the dark markings on his flesh and over the ridge of his jaw. And when their lips met, she didn't know why they'd waited so long. She'd had good kisses before, even from Dan. But as Toran's lips moved over her, as his tongue swept into her mouth and she tasted the unique flavor that was her powerful alien, those memories melted away and were replaced by all of the possibilities that this man offered.

His hands were on her hips; one dipped back low and cupped her ass. Iris let out a little yelp of surprise and found herself smiling against the wave of lust he brought out in her. It was an intense kiss, one she wasn't sure she could easily describe. She couldn't even explain what made it so special. But it was him and her, and for the first time it was them. And though she'd felt a pull to him since the first moment they met, now she could understand just what Toran said when he spoke of the bond between them.

Her back met a wall and she hadn't even realized that they'd been moving. But Toran's body trapped her there, shielded her from the rest of the room as he worshiped her mouth and showed her exactly how much pleasure he could bring to her. She gripped his shoulders tight and wrapped one of her legs around his waist, moaning against him as she felt his hardness brush up against her through the too thick layers of their clothes.

Why were they wearing clothes again? This would be a whole lot more fun naked, and all those crazy thoughts about waiting, about complications, were long gone. The only questions Iris now had were about when they could do it and for how long.

Hands brushed her wrist and Iris was confused. Toran's own fingers were playing against her hips and ass, and unless he'd been cleverly hiding a third hand, that meant someone else was touching her. She reached out and tried to push him away, but whoever was trying to join in on the fun seem to think her interaction was an invitation. She pushed harder and unbalanced herself, ending up draped against Toran as her lips were torn away from him.

Her eyes snapped open and she glared at the pale man with bright blue hair and eyes so green they had to be enhanced by either surgery or contacts. "Back off," she said, glaring at him.

Blue Hair looked confused, as if the fact that they were making out in a room as public as this meant anyone was invited to join in. "It's more fun with two." His eyes shifted to Toran, and he licked his lips and offered her man a flirtatious grin. "I can make it good for both of you."

In a flash, Toran was between them, his giant body shielding her from whatever threat or offer Blue Hair was making. "She's mine," he growled. "We don't share."

Heat should not have suffused her at that barbaric declaration, but if there was any question about how she and Toran would be ending the night, he'd just answered it in those words.

Blue Hair held up his hands and took a step back with a recalcitrant smile. "Sorry, sorry, I misunderstood." He faded back into the mass of bodies on the dance floor, but suddenly the heat of the room was too much for Iris.

"Want to get out of here?" she asked.

Toran grinned and she saw that his eyes had gone red. "I thought you'd never ask."

Chapter Nine

Maybe she should have learned from their near miss in the orgy dance club, but Iris didn't want to waste time getting back to their room. Ten minutes of walking was far too long when she was sure she was about to combust from the chemistry between them. They walked back down the hallway that they'd come through, and their hands were just as entwined as they'd been before. But this time whatever space they'd been letting stand between them was gone. Iris's shoulder brushed against Toran, and she half leaned into him as if she were too drunk to stand up straight. But what she was feeling now had nothing to do with alcohol. It was all down to the man beside her.

"Come here." She grinned as she pulled his face close with her free hand and stole another kiss. Why hadn't they kissed earlier? She wanted to do this all day. All night. All the time. Self-sacrifice, or whatever she'd been playing at, was dumb, and now she was making up for lost time. They could have been doing this for the last week.

The kiss took her over and Toran had her pressed up against another wall, and this time it was her hands on his ass making him groan. But Iris forced herself to pull away, and turned her head to one side. Toran took the opportunity to snake kisses over her jaw and down her neck, latching on and sucking like he was determined to leave a mark. She had to bite her lip as the thought crossed her mind. God, she was learning all sorts of new things about herself, about what she liked. And it was all because of him.

"Through here." It came out a moaned whisper and she doubted that it made much sense. She leaned towards the small door and Toran went with. Her hand triggered the sensor and they stumbled back through the door and into the semiprivate observation room of the hallway. She'd barely noticed it earlier when they were walking towards the party, but now she couldn't be happier that it stood out in her mind.

A dome of glass separated them from the harsh lunar surface. But it was the sky above them that was truly magical. Earth was spread out below them, a shockingly small blue marble that served as the perfect backdrop for this new beginning. The entire base was dotted with little observation decks like this. They offered a little bit of privacy and the ability to look at their home planet with new eyes. The room they were standing in could accommodate a dozen or so spectators, but at the moment Iris and Toran were the only people there. And at this time of night, they were the only ones likely to show up. But the door didn't lock, and adrenaline spiked in her blood as she realized that they could get caught at any moment.

"I'm not normally adventurous like this," Iris confessed. They were both taking a minute to catch their breath, and her heartbeat was going so fast that she could feel the blood pulsing in her veins. Excitement was one thing, but she didn't want to faint.

Toran played with her fingers, kissing the pads of each of them, and doing nothing to help with that racing heart. "What are you normally like?"

"Alone," it came out in a burst of self-deprecating laughter, but it was true, "and behind a locked door." She smiled. "But I don't want to wait anymore."

"I've been waiting for you for a long time." He sucked one of her fingers into his mouth and Iris's toes curled. His tongue didn't feel exactly like humans', she'd noticed strange ridges while they were kissing, and it was only more obvious as he played with her skin. Her body heated as she imagined his mouth between her legs.

"We've only known each other a week." And everything had changed since then. She didn't feel like the same person she was when she walked into that small gym and spied Toran for the first time.

"That doesn't matter." That magical mouth of his moved to lap at the pulse in her wrist and he grinned up at her as her pulse raced against his lips. Her heart did one of those strange little flips again, the one she was coming to associate with his smiles. And though she was aching, and ready, and desperate for him, she knew deep inside her that tonight was a lot more than simple sex. Even if he hadn't told her about the denya bond. There was a world, a galaxy, of opportunity waiting for them, all she had to do was be brave enough to hold tight and close.

Something he said made her stutter. "When you said waiting, you didn't mean... You've... I'm not..."

His grin turned into a warm chuckle. "This isn't my first time. But everything I've learned in my past, it's all been so I could give it to you."

Thank God. Someone might get off on introducing her partner to all the pleasures of the flesh, but Iris was in no mood to play teacher tonight.

And then they were kissing again, and whatever had seemed desperate before had nothing on the way their lips were devouring one another. It almost felt like a contest, a battle, but however this ended, they were both winners. Wide chairs that seemed built to accommodate two or more people were set up in a neat row to look out at the sky. Iris and Toran sank down onto the nearest one, and as Iris slung a leg over Toran's thighs and straddled him, leaning in close so their torsos were pressed together, the back of the chair gave way, reclining into something they could almost pretend was a bed.

Thankfully the chair was padded, or her knees might not thank her in the morning, but Iris wasn't really concerned about things like that at the moment. The only thing her body cared about was getting closer to Toran until they were connected on the most visceral level. Until she'd claimed him as her own.

Pants had seemed like a great idea earlier in the night when she thought she had some reason to resist the connection between them. Now Iris was cursing her past self, and wishing she'd worn a skirt to make this whole thing a lot easier. The hard press of Toran's cock was right there, teasing her under the thick material of his own pants. The only thing keeping her from howling out in frustration was that she could see that Toran was just as eager to be naked as she was.

Her hands went to the clasp of his pants and fumbled them open. It wasn't pretty or practiced, but it got the job done and freed him for her perusal. And peruse she did. There was no mistaking him for a human, not that there'd been any risk of that. She knew what Toran was and she wanted him just that way. But his penis was a reminder that though they were compatible, they weren't the same. The same dark markings that covered his golden skin dotted his cock, and at first she thought they were making some optical illusion to make it appear almost textured. But the ridges and bumps were far more pronounced than any vein on a human dick, and her mouth watered to taste him. He was different, but he was hers. And he was so hard that when she ran a finger down his length, he let out a harsh cry and one of his hands tightened almost painfully on her hip.

"Someone's excited." She grinned at him. She'd expected intimacy between the two of them to be a serious affair, all hot looks and scorching touches. And though she was about ten seconds away from exploding from the heat between them, her soul felt light. God, she was happy to be in Toran's arms, touching him like this.

She carefully wrapped her fingers around his shaft and slowly pumped up and down, savoring the enchanted look on Toran's face. He reached up and ran his fingers through her hair, cradling the back of her head and pulling her close until their lips met in another incinerating kiss.

He pulled her hand off of his cock and laced their fingers together while they kissed. But after a moment he let go, and his own hands dove for the clasp of her pants. "If we didn't need to cross the base to get back to our room, I'd use my claws to free you from these clothes." It was a low rumble that went right to her core and sent a shiver down her spine. Oh yeah, they were doing that at some point.

"Later," she breathed. "Right now, let me." His ruby eyes were twin jewels of impatience and Iris felt his absence as she had to lean back and pull her trousers off. They landed in a pile on the floor beside them, her shoes kicked haphazardly aside. When she crawled back onto Toran, she was completely open to him, vulnerable, and protected in his arms.

He tipped her to the side, encouraging her to lie back on the chair. "Let me taste you," he said, kissing her neck again.

Like she was going to say no to that. He knelt between her thighs and looked at her like she was some sort of treasure. His fingers danced under the hem of her shirt, tickling her stomach, but he didn't try to remove it. It was strange, from the waist up they were both fully clothed, but naked where it mattered. He bent his head and feathered kisses along her abdomen, heading lower until he found that place that made her arch up in the chair and bite back a loud moan. She didn't know if the room was soundproof and she didn't want them caught, not yet.

Any doubts she had about her mate's prowess were obliterated as he used his tongue like an instrument and played a symphony against her sex. She was delirious from the pleasure, covered in sweat, her shirt sticking to her all over the place, and her legs clenching around him, trying to hold them close.

And yet, when the orgasm came, it took her by surprise and she couldn't help but yell out his name and dig her hands into the padding of the seat below her. Toran brought her down gently and it took a few minutes for her heart to stop racing so quickly, especially when he didn't stop gently touching her and giving her those light kisses that were playing havoc on her heart.

He stood up at the same moment that Iris managed to sit, and that put his beautiful, impossibly hard cock at exactly the right level. "My turn." She rolled her eyes up to his and grinned.

Toran hissed as she took his cock in hand and slowly swirled her tongue around the tip. He was big, and though that sparked all sorts of possibilities in her mind, for the moment she had to take it slow, swallowing him centimeter by centimeter and tasting him all the way down.

As she got going, his hips twitched, and Iris reveled in the power that she had over him. He let out little groans and curses and she could feel him holding himself back when his fingers lightly curled in her hair. He didn't want to hurt her, didn't want to force her, and that consideration made her love him a little bit. But she was too busy at the moment to focus on that revelation.

He panted out a warning that he was close, and Iris kept going until Toran groaned out his pleasure and collapsed limp beside her.

She fell back into the chair and let his muscular chest act as her pillow. She wasn't sure if she could walk yet, and he didn't seem to be in better shape. "We're going to do that again sometime."

The breath that Toran let out might have been a laugh. "Yes, denya. Yes, absolutely."

Chapter Ten

Anticipation sang in Sierra Alvarez's blood as she waited beside her mate for the final security bot to pass. For a man suspected of engaging in interstellar conspiracies involving planetary destruction, Yormas of Wreet did not have the best security on his house. It was adequate, of course. But it had only taken her a day to determine the best way to get in and out without being seen. And the best part was she could afford to take Raze with her.

She'd missed this. Sure, it hadn't been long since her last mission, but chances of being reinstated to the SIA were slim. She'd gone against her orders in rescuing those women from Fenryr 1 and had lost an expensive military vehicle in the process. Maybe if she'd apologized for her actions things wouldn't be so dire. But there was very little about that mission that she regretted. And the main reason for that was standing beside her, a silent sentinel.

Toran and Iris had been gone to the moon base for nearly a day, and before they left the plan had been for Sierra and Raze to infiltrate Yormas's house and see if there was anything interesting once the coast was clear. And now it was.

"Now," she said, her volume barely above a whisper. And then they were moving, crossing the street and dodging through an overgrown hedge which had a gap just wide enough for a person to fit through if they were willing to endure a few scratches. "Thirty seconds." It was a warning to stay still. She wanted to reach out and hold Raze in place, not because she didn't trust him, but because she'd found that she really liked to touch him. But today neither of them could afford to get distracted.

The seconds passed and every security measure was invisible to the human eye. As the clock ticked down in her head, Sierra had to be confident in her research and her skills and when the time was up, she took off running, Raze keeping pace behind her before she made it to the back door. She placed a small device beside the security pad and tried not to tap her fingers in impatience as it hacked the code and the bio lock and disengaged the door's security.

Once inside, disabling the security system was child's play for someone who'd been a spy for years. "We're good now, you can turn on your flashlight." She did the same and she and Raze headed towards the upper story of the house, where Yormas kept his home office. If he kept anything incriminating, it was far more likely to be located here rather than at the embassy. As far as they knew, he was acting alone, or in concert with other shady individuals. He had just as much reason to hide from his own people as he did from Earth's governments.

The beam of Raze's flashlight kissed her own as he came up behind her on the stairs and trailed his fingers down her spine. He caught up to her and placed a kiss on her pulse before falling back a step. "I like to see you work," he said.

Sierra threw a grin over her shoulder, her heart light and soul happy even as they had to be cautious on this mission. "I like working with you." The denya bond sang between them, a connection stronger than the strongest steel and hotter than the surface of the sun. She wanted to kiss her mate all night, but that had to wait until they were done working. Once they were home, all bets were off. She'd never felt this way before, and she didn't know how she'd managed before she met Raze on that fateful night back on Fenryr 1. She would have never imagined that a cheap shot from his blaster that ended with her knocked out on the mossy surface of that desolate planet would lead them to this moment. But they were here now, and though the future was still uncertain, wherever they were going, they were going together. She'd never been more sure of something in her life.

They found the office easily, and Sierra wished they could afford to turn on the light. But enough people knew that the ambassador was allegedly on vacation that they couldn't risk someone seeing it from the street. Chances were low, but enough.

"I'll get to work on his computer," she told Raze. "Check out any papers he has lying around."

Sierra used another tool from her bag of tricks to hack into the computer, but was frustrated to find that most of his files were protected by an encryption that they didn't have long enough to try to crack. Still, she had access to his calendar, which gave them more information than they had.

"It says here that he has plans to meet with an Oscavian while on Gamma Base. I don't recognize the name, but I'm not that familiar with the Empire." She could name the major houses, and the important royalty, but outside of a mission she didn't need to know all of that. She made note of the name to do research once they were back home.

"I wonder if it's the same person who led the attack back at HQ," Raze mused.

"No way to know." They still didn't know who had attacked them, or who had tried to buy the women. They didn't know if Detyen HQ had survived the attack, and Sierra knew that it weighed heavily on Raze and his men.

"That would be—I think I found something." Raze cut himself off and snatched a paper from inside the binder he'd been paging through. "It references 'live testing.' I don't like the sound of that."

Sierra's stomach clenched. She didn't like the sound of that either. They'd assumed that the women on Fenryr 1 were being sold into sex slavery, but it was completely possible that they'd been collected for other nefarious means if there was some connection between Yormas and the Oscavian who tried to buy them.

"This is strange," Raze muttered.

Sierra made a copy of the calendar and shut down the computer, covering her tracks. She met him on the other side of the office and stood next to him to look at the page he was viewing. The header of the report was labeled 'Chemical Concentration in the Sol System.' A small note was affixed to it which simply read 'Detyen levels'.

"That is something. Let's get copies and get out." Her mind was trying to make the connections between what they found in Yormas's office and what they suspected him of. But she locked that away. Jumping to conclusions and skipping over evidence was one sure way to make a mistake.

Getting out of the house was just as easy as getting in, and in a matter of minutes they were back in their vehicle and heading towards home. Sierra drove and Raze laced their fingers together, gently drawing circles on her palm with his thumb. "We're getting somewhere, I can feel it."

She wanted to pull over and kiss her mate, but home wasn't far away, and once they were there, she could do a lot more than kissing. "Once Toran and Iris are back safely we'll have a lot to go over. I hope things are working out for them." In more ways than one. When Toran had revealed that Iris was his mate, Sierra was worried for him. After all, Iris held his fate in her hands when it came to his status on the planet. But seeing the two of them together, even though Iris was clearly still confused about what was going on between them, had assuaged that fear. She'd dove right into helping them as soon as she had all the information. She would be good for Toran, as long as they could communicate.

Sierra lifted up her and Raze's joined fingers and kissed his hand. "There is no place I would rather be than beside you." She hadn't been one for emotional declarations. But the more she made them, the easier they came.

Raze tugged their hands toward him and mirrored her kiss. "Nor I you, Denya."

***

There was a heavy arm wrapped around Iris's chest, and an inferno of a body at her back. Toran. After recovering from their lovemaking in that little observation deck, they'd stumbled back to their room, clothes askew, and fallen into bed. They hadn't done anything except sleep, and for that Iris was glad.

To call what had gone on between them intense was an understatement. Mind blowing, life-changing, incomprehensible. Those words might work, but her brain still hadn't quite caught up to any of that, and she snuggled further into Toran's muscular embrace and tried to put off her racing thoughts.

But now that she was awake, those thoughts and doubts and memories of things that had gone wrong battered her mind. She was more well rested then she could ever remember, and it was probably foolish to think that Toran's presence at her side was merely a coincidence. One side of her mind was screaming about all of the ways that this could go wrong, all of the ways that she could be hurt by opening her heart and her body to the alien beside her. But the other side, the one that had kissed Toran last night and taken pleasure from him, as well as gave it back, was busy pointing out that no one had ever made her feel this secure in such a short period of time.

Toran didn't lie to her, unlike Dan. No, she didn't want to think her ex's name. She didn't want him to tarnish whatever was growing between her and the golden Detyen who wouldn't let her go. Yes, there was information that Toran had kept from her, but he didn't seem to be doing that anymore. Not now that they'd begun to talk. Maybe this was all premature, a honeymoon period while their hormones went crazy and their bodies cried out for one another. But Iris didn't want to believe that, she wanted to open herself up and figure out exactly who she could be with Toran.

But she wasn't ready for that yet, wasn't ready to admit that to him. They hadn't talked about what the sex meant afterwards. Whether Toran realized that she was on the verge of freaking out if she thought too much about it, or whether he was just satisfied with getting off, he hadn't said once the orgasms were over. But she remembered the conversation from the restaurant, and what Toran had implied that he wanted from her. Not just sex, but a partnership deep in their souls.

Did what they'd done count? Where they bound together now? She didn't feel much different, besides being sated down to her bones. Maybe Toran would know. He was the one who knew about the bond in the first place. But she wasn't sure if she was brave enough to ask. If things were sealed between them, then it was done, no more decisions needed to be made on that front. If it wasn't, then she would have to deal with that.

She wanted to seal the bond, even if they didn't last. She found that thinking of the galaxy where Toran would die on some arbitrary birthday made her heart ache. At the very least she could stop that from happening. She had that much power.

As if sensing her roiling thoughts, Toran stirred. He placed a kiss on the back of her neck, but unwrapped his arms from around her and rolled over. He was silent for a long moment, and Iris wondered if he was waiting for her to speak. A few seconds later he answered that question for her. "Good morning," he said. She could feel him lying on his back, but she would need to turn over to get a good look at him.

She stayed lying where she was, one hand curled around the edge of her pillow. "Good morning. I'm going to take a shower." She fled the bed, but couldn't help looking back. Toran watched her as she walked, his gaze hungry and latched onto her. She was wearing all of her clothes; neither of them had stripped before going to sleep, but he knew what she looked like naked. At least what parts of her looked like naked. And from the way his gaze raked across her, he was imagining that right now.

Heat roiled through her and she wanted to hold out a hand and invite him to join her in the shower. But she stepped into the bathroom and closed the door behind her before she could gather the nerve. They had more they needed to talk about, and she wasn't going to complicate that with even more sex before they were ready. Before *she* was ready.

She washed herself quickly, and when she was done Toran took his own turn. While he was getting clean, she took the initiative to prepare them a small breakfast using their room's food processor and when he stepped out of the bathroom, steam billowing around him, he grinned when he saw the simple fare set out on the table.

Iris's mind stuttered to a halt, and suddenly any hunger for the food on the table evaporated, replaced by hunger for Toran. She squeezed her eyes shut and turned away, but that didn't stop her from hearing the masculine chuckle he let out. It went straight to her gut and trickled further down. It took a good deal of discipline not to squeeze her thighs together to try and get a little relief.

She rested her hands on the countertop and pressed down hard, taking several deep breaths before she forced herself to turn back around and face the man in the room with her. In the few seconds she'd taken for herself, he'd swapped his towel for a pair of pants. His chest was still bare, and her eyes roved over all that glorious golden skin. The dark markings that covered his arms, almost like tattoos, continued down one side of his torso, and she knew from experience that they continued even lower.

"Do my clan markings please you?" he asked, casually stretching to one side and giving her an even better view.

An inhuman sound escaped Iris's throat and she clenched her mouth shut to keep from making any other embarrassing noises. She pushed his plate of food towards him and gave it a pointed look.

"I like the way you look at me," he said, ruthlessly refusing to change the topic.

Something uncoiled inside of Iris. If he wasn't going to let her escape, she had no reason to hide what she was thinking. "If you like how I look at you, why did you put the pants on?" Her cheeks were on fire, but he seemed to like it when she blushed. If he was going to be bold, she would dish it back.

He grinned broadly and his face was transformed. Had she ever thought him an imposing, impossible warrior? Untouchable? No, he was none of those things, not to her.

"I'd take them off, but we do have some work to do today." He took a seat and dug into the food, making an appreciative sound as he ate. "What is this? It's delicious."

Iris sat beside him and looked down at her own plate. "Just pancakes and sausage, nothing special."

He glanced at her for a long moment, something deeper than lust and mirth in his eyes. "You made me breakfast. That is special."

Her first instinct was to tell him not to read anything into it, that it didn't mean anything. But they were beyond that now, and maybe it did. She still wasn't sure, was still figuring things out. But instead of denying him, she ate her food and didn't pull away when his thigh brushed against hers. In fact, she found herself leaning back into him, seeking his touch.

They ate quickly, and by the time they put their plates in the wash, Iris was wishing that they really were on Gamma Station for a vacation, just to enjoy each other's company. But they had more important things to do, and as soon as their breakfast was cleared, they got down to it.

Toran was setting up a device that Iris couldn't identify, but it quickly became obvious that it was used to analyze all the data and surveillance they'd picked up the day before. "We don't have time to listen to everything, not between the two of us," he said. "This device is programmed to listen for key phrases. It also has a predictive algorithm that can flag anything else that will be of interest."

The device didn't look like much. If she had to guess, she would've said that it looked like a holo player, though not one she'd ever seen before. A small black cylinder sat on a tripod in the center of the table and a red light flashed on top of it. "Does that mean it's on?"

"It means that the algorithm has flagged something," Toran responded. He pulled out his tablet and must have been controlling the device from that, because after a moment it started to play.

She was right about the holo player. They didn't just hear the sound, but saw what the tracker had seen. The angle was off, but Iris immediately recognized the scene playing out in front of them. Yormas sat next to the mysterious Oscavian that she'd watched him talk to the day before. It took a moment for her translator to catch up to what the men were speaking about. They spoke in Oscavian, not the far more popular Interstellar Common or her own native language of English.

"I'll have more details for you at lunch tomorrow," said the Oscavian. "It's a setback, but initial data is promising." They could have been talking about anything. The Oscavian's face gave nothing away, and her view of Yormas was obstructed by something in the tracker's path.

"Data from a single source is hardly conclusive. The study we've done suggests that you'll find the results we were looking for. But if you hadn't managed to—"

"Do you really want to talk about that here?" The Oscavian looked around and nodded at something. For a heart pounding second Iris thought he was looking in the direction of where she'd been standing, but a Gamma Station security guard walked past them and she realized that she hadn't been noticed. Not yet.

"You managed to recover one of them?" Yormas pressed.

"My brother did," the Oscavian confirmed. "And our luck..." His voice sank down to a volume the tracker couldn't pick up as he leaned in close to Yormas.

"No!" Yormas gasped, too overcome with surprise and disbelief to keep his voice down. But he regained enough control by the time he responded to be quiet once more.

"I'll have the data tomorrow. Late lunch in the observatory, I think you'll be interested."

The projections stopped and Iris looked over to see that Toran's fists were clenched and if his jaw was clamped any tighter shut he would've broken his teeth. "You think they're talking about what happened to you guys? About the women who were recovered? And the one who wasn't?" Though she hadn't come with him to find answers about Laurel, it now looked like her mission from the SDA was coinciding with Toran's. "What really happened to her?" He'd been cagey the first time she asked, but they were so far from that now, and whatever he told her, she would believe him.

"We were off the planet before we realized she was gone," Toran responded. He looked at her, and she saw agony in his eyes. "The slavers who'd kidnapped her had implanted a control chip in her head. At least Sierra thinks that's what happened, we never got a chance to confirm it. But I agree with her. On our way off Fenryr 1, the SIA ship broke down. It was sabotaged by Laurel. Luckily we were close enough to the Detyen home base. We took the women there, and offered Sierra and her crew the supplies they needed to repair their ship. But at some point Laurel got her hands on a tablet and managed to send a signal to someone. We don't know exactly who, but shortly after that an Oscavian warship attacked the planet. The same Oscavian warship that had planned to collect the women on Fenryr 1. In the course of our escape, a few of the survivors took it upon themselves to make sure that Laurel didn't make it to the ship. They insisted that they didn't harm her, that she was still alive when we left. But we have no way of confirming that."

Anger laced his every word, the frustrated kind where you knew that you'd never find an outlet for it. "And now you're thinking that this Oscavian might have Laurel?" she asked. "That he might have been involved with what else is going on?"

Toran nodded. "I need to be at that lunch, I need to see if I can get eyes on whatever data the Oscavian is talking about."

"No." The denial was out before she could even think of a reason to keep them back. She didn't want to send Toran into danger.

"I have to go," he insisted. "Don't worry, you'll be safe."

"You think that's what I care about?" The laugh that came out of her throat was anything but amused. "Yormas could recognize you, he can place you on Earth. And if he has something against the Detyens..." She didn't know how to finish that, and she choked on the thought of Toran getting hurt. "It makes more sense for me to go," she said, and as she suggested it the reason made itself clear in her mind. "He's already seen me on the station. Even if he thinks something's up, he can't be sure. I'm just one human among many. Besides, this gives you time to raid his and the Oscavian's quarters. You'll do that better than me, I don't have the skills."

Toran growled, and it really wasn't the time to find that sexy, but she found just about everything that Toran did sexy. "Fine," he bit out. "But if there's any danger, you get out. Don't put yourself at risk." She could feel the tension strung through him, and knew that there was a part of him that wanted to tie her to the bed to keep her from leaving the room. The fact that he was agreeing to let her go showed her just how important this mission was to him. But she filed thoughts of rope in the back of her mind, to bring up again when things were less stressful.

After going over a few more plans, Iris and Toran dressed for their missions and met at the door to their quarters. She swiped a quick kiss against his lips and her fingers clenched against his biceps. She forced herself to let go, and taking a step back was even harder. "Good luck," she said.

"Stay safe," he replied. Iris took a deep breath before heading out. She couldn't let Toran down, this was too important. And if fears tried to rear their head and she imagined all of the ways this could go wrong, she did her best to ignore that. It was going to be fine. Yormas had no idea who she was, and there was plenty of security on the station.

But the further she got away from Toran, the more hollow those reassurances rang. She had to do this right, had to find the information they needed and get back to her mate. She only hoped that Yormas and his Oscavian companion didn't catch on to them. If they were caught, they were a long way from home and no backup was coming.

Chapter Eleven

When Iris walked out the door Toran had to tamp down on every protective instinct that screamed at him to follow her, to protect her, to tie her up in their room and never let her leave. Yormas and the mysterious Oscavian were dangerous men, and if they found out that she was following them they could end her in an instant. Toran's claws flashed out and he swiped at the air, barely missing the hard metal of the door in front of him.

But Iris had a point; it was possible that Yormas could recognize him. And if Yormas had anything to do with the destruction of Detya then it was better to keep the Detyens out of his sight for now. His soul ached for vengeance, he needed to see justice done for his people and to protect his mate. But at the moment he could do neither. His mate was capable of protecting herself for now, and if that changed then he would do anything, would sacrifice anything, to keep her safe. Not yet though, not now. If he overstepped now she would pull away.

He'd been blessed with a mate just as strong as he was, just as dedicated to doing the right thing. And though he might feel more comfortable with a woman content to stay back and let him fight alone, he would not trade Iris for anything. The thought of her fighting at his side sent joy singing through him. It terrified him, but if she was the one that fate had deemed belonged to him it had to be right.

He hadn't dared hope that their relationship would progress so far so soon, but after the night before and the way Iris had opened up to him he thought that by the time they were home, she would be his in every way. She would let him claim her completely, and they would be joined in the most ancient way of his people. He already belonged to her in everything but the claiming, and he would do anything to make her see that. And for now that included trusting her on a mission dangerous enough to set his teeth on edge.

His claws slowly retracted back into his knuckles as he got himself under control. When Toran exited their room he spared a glance in the direction that he knew Iris had gone before turning the other way and resolutely marching down the hall. It hadn't taken much to figure out where the Oscavian was staying. He was registered as Nyden Varrow. Toran didn't know if it was his real name or a fake, but at least it gave him something to call the man other than 'the Oscavian.'

Varrow's room was located in a less expensive part of the station, though expense was relative on Gamma. These rooms did not have real windows, but instead looked out onto the moon and into space via media stations embedded into the walls. It was enough to remind a visitor where they were, but when Toran broke into the room and got a look at it, he was happy that he and Iris had the real thing.

If he wasn't certain that this room had been reserved by Varrow, he would have thought that it was standing empty, waiting for a new guest to reserve it. The place was tiny, with just a bed, the media station, a small bathroom, and a place on the wall that looked to fold out into a table and desk chair. No one would want to stay in there for long, it was practically a prison cell. And Toran turned over every corner looking for any hint of what Varrow had to offer Yormas. But there was nothing, no papers, no tablets, and not even any clothes. Had the man already packed up to leave? Was he keeping his things somewhere else? Toran didn't know, and he didn't want to waste time standing around and trying to solve the mystery.

As he let himself out of Varrow's room, he wished that he could get in touch with Raze to see how the infiltration of Yormas's quarters back on Earth had gone. Unfortunately, they'd made the decision that the information could not be shared over the comm lines between Earth and Gamma Station. It was possible to set up a secure line, but that involved coordination with the security forces on the base, and Toran did not want to bring that kind of attention to them. Instead, they'd established a code word, something innocuous that Raze could send to him if he and Sierra found anything that made the mission too dangerous or required Toran to get back to Earth faster.

So far he'd heard nothing, which meant that he and Iris had to continue on as planned. He only hoped that Raze and Sierra had found something useful.

Yormas's room was in a different part of the station, one frequently used by political officials of his caliber. His room would be similar to Toran's, but even bigger, with space built in to accommodate a meeting room. Toran knew this because he'd studied the schematics of the base before they left, not because he'd seen Yormas's room. He tried to get near the ambassador's quarters, but spotted a guard at the end of the hallway before he got close. He could make a distraction, but he wasn't sure it would be good enough. And he didn't know what other kind of security Yormas had put in place.

He hoped that Yormas's room was just as empty as the Oscavian's, and that he wasn't missing out on even more information.

A spike of fear lanced his chest, and rooted Toran in place, bile rising in his throat and sweat covering his arms. His breathing grew labored and for a moment he thought he'd been poisoned or otherwise injured. But whatever he was feeling, it wasn't coming from him. It was something he felt deep inside of him, through a connection that hadn't been sealed but was still strong enough to tie him to the human woman who completed him.

Iris was afraid. Iris was in trouble. Something had gone wrong. As those thoughts swirled around in his mind, he took off running towards the observatory restaurant. He had to find Iris, had to keep her safe. Because if she wasn't safe, he had no reason to live.

***

Everything was going fine. Iris arrived at the observatory after the Oscavian and Yormas had been seated, which worked out great for her. The android host tried to seat her on the other side of the restaurant, but when she asked to be seated near one of the windows nearer to her targets, it redirected without pause. She was out of sight of the men, but could make out the murmurs of their voices. That was where one of Toran's toys came in. The amplifier did exactly what its name implied, and when she enabled it she could clearly hear everything that Yormas and the Oscavian were saying.

272

He'd given her another piece of tech which was meant to allow her to view both Yormas and the Oscavian and whatever they were looking at despite the fact that she did not have a clear line of sight on the men. It looked like a little scroll and Iris anchored it to the table in front of her and unrolled it before following the instructions that Toran had given her to calibrate the device to her targets.

Yormas and the Oscavian sat across from each other, neither of them eating a meal despite the fact that they were sitting in a restaurant. They each had drinks which they casually sipped, and a small tablet sat open on the table in front of them. Whatever magic the device used to view them allowed Iris to see the screen of the tablet, but it was useless. The viewing device didn't act as a translator and she couldn't read what she thought was Oscavian. At least the device would capture a recording and if there was anything important they would find out about it later when they could run the images through a translation program.

"It would have been more private to meet in your room," said the Oscavian. Hearing them speak as clearly as if they were sitting next to her sent a tingle of fear and excitement down Iris's spine. This was nothing like her normal job. Though she occasionally ran into dangerous people, and often people with secrets, she never felt like she was putting herself at risk. She had the might of the Sol Defense Agency behind her and any harm done to her would be met with retribution. But not here, not today. The SDA had no idea what she was doing, and she doubted that either the Oscavian or Yormas would care if that wasn't the case.

"I did not leave the planet to stay cooped up in my room all day," Yormas responded. What was it about that man's voice that froze Iris's veins to ice? If she didn't know who he was, she would have said his voice was pleasant, melodic. Instead Iris was on the edge of shivers.

On the viewer, the Oscavian shrugged, satisfied with Yormas's explanation. Iris wondered if there was more to it, but she didn't want to get distracted by chasing the thought. She could worry about that more later.

The Oscavian pointed to something on the tablet and pushed it towards Yormas. "All the research indicates that we're falling within acceptable parameters. Even better, our new... friends seem more amenable to negotiation. We won't run into another incident."

Yormas placed two fingers on the tablet and scooted it close. "Good," he said, making small humming noises as he read through the data. "Is this all from the single source? Or have you managed to find new specimens?"

"The single source, mostly. As we've been instructed to scale back our collection efforts, most other sources do not fit the desired profile. However, we never expected to be able to compare the new subject to a living specimen. This is the closest match we found out of more than a thousand options." The Oscavian tried to keep the glee out of his voice, but Iris could hear it. He might have dressed the part of an intergalactic tourist, but at heart he was a scientist, she would bet her life savings on it. And with every word they spoke, she became more convinced that they were speaking of Laurel, and perhaps they had managed to get their hands on one of the Detyens from Toran's home world. That was a good, and if she could find the women who had abandoned Laurel to her fate, she would give them a piece of her mind.

"With data like this, I find myself eager to enter back into negotiations," said Yormas.

"Yes, well, showing your new friends what could happen to them has help negotiations before, has it not?" Asked the Oscavian. Did he mean the destruction of Detya? Had Yormas or whoever he was working for wanted something from them that they refused to give up? And had they got it from someone else in the intervening century? These were all questions that Iris would need to answer later.

Yormas peered at the Oscavian for a long moment. "You're too smart for your own good," he said with a note of warning.

The Oscavian snatched his tablet back and placed it in his pocket. "I'll be off then. When you give the word, we'll be ready."

"Good." And with that abrupt end, they were done. Iris knew she could try to make her escape before the two aliens left the restaurant, but she decided to stay in her seat so that she didn't bring any more attention to herself. As discreetly as she could, she shut down her devices and hid them away so that if anyone glanced her way, they would see nothing of importance. The Oscavian left without glancing her way and half of the knot of anxiety that had lodged in her chest began to dissolve. Once Yormas was gone, she'd be able to breathe again.

He stood up, and she forced herself to look away. Tracking him with her gaze would be too obvious. So when he slid into the seat across from her, she practically jumped out of her chair and had to fight back a yelp of fear. That ice she'd been feeling before froze her in place, and she knew her eyes were wide with fear, but she couldn't school her expression. She wished that Toran were there with her, or that she had let him do this part of the mission. He would know what to do now, while all she wanted to do was spring up from the table and run.

But they were in a public place, she tried to calm herself. Yormas wouldn't try anything here. That assurance ring hollow.

"Hello, my dear," he crooned. "You've been following me. Why?"

***

The spike of Iris's fear turned into a steady beat of terror as Toran got closer to the restaurant. Perhaps he should have alerted station security to a potential problem, but without knowing what Iris had run into, he couldn't take that risk. He could be putting her in more danger if he did that then if he went in alone. He would do anything to save her, if saving was what she needed. He could not say the same for station security. He couldn't guarantee that they hadn't been bought off by Yormas or Varrow.

The observatory restaurant looked innocuous as he skidded to a stop in front of it. The android attendant approached as if it were about to offer him a table, but Toran ignored it and burst into the restaurant, looking for the trouble. The pulse of the denya bond pulled him deeper inside, and he found Iris in a matter of seconds. His heart nearly stopped as he realized that Yormas of Wreet sat across from her at her table.

His mind raced, trying to determine the best course of action. Instinctively, he shrank as best as he could into the shadows, trying to stay out of sight and not alert Yormas to his presence. He had to trust Iris. Right now the ambassador just seemed to be talking to her, and she could learn a lot if he'd turned to gloating. From his position, Toran could offer her cover. If Yormas made a move against her, Toran would take him down. No one threatened his mate and lived.

His plan was interrupted by a heavy purple hand clamping down on his shoulder. Toran moved by instinct, twisting into the hold and taking control of his attacker, slamming him towards the nearest wall. But before the fight could even start, the cold barrel of a blaster jammed into his back against his spine and Toran froze. "Lift your hands up," said Varrow. "This is a modified blaster, and a single shot will lay you flat. You won't get up from it." Blasters were normally nonlethal, but it didn't take much work to modify that safety feature.

Even so, Toran momentarily considered fighting back. If he could give Iris those few seconds to get away, whatever happened to him would be worth it.

"We have your woman," Varrow said, seeming to sense the direction of his thoughts. "If you sacrifice yourself now, you'll do her no good."

He hated to agree with his enemy, but he would do anything to keep Iris safe. He raised his hands up and put as much space as he could between himself and the Oscavian guard. When Varrow instructed him to turn around, he did so slowly and with no argument. Anger poured off of him in waves as he saw that Yormas and Iris had joined the two of them. The ambassador was clutching Iris's arm tight, strong enough to leave a bruise. He would pay for that. They would all pay for that.

Toran risked a glance around the room and was surprised to find out that they were all alone. The door to the entrance of the restaurant had been closed, the heavy metal door as strong a barrier as a wall. Either they'd tipped someone off, or had somehow managed to reprogram the android. If it had just been him, Toran could beat three to one odds. He was a soldier, and had escaped much worse situations than this. But Iris didn't have those skills, and he couldn't risk her getting caught in the crossfire.

"We've met before," said Yormas, narrowing his eyes at Toran. "I never forget a Detyen. After all, there aren't that many of you to remember." The smile that curled his lips was evil, and any lingering doubts of Yormas's involvement in the destruction of Detya dissolved in an instant.

Toran remained silent, unwilling to play the ambassador's game.

But Yormas didn't like that. He curled his free hand in Iris's hair and yanked it back, exposing her throat to the room. "She's a pretty one, you chose well. Though I would suggest hiring your spies for skills rather than looks next time. Well," he huffed out a malicious little laugh, "if you had a next time."

"Why did you do it?" The question jumped out of his mouth and Toran wanted to call it back. They needed to escape this situation, not prolong it.

"You would have to be more specific than that. And I find I'm not interested in answering your questions." He turned to the security guard and nodded to Toran and then Iris. "Scan their IDs. I want to know who they are, and why they're here."

The guard did as instructed, placing a small scanner first against Toran's palm and then Iris's. The device beeped when it found a match for each of them, and the guard flashed the screen of the scanner to Yormas, who nodded in satisfaction. "Whatever you're doing, you shouldn't have gotten messed up in this," he said, almost apologetically. He leveled his gaze at Toran, but his hold on Iris relaxed slightly. "Especially you. You're lucky to be alive, and you're throwing it all away on some petty quest for what, revenge?

There's no such thing. The galaxy is far too big for something so small."

Toran had to clench his jaw to keep from responding to that, but it was obvious that Yormas hadn't yet figured out why he and Iris were observing him and Varrow. Yormas was close, assuming it had something to do with the destruction of Detya. But Toran wouldn't be the one to confirm it, and he turned his eyes to Iris, trying to signal by look alone that she should keep her mouth shut if she could. If he was reading her right, she understood what he meant.

Yormas shoved Iris towards the Oscavian guard and then clapped his hands together once. "Get rid of them. Whatever they heard, we don't want it spreading. Then find their quarters and see if they're keeping anything interesting from us." He turned to Varrow. "This is why I like meeting in public. You learn all sorts of things."

Varrow's face was impassive, but he nodded once. It was impossible to tell what he thought of this entire situation, but he wasn't objecting to anything that Yormas commanded. "I have two more of my detail that will join you," he said. "I think these two need more than one guard."

"Excellent," said Yormas. "Let's leave them to it." As Yormas and Varrow walked towards the restaurant door, it slid open to reveal a handful of Oscavians waiting to meet them. Varrow pointed to two of them and they walked back to join the guard that was already looming over them.

Toran took the chance to study Iris. She had gone pale, and her eyes were wide with fear, but otherwise she seemed uninjured. Whatever had happened, it hadn't been violent. Good. His mate was unharmed, and that would make escape easier. Because he was getting her out of this, no matter who he had to go through to make that happen.

The Oscavians were efficient. Two flanked Toran, one keeping a discreet blaster pointed at him, and the other pointing an equally discreet blaster at Iris's back where she stood in front of them with her guard. They took a moment to pat both Toran and Iris down. Toran was unarmed, but the guard found a device in Iris's pocket and took it from her. Toran recognized it was one of the tools he'd given Iris to listen in on the conversation today. The guard let the device fall to the ground, where he crushed it underfoot, destroying whatever information it had collected. Iris flinched and Toran tried to reach out for her, until his guard made a warning sound and twitched his blaster, looking for an opportunity to shoot.

Tourists on the station gave them a wide berth once they left the restaurant, and security turned a blind eye. In a matter of minutes, they had left the densely populated areas of the station and boarded a small platform that seemed designed more for employees than visitors. The head guard seemed to know where they were going, programming a destination into the panel in a matter of a few strokes. Toran tried to sidle up closer to Iris. Even if he could only touch her hand, it would be worth it. But his guards were too on point and kept him back.

They were nothing like the thugs who'd detained him and Kayde back on Fenryr 1. These Oscavians knew what they were doing, they must have been highly trained, and they understood exactly how much of a threat he could pose. He hated when his opponents were like that.

The platform came to a stop in a dark hallway in the bowels of the station. The guards led them even deeper down the pipe-lined walls. The air here was humid, and unexpectedly hot. He heard a dull roar come from the end of the hall, and Toran's heartbeat kicked up. He recognized that sound. Fire, an incinerator. No, the Oscavians weren't messing around. There would be no evidence of what had happened to them. And as they hadn't trusted the comm lines—probably a good move given the attitude of security here—Raze, Kayde, and Dryce would have no idea that anything was wrong until far too late.

The end of the hall terminated at a dark wall with heavy doors on either side. A small window on the door to the right danced with yellow flames as the incinerator fired. The door to the left was identical, but the window was dark, as the secondary incinerator was not active.

279

The guards shoved him and Iris in front of the darkened door. They couldn't open the firing incinerator, which he supposed meant they would live for a few minutes longer. Iris's hand found his and she gave him a squeeze. She looked at him and everything that they'd never been able to say, all the emotion they'd been dancing around, was laid out plainly in her eyes. But she said nothing, and Toran could understand that. This moment, their love, was meant for the two of them. To let the guards hear it would cheapen it, and he would not give them the satisfaction. He nodded once, as if to tell her that her message was received.

Determination firmed in Iris's expression and she flicked her eyes back towards the guards. Toran could read that too. There was no use going to their death willingly, and even if they harmed her, she was telling him it was worth it. That they had to try to survive.

This time Toran didn't acknowledge the flick of her eyes, didn't give the guards a second to read his intentions. He sprung towards the closest one, his claws flashing out between one breath and the next and raking across the exposed face of the nearest Oscavian. He went down with a cry as blood spurted.

A blaster shot took Toran in the shoulder, but as it seemed only set to stun, he was able to push through it and launched himself at the second Oscavian. But the second and third shots were stronger and Toran toppled over, unable to stand back up. The uninjured guard stood over him and aimed the blaster square at the middle of his chest. He fired a single shot and everything went black.

Chapter Twelve

Iris had never been so glad to wake up, and she'd never been more certain that waking would never come. It had been a desperate move to encourage Toran to attack the guards set on killing them, but better desperate than dead. For a moment she thought they'd blinded her, as the room they were stuck in was almost pitch black, but her eyes found the small sliver of light coming through a window on one of the walls. She'd seen that window before from the outside.

They were in one of the incinerators.

Iris sucked in a breath, and tried to keep her calm. It was warm in the incinerator, but the fire hadn't started, and she couldn't give up, not yet. Not while she was still alive. Not while Toran was breathing shallowly next to her. He was still unconscious. She ran her fingers lightly over his chest. It was a soft touch that wouldn't have woken him from a normal sleep, and it certainly wasn't enough to rouse him from unconsciousness. Iris took a step further and swiped her lips against Toran's forehead.

"Come on," she said. "I need you to wake up. We need to find a way out of here." She looked around, unsure of what she would find. She'd never seen the inside of an incinerator before, especially not one located on a moon base. But the contents seemed no different than what she would find on Earth. It was hard to see, but her eyes were quickly adjusting, and she could make out the dark lines and shadows of the piled refuse within the kiln. If she were standing, most of the trash would only come up to her knees. The ceiling wasn't high—Toran would have to stoop if he were standing—but the relative emptiness of the room gave her hope. Perhaps they had time and someone would discover them. Surely the base would want to fill the room up with more trash before wasting energy to destroy it.

She forced herself to take a step back from Toran and look for something that might be useful. Maybe there was something she could use to pry the door open, or a disposed med kit that still had enough supplies to tend to any of Toran's injuries. She worked her way through the nearest pile, navigating by touch and trying not to cringe any time her hand encountered something gross. In the first few minutes after waking she'd been too focused on the situation to notice the stench in the room. Rotten food and smoke, along with something acrid and chemical. It couldn't be healthy to breathe it all in, but she would worry about that later. It would be even less healthy to be in the room when the fire started.

Toran groaned as he stirred, and Iris gave up the search for anything useful and rushed back to him, kneeling by his side and holding herself back from hugging him to make sure that he was okay. His eyes snapped open, and in the darkness they glowed red. Iris had never seen a more beautiful sight. That ruby color of his impassioned eyes was quickly becoming her favorite.

"I'm okay," she said, somehow knowing that her well-being would be his primary concern. "What about you? Can you sit? Can you—" She cut herself off, afraid that she was rushing things and smothering him. If either one of them were equipped to handle this situation, it would be Toran. She'd lived a relatively cozy life back on Earth, and he was the interstellar space warrior who'd seen everything.

Toran sat up slowly and reached for her hand, linking their fingers together. He didn't seem to have any trouble seeing in the low light, and Iris wondered if Detyen night vision was better than human. "My head aches, but that is to be expected." As he looked around their surroundings, his hand squeezed hers involuntarily and she could feel the exact moment he realized where they were. "We need to get out of here."

"Yes, I've been looking for something to pry the door open."

"Can it be pried?" he asked, glancing towards the window, their only source of light.

"I was trying not to think of what would happen if it couldn't be," she admitted. Now that he was awake, she realized that she hadn't even checked to see if there was some sort of handle on the door that they could use to open it. She'd figured that the guards wouldn't have placed them somewhere that easy to escape.

Unfortunately, she was right.

Toran staggered to his feet and they both made their way over to the incinerator door, feeling around for any way to open it from the inside. But she couldn't find the edges of where it sat in the wall. The plan to pry the door open was dead on arrival. Toran's arms came around her and he held her close, one hand cradling the back of her head. She leaned into him and tried not to cry. A dark chasm of despair opened within her as she realized that this was the end. They couldn't open the door and eventually the flames would eat them alive.

Her mate was not ready to give up. "There might be another way out," he said, but from his tone she could tell that he didn't believe himself.

"You think that…" Iris trailed off as her mind latched onto a thought, half formed and as difficult to clutch as water through her fingers. "Wait, be quiet." Toran hadn't said anything, but she needed to chase this down. She squeezed her eyes shut and tried to remember a safety manual she'd been forced to read for work years and years ago. The old building that her office had been located in had an incinerator in the basement. She'd never needed to go near it, but company policy meant that everyone had to know the proper safety procedures relating to it. Including the safety release.

She pulled out of Toran's embrace and backed up towards the wall, turning around and running her fingers over the rough surface. "Look for a flap or a little door or something. It shouldn't have a lock on it." There was no guarantee of a kill switch inside this incinerator, but it was their best, their only, hope.

Iris closed her eyes as she felt along the wall, the light too dim for her to make out the subtle differences with her eyes.

"I found something!" said Toran. He flipped open a little flap in the wall and revealed a bright red button illuminated by a faint light. She couldn't see a label. Toran's hand hovered over the button, but he looked at her as if this was a decision they had to make together. "Is there a slight chance that this sets the whole thing off?" he asked.

Iris didn't want to consider that. "It's our only shot." She placed her hand on top of his and together they pressed down on the giant red button. For a moment, nothing happened, and a weird sense of disappointed relief washed over her. But then the door clicked open with a loud buzz and a strip of bright light practically blinded her. She and Toran didn't hesitate, running for the opening and throwing themselves outside. Even if the guards were waiting for them in the hallway, they had a better chance out there than they did inside the incinerator.

But the hallway was empty and as the door to the incinerator shut behind them, she and Toran were alone.

She took a few steps, but her legs were wobbly, and she leaned back against the wall and slid to the floor, her hands shaking as she realized just how close she and Toran had come to the end. Toran sank down beside her and placed his arm over her shoulders. "You're brilliant," he told her.

"Just lucky," she said breathlessly, as if she'd just run a marathon. They sat together for a long time, neither willing to make the first move to get up and tackle what needed to be done. Minutes ticked by, and Iris lost track of them. But at some point, she shifted in her seat and Toran started to move beside her, standing up and offering his hand.

"We need to get home before the ambassador realizes that we escaped," he said. He was right, though Iris's legs still didn't want to cooperate. She forced herself up and took a minute to stand steadily.

"Let's go home." Though, strangely, she realized that in the time since she'd met Toran, the meaning of home had changed, and as long as he was by her side it would never be far away.

***

Anger unlike anything he'd ever known threatened to consume Toran for the injustice done to his mate. She could have died in that tiny room and no one would have known what happened to her. The fact that he would have died at her side didn't matter. She was his to protect, and he had failed in that. But he kept a tight leash on the anger as he could sense that Iris was still fragile from the entire ordeal. She was keeping up a strong face, walking quickly and steadily beside him through these lower hallways of Gamma Station. Her face was set in a determined expression, and if it weren't for her quick thinking they would still be stuck back in that incinerator or worse.

But he could sense the cracks that she was trying to hide. As soon as they stopped she was going to shut down. It happened to the newer warriors sometimes, the ones getting their first taste of battle and carnage and death. And it was something that Iris should have never been forced to experience. He didn't bother to ask her if she was okay; she was physically fine, but if she had to examine her emotional state too closely that strong façade she was putting up might give out.

The hallways had seemed longer when Yormas's guards were leading them. Toran had known they were being led to their death and time had constricted in a way that he had never experienced. Now it was speeding up to make up for the discrepancy. They came to the platform that would lead them back to the main part of the station much sooner than he expected. He activated the sensor to call the platform to them and they were forced to wait, stopping for the first time since they'd stood.

"What's the plan?" Iris asked, her voice steady but a little too forceful. "They scanned our IDs. They could have us flagged in the system."

It was a possibility that he'd hoped Iris hadn't realized, but he should have known better by now. His mate was quick to think of all of the possibilities, good or bad. "I have something back in our room," he promised. "If we can get back there, it won't be our IDs that the computer scans when we return home." Sierra had given him an entire bag of tricks, and at the time he'd thought her collection of toys was excessive. Now he was trying to think of the proper thank you gift for her foresight.

"And if Yormas and that Oscavian guy got there first?"

"His name is Varrow. Nyden Varrow. There was nothing in his room when I checked, like he'd already left the place, even though that was obviously not true." Though now that Toran knew he'd come with a bevy of armed guards, it was possible that Varrow was keeping his things with them. Especially if they were traveling under assumed identities.

"That's nice, but you didn't answer my question." Iris looked at him expectantly. "I'm thinking we don't want them to get their hands on everything back in our room." She crossed her arms in front of her and tapped her finger against her forearm in a nervous gesture.

"Everything in the room is keyed to us. Even if they get their hands on it, they won't be able to use it. It's programmed to self-destruct." That feature hadn't seemed excessive, though Toran had hoped he'd never have to use it.

"So even if we get back to Earth, nothing we found here is coming with us. We learned almost nothing." She sounded defeated, and Toran wanted to take the time to reassure her that everything would turn out all right. They were alive, they were together, and they had both witnessed the fact that ambassador Yormas of Wreet was up to no good. But the platform finally arrived in front of them and Toran didn't want to risk continuing talking about this. The platforms were highly monitored, and they might have been wired for sound, though he wasn't sure. Even though the station was too big for them to get around by foot, he didn't like riding the platform; it felt too exposed, too controlled by the station. But his unease got to him and they got off long before the closest stop to their room. Iris didn't question his decision.

There were enough aliens on the station that Toran didn't feel like he stuck out too much. But he still wished that he had a cloak or a hat or something else to cover his head and obscure his skin and clan markings. It was no use to dwell on things like that and he pushed the thought aside rather than wallow.

Iris walked quietly beside him, her shoulders held tight like she was a coil ready to spring. It was a big station, and they were just two people trying to disappear into it. Yormas would be on the lookout for them, even if he believed that they were dead and reduced to ash. He seemed too smart a man to breathe easy until he had confirmation that his orders had been carried out.

As they entered one of the courtyards that featured several casual restaurants and shopping options, the skin at the base of Toran's neck prickled. He slowed his pace and casually looked around the room, trying to see if anything was out of place. The tourists around them were acting like nothing was wrong, running and laughing and enjoying their time on the station. But Toran couldn't shake the feeling in his instincts.

"What is it?" Iris asked. Her eyes darted towards the far exit, the hallway that would lead them closer to their room, and then her gaze swung around to the security station nestled into one of the walls. Two human guards sat there along with an android, their poses relaxed. They mostly existed to break up fights and provide first aid when it was needed. These weren't police, nor were they soldiers. They were employed by the station and answerable only to that authority.

Standing as close to the doorway as they were, Toran knew he and Iris were lit up like a beacon. He stepped further into the room, Iris at his side. He found them a corner with slightly more cover, but they were still in view of the security station, and it was only a matter of time before one of the humans or the android spotted them. "I don't know," Toran told his mate. "It's just a feeling."

"I trust your instincts," she told him as she brushed her hand against his arm. They kept doing that, touching each other in small ways, as if confirming for themselves that the other was still alive, still safe.

His instincts were screaming at him to turn around, but this was the closest way back to their rooms. Besides, if they took another path, they would need to travel closer to the central security hub of the station and he would much rather deal with two guards and an android than the centralized force that could be sent from the hub. "Let's keep going," he forced himself to say. The sooner they moved, the sooner they could get out of danger.

In the end though, it wasn't the security who tipped them off to trouble. They crossed paths with a human woman with long brown hair standing beside a young child. She froze in place, and her eyes widened as she caught sight of Toran. She tugged on the child's arms, but that only brought his attention to what she didn't want her kid to see.

"Is that the bad man from the report, Mommy?" the child asked.

Toran didn't run—running only made it obvious. But he grabbed Iris's hand and ducked behind an information stall near the edge of the room.

"Bad man?" Iris asked.

"It's one way to detain us," he replied. He brought up a generic information terminal and scrolled through the warnings and alerts that were available to all guests of the station. It didn't take long to find his picture alongside Iris's, and when he read their alleged list of crimes, he cursed. Theft, assault, stolen identity, and tampering with station life support. Nothing there would make them sympathetic to the guests of the station, especially not the last one. "We have to get out of sight," he said. "They'll have our room covered." Maybe it had been stupid to try and get back there, but the equipment and the information contained was important. They'd had to try. And now it was time to try something else, to try anything that could get them home.

No one else seemed to notice them as they ducked out of the area and back down one of the less populated halls. "There's no way we get on the transport with that over our heads." Iris didn't phrase it as a question.

She was right and Toran's mind reeled as he tried to come up with an alternate way off the station. "We need to find a place to lay low." They must have been caught on several of the security cameras by now, but it would take time for whatever algorithm was looking for them to analyze the footage. As soon as they were flagged, Yormas would know that they were alive and things would get even more complicated. "I swear on my life that we will return to Earth and you will be unharmed."

"I'm not just worried about myself, Toran," Iris said as she grabbed his hand. "We're both going to get back to Earth. And we're going to take that bastard down." They took off back down the hall, neither of them voicing the doubt that had to be racing through both of their minds. No matter the determination, returning to Earth had just gotten a lot more difficult.

Chapter Thirteen

For a luxury resort, Gamma Station's security was lacking. With the clever use of the cleaning bot, Toran was able to sneak them into an unused room without anyone the wiser. It wasn't as nice as their suite—nothing would have been—and all of their equipment was still lost, but at least in the room they didn't have to worry about cameras or security guards. Not for a little while. Gamma Station took privacy seriously, probably more seriously than security, and there were no surveillance cameras or devices in any of the rooms.

The door was the only way in and out, so if they were caught they would be trapped. Iris was trying not to dwell on that at the moment, and with all her other worries she was almost succeeding. She had never been so close to death before as she'd been in the last two hours. Her hands still shook with the aftermath of what had almost happened, and she found herself reaching out to brush those shaking fingers against any part of Toran that she could reach, needing to convince herself that he was still there, still alive and safe.

One thing had become clear. Toran was vital. Vital to her very existence. How she could go so quickly from not knowing that he'd existed to needing him to survive, she wasn't sure. Maybe she hadn't really been living before, just going through the motions until this life-changing cannonball of a man exploded in her path. She'd never understood before what it meant to need someone, not like this. It wasn't about what he could do for her or anything like that, instead he was a pillar, holding her up when she feared that she would collapse.

But right now her pillar looked ready to slump over as they both came down from the excitement and stress of their escape. He sank down onto the only bed in the room and kicked off his shoes almost defiantly. Iris stumbled across the room and lay down next to him, curling into his side and wrapping an arm around his waist.

"We can't stay here long, can we?" she asked, even though she was pretty sure of the answer. Gamma Station was no longer a safe place for them.

"No, we can't." His finger idly stroked her hair, wrapping a strand around in circles.

"Any ideas for what to do next?" Iris might've been the one to remember the failsafe in the incinerator, but her brain was turning to mush and she had no idea how they were going to get out of Gamma Station and off the moon. Each of the four moon bases had daily shuttle service, but those services were highly monitored. Even if they could get off Gamma and sneak into one of the other stations, they might just as easily be detained by security there.

"I'm working on it, but this mission is a little complicated." He turned his head towards her and smiled. Iris's heart leapt. Things were bad, and she didn't want to think about how they could get worse, but when Toran looked at her like that she could pretend that everything was all right, that it was just the two of them on this lunar paradise.

"Is it more complicated than your normal missions?" She wanted to know everything about him: his likes, his dislikes, his history, his hopes and fears, and everything else he was willing to give her.

Her mate grew thoughtful. "Every mission has its complications. Did you know that Kayde and I were briefly detained by the slavers on Fenryr 1?" He asked it like he knew she hadn't known, and he didn't sound too traumatized by the event. "They didn't catch Raze, and he was able to extract us, but that was a more unpleasant day than this one."

"So today is just unpleasant? I thought it was heart-stoppingly terrifying." How she could smile when she said that, Iris wasn't sure. It probably had something to do with the warrior pressed up against her side.

"I am with you, and we're safe for the moment. Though my heart did threaten to stop when they pointed their blasters at you." His hand stopped playing with her hair and his body grew tense.

Iris splayed her fingers across his chest and drew a pattern in the soft material of his top. She wanted to tell him that everything would be all right, but they both knew that they were far from safe. "You're the reason I made it through. I wasn't going to let them hurt you, not if I could stop it. And I knew that you needed me to be strong, to pull my own weight to get us out of there."

Toran turned more fully towards her, his eyes briefly blazing red. "I need you alive and with me. If you cannot walk, I will carry you. So long as you live, I will breathe. And I would gladly stand by your side until my dying day."

Her stomach flipped and Iris's mouth went dry at that declaration. "New rule. No talking about death and dying days until we're back on Earth. I don't want you getting any ideas." She met his eyes and her tongue darted out to wet her lips as she considered her next words carefully. In a way, opening her heart was far more terrifying than having a blaster pointed at her chest. That kind of pain was only physical; the chance of rejection, however slim, would melt her like las fire. "And I feel the same. About the living, standing by you. All of that." There was an easier way to express that, but Iris couldn't make her tongue form the words.

The smile that lit up Toran's face told her that he didn't need that word, not yet. He looked young and joyful, full of hope. Not like he was hiding in an unused room on a pleasure station hoping that security forces didn't figure them out.

They leaned in at the same time and their lips met in a gentle kiss. Iris's fingers curled in the fabric of Toran's shirt, but she didn't pull him forward. They held themselves still, as if leaning any further forward would detonate an unstoppable explosion between them. He tasted like home, his tongue a welcome intruder that she opened under with no resistance. Iris's body was on fire, the good kind, not the kind in the incinerator, and every move Toran made only heated her up more.

He broke their standoff first, pulling her towards him and rolling them on the soft bed until she was snugly under him and his heavy weight pressed down on her while they kissed. He was a blanket, and while he was huge, he was careful not to crush her. Iris let one hand explore, trailing it along his side and around his back until her fingers could trace the hard lines of his muscles through his top. "Off," she muttered against his lips. "*Off.*"

She only realized how that sounded when Toran pulled back, a puzzled look on his face, his eyes red with desire. "Is something wrong?"

Iris tugged at the bottom of his shirt. "Too many clothes. Shirt off." She wasn't quite capable of complete sentences anymore, but from the way Toran's nostrils flared and his eyes narrowed with a predatory intent, he was pleased with the situation.

He tugged off his shirt, exposing all of that glorious golden skin and those markings she still needed to trace with her tongue. No time like the present. She pulled him back down towards her and with a clever move she'd learned in a self-defense class years before, she thrust her hips up and rotated, ending up on top of Toran, straddling his hips. But self-defense was the furthest thing from her mind, and from the hardness she could feel growing in Toran's pants and pressing against her, his own mind wasn't on fighting. She leaned down and swiped her lips against Toran's when he angled his head for a kiss, but she didn't let herself get caught up, there would be time for that later. Now she had a mission, intent on exploring every bit of him that she could reach. The markings at his neck were the easiest to find and when her tongue found the edge of one, Toran bit out a curse and bucked against her.

Her lips curved. "Sensitive?" Nothing about them looked erogenous, but she loved having this effect on her mate.

"A little," he gasped. "More than expected." That was no good, he could still handle sentences.

Iris went back to work, tracing down his neck and working every mark she saw, no matter how small. While her tongue worshiped him, she used her hands to explore his muscles, and flicked her thumbs against his nipples. The cry that tore out of him was somewhere between anguish and ecstasy. And before she knew it, Iris was on her back, with Toran looming over her. The look on his face would've been terrifying if she didn't know how much he wanted her.

"When we get home I'm going to use my claws to tear your clothes off you until you are lying naked beneath me," he threatened or promised, she wasn't quite sure which. At least he was keeping his head clear enough to remember their precarious situation. Maybe Iris should have pulled back, should have stopped him from going any further, but she trusted Toran to keep her safe, and for just a few minutes she didn't want to remember. Okay, she bargained with herself, several minutes, maybe an hour. How much harm could one hour cause?

"I'm going to hold you to that," she responded. It took a little work, but she wiggled out of her top and Toran tossed it somewhere across the room, leaving her bare from the waist up to him. Somehow his eyes seemed to get even redder, rubies sparkling with a heart of fire. He leaned down and just like she had done, swiped a kiss against her lips before making a path along her chin and down her neck, down to her breasts, where he lavished them with attention until she was squirming under him, panting for more, her fingers curling into the sheets below her. She splayed her legs, wrapping one around his hip and rubbing against him, desperate for more friction. He rutted against her, and it was almost enough, but Iris hovered on the edge of something, not quite able to tip over the crest of pleasure. She needed more. With an almost supernatural sense of Iris's desires, Toran ventured further south, placing kisses along her stomach and gently opening her trousers and revealing more of her skin for his tongue to explore.

He pulled her pants down over her hips, and for a moment Iris was upset that she had to move her leg to let him maneuver. But when he settled himself between her thighs and placed his lips over the heat of her sex, her hips bucked up and all thoughts of disappointment were quickly replaced with the extremes of pleasure that his tongue brought her. She gasped out his name and arched up, one leg ending up over his shoulder to give him easier access to her.

Toran showed no mercy, playing her like a tightly strung instrument until all she could do was make high-pitched noises while vibrating with pleasure. The orgasm ripped through her like a crescendo, curling her toes and working its way up until she was writing from side to side and calling out Toran's name like a supplicant in prayer. He brought her down from the high, placing gentle kisses against her thighs and working his way back up to capture her mouth in a passionate kiss.

She could barely move, could barely think, her entire being attuned to Toran. She expected him to free his length and seat himself at her core, to push into her and claim her and make her come again, but he seemed content just to kiss her pleasure-sated body.

If he wasn't going to move, Iris would. She snaked a hand between them and worked at the clasp of his pants. "I want you."

Toran pulled back enough to look at her, his gaze intense. "I will not claim you until we are off the station," he declared, even as his eyes flared with passion.

It took Iris's pleasure drunk brain a moment to understand what he was saying. "Why?" They were together now, she wanted him, he wanted her, what was the problem?

He placed his hands on the bed at either side of her head, holding himself over her in a planking position. The air was superheated between them, and though she could barely feel his body, his presence laid over her like a ghost. "Because I need time to properly claim you. Not a few stolen moments where we could be discovered at any minute." He rolled to the side, laying beside her.

Iris turned towards him. "Okay, I can understand that." And maybe a small, infinitesimal part of her was a little bit relieved that she wasn't making this decision, this commitment right now. But she could still see Toran's length straining against his pants and she did not need to be the only one who was laying satisfied in the bed. "At least let me help you with that."

Toran sucked in a deep breath and for a split second, she thought he would reject her, but to her delight he freed his cock from its confines. Iris's sex clenched and she was ready for another round, but at this moment it was about Toran. She wrapped her fingers around him and watched his face intently as she stroked the hard heat of his length. He was leaking, and she ran her thumb against his head, using the lubrication while she brought him to the edge.

He gave himself over to it, his head tilting back and hips jerking as she stroked harder and harder. He leaned forward and clasped his hand around the back of her neck, pulling her towards him and capturing her lips with his, ending the embrace with a gasp and a groan as his pleasure exploded between them.

His skin was hot under her, and they couldn't stop kissing, even as they lay beside one another and recovered from the explosive pleasure they'd given and received. It wasn't safe to sleep, wasn't safe to rest, but Iris curled in beside Toran and her eyes grew heavy as the weight of the day and everything they'd done crashed over her.

Toran kissed the side of her neck gently and slung an arm over her. "It's okay, rest. We have a little time. I'll make sure you're safe." And even in the midst of everything, with danger closing in on them, Iris's eyes slid shut and she fell asleep with a smile in her mate's arms.

Chapter Fourteen

Toran knew that he should try to join his denya in sleep, but after several minutes of laying still with his eyes closed and breath steady, it became clear that sleep eluded him. He pulled Iris closer and buried his face in the crook of her neck, breathing her scent deep into his lungs. It wasn't sleep, but any of the tension he'd been holding close dissolved as her essence filled him.

What would it be like when they were bonded? Already he could barely keep himself from reaching for her every minute of every hour that went by. Would be intense hunger that he felt diminish? Or would his need for her grow until it was an all-consuming thing that defined his existence?

He wished he could ask Raze these questions. He wasn't close to the other bonded males at Detyen HQ. Many of them were much older than Toran and though they'd been his teachers and mentors throughout his entire life, the things he needed to know now were too personal, too intimate, to ask just anyone. He barely wanted to ask Raze. But if there was something that Raze knew about mating, about keeping his denya satisfied and happy, Toran wanted to know as well.

Iris stirred beside him, shifting slightly before sinking deeper into sleep. Toran's lips curled into a smile and he tightened his arms around her. They couldn't stay here long, but he could give his mate these peaceful moments while he set his mind to the next phase of their escape.

He doubted that Yormas or the Oscavian had enough clout to call for a search of each of the rooms. And even if they did, that would take hours. Still, it was better to be ahead of them, gone from the base as quickly as possible before security realized that they'd escaped.

He quickly dismissed any thought of attempting to stowaway on the passenger shuttles. Those were the most highly guarded exit and entry points on the base and the risk was too great. But the passenger shuttles were not the only ways on and off the moon. Despite years of terraforming and the large indoor gardens that had been built in the bases, the majority of the food available here had to be shipped in. It was a massive and expensive effort to feed the thousands of people living on or visiting the lunar surface. It wasn't just the food, either. All of the shops needed to be able to receive shipments, and though maintenance could use 3D printers to manufacture most of the supplies they needed, some things still needed to come from Earth.

A supply ship could get them home. They only needed to find one, avoid any of its security, evade the station guards, and keep off Yormas's radar. How difficult could that be?

Toran wasn't going to answer that.

He went over the logistics in his mind, losing himself to thoughts of what they could do and how things could go wrong. He got so caught up in the planning that time slipped away from him, and before long Iris was stirring and waking beside him. She rolled over and looked at him with a sleepy smile.

"You have intense face going on," she said.

Toran kissed her nose. "Are you ready to go home?"

***

Iris almost felt guilty about the nap. Especially when she woke up and Toran had devised an entire escape plan. But she didn't let herself dwell on that as they took turns in the showers and cleaned themselves up as best they could. She knew that Toran wouldn't want her to feel guilty for something as innocent as sleep. He wanted her safe and off this base as much as she wanted that for him. They didn't need to get into a contest, competing to save each other or come up with brilliant plans to get home. It wasn't a competition, wasn't a game, and there was no score.

Even so, next time maybe she would try to stay awake for the planning session. She just wouldn't tell Toran why she thought she needed to do that.

Her clothes felt dirty, as if she'd been wearing them for several days, and she wished they had access to their room. But dirty

298

clothes were the least of her worries, and she wasn't about to complain about something as simple as that. She tidied up the room as best she could, but there was no way to disguise that the two of them had spent time there. She only hoped that whatever cleaning bot was responsible for these quarters wasn't programmed to report that they had been illegally occupied. She didn't know how cleaning bot programming was supposed to work.

Once they were both clean and ready, she and Toran left the room without a backwards glance. Toran's hair was still a little wet from the shower and her mind flashed back to their sweat-soaked bodies grinding against one another on the bed. Arousal scorched through her and she had to clench her fists to keep from reaching out and stroking her hand against her mate. She had an insatiable hunger to touch him, and she might've been embarrassed about it if it weren't obvious that Toran felt exactly the same way.

But doubts were creeping up. She'd been ready to do everything with him, to seal the bond he told her held them together. And while she knew he had a point about taking their time and doing it right, that little voice that lived inside her and liked to whisper about how she wasn't good enough, how she wasn't worthy of love, and how she couldn't pick a good man to save her life, was saying some very hurtful things that she was having trouble blocking out. It was saying that Toran didn't need a weak mate, a woman who couldn't fight security guards who held her captive. A woman who fell asleep rather than finding an escape route.

Logically she knew that he didn't think those things. And even if he had reservations, he had every reason to want the bond sealed between them. After all, he would die if he didn't have sex with her. And wasn't that an ego killer? Did he only want her as his mate because he didn't have another option? Would he rather be alone than with a woman who'd been assigned to investigate him as a potential threat to the planet?

She thought she'd been doing well, keeping these doubts at bay. Things had been moving too fast for her to dwell on anything. But it looked like this quiet walk through the corridor was exactly the right moment to be freaking out. It didn't matter that they needed to be on the lookout for security and had to try to keep out of sight of the cameras, her mind had decided that it was safe enough to have a little freak out.

She wanted to reach out and take Toran's hand, to feel the comforting weight of his presence. But he needed his hands free in case they suddenly came upon someone who meant them harm, and she didn't want to be the reason that they couldn't fight back. She'd fallen back a few steps while they walked, and Toran glanced back over his shoulder and offered her that genuine smile that seemed to exist only for her.

The weight lifted from her heart. It wasn't as good as a caress, but it banished some of the darker thoughts. Not all of them; it would take time for those to go away. Iris caught up and kept pace beside him as he led the way to the hidden parts of Gamma Base.

There was a secret station behind secure doors, one that the tourists and guests never saw. It existed to make their stays pleasant and painless, allowing the staff members, robots, and androids to move about unseen and to allow them to move supplies between different parts of the compound without interrupting anyone. It was a lot like the old theme parks back home with their tunnels and secret passageways that no visitor ever saw.

They came to an unobtrusive door that Iris would have normally passed without a second look. It wasn't labeled, but there was a keypad on the wall beside it which suggested that it wasn't meant for guests to enter. Before she could ask how Toran planned to get through, he pulled a thin device out of his pocket and placed it on top of the pad. It looked like a pen, but she didn't see a pointed end. After a moment, the door unlocked with a click and Toran grabbed the device and hid it away again.

"Not everything got left in our room," he said with a grin. Iris smiled back, glad that at least one thing had gone right today.

The station hadn't bothered with much decoration for these hidden hallways. Unbroken gray ran in every direction, giving Iris a bit of a headache as she tried to judge the distance towards the end. The harsh light overhead didn't cast any shadows and there was nowhere for them to hide, but at least that meant that they would see anyone coming towards them. "Did you memorize a map of this place?" she asked Toran.

"Of course," he replied. They didn't waste any more time talking after that.

Whether it was the late hour or their location in the station, they didn't run in to anyone. Toran used his unlocking device to get them through two more doors until they came to a large garage that was their destination.

"We need to get in that one," Toran said, pointing to a large ship sitting beside one of the walls. Inside the garage it looked huge, but she knew that once it was outside it would be tiny. Cargo ships like these were built to dock with bigger ships that ferried back and forth between Earth and the moon, remaining in orbit at all times.

It all seemed too easy. Why weren't there any guards? Iris knew she should ask Toran, but voicing the question out loud felt like she would jinx it. Couldn't one thing go their way?

Apparently her thoughts were enough to cause an issue. A door on the other side of the room slid open with a hiss and she and Toran froze where they stood, half hidden behind a small forklift. Her heart beat loud enough that she was sure Toran could hear it, hell the guards could probably hear it. Two members of security spoke quietly to one another as they walked a circuit around the room. As they got close to her and Toran, she and her mate crouched low and scrambled around the vehicle in front of them, trying to remain as quiet as possible.

Iris would have given them away—a misstep sent her sprawling, and she would have smacked against the hard ground if Toran hadn't looped an arm around her chest and covered her mouth with his big hand to keep her from making a noise. She could barely breathe around his hand, but she was glad he didn't move it. Her lungs tried to drag in ragged breaths but the security members were still too close; they would hear her in the cavernous garage.

Luckily they didn't, and several minutes later she and Toran heard the door open and close again as the guards left. Her arms were shaking and she wanted to collapse down on the cold ground, but they needed to move. There was no telling when those guards would come back or when the cargo ship would take off.

She and Toran made a break for it. They slipped into two survival suits which would keep them warm enough and give them oxygen if something happened to the life support system on the ship.

On board there weren't many places to hide, but some creative squeezing that was sure to lead to cramping had them out of sight just in time. They couldn't see what was going on and couldn't speak to one another to try and figure it out, but footsteps sounded outside, echoing like metal against concrete. That was what it sounded like when someone ran up the entrance ramp. A guard? The pilot? Another stowaway? With no outlet for her thoughts, Iris was going to go crazy.

Escaping like this was insane; she didn't know why she ever thought it was going to work. No, she knew. Toran had told her and she trusted him. He would never let her get hurt, would do anything to make sure she was safe. She held those thoughts close and wrapped her arms around herself, trying to find a way to give herself comfort.

The ship rocked sometime later. She had no way of knowing how long they'd been stowed away. But the motion was unmistakable, they had taken off. It was dark in her cubby and she couldn't see the wall in front of her. Her legs hurt, as she was stuck in a half crouch, and she bit her lip to keep from crying out. The flight from Earth to the moon took hours and she couldn't afford to make a peep. It had to be worse for Toran, but if she hadn't known her mate was stowed away in a similar spot, she would have no clue he was there with her. He could become a statue, he had the training. She had to take her strength from that.

And somehow she did. Iris managed to fall into a half doze, half trance, and the time slipped by around her. Only when her ears popped and the shuttle rocked violently did she realize that they were close to Earth, close to home. Only a little more time and they would be safe.

A little while later, the shuttle landed gently on terra firma. They hadn't had a chance to discuss it, but Iris stayed in place. They needed to wait before they attempted to exit. They had made it off Gamma Station and they didn't want to get caught now.

A while later a light scratch on her door was all the warning Toran gave her before he opened it. She leaned out and stood as a gasp tore from her throat. Blood surged through the muscles that had been cramping for a long time. She bit down even harder on her lip and tried to keep quiet. Toran wrapped his arms around her and rocked her, and whether it was the gentle motion or her mate's arms, she started to feel better.

Hand-in-hand. they walked for the door, ready to go home. But when they stepped out of the ship five men in security uniforms were standing in a half circle with blasters pointed at the entrance of the ship, right at them. She and Toran raised their hands in surrender.

Chapter Fifteen

Iris had thought that sitting in that cramped cubbyhole on the shuttle was the worst place she could be stuck outside of an incinerator. It turned out that a relatively spacious detainment cell was even worse. From corner to corner she could manage four paces before needing to turn around, and if she sat on the ground she could stretch her legs completely, but the grime the floor left on her fingers made her quickly stand up and reconsider that decision.

No one was telling her anything. She didn't know where Toran was being kept, she didn't know if this was a private facility or if it was run by the government, and she didn't know if they were being accused of any crime or if punishment here was a more personal matter. She feared that the heavy steel door blocking her in would swing open and reveal Ambassador Yormas with that evil smile on his face. But he was still on the moon as far as she knew, and she doubted that he would do his own dirty work.

Lights embedded in the ceiling gave the cell a soft glow, but made it impossible to sleep or get a sense of time passing. She wasn't sure if she'd been stuck in that incinerator with Toran hours ago or if days had already passed. Things had been moving fast. She was so tired that her eyelids kept dropping shut and she felt the need to scratch the gravel out of them. She curled up on the small bench affixed to the wall and flung her arm over her head, trying to give herself a little darkness to make it easier to sleep. It didn't do much to help, but her limbs were so heavy that lying down was better than nothing.

When she got out of this she was going to find Toran and then sleep for a week. She couldn't rest until she was sure her mate was safe, but that needed to happen really soon or she was going to scream.

The sound of movement in the hallway caught her attention and Iris flipped back over and forced herself to sit up. If someone was coming for her, she didn't want to be caught lying down. She couldn't quite manage to stand. That took too much effort.

Her door opened, but it wasn't Yormas coming to kill her or Toran coming to save her. One of the guards stepped in and instructed her to stand before placing laser cuffs on her hands. He and his partner silently escorted her down the hall and Iris tried to get a good look at where she was in case an impossible opportunity to escape presented itself. After all, she and Toran had escaped the freaking moon, what was one little cellblock?

The guards led her to an interrogation room and affixed her cuffs to a sensor on the table. She could barely move, but some clever twisting let her rest her elbows on the flat surface. The guards left, but she wasn't foolish enough to think they were gone. There had to be cameras and other security measures in here to make sure the interrogators remained safe.

But when the door opened and her boss Selma walked in, Iris could have been knocked over with a feather. The older woman gave her a disappointed look and sat in the seat on the opposite side of the table. "When the police called me, I thought there must've been some sort of mistake," said Selma, unexpectedly answering one of Iris's questions. This wasn't a private facility, it belonged to the police. Was that a good thing? Or bad? She didn't know anymore.

"I'm sorry." The apology came out automatically. What must Selma think about her now? She'd lied about her whereabouts and ended up arrested. "Why did they call you?" Was that normal? Did the police normally call a person's boss? Then again, Selma worked for the SDA. They knew everything.

"You've never received even a traffic citation and now you're causing disturbances on other planets and illegally stowing away with the man you're supposed to be investigating?" Selma shook her head and glared.

Iris bit her tongue to keep from pointing out that the moon wasn't a planet. It wasn't important. She didn't have a response, and Selma hadn't asked for one, so Iris remained quiet.

"You have a bright future. When you got into that mess with your ex I thought it was just bad luck." The implication was a stab to her heart. She hadn't realized how much Selma knew about Dan, as she had tried to keep that information separate from her work life. But of course Selma would know. And she hated to be judged by that one mistake of a relationship. She bit back the urge to tell Selma that Toran was nothing like Dan, that the thing between them was real in a way she'd never experienced before. Selma continued. "You're not the kind of girl to make stupid decisions. I told you to investigate Toran NaLosen, not take off to a pleasure station to let him take advantage and get you into trouble."

If she bit her tongue any harder, Iris was going to bleed. This didn't feel like a dressing down from her boss. It felt like her mom was yelling at her.

"What's so special about this Detyen that you've lost your head?" Selma looked truly confused. Maybe if she'd seen Iris any time in the past few weeks she would've realized that something was different, she might've thought that something was wrong. But Iris had kept their communications to comm calls and emails to avoid uncomfortable questions.

A crazy part of Iris wanted to say exactly who and what Toran was to her, why she was acting this way. But she knew that if she explained, things would go from bad to worse. She didn't care about her job right now, didn't care if she got fired or was blacklisted or anything like that. But she couldn't bring more attention to Toran, she had to protect him. And at this moment protecting him meant keeping their connection a secret. "I was investigating another angle. Things got out of hand."

The raised eyebrow Selma shot her spoke paragraphs. But instead of saying them out loud, she merely sighed. "Ambassador Yormas of Wreet has issued a complaint against you and now I need to do a full investigation into your recent projects. I've never heard of this guy before, but it seems he made an impression."

If Iris explained, would Selma believe her? Selma had to know about the darker things that lurked in the galaxy, the dangers that faced their planet on a daily basis. Something caused light to glint off the lens of one of the security cameras and Iris decided kept her findings to herself. Even if she could trust Selma, she couldn't tell her here, not when anyone could be listening. "I didn't mean to cause this much trouble," Iris said quietly.

Selma just shook her head. "I've talked to the authorities here. You can go home. But no more off planet jaunts until this is all settled."

Iris wasn't sure she ever wanted to leave the planet again, not unless she had her own transportation to get back. "What about Toran?" Was he still here? Had someone come to fetch him? Did Yormas happen?

"This will go in his file, of course. He can talk to the judge at his hearing if he wants to go home, or back to his quarters, I mean. That's none of your concern anymore. You're suspended pending the outcome of the investigation." Selma stood from the table and was out of the room before Iris could put together any more questions. Everything happened in a whirlwind after that. The guards came in and released her from her cuffs. They had her sign several pieces of paperwork that she barely managed to read, and in no time she was outside the nondescript facility and shunted into a taxi on her way home.

It killed her a little to leave Toran behind, but she was out and much more useful to him from there. She was already making plans to call Sierra and Raze and all of his people. She'd raise up an army and level the building if she had to, he just had to hold on for a little while longer.

The taxi dropped her off in front of her building and Iris walked up the stairs in a daze. She opened the door and didn't realize that something was wrong until the cloying scent of an overly masculine cologne tickled her nostrils. She looked up and saw a blond man sitting on her couch. Had she really thought that he was the epitome of masculine beauty at some point? Had she really been willing to share her life with him and overlook all his flaws? Had she been that blind?

"Dan, what the hell are you doing here?"

***

Patience was key to getting out of a situation like this. Toran sat calmly on the bench in his cell and waited. He tried not to dwell on what was going to happen, on the things that could be done to him. And if he let himself think about the fact that his denya was somewhere in this building locked in a similar cell and facing an equally uncertain future he would go mad. So though it went completely against his nature, he forced those thoughts to the back of his mind. He couldn't help her while he was locked behind solid steel. He had to get out before he could find her.

Hours ticked by and no one walked near him. He'd have heard it in the echoes on the walls if they had, but his only company was his breath and his heartbeat. He wanted to pace, but the cell wasn't really big enough for that and he didn't want to give his captors the satisfaction of watching him stew. He'd known this was a possibility when they climbed aboard the shuttle to leave Gamma Station. But he'd said nothing to Iris. She was worried enough already and it was better to be imprisoned on Earth than on the moon. That had been his thought, at least. And he hadn't wanted her to worry during the long, uncomfortable ride. Maybe he should have warned her. Now he had plenty of time to think of that mistake.

He closed his eyes and tried to focus on the bond between them, but the connection was incomplete, and though he could feel Iris's presence nestled in his heart, he could not focus and pinpoint whether she was okay and what direction she lay in. He wouldn't regret his decision not to seal the bond under such precarious circumstances as they'd been in. Iris deserved a perfect moment, even if it would give him comfort to know through the metaphysical connection that she was all right. He had to go on faith instead, a difficult concept for a Detyen.

The sound of footsteps in the hall almost had him flinching, and he was standing at the ready when the door opened. It took him a moment to recognize the older man standing haloed in the bright light of the hallway, but when he did, Toran had to fight back a smile. Yormas wasn't the only man with friends in high places.

"General." He nodded in greeting at Sierra's father.

General Remington Alvarez glared at him. "Let's get you out of here." The older man turned to the guard standing beside him and waved him into the cell. "Take those cuffs off of him now." The laser cuffs that Alvarez was referring to were so lightweight that Toran had almost forgotten he was wearing them. He could move each of his hands independently, but if he got too close to any of the guards or one of the guards got jumpy and triggered the cuffs, they would be pulled together to immobilize him.

Toran held his hands out, ready to be freed. He had questions, foremost in his mind about the location of Iris. But for the first time today things were looking up. Another one of those questions was how the general knew he was in the cell. Had Sierra or Raze been keeping an eye out? They must have been.

In a matter of seconds the guard had undone the cuffs and stepped back, giving Toran a good deal of space. Once the guard was back through the door, the general began walking, expecting Toran to keep up. In a few quick steps he pulled up beside Alvarez and walked in step with him. "Are we going to retrieve Iris?" he asked. "Or is she meeting us somewhere?"

Alvarez shot him a look, his steely eyes unreadable. "Miss Mason was released two hours ago. She was sent home and the cab that dropped her off reported a safe entry into her quarters. She's safe."

But why hadn't she come for him? Who had let her out? He repeated that question to Alvarez.

"Do you think I have all of the answers? If you knew the amount of favors I was calling in today, you would be embarrassed. If it weren't for my daughter..." He shook his head and cleared his throat. "Whatever this mess is, it better not bring her down too. She's already in enough trouble, and now she has that man beside her kicking up enough dust to choke someone. Whatever game you're playing, you keep my daughter safe." Alvarez never raised his voice, and from his tone he might have been speaking about the weather. But Toran felt the threat to his bones. Alvarez loved his daughter, that much was obvious. And he hated that he couldn't protect her, that she was willing to throw herself into danger for people he thought were strangers and aliens.

"Sierra has given light to Raze where before there was only darkness. She is hope, and I will protect her as if she were my own sister." He might have been wary of her when they'd first met, but those days were long past. Sierra had proven herself to him, and after Iris, she and Raze were the closest thing he had to family, with Kayde and Dryce not far behind.

The general still looked wary, but he nodded and let the subject drop. "I'm to take you back to your quarters."

"Take me to Iris instead."

Though Toran had thought his tone invited no argument, Alvarez shook his head. "Let her rest, both of you have had a long few days. She needs sleep, and if you go and see her now can you guarantee she'll get some?"

That was not something he was about to discuss with a man he'd only just met. "I need to see my—I need to see Iris."

"You will. In a few hours. Let her sleep and then give her a call once it's morning. You have my word that nothing will happen to her before then. Besides, there's something you need to see." They were already at the entrance, having passed through several security gates where the guards waved them through with blank faces. Whether it bothered them that Toran was being removed without punishment didn't show on their faces. They probably didn't care about him at all. He was no longer their problem.

Toran wanted to fight, wanted to insist. The need to see Iris beat strongly within him, but he understood the general's point. He doubted that Iris had stolen any sleep while locked in her cell, and she would be most comfortable in her home. Morning was not far off. In a few hours he could call on her and reassure her that everything would be fine. And if they took the day to do more than sleep, to do the things they couldn't do on Gamma Station, well, that was just a bonus. But Alvarez was looking at him expectantly, and leading him to a black car.

Toran nodded at him and said, "Let's go."

Chapter Sixteen

It was too early for this shit, or too late. Iris wasn't exactly sure of the time. It was dark out, and she really wanted to sleep. But Dan was sitting on her couch, the same Dan who had cheated on her and stolen all of her things. The man who'd taken her car and ditched it in the middle of Oklahoma. The same man who the police couldn't manage to catch, no matter how much evidence he left behind.

Iris didn't know what she would be saying if she weren't about to pass out from exhaustion. A small sliver of her believed that he was actually a hallucination induced by all the crap she'd gone through in the past two days. He had to be a hallucination, there was no reason for Dan to smile at her when he got up from the couch and walk close like he was about to give her a hug.

She took a step back and put her hands up, pushing him away before he could make his move. No hallucination would be that solid. Iris's mind spun. Dan. Here. "How did you get inside?"

The smile he gave her called back wicked, sultry nights spent together in bed, and her stomach curdled at the memory. "You let me in, isn't that how it works?" He was grinning indulgently as he spoke.

Bile rose in her throat. Was this asshole serious? Was he flirting? "I changed the codes and the locks. How did you get in?" It felt like bugs were crawling over her skin to imagine Dan sitting in her sanctuary. He could have taken anything, or trashed the place, or done something worse. She wanted to throw up, but she took a big gulp and did her best to swallow that down. She wasn't about to show weakness in front of this vile creature.

His smile shifted, and a long time ago she might have called his expression sweet. Now all she saw was the condescension. "You didn't change the emergency reset question, babe. I knew you'd give me a way in." He reached out and gently placed a hand on her shoulder before Iris could evade him.

She stepped back out of his grasp, and backed up into the little half wall dividing her living room from her kitchen. Dan's eyes lit up as he realized that she was trapped. He took a step to the side, cutting off her easiest avenue of escape. It looked natural, but she had a long history of observing how Dan worked. If she called him out, he would say she was overreacting, that she could step around him easily and he would make no move to stop her. And that might be true, but she would have to sidle up next to him to do it, and she wouldn't be able to avoid his hands.

"That was a mistake, I don't want you here." And it was an oversight she would be correcting immediately.

"I know you have to say that," he said softly. He sounded understanding, caring. Everything he wasn't. "Those things I did, I know I was wrong, baby. I know you were hurt. I shouldn't have done that, but I was scared. Things were going so well, no one's ever understood me like you do. You know I sabotage myself. That was all that was, I've had time to think. That's why I'm here."

Her mind reeled trying to make sense of the gibberish that he'd just spewed. "You stole my car. You cheated on me. The only way you could make that up to me is if you marched down to the police station right now and turned yourself in." She should be calling the cops, she knew. But a part of her was afraid that if she reached for her comm Dan might think she was going for a weapon and attack her. He didn't usually get physical like that, but after the adventure on Gamma Station she was too keyed up.

"No." Dan was shaking his head, his jaw clenched. "No, you have to understand."

"Understand what?" She shouldn't be playing this game; she knew he was going to screw with her head. There was nothing he could say that would make her take him back, even if she wasn't in love with Toran.

In love? Really? She had to realize that now? Iris tamped down the thought and pushed it aside, she'd deal with it later. She didn't want Dan's presence to pollute thoughts of her mate.

"You understand me, baby." He stepped closer, but the look on her face must have warned him and he kept his hands to himself.

When they were dating the pet names had seemed sweet; now, like everything else about Dan, they made her sick. "Don't call me that."

"You're my baby, you love it when I call you that. Remember that time you made me say it while I was—"

"Don't finish that sentence." He was a reminder of all her poor choices, and she didn't need the play-by-play. "I'm calling the police."

He couldn't stop himself from placing a hand on her arm. "No, please don't. I came to apologize. I love you. I want you back. We can work this out."

Iris wrenched away from him and reached in her pocket for her comm. "We really can't."

"You understand me, baby. And you know I'm the only one who understands you. I wanted you when no one else would even look twice. You think anyone's ever going to love you like I did? Like I *do*? You work too much, but I can live with that now. I know you get obsessed and you don't think about me, but we can work on that, and when I get lonely I won't need to look for anyone else anymore. Not if I have you. I won't lash out, I promise." He should have sounded pathetic, but a small part of Iris, the one he'd sunk his hooks into years ago, couldn't help but listen and flinch.

They'd had these fights before, when her jobs took over her life for weeks at a time. When Dan came home smelling of another woman's perfume. When she found a pair of underwear that weren't hers. He'd made his excuses, and she'd believe him, because no one had ever loved her before.

But even if she didn't have Toran, everything Dan was saying would still ring false. She was a different woman than she'd been six months ago, she had grown. And now she had a strong Detyen warrior to stand at her side, one who respected her dedication and her competence. One who had never critiqued her body, or the things she wanted to do with him. One who belonged to her as wholly as she belonged to him.

"You love me?" she scoffed. "You're a slimy bastard who doesn't know the meaning of the word. You want to use me and I don't believe for a second that you can be faithful, that you wouldn't be up to your same tricks the second my back was turned. I spent way too much time dealing with your shit, and I'm not about to waste another second." She held up her comm and waved it at him. "I'm calling the police right now, and they're going to take you to jail where you belong with the other criminals. And then I'm going to forget about you, because my life is so much better without you. I never knew what happiness was when we were together. You were a mistake, one I've regretted since the day we met." She called up the number for the detective she'd been working with. "Now stay here. Don't make me hurt you."

But her exhaustion must've been getting to her. She saw Dan lunge forward, but she didn't have a chance to turn away before he pushed her to the side and left her sprawled on the ground, her comm flying across the room and smacking into the wall. He was out of the house in a flash, and by the time Iris pushed herself up to chase him he was out of sight. She let out a frustrated growl, a habit she was picking up from Toran.

She closed the door and took a moment to change the locks again and the emergency security question. Once that was done she found her comm and got the detective on the line, reporting everything that had just happened. The detective assured her that officers would be on the lookout for Dan, but Iris wasn't hopeful. He'd evaded them for this long, had somehow managed to get into the city without being caught. There was no reason to suspect that they would catch him now.

She felt a hollow sort of acceptance. She was done with Dan, and even if he was never punished for the shit he'd done to her, she couldn't quite bring herself to care. This confrontation here was closure. He'd come to hurt her, or get her back, or something like that. And she wanted nothing to do with him. A small part of her had always wondered what it would be like to see him one more time, whether he would still have the power over her that he used to wield. And now she knew he didn't. Now she was sure that she was over him, and she could move on with her life, could travel down the path that fate had set her on.

But to do that she needed her mate by her side. She used her comm to call up the quarters that Toran shared with his fellow Detyens. To her surprise, Sierra Alvarez answered. "I sent my dad to get Toran. He's on his way here. Can you come?"

"Yes." Anywhere her mate went she would go. Exhaustion momentarily abated, she called a taxi and headed out again.

***

Alvarez dropped Toran outside of his building and pulled away with a curt farewell. Toran watched the vehicle drive away and narrowed his eyes as a taxi passed the general and came to a stop in front of the building. Iris opened the door and stepped out, and suddenly the balance of Toran's world was right again. It was amazing how somebody could become so essential in such a short amount of time, and it was only now that he realized that he hadn't quite been able to pull in a deep breath since he and Iris were separated. Seeing her safe, here and now, banished the dark thoughts in his mind, and he truly believed that they could take on all of the evils of the world and triumph. As long as they were together.

He and Iris stared at each other for several seconds before they both moved forward as if released from some invisible hold and clutched each other close, hugging tight enough to crush. He breathed her scent in deep and let the soft curves of her body soothe him. It was more of an impression under all her layers, but even touching like this with no sexual component was satisfying in its own way.

"Who got you out of there? You were already gone by the time Alvarez fetched me." He was glad she was safe, but when she pulled away she looked shaken. Toran swiped his lips across her forehead, offering comfort. He stepped back to give her room to breathe, but didn't let go. He didn't know if he'd ever be able to stop touching her.

"My boss," Iris answered. She closed her eyes and grimaced. "I actually forgot about that, it's been a night." He opened his mouth to ask, but she shook her head. "I'll tell you later, I promise. It's nothing important." She laced their fingers together and tugged him towards the door. "Sierra said she has information for us."

"That's why I came here first, I wanted to give you time to rest." He could see from the dark circles under her eyes and the sag of her shoulders that she still needed sleep, but Toran wouldn't insist right now. She could say the same thing about him. There was probably no safer place on the planet than the room they were about to enter, and once they had the information they were about to be given they could nap together. That sounded like the human idea of heaven.

Inside the suite Sierra, Raze, Kayde, Dryce, and Quinn were all waiting for them. Quinn's presence was a bit of surprise, but she must've been working closely with the others while he and Iris were away. He wouldn't insult her by questioning her presence; obviously the other people in the room approved.

Toran and Iris collapsed beside one another on the couch and Sierra shot them a concerned look. "We can go over this in the morning if you'd prefer."

"Let's just do it now," said Iris. She snuggled into Toran's side when he slung an arm over her shoulders. Toran's heart warmed at the contact. Before he met Iris he might have questioned why someone would need to touch their mate so much, but now he understood. He couldn't be near her and not touch her. They were meant for one another, could comfort one another, and being beside her just felt right.

At Toran's nod Sierra took her place beside Raze at the front of the room. The others had settled into the chairs, except for Dryce, who was sitting on the floor instead of taking the open spot on the couch. Sierra engaged the holo player and a stream of data from a report appeared in front of them. "This is what we found in his office." She didn't need to say Yormas's name, they all knew who they were talking about. "It's a chemical composition report with entries for each of the planets in the Sol System along with their moons. Most of the attention was given to Earth, probably because of the native population. It is the only planet in the system where life evolved."

"They mentioned something about testing, about human subjects," said Iris. "Do you think this is connected? He was meeting with an Oscavian named Varrow who seems to also be involved."

"There was an entry in his calendar for that meeting," Raze confirmed with a nod. "That meeting was just one in a line of many with several different Oscavians."

Toran leaned forward and sifted through the data being projected. He wasn't a scientist, and this was far from his area of expertise, but it was surprisingly easy to understand, as if it were written for a layman. "Do you know what 99.97% match for D1 means?" he asked. It was easy to jump to conclusions, especially given the information they'd gathered and lost on Gamma Station. Toran forced himself to be careful.

"We think it means Detya," said Sierra. "We think this report shows a commonality in certain chemical compositions between Earth and Detya. Compositions that aren't found in other systems. And..." she trailed off and shook her head, as if dismissing her thought.

"What?" Toran insisted.

Sierra shrugged. "It's just a thought," she hedged. "But maybe that's why there are human denyai. I don't know, we haven't found any other links between Earth and Detya. I mean, I haven't thought about it much. Been a little busy." She huffed out a laugh. "Maybe it's dumb, it could be something else."

"I don't think it's dumb," said Iris. "It's not like we have a lot of information to go on. Aren't we the only two women mated to Detyens?"

Toran couldn't help the smile that nearly cracked his face in half. He reached back and grabbed Iris's hand to kiss it. "Not quite," he corrected. "Over the past two years or so, I've heard a few reports.

Perhaps half a dozen women not related to the Detyen Legion. All human, but not all from Earth."

"What about men?" Quinn asked, reminding Toran that he and Iris were not the only two people in the room.

"It's possible," Kayde responded, leveling his intense gaze at the human woman. Something was off, something tickled at Toran's senses, but he didn't know what. He hated to bring it up, but he would need to evaluate Kayde in the coming days. If the soulless Detyen was becoming unstable, they couldn't risk the destruction he could bring about. "There are far fewer female Detyens, but there is no reason that one of them could not find a mate among human men."

"Why is that?" asked Quinn. She placed her hand on her chin and leaned against the arm of her chair, posture casual but engaged.

"A matter of bad luck," Kayde responded, not giving anyone else a chance to speak. "According to our records, roughly equal numbers of men and women made it off Detya. However, in the years since, more boys have been born than girls. And early in the days of the diaspora, tragedy struck and a ship carrying many of our women was destroyed."

Toran, Dryce, and Raze stared at Kayde. That was the most the man had spoken in weeks. The soulless were not generally talkative, especially not about Detyen history. The women in the room didn't seem to understand just how strange that was.

"That's fascinating," said Sierra, turning them back to the matter at hand. "And you know my heart breaks every time I hear more about what happened. But let's focus on things we can change. We have people involved from two different nations. Do you think that Wreet is masterminding this endeavor? What about the Oscavian Empire? Or these individual actors?"

"From what we heard, they weren't speaking like they had a government sanction," Iris observed, and she tugged on Toran's hand and pulled him back towards the couch. He sat down beside her. "But they might have a mandate to keep quiet. We think Varrow, the Oscavian, has that girl you let go—"

"We didn't let her go," Quinn interrupted.

Iris's head snapped towards her. "Fine, the woman some of your group callously abandoned in the middle of a war zone. Is that better?" She jutted her chin out in defiance.

Quinn crossed her arms, her jaw set. "If you think I'm happy about that, you're wrong."

"Whatever." She turned back towards the center of the room. "We think Varrow, or the brother he mentioned, has Laurel. And he might also have a Detyen. They were speaking about it openly on Gamma Station and I overheard them."

"Where?" Quinn demanded. "We need to find her, bring her back. What happened wasn't her fault."

"We also need to warn the humans about the impending threat to the planet," Dryce cut in. "We can't let what happened to us happen to them."

"What we *need*," Sierra spoke over them loud enough to cut everyone off, "is more information. I want to get Laurel back," she nodded at Quinn. "And you know I don't want my planet to be destroyed," she said to Dryce. "But we still don't know enough to take action."

"So what do you suggest?" Toran might have been in charge of the Detyens, but this was Sierra's planet and she seemed to already have a plan.

"We need to bring my dad all the way in." She grimaced as she said it, and Toran was reminded that their relationship was not the closest or the friendliest between father and daughter. "Not only is he high-ranking, he holds enough social sway to ensure that he'll be listened to. If we can get him to believe us, that's half the battle."

There was chatter and discussion, but after only a few minutes the group agreed. General Alvarez was their best bet to warn the planet and to get more information about Yormas of Wreet and Varrow the Oscavian.

Beside him, Iris yawned and laid her head against his shoulder. "Are we done yet?" she muttered.

Toran kissed her cheek. "Almost," he promised.

It took a few more minutes of talking, but then the group broke up and agreed to meet again later after Sierra had spoken to her father. Though Toran had a room that was relatively private in the suite, he guided Iris out of the room and further out of the building, calling a taxi and punching in the directions for her house when they climbed in. The suite was too crowded, and never completely silent. His mate deserved an undisturbed sleep in her own bed, and he would lay by her side to make sure that was what she got.

Chapter Seventeen

There was a furnace lying against her back, and an iron bar draped over her waist. Given that, Iris shouldn't have been comfortable. But after a long night of sleep in her soft bed with no threats from evil ambassadors, security guards, or shitty ex-boyfriends, she found it easy to bear the weight. Especially when the furnace behind her shifted and she remembered that it was Toran lying next to her, holding her close. She didn't remember coming back to the apartment last night; the end of the meeting had gone by in an exhausted blur. She remembered Sierra promising to speak to General Alvarez, and then everything went hazy. Hopefully nothing important happened after that.

Iris tried to glance at the clock on her bedside table, but it was behind her, blocked by the huge pile of Detyen male sleeping in her bed. The room was bright, sunlight streaking in through the windows. And it wasn't the gentle light of early morning. No, if she had to guess they were getting close to noon. It wasn't just the light that told her; now that she was paying attention she could hear the sounds of the city alive around them, vehicles moving, horns honking, people yelling, everything come to life.

That was the best part of the city, the sound. Even when she was lonely, she was never alone. Though now that she had Toran, she didn't need to worry about the loneliness anymore.

She'd called herself his mate in front of everyone. She'd been speaking about it to him for days, but never when others were around. She might have expected it to be more difficult, but nothing had felt more natural. Technically they weren't completely mated, but her mind had been made up for a while. Any doubts she had had dissolved when she confronted Dan. Strange thought, that. She wouldn't thank her ex, but she was glad his unexpected reappearance had clarified some things. He and Toran couldn't be more different, and Toran would never try to use her in the ways that Dan had. Toran actually respected her and she deserved his respect.

She snuggled back against him and her eyes drifted shut once more. The next time she woke Toran was tracing a path down her arm with his finger. When she tilted her head towards him, she saw that he was connecting the small moles on her arm like they were a kind of puzzle.

"I like your clan markings," he said, leaning down and kissing one at the top of her shoulder.

Iris shivered. "Humans don't have clan markings."

He kissed another one further down her arm and raised goosebumps along her flesh. "I like them anyway."

"What else do you like?"

His fingers tangled in her hair. "I like the way your hair spreads out over your pillow, fanning out to frame you." He gently pulled on her shoulders until she rolled under him. He kissed her, tugging on her bottom lip until she opened for him. But just when it was getting good, he pulled back. "I like how soft your lips are and the way they taste against mine." He placed featherlight kisses over her eyes and then one on her nose, which made her grin. "I like the way you see beyond the surface and take your time to study what matters. I like the way you look at me when you think I'm not watching." Her cheeks flamed, but she couldn't look away, trapped in his gaze. "And when you look like that, your eyes go soft and hungry, and they don't need to glint red for me to know exactly what you want."

"And what's that?" she asked, breathless.

Toran grinned and all the trouble of the last few days dissolved. It was just the two of them in this moment, and they had all the time in the world. "Me."

He said it so confidently Iris tipped back her head and laughed.

"Is it not true?" He smiled as he asked and feathered kisses across her face and down her neck. "Let me convince you."

Her body wanted to arch against him, but Iris made herself push away. "What about me?"

He was a heavy weight where he laid against her, but not enough to crush. He rolled his eyes up towards her until their gazes locked. "What about you?"

"Don't I get to tell you what I like about you?" She'd expected a tidal wave of passion, a hurricane that picked them both up until they crashed together, unable to control themselves. Not this romantic morning, or possibly afternoon, of gentle kisses and exchanged vows. Because that was what they were, that was what this was. A wedding by Detyen terms, if not human. Two weeks ago Iris would have been terrified by that thought, but now there was no other place she wished to be. She would stand by Toran's side forever.

"Don't let me stop you," he said before returning to his onslaught of kisses, painting a track with his lips down her neck.

It made it hard to concentrate, but Iris was determined. He needed to know this, needed to know that she was here with him 100%. Fate had brought them together, but she was choosing to stay. When it came to him, she always would. "Let's start with these." She laid a hand against his naked arm, outlining one of his dark marks. "I like your clan markings," she said. "They make you look a little bit like a cheetah."

"A cheetah?"

"It's a kind of cat, a big one. They're very fast, and they're spotted like you. Or maybe you're like a leopard, another cat. They're very strong, dangerous predators. That's what I knew from the moment I saw you, that you would be ruthless whenever you were opposed. And in your pursuit of something that you wanted. Me. I never thought I would want that, but you've shown me things about myself that I didn't know." She ran her fingers through his hair, tugging on it a bit when he tried to move further down her body. "There will be time for that later," she promised. "Let me talk."

He placed a kiss at the base of her neck before crawling back up her body until they were face-to-face. "You have my full attention," he said. She could feel his full attention pressing hard at the juncture of her thighs, and that was making it even more difficult to concentrate.

"You play dirty," she accused.

"Ruthless, just like you like." They kissed again and it was several minutes before Iris could make herself pull away.

"I like your dedication to your people, and the way you would do anything to protect them. I like that you're smart, and quick, and you don't let yourself get blinded by your pride. I love that you respect me, and that you've accepted my help when I could give it. And that you've saved me when I needed it." Tears pricked the corners of her eyes as she thought of everything Toran had done for her, everything they'd done together. But now was not the time for tears, she didn't want to cry. She placed her hand against his chest and squeezed. "And your muscles aren't bad either," she told him with a grin. "I really don't mind looking at you."

Toran laughed. "I really don't mind looking at *you*," he promised.

"I'm glad that I'm your denya, that out of all of the billions of people in the galaxy it was me. And I'm glad we found each other, even though it seems impossible. You make me believe that anything is within my reach."

His face grew serious and he echoed her vow. "I am glad that you are my denya. You have given me hope and I could ask for nothing more."

Iris cradled her palm against Toran's face and brought his head down until their lips met. She sought him out with her tongue and he opened for her, their breath mingling between them as they devoured one another. Her clothes felt heavy where they pressed against her skin, but when she hooked one leg around Toran's hip she realized she wasn't wearing any pants. He must've removed them, or she had, before they fell asleep. At the moment she didn't care. In fact, she was grateful. One less layer to stand between them.

It was a dance of passion, twisting and tasting and moving together in a rhythm as old as the universe. They came from different species, different planets, but in this moment they were communicating in the most ancient and universal of languages.

Perhaps out of a misplaced sense of chivalry, Toran had worn pants to bed. Iris tried to hook the heel of her foot in the waistband and pull them down, but she wasn't quite flexible or dexterous enough to pull it off.

Toran smiled against her lips and spoke while barely pulling away. "What are you doing?"

"I need you naked. Now."

***

Anything his denya wished, Toran would give to her. And what she asked now was no sacrifice. He shimmied out of his pants and tossed them somewhere across the room, not caring where they landed. That was a problem for later; for now his denya deserved his full attention. She lay on the bed in her shirt and underwear, staring at him while biting her swollen lower lip. Her hair was fanned out against the pillow, just the way he told her that he liked it earlier. She was a picture of seductive beauty, a goddess whose altar he would worship at forever.

He knelt on the bed, the soft mattress sinking under his knees, and stalked forward until his hands found the hem of her shirt. "Up," he demanded, tugging on the fabric. Iris came with no resistance and in a moment, she was naked before him except for the flimsy scrap of her panties. Toran freed his claws and grinned at her. "I promised I would do this," he said. He held up his hand and waited for her nod of consent. When she gave it, his chest heated with the fire of the sun and the surety that this woman was right for him. He moved carefully, and in two flicks of his wrists her panties fell away, leaving her exposed to the warm air of the room.

"That'll be expensive if it becomes a habit," she teased, linking her arm around his neck, heedless of his claws, trusting him not to harm her.

Toran felt more powerful than he did behind the las cannon on a battlefield. The trust his mate placed in him could bring him to his knees, and raise him higher than he'd ever flown before. He'd never known that a person could have such power over him, that he would want someone to have that power. But she held his heart in her hands, and he gladly gave it to her. "I don't worry about cost when it comes to your pleasure," he said. "But I will never do anything that you don't like."

"I don't know how you're real," she said. She pressed against him, her soft breasts pillows against his hard muscles. There was no room for modesty or shame with them, this joining was natural and a long time coming. And while he knew that one day he would ask his mate to sit around naked in their quarters just so he could look at her, today was not that day.

"It doesn't matter how. All that matters is that I'm yours, and you're mine." Fate had smiled on them and the last thing Toran wanted to do was question the blessing. He dipped his head down to capture his mate's lips and after that, no words were needed.

His hands explored her, teasing her soft places until Iris moaned and writhed beneath him, arching closer as if any air between them was an affront to their union. Desire pulsed hard in Toran's veins and he bit back an animalistic growl when Iris shivered. Her hand found his cock and Toran let out a curse as she stroked him. He could feel his eyes flaring red as he was consumed by emotion, by the need to claim his mate in the most primal of ways.

Every second since their first meeting had been leading to this moment, and they had already denied themselves for so long.

His fingers found her hot and wet and when he pressed inside of her, Iris gasped. The sound pulled a smile from Toran's mouth and he captured her mouth in another kiss, stealing the noises she was making and making them his own. He added another finger and saw Iris squeeze her eyes shut from the sensual invasion. She rode his hand, moving in time with him.

After several moments, her eyes snapped open and she gripped his bicep hard enough to bruise. "Now," she demanded.

"Anything for you, denya." It came out guttural, barely understandable, but they were beyond the need for words.

Toran pulled his fingers out and stroked his cock once, lining himself up with her entrance. He sank in deep, his eyes falling closed as he groaned out. She was tight and hot and perfect. He held himself over her, covering her body with his own, shielding her from the rest of the world in their own little paradise of home.

And then they moved.

As she adjusted around him, her hips arched and Toran sank deeper, gnashing his teeth to keep from yelling out. He wanted her now, he wanted her forever, he was hers completely as the bond circled around them and tied them together from heart to heart.

But it wasn't enough, not yet.

They moved together in an ancient and universal ritual, taking their pleasure from one another and giving it back tenfold. Sweat poured off of Toran and it was sensual torture to keep himself from spilling. But not before his mate, not until she found her peak.

And then she was gasping under him, rippling around him and calling out his name as she sank into the grasp of her orgasm. Toran plunged deep, emptying himself with a growl and letting his body cover her. Without thought, his lips landed over her shoulder and he opened his mouth, biting down and marking her in the way of the ancients, claiming her primally as his own as the bond shot out from his body and latched onto her soul, tethering them together for all eternity.

Several minutes passed as their breathing evened out and they separated, but didn't fall far from one another. Iris burrowed into his side and Toran slung an arm over her shoulders.

"Holy... wow," Iris finally breathed out, sounding dazed.

"Wow," Toran echoed. What else was there to say?

Chapter Eighteen

Sierra wished that Raze was beside her as she parked her car in the garage under her father's building. But the relationship between the two men was still a bit rocky. If she had thought that her father took issue with her career as a spy, it was nothing compared to showing up on his doorstep with an alien warrior for a mate. Especially since she and Raze had only known each other for two weeks. But only time could mend that relationship, and she was strangely confident that things would turn out all right. Maybe it was that she had someone a hundred percent in her corner, or maybe she'd learned something from the last mission. She would give her father time to come around on Raze, and she hoped that what she was about to do wasn't a giant mistake.

The walk from the garage to his apartment went by far too quickly. A part of Sierra wanted to linger in the hall, but she didn't want to be seen by any potential enemy. Not that it was likely. She doubted Yormas or his Oscavian allies were tapped into the security feed to the hallway of her father's building, but years of spy work had made her paranoid and she was knocking on her dad's door before she could think of an excuse to leave.

It was late afternoon, and many people were still at work, but her father often left the office early on Thursdays. When he opened the door to her it was clear this one was no different. Her father gave her a questioning look but stepped back to let her inside and closed the door behind her silently. He led her further into the apartment and Sierra glanced around. Nothing had changed since the dinner a few weeks ago, before she left on her mission to rescue the twelve women abducted by a group of pirates and slavers working for a mysterious Oscavian. And yet since that night her entire life had been turned upside down.

"Would you like something to drink? A snack?" her dad asked. He entered his kitchen and grabbed two glasses from one of his cabinets.

Sierra slid onto one of the stools tucked into his counter and crossed her arms on the cool slab. "I'll take a water," she said.

He slid a glass over and she took a sip. They remained there silently for several more moments, drinking quietly, tension thick in the air. Her father broke first. "I had to call in quite a few favors to get your friend out of lockup," he said evenly. "I can't do much more if you refuse to give me any information." He chose his words carefully, as if he didn't trust her not to lie. It hurt a little, but Sierra supposed that she deserved it. She'd been keeping many secrets.

"There's a lot more going on than you know," she began. "And we need your help." And so Sierra explained everything, heedless of the fact that her mission to Fenryr 1 was highly classified. As a general, her father had the level of classification needed to hear the details, but she didn't have the permission to share them. With the fate of Earth in the balance, that didn't matter to her.

His expression barely changed as she told him the conditions they'd encountered on Fenryr 1, the state of the women, the battle with the Oscavians, the history of the Detyens, all of it. When she got to the part about breaking into Ambassador Yormas's quarters, he put his head in his hand and sighed, but let her continue speaking. And when she was done, her father looked at her for a long minute before draining his water like it was something much stronger.

"If you were under my command..." He shook his head and squeezed his eyes shut, grimacing. "*Thank God* you aren't under my command."

"This isn't the only reason it's a good thing you're not my commander," Sierra couldn't help but say with a smile. "So can you help us?" Despite their differences, she had never doubted that her father would be there for her. But this was different than anything else, far more risky, and if it went wrong his reputation would be ruined and he could easily be sent to prison. Or worse.

But her father didn't hesitate. "Do you really think that I didn't start looking into this the second you called last time?"

Sierra grinned. "I think it's your fault that I'm as curious as I am."

He glared, but it didn't have any heat. "Don't blame me for your career path."

Sierra rolled her eyes, and for the first time his comments on her career felt more like teasing than censure. "I'm good at my job. Hopefully they realize it and give it back to me." Then again, if Earth were destroyed it would be a little difficult to work for the Sol Intelligence Agency.

"You did the right thing," her father shocked her by saying. If she weren't already sitting on the stool, she would've had to brace herself against the counter to keep from falling over. But rather than descend into a tearful hug of acceptance, her father straightened and placed his glass in the sink. "The ambassador left Gamma Station not long after placing his complaint about your friends. However, he didn't return to Earth. He filed a travel plan that stated his intention to venture out to Mars. But I called a friend on that station, and the ambassador has yet to show. He's in the wind."

Sierra had feared that would happen, but her father's words confirmed that asking for his help had been the right call. "We need to find Yormas before he can do anything to destroy the planet."

"We will," her father promised. And for the first time in a long time they were on the same page.

***

The morning had begun with lingering kisses and smiles. Iris's body was still sore in all the right places, and she could feel the imprint of Toran's fingers against her skin, even if he was no longer in her home. They had planned to spend the day together, but when his men called with more questions about their time on Gamma Station, she'd sent her mate away. Spending the day in bed was a fantasy that would have to wait until the immediate danger was out of the way.

She wouldn't begrudge Toran his duty, and she would expect him to give her the same respect. That was how healthy relationships worked, or so she heard. And she was determined to make this thing between them last forever.

But after Toran took off, the bed felt cold and her plan to sleep in suddenly didn't sound so smart. She forced herself out of bed with a groan and took a look around the house. Dust had settled on the tables and shelves, and the time away at Gamma Station had given the entire place a slightly abandoned feel. Nothing a little cleaning couldn't fix.

Iris put on her raggedy clothes and got to work. Before she knew it, an hour had gone by, and she had only thought of checking in on Toran a half a dozen times. It was like she could feel him burrowed in her chest. She placed a hand just a bit under her heart and rubbed the tender skin there. Was this the denya bond? If she closed her eyes and concentrated, she could feel it tug her in the direction of his quarters. If she followed it, she would find him there.

Comfort and warmth pulsed through her and Iris couldn't help but smile. She concentrated, thinking hard about what it felt like to be held safely in Toran's arms, and then she sent the thought away, trailing down the bond towards her mate.

Her communicator rang and Iris's head snapped towards the view screen. She ran her fingers through her hair and pushed herself up from where she'd been kneeling on the floor. A quick glance around showed that the room behind her was perfectly clean, which made her relieved when she saw that the call was coming from Selma. Iris took a deep breath, suddenly fearful of what her boss would have to say.

She engaged the call and kept her expression calm, greeting the older woman with a smile.

Selma didn't return the expression, and Iris's heart sank. She supposed that was answer enough for where this discussion would be going. And while she was disappointed, she wasn't crushed, not like she would've been before Toran, before the adventures of the last few weeks.

"I see you're keeping busy," said Selma with a nod to the cleaning products sitting on the table behind Iris.

"I had the time on my hands," Iris replied.

"This call is a courtesy," Selma warned. "I wanted you to know that the investigation into the Detyens has concluded. Your initial findings were very helpful, and I'm sure you'll soon hear from them that we've determined that they posed no threat to the planet."

"That is good to hear." Iris had hoped that any suspicion that her actions had raised wouldn't reflect poorly on her mate, and she was glad to hear that it hadn't.

"That's not the reason I'm calling," Selma continued.

Iris nodded. "I figured."

"You, too, have been cleared of all wrongdoing. You were one of my favorites, Iris." Selma shook her head sadly. "But your contract with the SDA has been terminated. We thank you for the work that you've done for us, but we will no longer need your services."

That was what Iris had expected, and a strange sense of freedom suffused her. She had loved her job, had loved that it allowed her to protect her planet in her own little way. But it was time to move on from that, and she was capable of greater things. "Thank you for telling me yourself," she finally said. "I learned a lot from you."

"Is it worth it?" Selma surprised her by asking.

Iris couldn't help but smile. "It is." There was nothing more to say and they disengaged the call. Iris thought about getting in touch with Toran and letting him know what had happened, but he would be coming back soon enough and she didn't need to interrupt him about something like this. As soon as she told him about how she'd gotten out of detainment, they'd both known that she likely wouldn't keep her job.

Instead, she glanced at her food processor as her stomach rumbled, but there was nothing listed in her available ingredients that sounded appetizing. Iris changed her clothes and was out the door in a matter of minutes, walking down the street towards one of her favorite little cafés and soaking up the bright sun.

An unfortunately familiar light head of hair caught her eye, and Iris ducked into a small alleyway before Dan could see her. What was he doing here? She'd made it clear that she wanted nothing to do with him, and she doubted his presence by her house was a coincidence. Should she hang back to make sure that he didn't break in again? Or was it wiser to stay outside, so he didn't know where she was?

A vehicle pulled to a stop at the end of the alley and unease raced down Iris's spine. Had Dan planned something? Did he have accomplices? No one was getting out of the vehicle, and she glanced down the alley, contemplating making a run for it. But a high fence at the other end cut off her exit.

She was being paranoid. Vehicles stopped all the time, and she had no reason to think that Dan was about to kidnap her or something. He was a sleazebag, and a little violent, but not like that. Iris took a deep breath and started walking towards the car. Once she was back on the main street, she would be able to breathe easier. And if Dan was out there and he saw her, she would live. She could handle another encounter with him. She just didn't want to.

But as she got closer to the vehicle, she noticed the darkly tinted windows, and her unease iced into fear. Someone could force her into that vehicle and no one would see her struggle. No, she mentally shook her head, she was just being paranoid.

When she could practically reach out and touch one of the windows, the door flashed open and a tall man with purple skin and a sinister smile stepped out. Varrow.

She never thought she would've wished for Dan.

Iris tried to run, but a second Oscavian stepped behind her and placed something against her neck, and between one breath and the next she was out cold.

Chapter Nineteen

Something felt off all morning, but Toran convinced himself that it had to do with the newly minted denya bond. His body needed time to adjust to the connection that now thrummed between him and Iris, and it wasn't strange to feel a mild sense of discomfort. He kept repeating that reasoning to himself, and if Raze were there, he probably would have asked him to confirm that Toran's feelings were right.

But only Kayde and Dryce were at this meeting and neither would be any help, for completely different reasons.

As lunchtime rolled around, Toran finally gave in to the anxiety and tried to give Iris a call. When she didn't answer, the unease deepened into something stronger. He called again and there was still no answer. While it was possible that she was sleeping or in the bathroom or simply didn't hear the chime of the communicator, he couldn't make his nerves believe that. So Toran called the meeting to a close and promised his men that he would get in touch later. Neither questioned why he was leaving so soon, and when Dryce didn't make a joke about Toran sneaking off to join his mate, Toran realized that the younger man had picked up on Toran's unease.

Kayde said nothing, but that was expected. Toran was grateful for it. Before the journey to Fenryr 1, Kayde had shown some signs of instability, but despite all of the changes and uncertainty of the last several weeks, the soulless Detyen seem to be holding steady.

Traffic was dense on the drive back to Iris's house, and Toran grit his teeth the entire time, tempted to run over some of the smaller vehicles that wouldn't get out of his way. It was only a little after noon when he parked his vehicle, and as he approached the front door something still felt off.

Toran entered the silent house and immediately knew that Iris wasn't there. The door slammed shut behind him, but he barely heard it. Nothing was out of place, in fact the entire dwelling gleamed with cleaning polish and hard work. He hadn't noticed that it was particularly messy the night before, but Iris had clearly used her time to make the place immaculate. He didn't want to consider that someone might have come in, harmed his mate, and then cleaned the place to destroy the evidence.

He walked through each of the rooms, trying to convince himself that everything was okay. Iris hadn't mentioned the need to leave, but this was her neighborhood and she knew it well. She wouldn't feel in any danger if she needed to head to the store or one of the restaurants down the way. There was no note, but if she had no reason to expect him back this early then she might not have left one.

Toran checked his communicator again and saw no messages from Iris or from anyone else. He tried to give her another call, but she didn't answer. Where was she?

He paced back and forth in the living room, balling his hands into fists and clenching his jaw to keep from screaming in frustration. He had not just claimed her only to lose her immediately, he had to find her and make sure that she was okay. He looked back at his communicator and tapped his finger against the screen idly, contemplating whether or not he should call in the cavalry. His team, along with Sierra and Quinn, would come running the moment he called. Sierra had plenty of friends in the city, including Mindy and Jo, her partners for the mission to Fenryr 1, and he could have a huge search party at his beck and call in less than an hour.

But if this was just nerves, if he was overreacting, he'd never hear the end of it. It wasn't just his pride that had him putting his communicator back in his pocket. He and his team were in the middle of a crisis, and they had to trust his judgment.

Which meant he had to give it a little while and try to find Iris himself before he called for any help. She was fine, he told himself again, she had to be.

He took a steadying breath and headed for the door. He'd look in the shops down the street and in the restaurants, and if he didn't find her there he would ask around. And if he didn't find her *then*, he'd call his friends. But when he opened the door, a scrawny male figure was retreating at a quick pace, trying to dodge behind one of the plants in front of Iris's house, as if the spindly branches would be enough to hide him.

Toran was on the man in seconds, grabbing his arm and tackling him to the ground, his knee lodged firmly in the stranger's back. "Who are you? What are you doing here?"

The man sputtered and then groaned. "Give her back, or I'll call the police!"

"Where's Iris? Who are you?" His claws threatened to burst out of his skin, but Toran held himself in check. If his claws came out there was no telling what damage he would do to this guy, whoever he was.

"I'm her boyfriend! And you alien shitheads can't have her!"

***

The pain in Iris's head was worse than the hangover she had the first and last night that she got ragingly drunk. Her mouth tasted of cotton and vomit and when she turned to her side she curled into a ball and couldn't drag in a deep breath due the sharp pain in her ribs. Her mind was cloudy and she tried to think of how she'd gotten here. Hadn't she just been going to get lunch? Where was Toran? Was he okay?

She tried to sit, but it hurt too much and she couldn't quiet the moan of pain that escaped from her lips.

"You're awake," said a cold voice that she could almost recognize. He sounded a bit surprised.

Iris tightened further into her ball, as if she could make herself small enough to disappear and escape from wherever she'd been taken. She cracked her eyes open and the bright light of the room nearly blinded her. She flinched and slammed her eyes shut again, but even the afterimages were enough to make her headache worse. What had she been given? How long had she been out? The only way to get answers to those questions would be to talk to the man behind her, but that seemed like a very bad idea. Whatever he wanted to do to her, it couldn't be good.

"Pretending to sleep will do you no good," he warned. "I don't need you to be awake for what I plan to do, but it's just that much more fun."

A wave of dread washed over her, temporarily dispelling some of the pain in her head. She knew that voice. It wasn't the ambassador, but his Oscavian friend, Varrow. She opened her eyes slowly this time and squinted against the light. After a moment, Iris forced herself to turn over to get a good look at the man and the room he was keeping her in. It was bigger than a cell, but not as big as her room at home. She was laying on the floor near one of the walls, but there was a gurney sitting in the middle of the room, with a tray beside it. Varrow stood next to the bed, sorting through instruments on the tray.

Iris remembered that he had spoken of experiments performed on people. Was she about to be one of those victims? Or was this just recreational torture? She pondered that with an odd sort of detachment. She'd been ready to snap, given all of the trauma of the last few days, and she had been certain that when she did she would be reduced to a screaming, crying mess. But it hurt too much to cry right now, and she didn't want to give him the satisfaction of the scream. Not if she could help it.

"How did you find me?" Her voice came out a raspy whisper, her vocal cords practically shredded.

Varrow paused and looked over his shoulder towards her. "Your address was listed in your personnel file, along with all of your communicator information. It wasn't difficult to place a tracker."

"My personnel file?" SDA documents like that were highly protected, and if he had access to those, there was no telling what other information Varrow or his allies could obtain.

"You shouldn't sound so surprised. Any information written down or transmitted can be gathered. That's basic intelligence knowledge. Then again, spy work isn't your forte." He turned back to his work on the tray, dismissing her like she wasn't a threat.

Iris wasn't even tied up, and she hated that he was right. She struggled to a sitting position and had to stop, gasping for breath as another wave of pain washed over her. Moving slowly, mostly because she was trying to obscure her movements, she lifted the edge of her shirt and saw an ugly purple bruise blooming along her ribs. That would explain the pain and difficulty to breathe. But she hadn't gotten that from whatever drug they'd given her.

"You beat me?" She didn't mean to ask it, but she was having trouble keeping control of her thoughts.

Varrow's shoulders lifted, as if he were huffing out a laugh. "My brother is the scientist in the family. I've spent plenty of time in his lab, and you wouldn't believe the pain that he can extract from his subjects. But he has always needed the trappings. As for me, torture has always had its uses."

The blood in Iris's veins ran cold and ice froze along her spine. *Toran, where are you?* She was thankful that he didn't seem to be here, thankful he was out of Varrow's grasp. But she didn't know how she was going to get out of this one, and no matter what happened, it was going to hurt.

***

Toran's hand flashed out and gripped the back of the man's neck, squeezing hard enough to make a pathetic sound escape his throat. Boyfriend? Not a chance. But with those ill-chosen words, Toran knew exactly who he was talking to. "You're Dan, aren't you? Give me one good reason I shouldn't leave you bleeding?" The last bit came out a growl. He didn't know everything that Dan had done to his mate, but he knew enough, and he was already on the edge of violence.

"Wait!" cried Dan. "Wait! I didn't hurt her, I swear it." His arms shot out in front of him, palms flat against the short grass. He jerked under Toran, but didn't try to escape. It was obvious to both of them that Toran wasn't going to let him go.

"Talk," Toran demanded.

Dan sucked in an unsteady breath. "I was coming here to see if anything was wrong. She didn't look like she wanted to get into that van. Iris is a lot of things, you know. But she ain't no alien-fucking slut."

Toran dug his knee in deeper to where it was holding Dan down until the other man yelped; the human was lucky Toran hadn't done worse. "Just facts, no commentary."

"Who the hell are you anyway?" Dan got brave enough to ask. "I shouldn't be telling you shit."

"What van? Where is she?"

"I don't know! I swear." He sounded just honest enough that Toran was willing to believe him.

"Tell me what you saw," he demanded again.

"Let me up and I will," Dan countered.

Toran wasn't about to do that. The minute he let go, he knew Dan would bolt. "Talk." He raised his knee just enough so that Dan might not need to whimper in pain, but not enough that he could escape.

The fight went out of the man and he slumped on the grass under Toran. "Fine, whatever. Some big purple dudes surrounded her and shoved her into a white van. It headed north. That's all I saw."

Toran considered his options. Dan was a liar, and he had treated Iris terribly, but would he stoop to kidnapping? And would he blame aliens for it? Was he a good enough actor to pull it off? From the way he was trembling under Toran, the answer was no. And if he'd kidnapped Iris, the pathetic human had no reason to come back to her house like he had. With regret, Toran lifted his knee off of the shithead and removed his hand from his neck. Dan was up in a flash and running, but Toran didn't bother to chase him. He wouldn't offer any more help, that much was obvious.

But now Toran knew that his worry, his anxiety, was well-founded. He pulled out his communicator to get a hold of his team. It was time to get his mate back.

***

She tried to struggle as Varrow forced her from the ground up onto the gurney. But it was no use. Between her injuries and his strength she couldn't manage to fight back. In a matter of minutes, she was strapped down and completely at his mercy. She wished for the oblivion of unconsciousness; at least she couldn't feel the pain then.

"I tried to tell my friend that he was not cautious enough," Varrow said conversationally as he ran his hand over the assortment of instruments he could use on her. "But his arrogance, and your bumbling, have cost us years of work. And then he left me here to clean up the pieces. Not that I would want to go back to that waste of the planet he calls home." His smile sent a shiver down Iris's spine as he finally selected an instrument. It was a thick cylinder with a lighted tip at one end, and Iris had no idea what it was supposed to do. It didn't look like a laser or scalpel, but she had no doubt that it could cause a lot of pain or damage or both.

"So you just do what he tells you?" she asked, scrambling for a reason to keep him talking. If he was talking, she hoped he might hold off on the torturing.

Varrow rolled the cylinder between his fingers and glared at her. "I'm not a minion."

"You're his partner?" If he was going to talk, she had to survive this. She had to get this information to Toran, she had to see her mate again.

The Oscavian shrugged. "If you want to call it that. Are you trying to get me to spill the master plan?" He grinned. "Keep me talking until your friends can rescue you? They won't find you."

"That means we have more time to talk, doesn't it?" Her hope was running out but Iris couldn't give up.

Varrow tipped back his head and laughed. "Oh, I wish I had more time with you. I can tell you would be a fun one. You're not too clever, but you aren't dumb. It's people like you who always last the longest, you never know when to give up hope."

She already felt low on hope, but she wasn't about to tell Varrow that. Did Toran know she was already missing? Had anyone seen her get taken? "Why are you working with him? Or why were you?" She knew whatever was happening was Yormas's idea, he'd done it before. Why would an Oscavian be involved?

"Money. Power. Fun, take your pick." Varrow twirled the device between his fingers and Iris's eyes couldn't help but follow it. He saw where her attention was locked and tossed the device in the air, catching it before could fall to the floor. "Now let's play a little game, would you like that?"

She really wouldn't, but Iris kept quiet.

"I love this little shocker, it's been one of my favorite toys for years." He held it up and gave the dark metal a quick kiss. "But you're in luck, this one needs to be recharged between uses. So I offer you a deal. For every shot you take without passing out, you get one question. And I'll even answer truthfully. What do you say?"

Iris glared at him, but her mind raced. She needed answers to her questions, and it wasn't like she was going to get out of here anytime soon. She gritted her teeth and ground out, "Bring it on."

Chapter Twenty

Everything was pain, and it took Iris several moments to realize that the shocker had been turned off. She panted and tried to curl to her side, but the restraints at her wrists and ankles kept her in place. Had the room somehow gotten brighter? She'd never been tortured before, had never imagined that it would feel like this. She knew pain, she could manage pain, but the helplessness was the worst part. There was no way to escape it, no way to stop it, her only choice was to endure.

Something clattered down beside her, and Iris jerked her head to see Varrow lowering the shocker to the table. He clapped his hands together in genuine glee. "Oh, very good. I didn't expect you to make it through that first one."

"Will it—" Iris bit back the question, her mind clearing enough to remember the game he wanted to play. What could she ask? What would be useful? Her mind was all fuzz and mud and pain, and stringing two thoughts together was way harder than it should've been. "Is Yormas working alone?"

Varrow sighed, and though she couldn't see him she could tell he was disappointed. "You already know that he's working with me."

"That's not what I meant," she tried to explain. "Is he working on behalf of his government? Or for his own means?"

Varrow clicked his tongue. "That's not what you asked, and you only get one question. Do better."

Iris wanted to cry at the unfairness of it all, but she doubted her torturer would show any pity. Her eyes were laser focused on the torture tray beside her, counting down the seconds until he picked the shocker back up and started up on round two. She didn't know how she stayed conscious through the last one; it all blurred into one mass of pain and screaming, and if he'd said anything to her while the voltage ran through her body, she couldn't remember. But she must've stayed awake, and she would need to do it again, more than once, if she was going to make any use of what was being done to her. She might be able to live with herself, to live with the nightmares this was sure to give her, if she could convince herself that it was all done for a purpose.

She sucked in a deep breath and waited for Varrow to make his move. She wasn't going to argue, wasn't going to beg, not until she couldn't stop herself from holding the pleas back.

Varrow picked up the shocker and Iris's entire body went taut with terrified anticipation. The Oscavian sighed and looked at her for several seconds. Iris jerked her head towards him so she could glare straight at him, rather than at his table of horrors. "He's not working alone," Varrow offered. "That's the last freebie you get, so be grateful for it."

She wasn't about to thank him for it. Not when the bastard was practically vibrating with delight at the opportunity to extract pain from her. "They're going to kill you," she warned him. "The second you touched me, you signed your death warrant." Even if she didn't make it that long, Iris was sure of it. Toran would tear the world apart to find her, and he'd destroy it to get his revenge, if it came to that.

"You're so sure?" Varrow asked, seemingly unconcerned with the threat.

"Yes."

"Then isn't it in my best interest to kill you quick and make my escape?" He said it like it was a joke, but Iris's stomach curdled at the thought.

Before Iris quite realized what he was doing, Varrow scooped up the shocker and jammed it against her neck, activating the power switch in a blaze of pain. Everything around her went white as she screamed. Time stretched between the seconds, and while she tried to gasp in breaths, her heartbeat was so fast that it hurt her lungs to take in any air. Her fingers gripped the leathery cover of the gurney under her and she tried to ride, tried to escape the pain, but there was no getting away.

As suddenly as it began, it ended. Iris heard a curse, as she was trying to come back to her own mind, and by the time conscious thought returned the Oscavian had disappeared out the door.

She gulped down steadying breaths as her heart rate returned to something like normal. Her entire body was covered in sweat and the room had not seemed cold at first, but she was starting to shiver, whether from the temperature or shock she didn't know.

Where was Varrow? Why had he left like that? She needed to get a look around, but all of her muscles were shaky and she couldn't force herself to turn her head. *Okay, a five second break. You can do this.* She counted down the seconds and when she got to zero she still didn't move. Five seconds wasn't nearly long enough to recover. But Varrow could get back at any minute, and she needed to take this unexpected reprieve and use it to her advantage.

With a grunt, Iris turned her head and confirmed that she was alone in the room. She was still strapped to the gurney, but in his haste to leave, Varrow had upset the surgical tray beside her bed. Out of desperation she tried to flex her fingers far enough to reach for something, *anything*, but it was too far. She took a deep breath and tried not to panic. Her legs flexed, and her hips came off the gurney, but the straps were too tight and she couldn't wriggle free.

As her hips slammed back down onto the gurney, the surgical tray rocked with the motion. A small cylindrical object, possibly a laser scalpel, rolled near the edge, and almost fell off. It was so close that Iris could practically taste it, but it was still out of reach of her fingers and when she reared up, trying to reach for it with her head, she couldn't quite close the distance. Iris plunked down again and the scalpel moved some more, rolling even closer towards her.

She stopped breathing, holding herself completely still, afraid that any movement might send it rolling away. It was so close her fingers could practically brush it. There was a little give in the bindings at her wrist, allowing her to slide the binding cuff closer to her elbow to give her room to reach. She just needed a few more centimeters and she would have it.

Iris lifted her hips up off the gurney again and let them drop and the scalpel rolled. Her fingers brushed against it and she had to bite back a yelp of victory. She wasn't free yet, not even close. Varrow could be back at any moment. But now she had a weapon, and now she wasn't helpless. She had to get out of here before he could realize she was gone.

***

Each second that ticked by without a lead on Iris was a torture that Toran had never before known. The information that Dan had given him was solid, but it took more than an hour to find a way to tap into the security feeds and find identifying information on the vehicle. He felt like he was doing nothing while an algorithm trolled through the city's feeds, following the van back to its home base.

Raze had no words of comfort to offer him, knowing how awful it would be to lose his mate. Kayde was silent as always. Dryce paced back and forth in the center of Iris's almost unnaturally clean apartment, the only one of the four Detyens letting his feelings show.

"I've got it!" Sierra cried, looking up from the tablet she'd been using to track the truck. "They're in Arlington." She engaged the hollow display and pointed to an old brick building on the 3-D map.

"Let's go," Toran said, holding onto his composure by a thread.

Kayde held up a hand. "We don't know what we're facing. If we charge in without more intel, we could be walking into an ambush." His voice was flat and emotionless and Toran wanted to punch the sedate look off his face.

"They have my mate," he said, grinding out each word. "I'm not waiting another minute. Stay here if you want." Toran took off, pressing a hand against the blaster in its holster on his side and stomping towards the vehicle that his men had taken to the apartment. He let the door slam behind him, and a moment later it opened again as everyone rushed out of the apartment.

"Don't think for a second we're letting you go in there alone," said Raze.

Toran reached for the driver's door, but Sierra placed a hand on his arm and nodded towards the back seat. "I know this city better than any of you," she said. "Let me drive, we'll get there faster."

He wanted to control the driver's seat, but he knew Sierra was right. This wasn't his city, wasn't his planet. If he got lost than there was no one to save Iris. He got into the backseat without a fight.

As soon as the vehicle started moving, Sierra engaged the call display and contacted Quinn, who was waiting back at the Detyen's quarters. "Do you have news?" the woman demanded as soon as the call connected.

"Yes," Sierra confirmed. She told Quinn everything they knew. "Get in touch with Mindy and Jo," she said, referring to two of her partners from the SIA. They'd been instrumental in liberating the women from Fenryr 1, and saving the lives of Toran, Raze, and Kayde. Due to their actions, they'd been suspended along with Sierra. But unlike Sierra they didn't have a close connection to the Detyens, and they hadn't been called in to help with the investigation into Yormas of Wreet. Now that they needed backup, though, the two women were perfectly placed to help.

"I'll call them," Quinn promised. "What about the police? Or your dad?"

Sierra was silent as she contemplated, but she finally said, "Don't call my dad. If I haven't called you back in an hour, or if Mindy and Jo say to do it, call the cops. But give us time to get our girl out. We don't want to be hampered by any rules."

A moment stretched for several beats before Quinn responded. "Okay. Good luck." They ended the call and made the rest of the drive in a tense silence.

Toran tried to keep his thoughts focused, but the denya bond pulsed strong in him and he could feel Iris's fear and the echoes of her pain. Something was being done to her, something very bad, and his mind reeled as he tried not to imagine what. If he was too focused on the horrors being inflicted upon his mate, he would be useless as a soldier, unable to focus enough to do what needed to be done.

He clung to whatever calm he could and tried to send it through the bond, tried in this way to let Iris know that they were coming, that she only needed to last a little bit longer until she would be safe, until he would destroy the people who tried to harm her. But her fear spiked and Toran's claws burst out a moment before he ripped up the leather of the seat he was sitting on.

"You need to calm down," Raze said from where he sat in the front seat. His entire body was twisted around as he glared at Toran.

"How can you expect me to remain calm?" Toran practically yelled. He could feel Dryce flinch beside him, and Kayde was a silent statue on his bench in the back.

"I expect it because you are our leader and your mate needs you." If they'd been any closer, he knew Raze would have clutched the front of his shirt and held him immobile until he was sure that Toran understood. Luckily Toran was just out of reach.

"She can count on me," he promised.

"She better," Sierra said, pulling the car to a stop. "We're here."

***

Iris almost sawed her hand off the second the laser scalpel fell into her fingers. It burned a line of fire across the edge of her palm, but she was able to turn off the laser almost as soon as it ignited. She bit her lip to keep from crying out in case Varrow was anywhere nearby and manipulated the device so the laser was pointed out and away from her body. It took her a few minutes to figure out the best way to cut herself out of her bindings, but with careful contortions she was able to slice through the chain holding one of the cuffs to the side the gurney.

Once one hand was free, everything became a lot easier. Iris peeled out the second cuff and then freed her legs, but when she swung to the side of the gurney and tried to stand, the room went wobbly. She wanted to run away, wanted to find a way out of this place, but she couldn't do that if she couldn't walk. A few deep breaths made things much better and she barely swayed by the time she made it to the door.

Her hand froze on the handle as she realized that she had no idea who was out in the hall. It could be empty, or it could be crawling with guards. All she had was a laser scalpel, and while that weapon was certainly deadly, it was no match for a blaster. One shot and she'd go down, and she wasn't sure she'd be getting back up. Varrow didn't strike her as the kind of man who made the same mistake twice.

What would her mate do? How would Toran get out of the situation? As soon as she thought it, she knew it was a useless path to travel down. She wasn't Toran, she didn't have his training. He might bust out of the room, claws bared and ready for the fight. Iris knew how to throw a punch, but this wasn't the boxing ring at her gym, there would be no tapping out here.

But she couldn't just give up. If she stayed in this room, she'd end up strapped back to the gurney or worse as Varrow played with her. He'd give her no more answers, and she couldn't trust that anything he told her was truthful. She couldn't just wait for Toran to rescue her. She had faith that her mate was coming, but it would take him time to find her, time she couldn't afford to lose.

Mind made up, Iris tested the handle and found the door locked. Of course it was. She didn't let frustration get to her, remembering a trick she'd once seen on a media show. She glanced down at the laser scalpel in her hand before kneeling beside the door and using it to overheat the locking mechanism. Seconds ticked by, then a minute; the scalpel grew hot in her hand and the smell of frying metal burned her nose. Maybe she shouldn't have been relying on a media program to find a way to escape from the clutches of the sinister alien. But just as doubt started to assail her, the light on the lock went out and something in the door clicked.

She tested the handle and winced as her hand brushed hot metal. But the door opened and Iris's pain was soon forgotten. She listened carefully before sticking her head out, trying to figure out if anyone was waiting in the hall. But it was empty. Varrow had at least one accomplice; she remembered he'd captured her with one other person. He'd had more guards on Gamma Station, but she had no idea if they were with him now.

Every step she took tested her nerves, but Iris was relieved to see that she was in some sort of house, not a place designed to hold people captive. It might even be Varrow's house, she had no way to know. There was a fine layer of dust on the floor, and everything smelled a bit musty, as if the place hadn't been used in a while. A board creaked underfoot and Iris froze before she made herself move again. She felt too exposed as she walked down the hall, and she had to clench her fists to keep them from shaking.

A commotion somewhere ahead of her caught her attention. Fighting, that was what she was hearing. Every instinct told her to turn around and find another way out, but she forced her feet forward. The denya bond thrummed within her and she knew that her mate was near. The heavy ozone scent of blaster fire was in the air, and Iris moved carefully, afraid of being struck by a stray shot.

She came to a staircase and the sounds of fighting grew even louder. That was why no one was upstairs, they were too busy fighting off the intruders to guard her. Maybe that was why Varrow had left her alone.

With cautious steps, Iris descended, staying low and hoping the railing would do something to obscure her movement. Varrow, along with three of his guards, faced off against Toran and his team. She didn't know how many people Toran had brought with him, she couldn't quite make them all out.

If she had a blaster, her position would be perfect—she could've taken Varrow out from behind before he realized she was there. No one, not even her mate had spotted her yet. But all she had was the damn laser scalpel and she would need to get close to somebody before that was any use.

Two of the guards went down at almost the exact same time. Rather than stay and fight, Varrow left his man and retreated towards the stairs. Iris tried to scramble up, tried to get out of his path, but he was on her before she'd gone up two steps.

Varrow stared at her in shock, but his instincts must've kicked in. He grabbed her around the neck and spun around, holding her tightly and placing a blaster to her temple. "Put down your weapons or she's dead," he called to the fighting men below. He wasn't quick enough to save his third guard, who went down as Varrow was making his escape.

The fighting stopped. She met Toran's eyes and offered a weak smile. She expected anger, but she saw relief in his expression. She understood. Things might've been bad, but they were alive, and they could see each other. Even if this was the end, they were going out together.

Varrow forced her down the steps and she could see that Toran had Raze, Dryce, Kayde, and Sierra with him. Kayde had fallen to blaster fire and was propped up against one of the walls, clutching his shoulder. He was conscious, but was making no effort to get up. Toran slowly lowered his blaster towards the ground and the rest of his team followed suit. They couldn't take out Varrow when he was using her as a human shield.

"Let her go," Toran demanded. There was no quiver in his voice, nothing to give away his anger other than his flashing red eyes.

The Oscavian actually laughed, and Iris's body jerked as his chest bumped against her. "We both know that's not happening." He scraped the side of her head with his blaster and moved it down to rest the barrel against her neck.

The scalpel was heavy in Iris's hand, and she wasn't sure if it was pointed at him or not. Even if she hit him fatally, he'd be able to get off a shot. And with the blaster pointed point-blank at her neck, it just might kill her. She looked at Toran for strength, for some sign of what she should do. "They'll let you go if you don't hurt me," she tried to bargain with Varrow. "Just get to the door and no one will chase after you."

He shuffled his grip again and she tensed as the blaster dug further into her skin; it would leave a bruise if she survived this. "Even if you believe that, your beast doesn't," Varrow hissed at her.

Iris looked directly at Toran. "Give me your word, if he lets me go unharmed, you'll let him go." They could still get out of this relatively unscathed, but Toran had to leash his killing rage. He had to make Varrow believe his word.

Her mate's jaw locked and she could see his fingers curling into fists. Frustration and anger barreled into her through their connection and Iris wished she had some calming emotion to send him, but she was just as on edge.

Toran took half a step forward, and Varrow's attention shifted. The blaster slipped, not quite aiming directly at her. It was now or never. Iris lit up the scalpel and swiped back, aiming for anything soft and vital. Varrow cried out and turned her, letting off three blasts, and as one connected, the scalpel slid from her fingers as her body locked up and she fell to the floor.

Chapter Twenty-One

It was easier to deal with things like this in space. There was no paperwork when it came to disposing of the bodies of bottom feeders and sadists like Varrow. Toran sat in the hospital speaking with someone who had identified herself as a police officer and explained everything that had happened in the past few hours.

Well, he explained the story that he and his team had agreed to tell. The human police weren't particularly interested in dealing with alien crime, and Sierra had made it clear that once they got their hands on Varrow's house and declared it a crime scene there would be no hope of getting in to search for any relevant intelligence.

When she'd said that, Toran's only concern had been getting Iris the medical care she needed. The blaster had clipped her face and knocked her out, and a nasty scorch mark scored her chin. He'd rushed her to the nearest hospital while the rest of the team scoured Varrow's house.

The officer bid him farewell, promising to look into the false crime that he'd described. He'd told her that he and Iris had been mugged by an alien matching Varrow's description. He kept the details bare, another piece of advice from Sierra, and he didn't have to pretend his worry for Iris. Whether he would get in trouble for lying depended on what the police found, but at the moment he couldn't care less. He just wanted to know that his mate would be okay.

An android attendant wearing a lab coat came down the hall and asked for him by name.

Toran stood and greeted the bot. "Is she okay?"

The android gave him a flat smile, like something one of the soulless would try. "She's asking for you, sir."

The walk down the hall seemed to take longer than the wait, though it in reality only took a minute. Toran was led to a private room, and the android left him there. Iris lay in a small bed, her hair fanned out against the pillow, and her skin disturbingly pale against the white sheets. But she was awake and her face lit up with a smile when she saw him. A bandage covered the bottom half of one of her cheeks and part of her jaw. Toran closed the door behind him and took a seat beside her. She reached out and he laced their fingers together and they enjoyed a moment of silence, peace settling over them.

"What happened?" she asked, her voice raspy and a little slurred. "Didn't want to pass out."

Toran involuntarily squeezed her hand, the memory of her falling down washing over him like an icy wave. "You got him. Must have nicked something important. He went down not long after he got the shot off. By the time I was across the room, he was gone."

"Gone?" she whispered. "He got away?" Whatever painkillers they had her on must have been making her think slower. A moment later she stiffened and shook her head slightly. "He's dead?"

Toran nodded, unsure of how his mate would feel about this. He was a warrior, one who'd dealt death across the galaxy where it needed to be dealt. He would've taken Varrow down in an instant for the crime of threatening his mate. But Iris was not him, and he knew she'd never killed anyone before.

But Iris let out a relieved sigh. "Good," she mumbled. "Can't hurt you, good." Her eyes drifted shut but she forced them open after a second and looked at him seriously, the expression almost comical on her tired face. "He said Yormas wasn't working alone. More than just Varrow. Maybe his planet is involved. Don't know."

Toran leaned forward and brushed his lips against her forehead. "You did good. You're so strong."

"Had to make it for you." It was hard to make out exactly what she was saying as drowsiness started to win the battle. "Had to tell you I love you."

Toran's heart clenched and he kissed her again, but before he could say anything else she was already asleep.

***

Iris examined her face in the mirror, looking for any sign of scarring from the blaster shot, any hint of the injury she'd taken three days before. But the miracle of regen gel and a few other medical tricks made it impossible to tell that she'd been seriously injured, except for a little redness that she'd been promised would disappear.

She'd been in the hospital for less than a full day before being released to return home. Toran had gone with her and he hadn't left. He seemed to be getting joy out of playing the role of nursemaid, but Iris was now healed and all of the threats and worries of life were still waiting for them.

She left the bathroom before Toran caught her staring again and plopped down on the couch. Her mate was in the kitchen, arguing with the food processor. He claimed it didn't like him, and Iris had not yet given him the trick to making the finicky device work properly. A part of her liked to watch him struggle.

After letting out a series of curses, Toran came out of the kitchen holding a tray of food, his expression serene, as if she couldn't hear what he'd been saying to her electronics.

"My face was broken, not my ears," she said with a smile.

"That machine is possessed by evil spirits, I take no blame for what I said." He sat beside her and placed the tray on the table in front of them.

Iris leaned forward and plucked up one of the vegetables before popping it into her mouth, leaning against her mate. "Evil spirits?"

"The most sinister," he said in his gravest voice.

Iris smiled. She loved seeing this side of her mate, the playful side that was just for her. He was so serious, so in charge around his team, that they probably wouldn't recognize him when he spoke of the evil spirits living in her food processor. "When is everybody coming over?" she asked.

"Soon," said Toran.

"Do you have any more information about Wreet? Or about where Yormas went?" On the first day after her injury Toran had told her nothing, insisting that she rest up and not worry. On the second day he fed her small bites of information that had only whet her curiosity. Now everyone—Raze, Sierra, Kayde, Dryce, and Quinn—was on their way to go over what had happened to Iris and what they needed to do next. She'd heard mention of two other women, Mindy and Jo, but apparently they'd been reinstated at the SIA and weren't available to join the meeting.

"I'm sure we'll know more soon," Toran promised. He slung his arm over her shoulder and pulled her closer. "You told me you loved me in the hospital," he said quietly, as if it had been eating at him for a while.

Iris tilted her head towards him and offered a smile. "I know." She had been a bit loopy, but she remembered everything that happened after she woke up. She hadn't been *that* injured.

"You fell back asleep before I could say anything." Her mate wrapped a finger around strands of her hair and played with it idly.

"What do you have to say?" She couldn't help but grin, and her tone was a bit teasing. She knew that Toran cared for her, that he would do anything for her. And she could feel the tender beat of his emotions through the denya bond. She'd never felt more secure in a man before, and knew that he was the only one for her.

"I love you, my denya," he said like a vow. "I should have said it sooner."

Iris laughed out loud at the thought that two weeks was too long to go without admitting love and Toran gave her a harsh look, but she swiped a kiss against his lips to soften the blow. "We have a lifetime, there's no need to rush."

Toran placed his hand against her hip and leaned over her, swiping his lips over hers and tasting her with his tongue. "We may have enough time to rush before the others get here," he tempted.

"How soon is soon?" Iris wanted to take him up on his offer, but she didn't want every person he knew to catch them with their pants down. They would never hear the end of it.

Before Toran could answer, there was a knock at the door, and all thoughts of rushing washed away on a wave of frustrated desire. "Later, you are mine," he declared.

Iris pushed him off of her and gave him a kiss as she got up to answer the door. "I'm always yours," she said with a smile. But for now the team was waiting. With the threat of Varrow taken care of, and the information they'd found at his house, they were that many steps closer to hunting down Yormas of Wreet and getting justice for the destruction of Detya. Their group was small, but they had allies, and Iris knew that as long as she stood at Toran's side she would do anything to help him heal this generational wound.

So she opened the door and greeted her guests, ready for the things to come.

***

Heartless: Detyen Warriors

By

Kate Rudolph

and

Starr Huntress

Published by Starr Huntress & Kate Rudolph.

www.starrhuntress.com
www.katerudolph.net

Chapter One

Beer beat therapy, that was for sure. Five women sat around the table in the beat up little bar that CJ had summoned them to. It was the first official meeting of the survivors' club, not that they had agreed on the name. But it beat *victims* or *abductees* so Quinn didn't think that she was going to get a lot of pushback on it.

CJ lifted her mug and proposed a toast. "To two months back, I can't believe we all survived."

Quinn winced and Muir scowled. "Not all of us survived," said the senator's niece. She was the youngest among them and the only reason that they had been rescued in the first place.

"We don't know if she's dead," Davy tried to reason.

At the same moment, Valerie said, "Good riddance, she was a traitor."

They were all survivors, but none of them were unscathed. "Maybe we don't talk about Laurel right now," said Quinn, trying to keep the peace. It reminded her of her childhood, when she had been the oldest of four rambunctious foster siblings. She had learned at a young age that peace was better than agreement, if only because agreement was usually a pipe dream.

Muir didn't share Quinn's philosophy. "I'm not the one—"

"She would've killed us all," Valerie doubled down on her earlier statement. "We did what we had to do."

"*You* did what you thought you should do," Muir corrected. She had come a long way from the fragile blonde waif who Sierra Alvarez and her crew had rescued from slavers on Fenryr 1. Quinn was glad to see the girl recovering, but the headache brewing behind her eye made her wish that the younger woman was a bit more timid.

"Who wants another round?" Quinn asked before they could descend into further argument. "It's our two month anniversary, let's celebrate." That distracted the women, and she took their orders before pushing up from her seat and heading for the bar, where an android waited to serve her.

The five of them: Muir, CJ, Valerie, Davy, and herself weren't a natural group of friends. They weren't *any* kind of friends, but all of them shared the same horrifying experience that bound them together through trauma and perseverance. Along with a handful of other women who had left Washington in the two months since they were safely returned, the survivors club represented the women who had been abducted by slavers from Earth and recovered on a faraway planet called Fenryr 1. They'd endured horrible, unspeakable things at the hands of those monsters, but they were all alive now and only the memories and the nightmares could hurt anymore.

Eleven women had been held captive on Fenryr 1 at the time of their recovery. Ten had been returned to Earth. One of the slavers' victims, Laurel, wasn't so lucky. She had been implanted with a control chip and had led the slavers to their location after they'd escaped. It led to a vicious attack on their allies and in that final fight, some of the survivors, Valerie included, had taken it upon themselves to ensure that Laurel didn't make it to the ship that was going to take them home. Valerie insisted that they hadn't killed her, but Quinn wasn't sure if her fellow survivor was telling the truth. One thing she had learned in the last two months was that she couldn't think of some things too hard, and what happened to Laurel was one of them. If she started thinking about what could be happening to Laurel right now, if she was still alive, then she started to remember everything that had been done to her.

Those were the nights where she woke up screaming.

The hairs on the back of her neck prickled, distracting her from the dark road her mind was trying to venture down. She looked away from the bar, and cast her gaze around the room. Her companions had settled into a more sedate discussion, two human men played billiards in the corner, two aliens cheered them on near the jukebox, and a few more groups of humans clustered around the tables. Nothing weird, nothing wrong, but she was still almost certain that she was being watched.

You only needed to be snatched from the planet by nefarious forces once to develop a healthy sense of observation and paranoia. But by the time the android placed her drinks in front of her, Quinn hadn't seen anything out of place. Okay, she conceded, sometimes her paranoia edged into the unhealthy category.

It was a careful balancing act to get five drinks back to the table and she realized that she should've asked for a tray, but by the time that thought crossed her mind, she was already halfway across the room. She made it back to the table without spilling a drop to the cheers of everyone around her. The women grabbed their glasses, and everyone sat back, drinking quickly, like they'd been lost in the desert for years.

Muir was the first one to set her beverage down. She looked over at Quinn and said, "I was just telling the others. My uncle is introducing legislation to combat the slavers who've been preying on people. He really thinks they could make a difference."

Quinn couldn't stop her scoff. "Kidnapping is already illegal. I don't think that's been any deterrent."

"He's allocating funds—"

"Please," CJ interrupted. "If we have to talk politics, I'm going to get myself abducted again to escape it."

Muir sat back, chastened.

"I want to know what's going on with those aliens who rescued us," said Valerie. "Especially that one, you know, the sexy one. With those *eyes*." She shivered.

"They all had eyes," said Muir. "Do you mean Toran?" she asked casually, but Quinn already knew the girl would be disappointed when she learned that Toran was newly mated.

"Ew, no!" Valerie was shaking her head and scowling. "He seems like one of those by the book guys. All rules, all the time. No thank you. I mean the other single one, the intense one."

Quinn got very still. Of the four aliens who had come to Earth with them, there was only one that Valerie could be talking about. "You mean Kayde." *Intense* was one way to describe him, or cold, or heartless. She'd been around him several times already and there was something about that man that made her feel weird. Off in a way she couldn't quite wrap her mind around.

This time it was Davy who saved her from this unpleasant turn of conversation. "I want to know what's been happening with them. And I don't mean like Valerie does. I wasn't into men, human or otherwise before we left the planet, and nothing about the experience has changed my mind."

Quinn latched onto the subject change. "They've been on the lookout for this guy. Ambassador Yormas of Wreet. They think he had something to do with the destruction of their planet like a hundred years ago."

"Destruction?" asked Muir, leaning closer, intrigued.

Quinn nodded. Dryce, the playboy Detyen and youngest of the group, had told her the story weeks ago. "The place was called Detya. It was peaceful, or so they say. But apparently someone had a problem with them. A hundred years ago the entire planet was destroyed with a weapon that hasn't been seen before or since. The only people who survived had easy access to space ships, or were already off planet at the time. Kayde and the rest of them are descendants of the survivors. Their mission, I guess, is to find out who destroyed the planet and get revenge."

"And they think the same guy who attacked them a hundred years ago is still alive?" Davy was skeptical.

Quinn shrugged. "Aliens," she said by way of explanation, waving her hands like she could make a point. "Anyway, the ambassador disappeared a couple of weeks ago. We've been following up on leads, but it's slow going."

"Why are you helping them?" asked Valerie, her eyes narrowed in suspicion. "How did you get involved in all that?"

"It's not like I have anything else to do right now." She didn't have a job to go back to, and there was no real family to miss her. Those foster siblings that she had looked out for when she was young had all scattered as they aged out of the system, just like her. Before Sierra and her crew had shown up on Fenryr 1, Quinn had been certain that no one was coming for her. Her only way out of that hopeless situation was to rely on herself. But now she was home, and safe, and until she had started working with the Detyens she'd been at a loss. The only way to keep sane, to keep from screaming in horror from all that had been done to her, was to keep moving.

That prickle of awareness was back. Quinn looked around the room but didn't see anything out of place.

"Excuse me," she said as she pushed up from her seat. She made her way back to the small hallway that led to the bathrooms near the rear exit. The door slammed shut just as she turned down the dimly lit hall. Without pausing to think, Quinn followed outside. The back door led to a short alley behind the bar which ended at a busy street. A figure in black, whose exposed skin glinted bluish green under the single yellow light of the alley way, moved quickly, not bothering to look behind him. "Kayde?" Quinn called before she could think better of it. But the figure didn't stop, didn't even pause. If it was him he didn't want to talk.

She stood frozen for a minute, unsure if she should pursue or go back to her friends. But in the end Quinn turned around and headed back inside. If that was Kayde, he could handle himself. She had no reason to follow him, no reason to talk to him at all. But that didn't mean she felt any better about the decision.

This wasn't the first time she'd seen Kayde out in the city. She didn't want to accuse him of following her, but it was getting to the point where she didn't know what else to call it. It seemed like she had an alien stalker, and given her history that should've made fear run cold in her veins. But when it came to Kayde, all she felt was a bit of curiosity.

What the hell was he doing?

* * *

What in all the hells was he doing? Kayde knew that he should be back in his quarters preparing for sleep. His schedule would be insistent on that point. And a man like him lived and died by his routine. It was all he had left. Until two months ago, when this obsession started to blossom. He hadn't said anything to Toran, or Raze, or Dryce. They were all wrapped up in the quest to find

Yormas of Wreet and bring him to justice for the destruction of Detya, if he had been the one to destroy it. The evidence pointed towards him, but they had yet to find definitive proof.

He knew his companions were excited and getting a bit impatient, the longer the ambassador was absent from his post. Kayde could almost remember what those things felt like, but all he had left now were echoes, hollow memories of the emotions that used to beat hard and fast throughout his system.

Like Raze, he had let the Detyen Legion remove his soul, and with it all of his emotions, to lengthen his life. Unlike Raze, he hadn't been handed a miracle. Soullessness was the final step before death. The average life expectancy of a soulless warrior was thirty-five years. They traded away everything for five cold, heartless, empty years that personally meant nothing, but could mean everything to the Legion. There weren't enough soldiers to go around, and the Denya Price meant that there were fewer and fewer every year. Kayde had never questioned whether or not he would surrender his soul for his people. That was his duty.

If the planet had still existed, he would have owed his life to them anyway. As a descendent of one of three royal families who had reigned over their kingdoms, Kayde knew the cost of existence. Some people were born to lives that weren't their own, and his fate had been decided long before the planet was destroyed. He had a duty, and that duty had kept him strong in the years since he gave up everything else.

The memory of that duty was growing faint, replaced by something he didn't understand. Some compulsion that led him out into the night to follow a path he never knew he was on until it ended with her. Quinn. His companions might accuse him of fixating, an unfortunate side effect that appeared for some of the soulless. They grew obsessed with a person or place, until that obsession lead to destruction and death.

Kayde wasn't going to hurt Quinn. Everything left within him rebelled at the idea. Then again, it would not be difficult to believe that other fixating soulless warriors held that same thought close until it was too late.

The streets were dark, and many might have feared walking alone at this late hour. It would be wise to catch a taxi back to his quarters, but restlessness pounded in Kayde's veins. If he stopped moving now, he wouldn't sleep this night, and he could not come up with a good excuse to explain tomorrow's exhaustion to Toran. So he would beat the energy out of himself, walking darkened streets and long roads back to home.

No, not home. No Detyen had a home, not any more. He and his brothers in arms had the Detyen HQ, or they had before the attack a little more than two months ago. None of them knew the outcome of that battle, and though it was difficult for Kayde to discern emotion, he could tell that Toran, Dryce, and Raze feared the worst. They feared that the Oscavian warship that had attacked their people was successful in destroying everything the Legion had managed to cobble together in the last hundred years. They feared the decimation of the remaining members of the Detyen race.

Maybe if he had a soul, Kayde would fear these things as well. And perhaps if he had a soul, he'd be grateful that he couldn't feel that desolation.

Time and distance got away from him, and before he knew it he was placing his palm on the bio lock of the Sol Defense Agency building that housed the Detyen quarters. They'd been given these rooms when they arrived on the planet, and had been forced to stay in them while they were under investigation. At first, the forces of Earth's defense had believed that he and his companions were a threat to the planet. The SDA no longer believed that, and they were free to leave the planet at will. Unfortunately, they had no idea where Ambassador Yormas of Wreet had gotten to, and until they had information of his location, leaving the planet would surrender their last connection to their only lead.

No, Kayde realized. Not their *only* lead.

He took the stairs up to the suite of apartments they were staying in and noted the silence when he opened the door. Unsurprisingly, Raze was gone. These rooms had never been his home. As soon as they landed on the planet, he had moved in with his denya, Sierra Alvarez, in the apartment she kept in the city. Since his mating, Toran had tried to split his time between Iris

Mason's home and here, but tonight it appeared he'd chosen to stay with his mate. Dryce would be back sometime before sunrise, Kayde was certain. The younger Detyen was wasting no time soaking up all of the experiences and pleasures that Earth had to offer. With his looks and cheery attitude he could find a new lover every night, and when he wasn't on duty he made a point of doing so.

That left Kayde alone with the silence. Of course, it didn't bother him. Nothing bothered him. He entered his room and showered quickly, but took a few extra seconds to let the near scalding heat of the water pounding against him soak into his skin. It loosened the tight muscles in his back and if he had a little less control, he might have groaned from the sensation.

The counselors back at Detyen HQ warned that the soulless should not revel in physical sensation. It could hasten the path to destabilization, but Kayde had learned that some warnings were better to ignore. He compromised with himself, experiencing the heat of the water and its physical effects for only a short time. When he climbed out of the shower stall, he wiped himself down efficiently and changed into a pair of sleep pants and a loose shirt. He kept his blaster on top of the small shelf beside his bed, in easy reach in case of a threat came upon him in the night.

But with his walk concluded and a shower over, Kayde found himself at loose ends, and his thoughts began to travel back to the one person he knew he shouldn't be thinking about. He couldn't be fixating on Quinn, of that he was certain. Counselors and other high ranking members in the Legion spoke of fixation as something terrible, some dangerous obsession that destroyed not only the warrior but the focus of his desire. Kayde wasn't obsessed, not like that.

There was just something about Quinn that posed a question he didn't know how to ask. He saw her strength, her resilience, and knew that she would become a powerful ally to his fellow warriors and their mates. She had shown herself to be a leader from the moment she and her fellow survivors had been rescued, and now she threw herself into helping in the hunt for Yormas with little regard for her own safety.

He respected her, admired her.

And he knew that those instincts were dangerous. A soulless warrior could not respect, could not admire. He only had the memory of what he'd felt before to keep him going—if he said he admired other members of the Legion, it was because he had known them before. He could not develop those feelings anymore, and he couldn't explain why he felt that way for Quinn.

The safest thing for all of them would be to remove him from the equation. Toran needed to evaluate his stability and decide whether he could continue to function or if he needed to be put down like the rabid animal a soulless warrior could become. Though he was not sure if the leader of their team would be willing to take that action. Before they had come to Earth, he would have had no doubt. But in the time since then, Toran had softened. His mate had brought out a new side of him, one that smiled more, one that laughed, and one that might care too much to kill a man he thought of as his friend.

But Kayde had to trust him to do his duty, and he had to report any concerns that he had about himself. Perhaps there was another way, one that would remove him from dark temptations of fixation and obsession and save his former friend from staining his hands with the blood of a man whose only crime was wanting to save his people for as long as he could.

Yormas of Wreet was not the only lead they had when it came to the destruction of Detya. He had been working with the people who had attacked the Detyen HQ. Now that Kayde and his companions had been cleared to leave the planet, someone could take their ship back home and find out what happened. And if Toran could not kill Kayde for failing as a soulless warrior, as long as the HQ had not been destroyed by the Oscavians, someone back home would. Kayde could save Toran that pain. He just had to convince his leader to let him go.

Chapter Two

Kayde didn't wait for Toran to return to the suite. Once morning rolled around, the sun sitting high in the sky and baking the city in a wet heat, he was out the door and headed towards Iris's house. Dryce's door was still closed, and he did not expect the younger warrior to be awake for hours yet. They'd fallen out of strict disciplines that they practiced in the legion, and if they ever returned, Dryce was in for a rude awakening. Then again, in a few years he would be forced to make an impossible choice if he didn't find his denya, so a part of Kayde could understand why the warrior was living his life at warp speed.

When the taxi dropped him off at the small house that Iris called home, Kayde took a deep breath before starting up the path and walking up the short flight of stairs to her door. He wasn't nervous, he couldn't be nervous, but he didn't know how this meeting was going to go, what Toran would ultimately decide, and he didn't relish the uncertainty.

After his knock, Toran greeted him with a bright smile that was lost on Kayde, who only nodded in response. Toran summoned him inside and Kayde glanced around, not seeing his leader's mate in the living room or kitchen, which were visible from the front door.

"Iris isn't home," Toran told him, watching him look around.

It wasn't a question, so Kayde wasn't sure how to respond. He remained silent.

Toran must have been getting out of practice with interacting with the soulless. Now that Raze could feel again, Kayde was the only one of their group left in emotionless limbo, and in the past weeks, Toran had seemed to be avoiding him. "What are you doing here?" Toran asked after a moment, seeming to remember that there was no need for small talk. "Is something wrong? Did something happen to Dryce?"

Was he meant to be Dryce's keeper? Wouldn't that job fall to Raze, who was Dryce's older brother? Kayde didn't ask these questions. "Everything is fine, as far as I know. When I left our quarters, Dryce appeared to be sleeping. He was in his own room."

Toran's eyebrows drew together and he took a deep breath. There was a name for the expression he was giving Kayde but Kayde could not define it. "You didn't answer the most important question. What are you doing here?"

Of course. This kind of distraction might be another sign of deterioration, Kayde noted dispassionately. "I came because I need you to evaluate me."

Toran drew up to his full height, as if preparing for a fight, but after a moment he stepped back and motioned Kayde further into the room. "Has there been a development since your last evaluation?" Toran asked.

"I haven't been thoroughly evaluated since we left Detyen HQ. You have mentioned the need several times, but you seem to be putting it off."

Toran opened his mouth as if to say something, but closed it after a moment and turned his back on Kayde to head into the kitchen. He pressed a few buttons on the food processor and a moment later had a glass of some green drink that smelled like nature. He didn't offer one to Kayde, trusting Kayde to be closely monitoring his own nutritional needs. "Are you unstable?" Toran finally asked, gripping his glass tightly.

Kayde took a few steps, so he wouldn't need to raise his voice to be heard. He stood stiffly on the border between the kitchen and the living room, aware that he had ruined Toran's morning, but unable to think of what else he should've done. He didn't know how to explain what was happening in his mind without talking about Quinn, but something inside of him rebelled at the thought of explaining his fascination to Toran when he couldn't explain it to himself. So he offered a half-truth, knowing the instinct to lie was another sign of destabilization, of fixation. Perhaps he was further gone than he had previously thought. "This planet is loud, full of disruptions. Humans don't understand the need for discipline, the need for order. I have found myself growing distracted and need a mission. A warrior like me is meant to be used, and if I cannot be used, I need to be..."

"If you aren't a danger to these people, I'm not going to kill you," Toran interrupted before Kayde could make his point.

"This existence of mine, it isn't living. You are letting your own emotions cloud your judgment. Use me or dispose of me, but make your choice." He would have never dared to say something like that back home. But they were a long way from home, and the rules were different here.

"Do you have a suggestion? There's not much we can do until the ambassador makes his next move." Ah, now Kayde could identify what had been thrumming through Toran since he opened the door. Frustration.

And that frustration gave Kayde the opening he needed to make his proposal. "Let me go back to HQ, let me take the ship. We need to know what happened there since none of our communications have been returned."

"You and I both know that the channels we were forced to use could mean that it will be months before we hear back, but so long as there are survivors we *will* hear back." Toran countered.

"I don't have months."

Toran closed his eyes and drank down his green concoction in a single gulp. He set the glass on the counter with a resounding clink. "You want to do this?"

"It's the only choice if you won't—"

Toran cut him off. "Very well. Make your goodbyes. You have three months, make sure you file your report then."

"You have my word. Either way, we'll know what happened soon enough." And Kayde would be free of this planet and all its distractions, and maybe he would be able to stop thinking about the one woman who had burrowed herself deep into his mind and thrown his life into chaos.

* * *

Sneaking onto a spaceship was not her brightest move, especially since Quinn was determined never to leave the planet again. But as the beer had been replaced by liquor last night and the

371

stories turned maudlin and depressing, the only thing that had staved off Muir's tears was a promise that Quinn would find her a keepsake from the ship that had brought them home. And it wasn't exactly sneaking. After all, there were plenty of security guards at the airstrip where the ship was sitting vacant, and she had had to sign in on the visitor log before they let her anywhere near a piece of equipment as expensive and delicate as the Detyen ship.

She'd been assured that though the ship was space ready and fueled up, no flight plan had been filed and as far as the airstrip knew, no one would be getting on the ship that day. She'd considered slipping a few credits into the hands of the person minding the log to keep her visit a secret, but at the last moment she thought better of it. She didn't have many credits to spare, and she doubted that the Detyens would mind what she was doing.

But what could she get for Muir? The girl seemed a bit sentimental, which meant that she would most likely want something that triggered a happy—well, not happy, but not unpleasant—memory. Was there anything on the ship like that? Hell, she could probably just take a picture and frame the thing. No need to hack up the inside and strip the thing for parts. Still, Muir had asked for a piece of the ship, not a picture. Quinn was going to deliver. This was an easy mission, one that didn't need extensive planning or scary looking weapons and high-tech spy equipment. Her folding knife was more than adequate to the task.

She stood in the passageway for several moments before turning away from the cockpit and heading back past a small seating area, through a hatch, down another hall, through the galley, through another hatch that closed behind her with a resounding clank, until she finally got to the open crew quarters. Half a dozen bunks were built into the walls, and the only privacy offered came from brightly colored curtains that could easily be pulled open or closed. For a week, this was where the survivors had called home. It had been crowded, and loud, and the exact opposite of private, but given what they had all been dealing with for the months before that, it had been a little slice of heaven.

Quinn placed her hands on the bunk that she had shared with CJ. There hadn't been enough for most of the women to sleep alone, and the beds were narrow enough that cuddling had been required.

But in those first nights, that was exactly what she had needed. Knowing that there was someone beside her who didn't want to cause injury, who didn't want to take her to bed, who didn't want anything from her except perhaps a little warmth, had kept her from waking up screaming. It hadn't stopped the nightmares—she didn't think that anything could stop those—but whimpering was better than screaming. She climbed up into the bunk and pulled the curtain closed while burrowing into the far corner, wedging herself deep inside. It was a tight fit. Her feet brushed the far wall and she wondered how those bulky Detyen warriors could ever hope to squeeze themselves in.

Light leaked around the curtain, highlighting it as if to say that it was the perfect gift. Yes, Quinn thought, that could work. She reached into her pocket for her knife and was caught off guard by a yawn that wracked her whole body. She hadn't gotten home until late last night and she'd woken early from disturbing dreams. She lay back in the bunk and pulled the blanket up around her shoulders. No one was coming for the ship today, and there was no danger of discovery. She felt safer here than she had anywhere else on Earth in the past month and there would be no harm in closing her eyes for a few minutes and enjoying the cocoon of false safety that this little bunk was giving her.

With a sigh, Quinn's eyes drifted shut and she fell into a dreamless sleep before she even realized she was going to pass out.

She woke when the ship jolted and rolled towards the curtain. The only thing keeping her from falling to the floor was the death grip she managed on a small handhold built into the wall and the way she shot out her foot to keep herself wedged into her sleeping cubby.

Her ears popped and she couldn't drag in a deep breath, as if the air around her had suddenly gotten thin. Her cheeks felt heavy, as if they were being pushed around by some invisible force, and everything around her was so loud that she wouldn't be able to hear herself scream. The ship was rocketing into space and with a final jolt and a final pop of her ears everything went silent, and the air around her thickened as the life support system kicked on.

What was going on? Had there been some kind of miscommunication? Was the ship being stolen? Was this some sort of maintenance run? Questions ran through Quinn's mind at a hundred kilometers a minute, then her teeth chattered as her body shook with the realization that she had been unwillingly taken from Earth a second time.

No. No, no, no, everything rebelled at the thought and for a suicidal second she wondered if there was a way to jump out of the ship and somehow make her way home. Of course that was impossible, she knew that. She had survived way worse than this. She didn't even know who was flying the ship and where they were headed. It was probably the Detyens, or a maintenance crew, and they'd be back on the ground in no time. She clung to that thought, but it took several more minutes of convincing herself that she wasn't about to get hurt to force herself to climb out of the cubby and slowly make her way towards the cockpit. If the ship was being stolen, she didn't want to give her presence away, but she needed to see who was flying the thing, needed to see if they were friend or foe.

This was probably one big misunderstanding, she told herself again, but she could remember the painful grip of the slaver's hand on her wrist, holding her tight enough to bruise, almost tight enough to break. She had thought that was a misunderstanding too, at the beginning.

By the time she made it to the seating area outside the cockpit, she could see a dark head of hair over the top of the pilot seat. There only appeared to be one person in the cockpit, but a ship like this usually had a much bigger crew. Why would someone fly it alone? Not for legitimate purposes, she was almost sure. If the Detyens were on a mission, surely they would've sent at least two. So if that was one of the Detyens, was he going rogue? If he had checked in with security before taking the ship, he would have known that she was on it.

The pilot shifted in the seat and Quinn got a good look at his profile. Bluish-green skin, straight nose, sharp jaw, and lips that she had spent absolutely no time thinking about whatsoever.

Kayde.

This was okay, she tried to tell herself. The Detyens were her friends, and though there was something off about Kayde, something she couldn't stop thinking about no matter how much she tried, she knew that he would take her back home. Whatever he was doing right now had to be legitimate. She had to believe that.

She took a deep breath, trying to center herself, trying to psych herself up to what she had to do, and closed the final distance to the door to the cockpit. "I think there's been some kind of mistake," she said after clearing her throat. "Did you know I was here?"

At first she didn't think that Kayde had heard her. He was frozen in his seat, still as a statue. But after a long moment he turned to her, the moment slow, beginning with his head and moving down his body until he was sitting at a strange angle in his seat. He stared at her for several moments with unfathomably dark eyes. His face was completely expressionless, something that wasn't strange for him, even if it was a bit unnerving. "Of course you're here," he said in his flat, robotic voice. From anyone else she would have thought those words were sarcastic, but from him he was stating a fact.

She waited for him to say something else, to say *anything* that would make it clear that this was a mistake. The silence stretched around them and the sinking feeling in her stomach told Quinn that Kayde wasn't about to add anything else to his statement. He'd known she was here, and he'd taken her anyway. He wasn't about to explain where they were going, and he wasn't about to let her go.

It was happening again. Her folding knife pressed against her leg where it sat in her pocket, reminding her that she wasn't as defenseless as she looked. But Kayde was a trained warrior, a dangerous man, and from the looks of it he had gone off the deep end. So she needed to wait for her moment, play this right, and find a way to get home. She wasn't about to be a victim again, and she would die before she submitted to anyone.

Chapter Three

Quinn was on his ship. They were rocketing away from Earth, halfway to the jump gate, and the one person on the planet that he was trying to avoid was standing only a few meters away, the brown skin on her face gone pale and her eyes wide. He'd been given his orders, had requested his orders. And now his mind stuttered at this unforeseen complication. How could she be here? The airfield was guarded, and the ship should have been locked.

He could ask those kinds of questions all day, but they were useless. She was here now, and if he wanted to make his scheduled time to exit the solar system through the jump gate, he couldn't afford to turn around. But he needed to do something to calm her down. Yes, calm. He recognized the symptoms he was seeing on her face. She was panicked, afraid. Perhaps she wanted to be away from him as much as he needed to be away from her.

"I mean you no harm," he said. "I did not realize you were on the ship."

She choked out something that might have been called a laugh under other circumstances. "That isn't what you said a minute ago. Take me home, I want to go back to Earth." She reached for the seat in front of her with one hand and gripped the headrest tightly. The soldier inside of Kayde noted that she kept her other hand out of sight. If she hadn't been an ally, if she had been someone other than Quinn, he might think that she could have a weapon, that she could be a threat.

No, she *could* have a weapon and she *could* be a threat. His own obsession, or fixation, or whatever madness had bungled his brain didn't extend to her. Whatever connection he felt, it had to be a one-way street. He could not underestimate her, could not trust that she wouldn't do him harm.

He turned fully toward her, the autopilot doing most of the flying at this point. "Could you put your other hand on the chair?" he asked, trying to sound nonthreatening.

Quinn stiffened and her jaw clenched, further signs that she wanted to keep her other hand out of sight. "Can you take me home?" she asked, unmoving.

"There's a tight exit schedule," Kayde replied. "If I don't make my time at the gate, it will be more than a week before my mission can be rescheduled." He had his parameters, had his goal, and he wasn't designed to deviate. Perhaps Toran, or Dryce, or even Raze would approach this problem differently, but Kayde was none of those men and he could only do this the way he knew how.

"No," Quinn insisted, the hint of a quaver in her voice. "Take me back home right now, you can't keep me here."

"It's my ship, how do you propose to stop me?" He only realized it was the wrong thing to say when Quinn's mouth dropped open and a helpless little sound escaped her throat.

The next thing happened very fast. In a blink, Quinn was around the chair, launching herself towards him with one of her hands, the one that had been hidden, holding a small, wickedly sharp knife that could do damage in the hands of someone properly trained. As she came at him swinging, he took in her form and acknowledged that she wasn't a complete novice. But whatever she knew, he knew far more. If he were a betting man, he would place credits on the fact that she had never sliced someone up before.

They grappled for a handful of moments, the fight dragging out not because of Quinn's surprising skill, but because Kayde was unwilling to cause her pain. A simple lock on her wrist could have ended this all in a matter of seconds, but as angry as Quinn was, Kayde was certain he would have to snap the bone before she would stop attacking. He couldn't do that to her. But before he even had a chance to get winded, he managed to loosen her grip and tossed the knife away, where it slid out of reach. He was straddled on top of her hips, his hands pinning her wrists to the floor, the fabric of her long sleeved shirt sliding under his fingers. Anger, no *rage*, washed over her face, making her look alive in a way that captivated him.

A spark of awareness shot through him, something that Kayde could almost define, something just out of reach. His eyes locked with Quinn's, and both of them were frozen in the moment. This was unlike any battle he had ever fought before. In the heat of combat there was no time to pause for longing glances or loaded looks. But this was no battle.

"You'll have to kill me," Quinn spat. "I won't submit."

From where Kayde was sitting, he didn't need Quinn to submit. The fight was already over. She tried to struggle against him, and he tightened his grip just enough to make it a warning, but not strong enough to bruise. In doing so, he pressed the rest of his body down against her, and that set Quinn off. She struggled in earnest, almost succeeding in bucking him off as he was surprised by the vehemence of her response. It only took another moment for his brain to catch up to what she meant.

"I mean you no harm. I would not touch you without your consent." He managed to press her back down against the floor, and tried to position himself so that he was touching her as little as possible.

"Your dirty hands are all over me right now, you fucking—" she let out a frustrated scream rather than complete the insult. "Let me go."

In other circumstances, if she were someone else, he wouldn't even consider it. The proper action at this point would be to restrain her and confine her to one of the rooms on the ship. But this was Quinn, and Kayde knew he wasn't going to do that. "Are you going to attack me again?" He focused on a small freckle just above one of her eyebrows, rather than risk looking her in the eye again. He didn't want to be caught up a second time, didn't want to risk that connection again. An impossible suspicion rose from his subconscious, whispering the seductive possibility that he couldn't afford to hope for. That was, if he were even capable of hope.

"Let me up and see," Quinn challenged. Her entire body was still taut, balanced on the knife edge between action and inaction.

If he let go, she was going to come for him, and they were going to end right back in the same position. And every time he let her fight back, he risked injuring her, and she risked injuring herself. But Kayde found himself loosening his grip and rolling back off his knees until he stood over her. He reached down and offered a hand to help her up, but Quinn scooted back and put space between them rather than take his assistance. At least she didn't attack him again.

Kayde's mind scrambled, trying to come up with the right thing to say to calm the human down. He'd already screwed up once, and he wouldn't have many chances to fix it. She would be stuck on the ship with him for some time, and at some point he would have to sleep. "There's a waypoint not far past the jump gate. From there you could book passage back to Earth fairly easily." Yes, that would work. According to his maps, the waypoint was little more than a fuel stop, but this close to Earth, Quinn wouldn't be forced to wait long to go home.

"With what credits?" Quinn scoffed. "You're not even a creative kidnapper. The guys who nabbed me at first tried to say it was all one big misunderstanding, they told me they booked me passage back home and I walked right onto that slaver ship without a backwards glance. I'm not going to be that stupid again." She sucked in deep breaths, her chest rising and falling in time.

"I'm not a slaver." Was that even in question? How could she think that? He had been one of the people who saved her from the slavers. He would never condone something so barbaric. Even in the cold winter of soullessness, whatever remnants of emotion still lived within him rebelled at the thought of trying to own someone.

For a moment, Quinn seemed lost for words. She took a final deep breath, and met his eyes. "Yeah, well, convince me."

* * *

Quinn was beginning to think that she'd made a hasty accusation. Kayde's expression never changed, but that was nothing new, and there was something in the way he held himself that made her think he was telling the truth. He hadn't known that she was on the ship, he hadn't meant to take her. She still didn't understand his bullshit about not taking her home, but she had been around the Detyens long enough to trust that he wasn't about to sell her to the nearest convenient scumbag who liked owning people.

"I can send a message to Toran right now," Kayde offered, taking up the challenge she had laid down. "We're getting close to the gate, and there will be interference, so it can't be a two-way call. But I can tell him where you will be, and I'm certain that he can arrange for you to be transported back home as swiftly as possible."

She was already so far in debt to the Detyens and to Sierra Alvarez that she had no hope of ever evening the score. Waiting for Toran to send an interplanetary taxi to take her home would only be a drop in the bucket. Of course, Sierra and all of them would insist that they'd only been doing their duty, that Quinn and her fellow survivors owed them nothing. But Quinn couldn't work like that. Where she came from, a person paid her debts or had those debts called in. There was no such thing as forgiveness, or a free ride. She volunteered to work with the Detyens in part to discharge some of what she owed, even if they never knew it. She'd had to tell them that she was working for them out of boredom, and even if it was the partial truth, it was only a small sliver of the greater whole.

"Where are you going? What's your mission?" An idea began to take root in her mind, something she would've never volunteered for, but since she had been thrown into the middle of the action she might as well go along with it. She owed Kayde just as much as she owed all the rest of them. For a moment, she was concerned that he wouldn't tell her. His always neutral expression seemed to shudder and she realized she was beginning to learn how to read the small tells that he had. He didn't like to give anything away, but no man, or alien, was made of stone. At least she didn't think so, how would that work? She gave her head a mental shake to dislodge the errant thought. Diving down mental rabbit holes was a nice way to ignore all the terrible shit that was happening to her, but those kind of tangents were practically useless when she needed to stay in the moment.

"Would you take a seat?" Kayde asked. "We'll be approaching the gate soon and need to be buckled in for safety."

If it were another man, she'd think he was stalling, but if Kayde didn't want to answer her, she knew he would just tell her no. So she sat and buckled into the copilot seat and waited to see if he would talk.

"While the rest of the crew is waiting for the ambassador to make his next move, I am following up on another lead," Kayde said after several moments. He didn't bother to explain everything that the Detyens and their human mates had been doing back on Earth for the past two months, knowing that Quinn had been involved with it all for some time. If she ever met Ambassador Yormas of

Wreet, she didn't know if she'd be able to stop herself from punching him in the face. He and his men had almost killed Toran and Iris, his accomplice had injured Kayde, and he might be masterminding a plot to destroy Earth. He was definitely not her favorite alien.

The alien sitting next to her—and it disturbed her to realize that he might be her favorite, current situation notwithstanding—continued to speak. "We need to know what happened back at HQ. Nyden Varrow said Yormas wasn't working alone. We know there was an Oscavian warship, obviously. But none of our communications have been answered."

"Is it a little soon for that? I assume you can't make a direct call." The location of Detyen HQ was a tightly guarded secret. Even though Quinn had been there, she couldn't have directed anyone to the place, no matter what they offered her in exchange for the information, or how much they threatened her. All she knew was that it was an icy planet, one that seemed completely hostile to life, yet where the remnants of the Detyen race cobbled their lives together, in a search for vengeance for a planet that had been destroyed before any of them were born.

"That's true," Kayde conceded. "But by now, we should have heard something."

"So you're going back to HQ to see what happened, right?" What must he be feeling right now? He might be flying directly into a graveyard, might be only days or weeks away from the confirmation that most of his kind had been annihilated. Something knotted deep inside her chest, an emotion strong enough to nearly choke her. "You're doing this all alone?" The answer was obvious, but she couldn't stop the question from escaping.

"It isn't dangerous, or it shouldn't be. I am merely a scout. With such a small team, we cannot afford to send anyone else back." He thought that she was concerned for his safety, perhaps that she was worried that the Oscavians were still lurking. And now that she thought it, that was true too. Concern for Kayde had buried itself deep in her skin, something she was scared to acknowledge, but couldn't extract without a lot of blood and pain.

"You shouldn't have to do this alone." No one should be forced to reckon with the possible loss that he was flying straight towards.

Kayde stared at her for several seconds, his stare a heavy weight everywhere his eyes landed. "It needs to be done."

If it was so important, why had they waited two months? Why hadn't they alerted the human authorities to potential threats? She didn't ask these questions. She didn't want Kayde to lie to her, and she suspected that he wasn't willing to tell the truth. "Are you heading back to Earth once this is done?" He would have to, right? How else would he relay his information? Clearly whatever lines of communication had been set up were compromised.

"Those are my orders," Kayde confirmed. Again, there was something in his voice that told her it wasn't the whole truth.

"And how long do you think this will take?" She couldn't be about to do what she was about to do. It felt like she was possessed, watching herself from somewhere else as her body volunteered for a task she had no place signing up for.

"It could be a couple of months."

Months. If she took him up on his offer to get off the ship and the way station, she would be home in a day or less. She could find a way to put together tattered pieces of her life, to clean up the mess the slavers made of her psyche, and create bonds with her fellow survivors. She could find a way to move on from the nightmare that she'd been living in for the past year, and let go of the balance sheet that only existed in her mind. But if she got off of the ship and went back to Earth, Kayde would be alone. He wouldn't be there when she turned her head, wouldn't be lurking in the shadows when she looked for him. In a strange, creepy way, he'd become a security blanket. A part of her had known for a long time that he wasn't a threat, and even when he'd wrestled her down to the floor and cast away her knife, he'd done his best to do her no harm. Absently, she wore at the cuff of her sleeve, tracing over the sensitive skin of her wrists. If she pulled back the fabric, she doubted that she would even be bruised.

Could she really let him do this mission alone? *Yes*, the sane part of her insisted, *let him go. Go home. Live your life away from this madness.* But even as the thoughts filtered through her mind she knew what she had to do.

"Don't drop me off at the way station. I'm going with you."

Kayde continued to stare at her for several long moments, his silence almost loud enough to drown out the distant drone of the engines. He had still said nothing when they came to the jump gate, and as they queued up to travel through it, he remained silent. Quinn gripped the arms of her seat tightly as they prepared for the jump, and once they flew through, her body feeling squished and stretched in the strangest ways, Kayde continued flying. They flew close enough to the way station that Quinn could see the distant sparkle of ships surrounding it, but Kayde never slowed. She leaned back in her seat and pulled her legs up, wrapping an arm around them and telling herself that she had made the right choice. The darkness of the view screen in front of her, the black stretch of space that seemed to reach out and to forever, offered no reassurance. But she was in this now, for better or worse. With Kayde.

She hoped she hadn't made a huge mistake.

Chapter Four

Quinn was beginning to regret her decision to stay on the ship. The only surprising thing about that was that it had nothing to do with Kayde. She hadn't realized just how *boring* space travel could be, especially when her only companion was a silent warrior who seemed determined to keep a polite distance between them at all times. Not just physically, but conversationally and emotionally too. If she didn't know better, Quinn might've thought that Kayde was a robot. He wasn't, right? Surely someone would've mentioned that before. Besides, she had seen him eat, and he had ducked into the bathroom on enough occasions to convince her that he had necessary bodily functions not found in mechanical people.

No, he just acted like a robot. The first day after she decided to stay, she had tried to chat, using the team back home as conversation starters. After all, that was all that she and Kayde really had in common. But when she asked after his fellow Detyens and Sierra and Iris, he had given one-word answers, effectively cutting off that conversational path. She got a little success when she asked him about the ship, letting him instruct her on how to read the navigational maps and how to chart a flight plan. That had taken all of a half hour. Nav systems were designed to be easy to use and she could only ask him to repeat himself so many times. Eventually Quinn had retreated into the heart of the ship, claiming one of the rooms for her own. Since it was just the two of them, she wasn't about to sleep in the open crew bunks. The room wasn't much, a small bed attached to the wall, a water station, a small mirror, and a cubby for her luggage. That only served to remind her that she had no luggage, no clothes, no cleaning supplies, and months ahead of her with nothing but what she was wearing.

The rest of the first day had been dedicated to scavenging any supplies that she could find. She found the room Kayde was going to use for himself, which was bigger than her own, and she thought it must've been the captain's quarters. The bed was huge, and soft, and inviting, but she wasn't about to lay down in it. She'd screwed herself over once by falling asleep in the wrong place on this ship, and she wasn't about to do it again. Especially not so soon after that first mistake. She ignored Kayde's bag and stuck her head into the private shower that was unique to these quarters. She found a small bottle of soap and debated with herself for about three seconds before sticking it in one of her pockets. Kayde's bag had still been sealed when she walked in, and she doubted he had unpacked his toiletries. There was no toothbrush, no razor, nothing else in the small bathroom to suggest that the soap she'd found was his.

In the empty room, the quarters not occupied by her or Kayde, Quinn hit pay dirt, finding a small bag which contained three pairs of pants, four shirts, and one extremely fluffy sweater. There was even an unopened package of undergarments. She said a silent prayer of thanks to any god watching, and slung the bag over her shoulder, ferrying it and her soap back to her room. In the large communal bathroom she found a closet well stocked with more soap, towels, and toothpaste. She didn't have much, but she had enough. As long as she had some way to clean her clothes, she would survive until they made it back to Earth. Hell, she didn't really need clean clothes. It wasn't like the slavers had cared that much about cleanliness.

The second day was spent much like the second half of the first, scavenging through the ship, this time for something to do, some form of entertainment. Kayde didn't seem to care about that stuff, when she asked, and he told her he hadn't even brought an entertainment pad with him. The ship did have an entertainment room with some sort of gaming system she didn't recognize and a holo player stocked with unfamiliar films.

On the third day she started pacing, clearing the distance from the cockpit, through the kitchen, to the crew quarters, and back, her long stride eating up the distance way too quickly to burn off the excess energy she found within herself. If anything was going to annoy Kayde, she'd expect it was that. But he said nothing, he didn't seem to be paying attention. Not that she wanted him to be paying attention. But it was strange to be around him with no one else with them. Back on Earth, they'd never been alone, not even when he went out stalking her. Stalking? Was that fair? Maybe. But if he was a stalker, why was he ignoring her now?

She just made it to the kitchen on her tenth or eleventh lap of the ship when Kayde came out of the cockpit. He spared her half a glance before making his way to the food processor. There wasn't much to eat, and it was all practically flavorless, but Quinn had had worse. That was her entire philosophy when it came to this trip. She'd had worse, she would survive.

"Why did you follow me back on Earth?" That was the problem with being cooped up, inappropriate questions just sort of popped out the second that she had any sort of intelligent companionship.

Kayde took three agonizing seconds to finish punching in the program on the processor before he swung his gaze around to look at her. How did he stay so blank all the time? There was something not right with him. And the longer she was in his company, or at least in his proximity, since they weren't exactly chat buddies, the more some things that she'd heard the Detyens and their mates say began to make sense. They didn't mean for her to hear them, that had been obvious. They only spoken when she'd walked out of the room, but her hearing was good, and they weren't nearly as quiet as they thought they were. From the little hints, she knew that Raze used to be like Kayde, used to be cold like him. And she knew the Kayde hadn't always been like this, that he'd been a happy child, joking around their base, and when he was a little older he'd become quite the playboy, just like Dryce. She wondered what tragedy had struck to make him so closed off. She didn't know how a person could go from being full of life, full of vitality, full of love, to being one step removed from an automaton. But here he was, and she doubted that he would appreciate her asking probing questions about his past. After all, she wouldn't be too keen to explain all of the things that she had done to survive, and that went well beyond the previous year and what the slavers had done to her.

Another man would've lied, or evaded the question, but that wasn't Kayde. He grabbed his meal, something that looked like a bowl full of protein slush, and stepped back from the processor, never looking away from her. "Something about you called to me. I can't define it."

"Called to you?" What the hell did that mean? Though, as her mind twirled the words around inside her head, she thought she might understand. She hadn't been following him, but every time he'd been near, it was like she could sense him at the outside of her consciousness. Was that a calling? Some kind of almost psychic connection? Not that psychics existed, at least not on Earth. That wasn't a human thing.

"It isn't something I can define any better than that. You shine brightly and I... That's all." He made it clear the conversation was over by taking his bowl with him back down the hall towards the cockpit.

* * *

Kayde had barely taken his seat again before Quinn was through the cockpit door, practically jumping around the copilot's chair and sitting in it sideways, one leg hooked over the armrest. "We weren't done talking," she said. "You can't just drop something like that and walk away."

She had asked the question, he had answered it. What more was there to say? He kept silent, unsure of what she wanted to hear.

"You followed me around all over the city, I saw you a bunch of times." It wasn't an accusation, she was just stating facts as she knew them. Kayde couldn't contradict her; after all, it was the truth. "You're really just saying that you followed me all around because you were drawn to something about me? And it never occurred to you to strike up a conversation? I'm not some—I don't know—*thing* that you can hunt. I am a person."

"I know you're a person. I know you're not a thing." Kayde wasn't sure how he had expected this conversation to go, but it wasn't like this. He certainly hadn't been prepared for the rawness in Quinn's voice, the emotion that he no longer could define. "And you had no reason to speak to me."

"You don't need a reason to start a conversation. That's *why* you start a conversation." Now she was looking at him, and this was an expression he could easily interpret. Confused. That was the look that all people that were members of the Detyen Legion eventually leveled at him. They didn't understand his way of thinking, and they couldn't understand why he was the way he was. It was the biggest kept secret of his people.

And he needed to stop this conversation before it could go much further. Soon Quinn would have questions, questions he couldn't answer, not without betraying the only things he stood for. "There are things you don't understand about me, things you don't know." That warning ought to do it. With any luck, she would back away. She would go back into the belly of the ship and leave him alone with his thoughts. Kayde felt a pang somewhere in his chest, but he ignored it. There was no use lingering with Quinn, no use making his pseudo-fixation worse.

If anything, though, his warning seemed to have the opposite effect. "Things I don't know?" she scoffed. "Yeah, I don't even know your last name. There's a ton I don't know about you, just like you don't know about me. That's why people have conversations. Are Detyens not like that? Are you... I don't know... All psychic or something? Do you have like pheromones, or whatever, that take the place of conversation?" He thought she might've been laughing at him, that she might have been teasing.

Kayde couldn't remember the last time anyone had bothered to tease him. It must've been before he lost his soul. Something unfurled within him, and for half a moment, his cheek twitched as if he were about to smile. He could almost remember what that was like. Smiles had once been easy, freely given, and taken as his due. He tried pulling his lips back, tried to find the right configuration of his face. His muscles became taut, and when he bared his teeth, Quinn sputtered.

"Um... what are you doing? Are you... Seriously... What are you doing?" She narrowed her eyes at him and leaned in a few centimeters, as if to get a better look.

Kayde wiped the expression from his face. What was he thinking? Smiling? He was soulless, he no longer had the right. But something inside him felt hollow, maybe the hole where his soul used to be. "It's NaDetya." He could not give her a real smile, but he could give her this. He wanted to give her this, even as some alarm went off inside his head, warning him of the danger of want.

"What is?" asked Quinn.

"My family name. Kayde NaDetya. What's yours?"

"Porter." Quinn scowled. She didn't like to use her surname, didn't like the memories of her childhood that it brought up. "Isn't

388

that basically Kayde of Detya? Like for me it would be Quinn of Earth? I thought you all had clan names. Dryce was telling me about it once."

An unexpected wave of something curdled inside Kayde at the mention of the young Detyen male. He had no claim on Quinn, she could speak with whoever she wanted, but he knew Dryce's attitude toward available women. "Have you spent much time with Dryce?" Even he could hear the bite in his voice.

Quinn's eyebrows skyrocketed, and she stared at him for several seconds before tilting her head to one side and blinking rapidly. "A little, I suppose," she said. "He actually knows how to carry a conversation."

Kayde didn't need to feel emotions to hear the pointed tone in that sentence. "That isn't the only thing he carries." Why had he latched on to this? Dryce was an honorable Detyen male, an accomplished soldier, and well respected among their people. Kayde could not fault the young man for doing exactly the same things that Kayde had done when he was his age. He just didn't like the thought of Quinn doing those things with him.

Like? No, he had no right to like or dislike anything. Whatever this was, he needed to get rid of it. He would schedule in time for meditation as soon as Quinn grew bored of them. He needed to center himself once more.

"Are you jealous of Dryce?" She sounded truly puzzled. "Why would you care? You said it yourself. We don't know each other."

Jealous. No, that couldn't be it. But his atrophied imagination provided an image of Quinn in Dryce's arms and the claws that lived beneath Kayde's knuckles itched to shoot out and attack the absent man. Quinn was his, Dryce couldn't have her.

No. Kayde shot up from his seat and turned his back on his companion. She wasn't his, he had no claim to her. This obsession was a danger to them both and he needed to get a hold of himself. He could not risk Quinn getting hurt because he was malfunctioning. He didn't think he could live with himself if he did anything to harm her. The remnants of his soul rebelled at the thought of causing her harm, but he couldn't trust himself, not anymore. He was no longer a man, he was simply a beast with a task: defend his people, seek revenge, follow orders. And none of those orders had anything to do with Quinn.

"Come get me if any of the alerts sound. I must take my rest." He escaped the cockpit before Quinn could say anything, and he wasn't sure if he heard her voice calling after him, or it was just the whistle of the life support system blowing through the ship.

Chapter Five

Yep, this was a terrible idea. As Kayde's footsteps retreated down the hall towards the sleeping quarters, Quinn settled back into her seat and crossed her arms, hugging herself tightly. That whole thing had been unexpected. Not that she expected anything from Kayde, not that she knew anything about him. The jealousy of Dryce? What was that about? Okay, maybe she had had an inkling about that. After all, the guy had practically been stalking her for the last month. Well, not stalking, not exactly, but he'd been paying close attention.

Did he want her? Was he attracted to her? Did she want him to want her? Did she want him? Quinn groaned and let her head fall back against the headrest, rolling it from side to side as if she could ward off some uncomfortable questions. Did she? Could she? She hadn't had any pleasant thoughts about sex, about being with someone in that way, since she had been home. Relationships had never really been her thing, and even before all of the horrors that the slavers had inflicted upon them, she hadn't had a spectacular experience. It had never been something to write home about, even if she had a home.

But Kayde was different. For one thing, he obviously wasn't human. Over the past few months she had been wary of human guys. She could remember the hard press of human fingers gripping her, hurting her, doing things to her best forgotten. But almost all of the slavers that had bothered her had been human. None of them have looked like Kayde, and that seemed to be some sort of blessing. She didn't feel uncomfortable around him, and those dark memories that swirled around at all hours didn't rise up and try and drown her when she was next to him.

And, yes, maybe she liked looking at his face. And his muscles. And those dark markings she had caught a glimpse of peeking out of the collar of his shirt. Was that attraction? Would she freak out if he tried to kiss her? If he touched her? She shifted in her seat as an unexpected flash of heat washed over her. No, she didn't think that she would have a bad reaction to him. Not at all.

What was she thinking? It was just the two of them stuck on the ship, potentially for months, and she was going to complicate that by developing feelings for him? By wanting to sleep with him? No, that way led to trouble. She couldn't walk down that path. And certainly not alone. The only thing worse than a frustrated attraction was a one-sided one.

Was it one-sided? Her mind circled back to the Dryce issue. For a man who never seemed to give anything away, Kayde's expression and body language had been practically screaming when she mentioned the younger Detyen male. Maybe that should've annoyed her. Kayde had no claim on her, and she had dumped more than one man for being consumed by his petty jealousies. But just as with everything else, Kayde was different. He made her feel different.

It would be really, *really* stupid to try something with him. He was her only way home, and if things went south she might end up stranded in space. She doubted Kayde would do that to her, no matter what happened. But she hadn't survived this long by believing the best in people.

Quinn needed to get a hold of her hormones. This probably had nothing to do with Kayde. It was just her body calling out for contact, a sign that maybe she was starting to heal after everything that had been done to her. Kayde was merely convenient, the closest male body that didn't make her shudder in terror. No, she had a feeling that if she were shuddering around him it would be for a completely different reason.

She locked down those thoughts, stuffing them in to a little box and burying it deep in her psyche. Kayde was the most closed off person she had ever met. He was practically a robot. Whatever she was seeing, she was just projecting it onto him. Even that jealousy thing. Maybe he had just been tired. After all, if he was attracted to her, wouldn't he have stuck around? Instead, he had stormed off in the middle of the conversation as if she were less interesting to him than the pillows and blankets in his bunk. Not exactly romantic material. Not exactly someone to fantasize about.

Quinn leaned forward and looked at the control panel, her eyes dancing over the blinking lights. One of her hands hovered over a control screen, but she was careful to keep her distance, careful not to touch. She wasn't about to screw up their flight by accidentally changing their destination, or expelling all of their fuel into the vacuum of space. That wouldn't be good. And if she did something like that, that would ensure that she was stuck with Kayde for more than the few months that he had anticipated.

She pulled her hand back quickly and tightly gripped the arms of her chair to resist the temptation to touch anything. She wasn't about to tempt fate. Quinn spared a glance back down the hallway towards the rest of the ship. It had gone quiet; Kayde must have made it back to his room all right. That left her alone, monitoring equipment she didn't understand, and questioning what the hell she was doing. Hopefully one day she would figure it out, and hopefully she wasn't going to go crazy with want for a man who wouldn't give her the time of day. She wasn't that desperate, and she was much stronger than that.

Kayde NaDetya could stay in his room for all she cared. She had no claim on him, and that wasn't about to change. And that was just how she liked it.

* * *

When Kayde resumed his post several hours later, Quinn switched off positions without a word. That was good, that was normal. That was what he was supposed to want. Well, not want, but it was difficult to find the right words to describe the way he experienced the world. So many languages were deeply rooted in emotion, and functioning without it could leave him adrift in vocabulary that no longer suited him. So he would have to settle for the word want, even if it wasn't quite right.

They didn't speak at all over the next day, and the trend might've continued indefinitely if Kayde hadn't checked the supply levels in their food processor and water containment systems. He'd been aware of the levels when he boarded the ship, of course. But with Quinn on board, they were going through their supplies twice as fast as anticipated. There was enough to survive to get them to Detyen HQ, but if his people's home had been destroyed, and if they could not scavenge once they got there, their situation would soon grow dire.

And even if everything was completely fine at HQ, Kayde doubted that Quinn wanted to subsist on flavorless protein packs and vitamin powders. Taste was no issue for him; in fact, the blander, the better. It was a survival tactic of the soulless. They avoided strong flavors, strong sensations, strong colors, anything that could trigger the remnants of emotion, of desire. It was a long-held theory that keeping all experiences as neutral as possible would lengthen the useful existence of the soulless. Kayde was willing to believe that. On Earth, with all of its noise and sensuality, he'd been strung like a tight wire. Back on the ship where there was much less to distract him he could feel his muscles unwinding. So long as he ignored Quinn.

It was a big ship for two people, and the task was simple when they each seemed determined to ignore one another. But with a supply stop imminently necessary, Kayde knew he would need to find his companion and inform her of the change in plans. She would not want to be kept in the dark.

He thought he would find her in the kitchen, but it was empty. She didn't answer when he knocked on the door to her room, but he remembered the ship came with an entertainment station and he realized that it was the most likely place for a human to spend her time.

The door was open and he could hear the sounds of the holo player as he got closer. Quinn's laughter echoed around him and Kayde froze in the doorway when he saw her face lit up with delight at whatever she was looking at. She was transformed, bright with emotion and looking years younger now that the worry she carried with her everywhere was nowhere to be seen. She was just the kind of woman he would've pursued before he lost his soul, beautiful with a hint of danger, who could laugh because she knew just how bad the universe could be and didn't let the darkness destroy her. If he could still wish, he would have wished for her. Would've wished that they had met years ago, before he lost his soul, before she had been subjected to terrors that kept her up at night. What would she have meant to him back then? Maybe everything.

She was the kind of woman he would have wanted for a denya. But even if Raze had been lucky enough to find his after losing his soul, Kayde held out no such hope for himself. The universe did not hand out miracles like that, and he certainly didn't deserve one.

The holo player went silent when Quinn realized he was standing there. Their eyes locked for a moment and a sharp echo of desire stabbed Kayde in the gut. He would've wanted this woman so much, would have done anything to claim her back when he could.

"When did your eyes get red? Are you okay?" Quinn asked.

Red? No, that was impossible. "It must be a trick of the light," he said. None of the soulless had the inner fire that allowed their eyes to shift color when they felt strong emotion.

Quinn looked at him, looked at his eyes, for several moments, but eventually shrugged. "Whatever. Did you need something?" And just like that, whatever connection had flared between them for a moment was gone. She hadn't moved physically, but somehow she had put hundreds of kilometers between them.

"We're low on food. Not critically, but I'll be making a stop soon. We don't have many options in this sliver of space, but there's an outpost not far out of the way of our journey. I thought you would want to know." Message delivered, Kayde turned to go.

"Thank you for telling me," Quinn called after him.

"You're welcome." He didn't stay to chat, though his feet wanted to turn around and take him back to Quinn. He wanted to see if he could close that distance between them once more, wanted to see if she would open up and speak to him, even as he realized that he was the one who kept ending their conversations by walking away. A lifetime ago he had understood how to talk to people, had understood how to be a person. He would have to dig deep to resurrect the memories of who he'd once been. He wouldn't be able to re-create that man, he couldn't feel like he once did, but he could take the skills he used to have and apply them to the life he was living now. He could give Quinn a conversational companion, even if he could give her nothing else. She deserved the choice of whether or not she wanted to be left alone. She shouldn't be forced to be alone because he couldn't handle spending five minutes in her company.

Kayde would dig deep, would do what needed to be done. He couldn't change his past, but he could give her this. It wasn't much, but it was all he had.

Chapter Six

Beznifa was nothing to write home about. That was Quinn's first thought as she and Kayde climbed out of their ship. The spaceport was bustling with dozens of small craft and a bunch of aliens that she couldn't identify. Mixed among them were Oscavians, humans, and a few other races that she had seen on Earth. The native population of Beznifa, the Beznens, looked kind of like humans. But their necks were too long, they all had pearlescent white hair, eyes that took up half of their faces, noses that seemed so small they were barely slits, and creepily long fingers. But they had two legs, two arms, and one head, and they spoke out of their normal-sized mouths.

For a moment Quinn was struck by what a human from two hundred years ago would have thought about all this. Back then they'd all thought that differences in skin tone and musculature were enough to determine one's superiority or inferiority. There were still echoes of those prejudices embedded in their society, but ever since aliens came to Earth, the small differences among humans grew smaller every day. Centuries gone by, a human would've looked at the Beznens in fear, only seeing the ways that the aliens were different, but when Quinn looked, she was relieved to see their similarities.

"Is there a supply depot?" she asked her silent companion. In the day it had taken to get to Beznifa, Kayde hadn't spoken to her. But this time it was a little different than the days before that. He didn't seem to be ignoring her, he just didn't know what to say. That made two of them.

"According to the directory information, there is a market not far from here. We should be able to find everything we need." His eyes scanned the perimeter of the spaceport, looking for threats, reminding Quinn that he was a warrior and that they weren't on vacation.

"Are there any points of interest? Fun landmarks? This is my first time off Earth when I'm not..." She trailed off, not wanting to remind him, or herself, of all that had been done to her.

Her slip didn't seem to affect Kayde's mood. "We have a schedule to keep to. We should stay the night here to let our ship run its cleaning protocol, but we should not linger."

Of course not. They wouldn't want to risk having any fun. Quinn kept those thoughts to herself. She and Kayde were operating under an unspoken truce, and she wasn't going to be the one to break it.

Open air shuttles manned by smiling Beznens took interstellar visitors from the spaceport to the market. She and Kayde climbed onto the small vehicle alongside two glowering Oscavians. She wondered if these men knew Nyden Varrow or Ambassador Yormas, but chastised herself or even thinking it. It wasn't like she knew every criminal on Earth, and she would be offended if someone asked her questions like that just because she was human. The Oscavian Empire was much bigger than Earth, almost too vast to comprehend. Two Oscavians on a minor outpost in the middle of nowhere were unlikely to know anything connected to what Quinn and her Detyen friends were dealing with.

She turned her attention to the streets of Pelinfa, the city they'd landed in. Dust seemed to coat everything, giving the world around them a slightly aged and yellowed look. The Beznens didn't seem to mind; they walked around all smiles, greeting each other with nods and embraces. All of the buildings around them were single-story, and Quinn looked around for anything taller. In the distance she saw a collection of poles that had strips of cloth that could've been flags hanging off of them.

Curious, she waved at their Beznen driver and asked, "What's that up there?"

The Beznen smiled and followed her finger. "That is the governor's palace," she—he? Quinn wasn't sure—responded in her melodious voice. The words seemed to wrap around Quinn like a hug and she wanted to ask the Beznen more questions just to hear her speak further. If she were an enterprising sort, she might've recorded the alien and sold the files back on Earth to someone looking for a new kind of high. She was sure if she listened for long, that was what would happen.

But Quinn didn't ask any more. She settled back into her seat beside Kayde and let the rest of the ride go by in silence. Well, not complete silence. She nearly jumped out of her seat when a disembodied Beznen voice wrapped up around them, welcoming them to Pelinfa and entreating them to have a blessed and peaceful visit. The voice warned them that violence of all kinds was prohibited outside of designated areas and that the use of weapons was punishable by death. They were told that a collection of androids and willing aliens were available for any kind of desire and that they should inquire at the market for more information.

Quinn's veins turned to ice at that announcement and any magic in the Beznen's voice dissolved. Slavery was a too common practice out in the galaxy, and she couldn't help but imagine that she might've ended up in a place like this, a slave to any trader's wants, provided as a perk of tourism.

She practically jumped out of her skin when Kayde placed his hand on her knee. From someone else it might've reminded her of the things she was trying to forget, but Kayde only offered comfort and gave her a moment to center herself. She wanted to run through the marketplace and free everyone she found in chains, but there were only two of them and they were only going to be on the planet for a day. What kind of person did that make her? She had almost suffered the life she was about to be forced to witness, and she was about to do nothing to save the victims from it.

Kayde leaned in close and spoke directly into her ear, his lips almost brushing against her skin. "I would offer to take you to a different planet, one that has outlawed slavery, but this was the only prospect on our entire journey. We have enough fuel to make it to our destination. We can turn around right now."

For a guy who didn't seem to understand how people worked, he had read that situation correctly. "No, it's okay," she whispered back. "Let's get this over with."

She didn't see any slaves in the marketplace, and that almost made it worse, knowing they were there, that their suffering underpinned the economy of this little city and yet seeing no evidence of it. Talk of the trade already had her on edge, and as they passed more Beznens, both those shopping and those manning their stalls, she couldn't help but feel that something was off about them. No matter what they were saying, who they were talking to, or whether they were talking to anyone at all they smiled as bright as the midday sun. It was kind of creepy. And they kept looking at her. Quinn had developed a keen sense of figuring out when she was being watched. It had been necessary for her survival back during her days among the slavers, and every sense that she had picked up back then was ringing in her head, telling her that she had fallen under the eye of someone dangerous.

But when she looked around, no one was looking at her inappropriately. Sure, some of the stall vendors were trying to get her attention, but that was nothing special. And then she realized that she was the only human in the market. Was that weird? It felt weird. Hadn't she seen some people back at the spaceport? Or were they some other race that just looked human from a distance?

"Do you feel like this all the time?" she asked Kayde, keeping her voice down. She didn't want the people on this planet to hear her every thought, and the feel of eyes on her back was making her paranoid.

Kayde looked up from the collection of fabrics he'd been examining. "What do you mean?" His eyes scanned the perimeter around them again. He hadn't stopped doing it since they hit the ground, as if he were subconsciously sensing the threat that neither of them could see.

"There aren't any other humans around." Only as she said it did she realize that it might be insensitive to remind him of the fact that he was one of the last surviving members of his race.

But like everything else, Kayde didn't seem bothered by that. "I highly doubt that what you're feeling and my state are similar." It could have been a rebuke, but she didn't get any sense of censure.

"In your state? What does that mean?" It might have been a trick of their translators—sometimes words got garbled—but they hadn't had any communication issues so far. At least not when it came to words.

Kayde looked at her for so long that the feeling of being watched started to fade as all of her focus narrowed in on him. "I meant nothing by it."

Quinn wasn't sure she believed that, but she wasn't about to get into an argument in the middle of the marketplace. When Kayde looked away, the feeling of being watched returned. "Do you feel—"

"No," he interrupted before she could finish her question. Was it the planet making Kayde snippy? Or was it just because she was seeing him around people now that she realized how cold, how heartless he could be?

"If you don't want to talk, just say so." She was a little hurt from the tone that he took, a little put off. They were friends, or if not that, companions. And on this planet they were all each other had. He didn't need to start acting like a bastard just because she'd asked a few innocent questions.

"We should try to find a hotel or an inn for the night," said Kayde. He nodded towards the horizon. "I don't think we have much more daylight left."

"I wouldn't mind getting off the streets," Quinn said, taking one more stab at conversation. "Something about it... I don't know, there's something weird here."

Kayde did his warrior scanning thing again before looking back to her. "Weird how? What do you see?"

"It's what I'm not seeing that's freaking me out," Quinn admitted. "I just feel like everyone's looking at me? Like I'm being watched. It's like eyes are crawling all over me."

"Crawling eyes?" He might have been speaking in his normal monotone, but even she could catch the hint of sarcasm. Or maybe she was just reading into it.

"So nothing feels off about this place to you?" Kayde was the one experienced in space travel, the one who had freely traveled to dozens of planets or more and seen so many things that Quinn couldn't begin to imagine. "Maybe it's just because this place is different from Earth. I'm probably overreacting."

"If you're uncomfortable—"

Kayde was interrupted from whatever he was about to say by a smiling Beznen wearing a bright red cloak and a giant gold medallion around its neck. His. All the Beznens kind of looked the same when it came to determining gender. Quinn realized that none of them had beards or breasts and that might have been why she had so much difficulty telling them apart. It was just another reminder that they were aliens and she couldn't use her human standards to judge them by.

"Welcome, welcome," said the Beznen in that comforting, soporific tone they all had. "I have been greeting visitors all day and I was worried that I would miss you." He held out his hands to Quinn, palms down, as if he expected her to clasp them. She glanced at Kayde to see if he had any idea what was going on, or if he knew who they were talking to, but her stoic companion was no help. "I am Yile, and the governor of this fine region has tasked me with welcoming all newcomers to our beautiful city. It is not very often that someone so exotic and radiant blesses our humble land."

Quinn darted a glance around, looking for whatever exotic, beautiful creature this guy was talking about. Could he mean Kayde? To her eyes he was definitely beautiful, or handsome, but Yile was looking right at her and the discomfort that she'd been feeling since they landed only amplified.

"It's... a good market you have here," Quinn finally said when Kayde let the silence between them go on for too long.

"Oh yes," said Yile. "We may be small, but we sit on plenty of trade routes. Tell me, do you plan to stay long with us? There is so much to see, so much to experience here. Even if you would not know it from what we have on display."

"We're just here for the night." Quinn offered him a regretful smile, even if she wished they were going to the shuttle right now and about to head back to their ship. "I'm sure your planet is great."

Yile sighed. "Of course you haven't decided to let us keep you," he said, laughing for some reason. "Have you chosen your lodgings? I would be happy to provide recommendations."

"We have not," Kayde said before Quinn could demur. She didn't want this guy knowing where they were sleeping. There was something predatory about him, something that made her not want to turn her back.

Yile clapped his hands together in delight. "You must take rooms at the Governor's Inn. It is just down the main road and caters to all sorts of foreigners. I shall call on ahead and ensure that you have quarters for the night. Please give me your name."

Quinn opened her mouth to tell him, but the word wouldn't come out. "I'm Q," she said after what must have been an obvious pause. "That's K."

"Wonderful, wonderful," said Yile. "Identify yourselves at the Inn and you will be led to where you belong." He made his farewells and left Kayde and Quinn to finish their shopping.

Once Quinn was sure the Beznen was out of earshot she shot Kayde a look. "He was weird, right?"

"He welcomed us," said Kayde. "How is that weird?"

Her companion couldn't understand subtext to save his life. "It wasn't what he said, it was how he said it. And there's something in the way these Beznens speak, I'm not sure I like how it makes me feel."

"You feel different when they speak?" he asked.

He didn't? How could she even describe it? "It's like a hug, and at first it's all soft and warm, but then I remember that it's a stranger that's hugging me, and I never told them they could touch me. Does that make sense?"

Kayde was silent, a clear sign that it didn't.

"Whatever, let's go to the hotel. Maybe then this whole place won't seem so creepy."

Chapter Seven

If anything, the feeling intensified once they got to the hotel. A smiling Beznen host directed Quinn to her room and instructed Kayde to remain at the front desk, promising that someone would be along shortly for him. She was being shepherded down the dark, narrow hallway before she could remember that they should make plans for dinner, or at least decide when they were going to meet up in the morning. She tried to get her guide to pause for a moment so she could turn around and speak to Kayde, but every time Quinn tried to speak, she lost the train of her thought and before she knew it they were standing in front of a bright blue door and the host invited her to enter and make herself at home.

"A meal is prepared and waiting for you," said the host. This one had not offered a name, and the dark light inside the hotel made it even more difficult to judge the correct pronouns to use. "Please make yourself at home."

Between one blink and the next Quinn was left alone in a small but finely appointed room. There was a soft looking bed, piled high with blankets and pillows that looked like they would suffocate her with softness. A small table pushed up against the far wall held the promised dinner; at least, Quinn assumed that was what was hiding under the opaque plate cover. An open door led to a small bathroom, and a soft robe hung on a hook, just tempting her to undress and get comfortable.

Quinn reached out and ran her fingers along the satiny material. It was almost cool to the touch, which surprised her. She'd been expecting something like flannel, but things were not always what they seemed.

She darted her head into the bathroom and was glad to see a nice assortment of toiletries. She hadn't bothered to bring a bag down to the planet, hoping she could buy anything she needed at the market. But she and Kayde had arranged to have all of their supplies delivered directly to the spaceport and she'd been so preoccupied with the weird cloud of observation she'd been under all day that she forgot to set a few items aside for her overnight stay.

Her clothes would survive another wearing. They were covered in that yellowish dust they'd been surrounded by all day, but though the dust made the planet look hazy, it hadn't been hot, and she hadn't even sweated much. Besides, who was going to judge her? Kayde? He'd seen her in much worse, and she had never felt self-conscious around him. Yeah, maybe sometimes she got the urge to pretty herself up and show off, but he never expected it of her, and he never made her feel like a slob when she walked around the ship in the pajamas she'd managed to scrounge up on her first day.

A wave of hunger washed over Quinn and she realized that she couldn't remember the last time she'd eaten. Had it been on the ship? She and Kayde certainly hadn't stopped for food while they were in the market. She sat down at the small table and lifted the cover over her dinner. It didn't look like anything she recognized, but it smelled good and her stomach clenched, rippling almost painfully at the thought of eating it. She picked up a spoon and before she knew it the food was gone. She couldn't have described the taste, she'd eaten so fast. It was good. She thought. She really wasn't sure. She really didn't care.

Meal completed, her body decided to shut down. She stumbled over to the bed and barely pushed back the covers before falling in and surrendering to sleep.

It took her a little while to realize she was dreaming. All of a sudden she was back on the ship hurtling through space to destinations unknown. The ride wasn't nearly as smooth as usual and her steps faltered, sending her crashing into one of the walls. She righted herself, leaving two arms out for balance. The hallway was longer than it should've been. Whether she was going towards the cockpit or towards the sleeping quarters, she should have gotten there by now. But the gray walls stretched and stretched and stretched as far as she could see, only vaguely flickering lights giving her a sense of distance. A smudge in the distance resolved into Kayde and he ran towards her, his expression almost comically easy-to-read.

Worried.

Worried? Kayde didn't get worried. He kept himself frighteningly contained. Even if some space dragon were about to bathe them in fire before swallowing them whole, there wouldn't be a flicker of concern. So what was the problem now?

He was saying something. She could see his lips moving and even heard a garbled noise, like she was underwater and the sound was all distorted. But she couldn't make sense of the syllables he was trying to push out.

When she tried to ask him to repeat himself, his face scrunched up in confusion, as if he were having the same problem. Quinn tried to speak again, louder this time, but it didn't help. What was going on? Where were they? This wasn't the ship. She reached for Kayde and tugged on the lapel of his jacket, relieved to find that she could touch him just fine. She didn't want to be stuck in this hallway for long. She didn't know what was coming, and she didn't like it.

But no matter how far they walked, and after a few minutes ran, they didn't seem to be getting anywhere. The hallway just went on and on and on, gray walls suffocating them. Quinn stopped running. She stopped walking. It wasn't doing anything, wasn't helping. She turned back to Kayde, almost afraid that he would have disappeared or turned into some kind of monster while she wasn't looking. But he was the same old Kayde, at least the dream version of him, the expressive one. His worry had deepened and he tried to speak again, but it was just like earlier and she couldn't hear anything.

She let go of his jacket and reached for his hand, but as her fingers brushed his flesh something jolted through her, knocking her out of the dream and waking her up.

Quinn opened her eyes and practically jumped out of the bed. She wasn't in the hotel anymore. What the fuck was going on?

* * *

The last thing he remembered before everything went wrong was standing in the lobby of the inn and watching Quinn be escorted to her room. Kayde's reflexes must have been getting dulled, or the sense of anxiety that had dogged Quinn, and therefore him, all day had put him too on edge to recognize the threat when it came for him. Something bit at his neck, a nuisance nick like some kind of bug, and before he could swat it away, he was falling to the floor, the world going gray around him.

Kayde woke up groggy, his mouth full of cotton, with the nagging sense that he had forgotten something important. The first thing he noticed was the smell. Death, decay, pain, and something like bleach trying to mask it all. It didn't work at all. He kept his breathing even and his eyes closed, not wanting to give away that he was awake if some enemy or guard were looming over him. But this wasn't his first time being held captive, nor his second, and Kayde soon realized that he was alone. And unbound, even better.

Still, he moved slowly, cautiously. Anything could have been done to him while he slept. He took stock of himself and found no injuries other than a few bruises that had probably happened while he was being transported to wherever he was. The room he was being held in was dark and small, but there had to be light coming in from somewhere. He couldn't see well, but he could see enough. If he stretched out both arms he could touch either end of his cell, and when he tested the handle on the door, it was unsurprisingly locked. The cell was absolutely bare. No cot, no chains hanging off the wall, not even a blanket to ward off the damp chill in the room. He was wearing the same clothes that he'd been wearing all day, though a check of his pockets turned up empty. They'd removed his communicator and anything else they could find.

A more paranoid Detyen would have sewn something into his clothes, some hidden tool that could be used to mount an escape or an attack on whoever lay in wait. But Kayde had expected no threat on Beznifa. Nothing in the published information about the place suggested anything dangerous. He would have never taken Quinn to any place dangerous if it could be avoided.

Where was Quinn? Now that he assessed the immediate threat level, his mind was able to expand to the other important things. Had Quinn been imprisoned as well? Was she in a similarly dark room, scared and alone and remembering every horrible thing that had been done to her on Fenryr 1? Something dark rattled within Kayde's chest. He would kill anyone who touched her. No one on this planet had the right.

Besides him, that dark voice inside whispered. She was his to protect, his to cherish, his...

He lost the thought as something clanged in the distance, perhaps a door opening. Something dragged outside, heavy and slow. A body? Supplies? No way to know. He listened as the dragging sound faded, trying to draw a mental map of what it looked like outside of his cell. After a minute it was silent again and Kayde was fairly certain that he was sitting somewhere in the middle of a long hallway. If he got the door opened and turned left, that loud clanging door would be several meters away. If there was a door to the right, he hadn't heard it open or close. There could just as easily be a turn in the hallway that muffled the dragging noise. It occurred to him that his captors could have been deliberately making the noise as a way to trick him. If they had a camera watching him, they knew he was awake. But he doubted the noise was a trick. It was too subtle. Anyone without training on how to deal with a situation like this wouldn't have been able to map the hall outside with so little information.

But he would keep the thought in mind and keep listening, waiting for his moment.

His stomach growled and he realized that he hadn't eaten all day. He wasn't at any risk of starving, not yet, but the longer he went without food the less effective a warrior he would be. He'd already failed to stop himself from being captured, and it would be difficult to rescue Quinn, wherever she was, if he was delirious from hunger and thirst.

Where was she? He couldn't hear any sounds of feminine screams, but he took that as a good sign. He hoped that it meant that if Quinn were in a cell near him she wasn't being tortured. He decided not to dwell on the possibility that there could be some level of soundproofing that would make it impossible to hear her.

The door down the hall clanged but this time it wasn't followed by any dragging. Kayde listen closely and when a sound scraped outside his own cell, he stepped far enough back from the door to give himself a little room to maneuver. It wouldn't have mattered. A bright light flashed, temporarily blinding him, and before he could get his bearings a net was thrown over him, clamping his arms close to his sides and tripping up his feet. He struggled, but he couldn't get his bearings about him to give a good fight, and the bite in the material of the net told him that his claws would be useless in freeing himself.

The hallway outside was almost as dark as his cell, and the flash of light had completely obliterated his night vision. No matter how much Kayde tried to look around, he couldn't tell how long the hallway was or how to get out. He didn't know where they were taking him. Was he about to face some sort of judgment? Execution? Release? The last one at least was highly doubtful.

If he had his soul, he might have been panicking, but Kayde had little concern for himself. He needed to survive to rescue Quinn and to complete his mission, and he could realize that at some point his priorities had become skewed. His duty to his people was supposed to come first, it was supposed to be the only thing that mattered. But he knew that if he were given the choice, Quinn's safety would come before the mission without the slightest bit of hesitation.

His own life didn't matter, but Quinn's did. She had continued this mission for her own reasons, ones he didn't quite understand, and it was his responsibility to see that she made it home.

They went through the door. As it clanged shut behind them another one opened, and the scent of death and despair grew even worse. He stepped forward and the ground felt softer under him, like he was laying on dirt rather than concrete. His captors grasped the net around him and picked him up, pitching him forward onto the hard, dirt covered ground.

Near him, too close to escape, something roared, ruffling his hair under the confines of the net. Kayde's heartbeat picked up as the song of battle called to him. His eyes began to adjust and he rolled to one side, taking in the small arena-like room he'd been thrown into. The walls were too tall for him to climb, at least twice his height, and even if he managed to make it, a strong but delicate cage climbed all the way up to the ceiling, keeping whatever spectators were watching safe from the monsters in the arena.

No, arena wasn't the right word for this kind of place. It was too small, too dingy. This was a fighting pit.

Kayde struggled against the net, trying to free himself while looking for the source of the roars that seemed to be getting closer.

The wall opposite him opened up, the door appearing solid stone, and from the black hole that had to lead to another darkened hallway came a beast that belonged in a monster's nightmares. Kayde worked faster to get free of his bonds. He didn't need anyone to tell him that this was a fight to the death. He said he would kill anyone who put Quinn in danger, this was only the first step.

One of the monster's tentacles hit the ground and something oozed out of it, sizzling against the dirt. Kayde finally freed himself from the net and rolled away with barely a second to spare before another tentacle hit right where he'd been lying. It grabbed hold of the net and that sturdy material seemed to dissolve in a matter of seconds.

Kayde tried to center himself, focusing on his opponent and letting all thoughts, all the rest of his concerns float away. He had to win, there was no other choice.

Chapter Eight

Quinn was out of bed like a shot, tangling in the covers and stumbling when her feet hit the softly carpeted floor. This wasn't the room at the inn. That place had been quaint, just a bed, a table, and a bathroom. She looked around now agog, and briefly wondered if she and some princess from an ancient fairy tale had switched lives. A quick glance down showed she was no longer wearing the clothes she'd slept in. They'd been replaced with a frilly light blue sleeping gown with bright green cuffs and delicately embroidered silver stitching in a pattern she couldn't quite make out.

Bile rose in her throat as she realized that someone had undressed her while she slept, had touched her without her consent. Her hands trembled, and she had to clench her jaw to keep it from quivering. She wanted to dive back into that bed—even if it was the wrong one—and close her eyes on the faint hope that she'd wake up shortly and find out that this was all one bad dream. But she didn't need to pinch herself to know that wasn't the case. She'd already filled her weird dream quota for the night.

Quinn closed her eyes where she stood and took a deep breath, quelling the quickly rising panic. She counted down slowly from ten, keeping in mind all the ways that she was still okay. It was easier to do here than it had been back with the slavers. She wasn't injured and she didn't hurt, she was fully clothed, she wasn't hungry, she was clean. That was more than she'd had for a long time, until the past few months.

She let her eyes open slowly and took a look around. The room hadn't changed. It was bright and big enough that a hundred people could stand inside with room to spare. If she spoke, she wouldn't be shocked if her voice echoed, but her throat felt like it was clamped in a vise and she didn't think she could speak right then to save her life. If that was the only way the panic manifested, she'd be lucky.

The walls were the same pale blue as the outfit she'd been dressed in, and the dark wood ceiling seemed strange, unlike any design trend on Earth. But Quinn was a long way from home. The bed was proportional to the room, huge and soft, with a pale green quilt that could cover a dozen people if they squeezed in tight. There was only one other person she might be willing to share that monstrosity of a bed with, though.

Where was Kayde?

Why hadn't she protested when the proprietor of the inn had separated them?

There was no use dwelling on that now. Quinn needed to find Kayde and see what the hell was going on. Maybe there was some innocent explanation for this. Maybe this was just how things worked on Beznifa. After all, the only aliens she'd ever willingly spent time around were the Detyens, so while she'd learned some of their customs, she knew nothing about how the Beznens operated.

No, none of those excuses were ringing true. Something fishy was going on, something that she didn't want to get mixed up in. She and Kayde needed to get away from this place before something terrible happened. She could feel it coming, she just wasn't sure what *it* was and she didn't want to find out.

First things first, Quinn needed real clothes. She wasn't about to run around in a borrowed nightie, especially when there could be lots of running involved. How far away was she from the ship? Had the Beznens done anything to damage it? She really hoped not. She wasn't a mechanic, and though she trusted Kayde's flying skills, he'd never said anything about being able to fix the ship.

That was a problem for later and they'd deal with it if it they needed to.

Quinn tried to find a closet or a wardrobe, any place that might hold a convenient pair of pants and some sturdy shoes, preferably the ones that belonged to her. She spun around, trying to take the whole room in, and her sense of unease grew, pounding insistently at her consciousness. The place was huge and brightly lit, but though the light seemed natural, like the sun was shining down on her, she didn't see any windows, and there were no bulbs hanging from the ceiling. She couldn't tell where the light was coming from.

And there wasn't a closet. Or a bathroom, or any door at all.

That panic from earlier tried to claw its way out of her gut again, but Quinn tamped it down, taking a tight grip on her emotions and burying them deep. She could freak out later, and it wouldn't be pretty, but right now she had to stay in the moment, had to figure out what was going on.

No doors. Not good. That took the situation from *funny misunderstanding* territory and transformed it into *prison*. Cold sweat covered her arms, making the pretty outfit she'd been dressed in stick to her in clammy clumps. *No, no, no panicking, not yet.* The sweat didn't stop, but a few deep breaths helped to pull her back from the edge.

Just because Quinn couldn't see a door didn't mean that one wasn't there, she reasoned. After all, she'd been placed inside of the room, somehow, and that meant there had to be a way in. And if there was a way in, that meant there was a way out. Right?

She crossed the floor, almost angry at how soft the carpet was against her feet. Prison shouldn't be comfortable. It shouldn't make a person forget to dream of freedom. But between the bed, the plushness underfoot, and the fancy clothes, she could almost imagine thoughts of Earth, thoughts of her life before drifting away if they kept her in here for long enough. Give her an entertainment system and this place would be a hundred times fancier than any place she'd ever lived. A girl could get used to it.

And that was why she needed to escape.

* * *

Kayde sank into memories of blood and death, of defeat and triumph. The monster came at him, all claws and tentacles, and it was no secret that if the beast touched him it would all be over. His skin was thick, but it could not sustain contact with whatever acid the creature was secreting for long. It was taller than Kayde by half and had too many tentacles to count. That should have given Kayde an advantage of movement, but the being seemed adapted for life on dry land. It used its limbs deftly, a dance Kayde might have been able to respect if he hadn't been about to die.

There were no weapons in the pit, nothing but the sand on the ground and the high walls. Even the net used to bind him was gone,

413

dissolved in a sizzling pile of goo that Kayde was careful to keep his distance from. This was unlike any battle he'd ever fought. The simulators at HQ training offered nothing in the way of pit fighting and he had no idea where the alien trying to kill him had come from, let alone its strengths and weaknesses. But now it was time to learn.

Perhaps the smart move would be to wait until the creature tired itself out. The tentacles looked heavy and it was heaving them with abandon. However, Kayde couldn't count on the fact that the being *could* be worn out. He couldn't stake his life on it. The thing came for him again, and when Kayde went to roll out of the way he misjudged by a few centimeters and fire flared along the side of his ankle where a bit of venom had landed on him. He kept moving while the crowd went wild and let his claws flash out.

There crowd quieted to a murmur as the question went around, wondering what he was going to do next, pointing out that he wasn't as helpless as they'd first thought. But Kayde didn't attack the creature. The fire was burrowing deep down into his muscles and he had no doubt that if he let it, it would eat through to the bone and destroy his leg, finishing him off if the monster didn't kill him first. He swiped his claws against the fabric of his pants, tearing a ragged hole and exposing his skin to the harsh air of the pit. Green blood oozed out around the sizzling venom and Kayde's first instinct was to wipe it away, but sense prevailed. He grit his teeth and flipped to his side, quickly rubbing his leg in the coarse sand underfoot. It abraded his wound, tearing at the flesh and getting grit where it shouldn't be. He hoped he'd be able to clean it later, but he had more pressing concerns at the moment.

The creature had fallen back, perhaps pleased that it had drawn first blood and playing it up for the crowd. But that victory had only lasted seconds and then it was coming back toward Kayde, who sprang up to his feet and tried to ignore the pain in his leg and the weakness it could bring. They fell into the rhythm, the beast and him. It attacked, Kayde defended, it pushed forward, Kayde retreated. Every time he stepped a new wave of agony flashed down his side, but Kayde pushed all of that down into the smallest recess of his mind. Pain he could deal with, there was no recovering from death.

Already his limbs were starting to feel heavy as the fight dragged on and on. Only battle for sport lasted this long. A fight on the streets was over in seconds, and war was another monster altogether. The strongest weapon of all was no blade or blaster, it was a sharp mind and acute senses, ready to act before he was even fully conscious of the opening in his enemy's defenses.

Kayde's claws flashed out, and as he made contact with the beast, wrapping his legs around one of the tentacles and leveraging himself up to hit at the pulsing core of the monster's center mass, Kayde yelled in agony. The entire thing was covered in that same slime that had tried to eat through his leg. He could feel it coating his claws and his arm, but that didn't stop him from digging deep until blood spurted and the animal beneath him went taut and then limp as life fled.

The crowd went wild as the creature's body collapsed to the floor, leaving Kayde the victor of this death match. He ignored them, even knowing that doing so could mean his own peril. He wiped his hands as thoroughly as he could on the dusty ground, removing the thin coating of slime that was trying to eat through his clothes and flesh. It didn't seem to be as potent as what had been shot at his leg, but he hated to think what it would do to him if he left it there for long.

Lights flashed rapidly, the blink of them disorienting, making Kayde dizzy. Or perhaps that was the injury catching up to him. He heard the door open and looked back the way he'd entered, falling into ready position and expecting another flight. Would they keep throwing monsters at him until he fell? Or was he to be named victor and showered in accolades?

Neither, it turned out. A half-dozen guards, all covered from head to toe in heavy duty armor, marched out, blasters at the ready. Kayde stayed in position, ready to fight. Was this another test? He could take one or two men with blasters. But six? He didn't have the skills or the speed. Not while he was injured and stuck in the middle of this bloody spectacle.

He was so focused on the guards that he never saw the shot coming. Something nicked his neck and before Kayde could reach up to swat at it, he was already falling to the ground unconscious.

415

*　*　*

The hours dragged on and Quinn was about to go out of her mind from the mix of boredom and terror she couldn't ignore. Though the room was huge, pacing ate up all the distance from one wall to another in a few handfuls of steps. She didn't know what she expected, but it sure wasn't this. Shouldn't a guard have come for her by now? Shouldn't someone have been there to terrorize her? If there was one thing she could consider herself an expert in, it was being held captive. She practically had a PhD in that subject. But she was quickly learning that they did things differently on Beznifa.

She was still wearing the pajamas she had woken up in. Despite a thorough search, she'd been unable to uncover any other clothes or shoes. The walls weren't hiding any cleverly disguised storage containers, and whatever door they had brought her into the room through, it had disappeared. But she wasn't actively panicking. If there had been a seedy-looking guard making comments about how soft and pretty she looked, then she wouldn't be able to contain herself. But right now she was only being tortured by the memory of those men. People said that the worst kind of torture was the kind that lived in your own mind, but Quinn would take that any day over the shit that had actually been done to her. The people who made asinine comments about mental torture had clearly never experienced the real thing.

Quinn practically jumped out of her skin when bells rang faintly behind her. There hadn't been any noise in the room except for her footsteps, which had been swallowed by the plush carpeting, and her breathing, which practically echoed in the cavernous space. She spun around, hands raised in defense. She knew a few tricks, but she was no fighter. That didn't mean she was going to go down easy.

But the person standing haloed by a bright light in a doorway that hadn't been there a minute ago didn't seem like she was getting ready to smack Quinn around. This Beznen looked like all the other ones that Quinn had met, pearlescent skin, large features, long limbs, serene face, but she was dressed in a fine wraparound gown

416

in pale lavender. If this were Earth, Quinn would've said that this was a rich woman, someone with power, someone who could hurt her or help her depending on a whim. Was the same true on Beznifa? Quinn would have to wait and see.

"I'm so glad to see you are awake." The Beznen's words wrapped around her in the soft hug that they all seem to speak with.

Quinn's skin crawled and she shuddered at the thought of any of them touching her. "What's going on? Where am I?" She tried to keep her voice even, tried to act like she didn't suspect that anything was wrong. She didn't know if she would be able to lull the Beznen into a false sense of security, but it was worth a shot.

"You are confused, and that is regrettable. You have my apologies." The Beznen's serene tone never changed. She spoke like Quinn was having an issue at a shop or a restaurant, not like she was being held prisoner on a planet far from home.

"What's going on?" she repeated. She almost asked after Kayde, but some instinct held her back.

"Follow me, and all will be well," said the Beznen, still not giving her anything approaching an answer to her question.

For a moment Quinn almost rejected the instruction on principle, but spite wasn't going to get her and Kayde out of this mess. Hell, maybe Kayde was waiting for her wherever the Beznen woman was taking her. So Quinn followed.

Her captor or tour guide, the distinction wasn't clear, led her down the brightly lit hallway. Just like in her room, or holding cell, Quinn couldn't tell where the light was coming from, and there were no windows so she couldn't determine the time of day or if the building she was in was near any place she recognized. She was almost worried that they were on a space ship hurtling towards the slave markets or some other equally disgusting place. But Quinn had been on enough ships to know the feel of artificial gravity, and right now she was almost certain that they were standing on solid ground.

Her captor/guide waved her hand in front of a small panel on the wall. It was almost invisible, and the only thing giving it away was that it was a shade or two darker than the bright paint that practically glowed. Quinn would've thought it was just a shadow, but a panel slid to the side and revealed a small room with a table laden with food waiting for the two of them.

"Do you have a name?" Quinn asked her captor/guide.

The woman studied her for a moment. "Of course," she said, as if Quinn were a child who had just asked a very stupid question. "But you may call me Mara."

But? Was Mara not her name? Quinn wasn't going to dwell on that; at least she had something to call the woman now.

"Please partake of these refreshments. We have much to do, and the day grows short." She stood in the doorway and waved Quinn into the room.

Quinn remembered how quickly she'd fallen asleep after the last meal she'd eaten, and she suspected that she'd been drugged. But her stomach grumbled and she briefly warred with herself. Did she take the risk and eat? Or did she suffer and starve, holding off until she couldn't say no?

Delicious smells wafted out of the room, and Quinn's stomach clenched. That decided her. If the Beznens wanted her to do things today they weren't about to knock her out. At worst they might give her something to soften her up. That thought was enough to make her second-guess her decision to eat. But by then Quinn was already sitting down and Mara was fixing her a plate filled with things she couldn't identify.

Eat or refuse? Quinn's fingers hovered over something that looked like a pastry, and after a final moment of indecision she picked it up. Mara didn't look particularly triumphant as Quinn took a bite, and Quinn hoped that meant the food wasn't tampered with. Her plate was piled high with enough to leave her stuffed until she was fattened up like a beast for the slaughter. That possibility hadn't occurred to her at first, and Quinn wasn't sure if it was better or worse than the prospect of slavery.

Still distantly worried about drugs, and more directly worried about becoming a fattened calf, Quinn left off eating after the first edge of hunger was sated. She could have eaten everything on the plate, but she still had enough self-control to hold back.

"I'm done," she told Mara. She didn't feel dizzy or drunk or anything like that, but Quinn was keeping close monitoring on her physical state. Not that there was much she could do about it at this point.

Mara smiled, her lips seeming to stretch too far, as if she wasn't quite sure how a smile was supposed to work. "Excellent. Now come, we must prepare you."

"Prepare me for what?" Yeah, that was a little testy, but Quinn was getting tired of trying to pretend she wasn't freaking out.

"For your coronation," Mara replied, leaving Quinn even more confused.

"Coronation?" Like a queen? No way was that what she meant.

"You have been long awaited, your highness."

Queen sounded a lot better than slave, but the way Mara addressed Quinn sent a shiver down her spine. Somehow she feared that things were about to get a whole lot worse.

Chapter Nine

Time lost meaning for Kayde. He fought, he ate, he recovered, and after every victory the guards surged onto the floor and he was knocked unconscious by an invisible shooter. The second time it happened, after he'd defeated someone who seemed human until his body shifted into a giant stalking cat with wings growing out of his back, Kayde had turned his back on the guards, fairly certain they wouldn't shoot him, and looked for whoever was carrying the sedative. And though he'd been turned in the same direction the shot had come from the first time, the back of his neck still pricked as the needle pierced his flesh, and Kayde went down like a heavy sack.

He didn't know what kind of drug or technology they were using, but it didn't keep him out for long. After each fight he woke in his cell rested as if he had enjoyed hours of sleep. A meal waited for him, little more than vitamin enriched protein bars and a jug of water, but it kept the hunger at bay and kept his strength up. But while he felt like he had slept for hours, the pain in his body told a different story. He knew how long wounds took to heal. He knew what his body felt like after a fight. There was only so much healing regen gel could do in a handful of hours. His leg had been bandaged where his first opponent had marked him, but when Kayde risked a peek under the wrapping, the wound had still been red and barely closed, still slathered in healing gel.

His captors were trying to confuse him, trying to make him think that a lot of time had passed when in reality he couldn't have been in the cell for more than a day or two. He'd already won six fights, but his body was stiff and he was starting to slow down. He wasn't ready to give up, but there was only so much activity that was physically possible. He would keep fighting until he collapsed or until he found Quinn and got her out of this mess, but with each fight he grew more concerned.

"They're prepping the grand arena for the coronation," someone said outside the door to his cell. Kayde didn't know if he was in the same room that he had originally woken up in or if he'd been placed in a different hallway. It was like he was sitting in an empty box, and there weren't any distinguishing marks on the floor, or the wall, or the ceiling to give him a hint that he'd been here before.

But that gave him an idea. Even as his ears strained to hear, he let his claws flash out and started to score a line on the ground beside him. He did his best to keep it close to the wall, to make it something that wouldn't be noticed in a cursory glance. Who counted the cracks on the floor in a prisoner's holding cell?

Kayde did, and there were none, which was why he was making his own.

"I never thought we would see another queen," a different voice said. They both had the somnolent tone of the Beznens that Quinn had pointed out to him. He didn't understand what she meant when she said it was like being hugged, but the words did seem to almost rub against his flesh like they were trying to burrow under his skin and take hold of him. It wasn't natural and a part of him wondered if they did something to themselves to enhance their voices.

"The timing is fortuitous," said the first Beznen. "The solstice approaches."

"Yes, but when will we find a proper champion? To do this right, we would need months to prepare. Instead we are forced to rely upon these... *creatures*. They do not deserve her." The second Beznen was probably scowling.

Kayde could almost imagine that, and distantly he wondered if that awareness was a sign of degradation. Since flying away with Quinn, Kayde hadn't noticed any more problems with his mental state but he knew that he could not rely on his own judgment. It didn't matter. He was already locked in a cell and being forced to fight for his survival. A full devolution might be a blessing in disguise. If he lost the last bits of himself, the last vestiges of whatever it was that made him a person, he would destroy everything in his path until he was put down. Blood would flow until it drowned everyone around him, and Kayde would have his vengeance against those who had presumed to use him for cheap entertainment.

But that would leave Quinn unprotected, or even worse, it would leave her harmed by his hands. Kayde's focus sharpened, and he was determined to hold onto his sanity. He could not betray Quinn like that—he was responsible for her since he was the one who had brought her here—and he would do everything in his power to see her away safely. And then he would make sure that his mental state remained stable, even if he had to meditate every hour and keep a tight guard on whatever remnants of emotion tried to flare to life.

"We must take our opportunities as they come," said the first Beznen. "I know that I would wager on our reigning king of the ring. He has survived for more than a month. I came out of the valley for his first fight, and have only missed a handful since. If any of this batch deserves to be our champion, it is him."

"What about the blue brute?" asked the second. Kayde had the uncomfortable suspicion that they were speaking about him, and it was only confirmed as they continued to speak. "Six fights in two days, and he should have been destroyed in the first. Krallgin was our former reigning contender. That was his first fight back after he'd been granted a stay by the governor."

"Very possible," agreed the first. They began to move and their voices trailed off, leaving Kayde in his cell to wonder what in all the hells was going on. A new queen? The champion? Why couldn't they talk about something useful? Like where Quinn was being kept, or if she was even a prisoner. They hadn't mentioned a human contender, but would they if she had been defeated in her first fight?

Kayde's stomach flipped at the thought and he dug his claw hard enough into the ground that it began to pull away from his hand, straining enough to hurt. He quickly pulled back, and sheathed his claws to give them a little time to rest. He glanced down at his handiwork. It was nothing fancy, but he only needed to mark the room so that he knew if he was brought back here. For that, it would do.

Could Quinn be dead already? Kayde's entire being rebelled at the thought. He could not let himself believe that she had been thrown into the pit for the entertainment of the Beznens. Why would they do that? She was worth so much more than that. If anyone deserved to be crowned queen, it was her. He didn't let himself dwell on the thought of Quinn being dead, or on why the mere idea of that affected him so much. He didn't know where she was, but the Beznens had done him a favor by speaking outside of a cell. The first monster he'd fought had earned a reprieve somehow, and the reigning master of the ring seem to have the respect of the Beznens. They were looking for a champion, and it was possible they wouldn't leave a champion to rot in an anonymous cell.

Kayde had his goal. It was the only way out, and if he could meet this queen and bend her ear in his favor, he and Quinn just might be able to make it home.

* * *

This queen thing wasn't making any sense, though Quinn wasn't sure what she had expected. Probably etiquette lessons, or law, or tiara fittings, something like that. Sure, there were fancy clothes, all in the same soft, pale fabrics that didn't look like they could sustain the slightest contact with any weather. But the light colors looked great against her dark skin, she had to admit. They wouldn't give her any regular shoes either, and she had asked. Her attendants, or captors, paid lip service to her requests, but any time she asked for sturdier footwear, or to go outside, or what had happened to Kayde, they found a way not to answer her.

Some queen she was.

No one was giving her any information, at least not beyond the basics. There would be some kind of ceremony on the solstice, a coronation, and a champion would be chosen by some means that no one had bothered to explain. What would happen after the coronation? No clue. What was the champion supposed to do? Who knew? The ignorance was putting her on edge, and though the Beznens were being very careful with what they said, Quinn could tell that something bad was coming. Whatever queen meant on Beznifa, it bore no resemblance to monarchy on Earth.

She was pretty sure they were going to kill her. And life had gotten so crazy in the past handful of days that the worry about her impending death was only her third or fourth most urgent problem. For one, she wasn't sure how long it had been since she and Kayde had landed on this damned planet. Since first waking in her quarters, she'd gone through three days, but she hadn't been able to look out any windows to observe the time of day or the location of the building she was in. There were no clocks or other timekeeping devices anywhere around her, and it was only her attendants who told her where to go and what to eat and went to sleep. So either it had been three days, or they were purposely fucking with her perception of time to keep her off her game. Quinn wouldn't put it past these manipulative little shits.

Well, not little. Most of the Beznens she met were taller than her, but they sure as hell were manipulative.

In the time since she had been taken, doubts had begun to creep in. Doubts about Kayde. She'd already suffered through imagining his death, or imprisonment, or injury, but by the third day another possibility occurred to her. It was possible he wasn't on the planet at all. He could've taken off at any time, could have sold her to these aliens for use in whatever ritual they were about to undertake. The fact that this possibility had not occurred to her almost immediately showed her just how much she had come to trust her stoic Detyen.

And the fact that she almost immediately rejected the possibility that he had abandoned her told her that maybe her feelings ran a little deeper than trust. A lot deeper.

Feelings. She scoffed at herself. She didn't have time for feelings, certainly didn't have time to consider what it meant that she had been imagining what it would feel like to taste Kayde's lips and press his body close, until every bump and ridge of his hard muscles was imprinted on her mind. Yes, she had found him attractive before, but this was more, this was deeper. And it wasn't just because she was worried for his safety. These feelings had been growing since she climbed aboard his ship and decided to stay with him. Maybe they had been growing for even longer than that. When she had first caught sight of him, she'd been in no position, mentally or physically, to contemplate an attraction to any man. But she had come a long way in the months since then, and it wasn't like she had much else to do right now. The Beznens left her alone with her thoughts much of the time, and they couldn't even spare a book or an entertainment tablet to leave her occupied.

Escape. Kayde. What she could do with Kayde. Those were the things her mind kept circling back to every time she was deposited in her room or left alone for more than a few minutes. And she really needed to stop thinking about what she and Kayde could get up to together, not just because it would complicate things once she had to face him again, but because there was no way in hell she was going to try to relieve her sexual frustration by herself when the Beznens surely had her under constant surveillance. She didn't see any cameras, but that didn't mean anything. Mara had dropped enough subtle hints to make it clear that there wasn't a moment when Quinn wasn't being watched. That made using the bathroom and showering especially nerve-racking, but she knew how to survive with a lack of privacy. The slavers on Fenryr 1 hadn't exactly been sticklers for it.

Quinn was undertaking what she was beginning to think of as her morning routine. She rolled out of bed and began to pace. If she'd thought she was cooped up on Kayde's ship, she never could have imagined what it would be like to be confined to a single huge room, only let out when strangers deemed it necessary. Energy thrummed through her veins, the need to move, to run, to jump, or to get into plenty of trouble with her missing alien. But she couldn't do anything but pace. She had covered every square centimeter of the room, sometimes walking a straight line back and forth, other times making a square, other times a circle. It could be a while before Mara came to collect her, she knew. So Quinn paced and she thought.

Was today the day they were going to explain what this whole coronation thing was? Was she going to find out what happened to Kayde? Were they going to admit this was all a giant ruse and lead her to the slaughter? She had plenty of questions to think about, and no answers.

When she turned around to begin another lap of the room, Mara was standing there, haloed in the familiar light, having made no noise when she opened the door that Quinn had still not figured out how to operate. Quinn didn't jump, not like she had on the first two days. She was growing used to this, and she didn't know whether that was a good or a bad thing.

425

"Good morning, your majesty," said Mara with a smile. "Are you ready for your coronation?"

"I thought that wasn't until the solstice," Quinn replied. Not that she knew the exact day of the solstice, seeing as she hadn't been offered a calendar or anything like that. She didn't answer Mara's question, pretty sure her answer wouldn't make any difference.

Mara clapped her hands together once, her expression like that of a proud owner of an especially precocious pet. "You've been paying attention! How delightful."

Quinn didn't respond; she had decided early on that she would speak to the Beznens as little as possible. Unless they were going to give her information that led to her and Kayde's release, she wasn't willing to play their game.

Mara was undeterred by Quinn's silence. She held up both of her arms and Quinn noticed the piles of fabric she was holding. "We must dress you for the ceremony. We have no time to lose. Strip."

That order sent a dark wave of memory crashing over Quinn and her hands shook a little as she reached for the hem of her nightshirt. No one had touched her inappropriately on Beznifa. They had held her prisoner and controlled her every move, but they hadn't taken those liberties. That didn't mean that the possibility didn't live in her mind. She knew what it was like to live under the absolute power of a group of sadists who saw her as a thing to use rather than a person.

"Hurry up, we don't have all day," Mara urged while Quinn hesitated.

The urging only made it worse, only dragged up memories that she was doing her damnedest to suppress. Her tongue darted out and she licked her suddenly dry lips. "Can you just leave the clothes in here?" She hated to hear the tremble in her voice, hated to make any request of these aliens and prove just how much she was under their power. But she wasn't sure that she could make herself fully undress in the presence of her captor.

A look that Quinn couldn't quite describe flashed briefly across Mara's face, but it was gone between one blink and the next. "Of course, your majesty," she said, as if there was no problem with the demand. "I will return when I see that you are ready. Do not tarry." Quinn didn't care about the reminder of her constant surveillance. She could ignore a camera, could pretend it wasn't there. She couldn't ignore Mara.

The Beznens handed over the outfit, a surprisingly dark ensemble in browns and reds made of a tough fabric that reminded her of leather. Whatever this coronation was, it was just about to happen, and she had to survive it. Hopefully, she'd have a bit more freedom once it was done. She knew that as soon as she found Kayde, they'd be able to come up with a plan, something that would get them both out of here quickly. One more day of survival, she could do that. She had already lived her life by stealing one more day despite the horrors visited upon her, despite the freedoms she was deprived of, and despite the hope that had been stolen from her. Whatever this coronation was, she would survive it too, and when it was done she would find Kayde, and they would escape. She was placing all of her faith in that belief. She needed something to hang on to, and faith in a stoic alien warrior was the one thing she wasn't going to give up.

Chapter Ten

"So what is it exactly that I'm supposed to do?" Mara and a fleet of attendants were leading Quinn down a narrow hall towards the coronation chamber. Or at least that was where she assumed they were heading; she still didn't have much information to work with. She'd put on the outfit that Mara gave her and had to keep pulling her arms back from where they crossed over her stomach, trying to cover up her naked skin. The outfit covered the important parts, but except for a series of straps that had taken quite some time to figure out how to put on, more of Quinn's skin was exposed than she would have ever allowed. She kept telling herself to be grateful that she wasn't naked, but that wasn't much of a reassurance.

"When it is time, you will do what you need to do," said Mara. That wasn't helpful at all and Quinn couldn't quite suppress the sound of frustration that tried to escape her throat.

"I can't—" She clamped her mouth shut to keep from saying anything that could get her beaten. The Beznens had not resorted to physical abuse, but she didn't know if that was because she had been cooperative, or if they were morally opposed to it. She didn't want to find out until it was absolutely necessary.

The coronation seemed to be taking place in the same building that she had been housed in for the past several days. She hadn't been placed in any sort of vehicle, and they had not gone outside, so she didn't see how they could have gone anywhere different. They arrived at the end of the hall which was blocked by a large metal gate. The place smelled almost like a fairground, but with an underlying scent of blood and violence. Quinn didn't like it, not that she liked anything about this situation.

"Face me, please," Mara instructed.

Quinn waited several seconds, trying to get a look through the gate to figure out what was going on. Before Mara could get fed up with her hesitation, she turned. "What?"

"Hold out your hands."

No, Quinn really didn't like that idea. She kept her hands steadily at her sides. "Why?" Not that asking questions had done her any good thus far.

"It is part of the ceremony," Mara explained. "Hold out your hands," she repeated.

"That's not an explanation, tell me what you're going to do." It was one thing to dress as instructed, and eat when told, but whatever this was, Quinn didn't want to go along with it without understanding exactly what they were asking of her.

But Mara wasn't about to be refused. She looked towards the two guards flanking Quinn. "Hold her," she said. It happened swiftly, before Quinn could try to run, or could try to twist, they had a hold of her arms and made her stretch out in front of Mara, palms up like she was some sort of supplicant. Mara produced a heavy set of manacles embedded with fine jewels and carved with details that spoke of a delicate craftsman. They were almost pretty, if one didn't pay attention to the chain. When Mara let go of her arms, Quinn's hands fell, not expecting the heavy weight of the metal and jewels.

"What kind of people treat their queen like this?" Not that she expected pulling rank to work, but it was worth a shot. Anything to delay the inevitable.

"You have not yet been crowned," said Mara. "First you must make it through the coronation. Choose your champion, bring him to heel, and once it is done, claim your crown. The governor awaits his entertainment." Mara flicked her fingers, and that must've been a sign. The gate in front of them began to rise and Mara and the rest of the attendants fell back, one of them giving Quinn a push through the archway.

The roar of the crowd almost knocked her off her feet. It was like something out of an ancient movie, where gladiators battled lions and tigers for the entertainment of the Roman masses. A high wall made it impossible to climb off the floor, even if her hands hadn't been bound. Seats in the stadium went up and up and up, and there must have been thousands of people gathered to watch the spectacle.

A voice was saying something, and as it spoke the crowd cheered even louder, too loud for Quinn to make out the details of the words. The ground was covered in sandy dust, and the killing floor was so big that she could just barely make out the outline of another gate on the other side of the arena. A beat reverberated through the arena as the spectators stomped their feet in anticipation of what was coming. It echoed around Quinn's head and for a moment her heartbeat pulsed in time before the spectators sped up their rhythm until it lost all definition and burst into a chaos of applause and stopped.

Her eyes darted around madly as if she could find a place to hide or escape, but just like the past several days, the Beznens showed complete control of her environment, leaving her not so much as a shadow to cower in. The sound of metal grinding on metal had to be an effect. When her own gate opened, the door had slid easily, as if the hinges were oiled every day. The gate was too far away for her to actually see it open, but she saw the shadows of a dozen beings walk out into straight lines. Had her heart been beating fast before? Now death was marching toward her and all she could do was meet it with dignity. She stood up straight and pulled her elbows back, holding her arms as if she meant to display her manacles, as if she were not bound by them, but help them proudly.

A flash of blue caught her eye, a tall man standing behind an alien that looked like some mix of a dog and a tree.

Kayde. Her champion.

***

After he heard the Beznens speaking about the coronation the fights got harder and Kayde grew more determined. He took out his enemies with a single-minded focus, and ended the fights with no flourish, knowing the less time he was in the arena the less likely he was to sustain a life-threatening injury. It must've been a challenge for his captors. After he flattened an Oscavian in under two minutes, they had taken to sending two or more opponents at him at the same time. Kayde did not lose, he adapted. And he did it well. He did enough to make it onto the champions roster.

He was among a dozen warriors, none of whom he had faced in battle before. But if they were here, they must have all faced similar challenges, and he could not underestimate any of them, not even the bright orange alien who barely came up to his hip.

A Beznen guard stood before them, his blaster holstered, but his hand resting on the gun. "Today is the day of our glorious coronation," he announced, practically yelling over the crowd which roared in the distance. "There are two ways to gain your freedom." A murmur went through the group at that announcement, and even Kayde's posture straightened. "Become the queen's champion, and if she is crowned she may grant you a reprieve. Or take her out and prove that she is merely a pretender to the throne. If that is your goal, only the one that takes her final breath will be granted freedom. The battle begins when the gong sounds. Move before then and you will be put down."

Kayde had his goal, and the rest of his competitors were his only obstacle to freedom. The choice of what to do with the queen was obvious. If he killed her, he would be free. If he protected her, she might choose to keep him as a slave. From the murmurs around him, and the unsettled movements, Kayde could tell that his competitors were coming to the same conclusion. With twelve warriors determined to see her end, the queen didn't stand a chance. But only one of them would gain their freedom tonight, and it would be a battle to the death to see who claimed the honor of killing the queen.

That was Kayde's plan until he stepped through the gate and the roar of the crowd washed over him. It wasn't the crowd that captured his attention, though. It was the woman in jeweled manacles standing proudly in the center of the arena. Quinn. Alive. For now.

His plan shifted between one second and the next. Even if the coldly logical, soulless part of him knew that it would be easier to escape this planet without Quinn slowing him down, he didn't for a second consider doing anything but protecting her. That was why he was here.

A breathless air of anticipation surrounded them as he and his competitors stood calmly into lines, waiting for the gong to sound. They all thrummed with energy, waiting to explode. Kayde darted glances around, making and discarding plans of attack. He had not seen any of these warriors fight and could not begin to guess what strengths and weaknesses they were hiding. He had his claws and his skills in the determination to see Quinn safe, but he had seen enough of the universe to know what kind of tricks these other aliens could be hiding.

It was a comfort to know that all of them had been held prisoner and forced into the arena, just like him. It meant that whatever tricks they possessed, it wasn't enough to overcome the guards and find a way out by themselves.

Now there was an idea. Twelve warriors all strong enough to survive a handful of arena battles could easily overpower the guards and find their way out of here. But the idea dissolved almost as quickly as it formed. Given time, and with a better ambassador than himself, Kayde might have been able to convince some of these men and women and beings of indeterminate gender to fight by his side, but the gong sounded before Kayde could even try to catch anyone's eye and communicate his plan through looks and gestures.

The tree dog jumped for him first, but Kayde was already rolling before his opponent's paws had left the ground. Dust burst all around him in a cloud of violence, obscuring his opponents and filling his lungs, thick enough to make him cough. Kayde used that distraction to his advantage, taking off running towards Quinn and closing half the distance between them before anyone realized what he was about to do. He expected an attack from behind, so when the ground erupted in front of him, a shower of fire exploding from nowhere, he was almost too slow to avoid immolation. Almost.

The fire was a wall, cutting him off from getting to Quinn and keeping her safe. But in its own way, it was a blessing. If he could not get to her, then neither could anyone else. Not unless they could fly. Kayde spun back around to make sure that no one was attempting to get to her by air, and was relieved to see that already half of his opponents lay dead in the dust.

Those were that easy ones, the ones who needed time to think while they were fighting. Now it was only the best of the best left.

Kayde thought that he could hear Quinn yelling through the veil of flames, but he didn't look back, shutting off his heart to her cries of distress. He had to take care of the rest of the would-be assassins before he could get to her, and she would need to survive long enough for him to make it.

* * *

The heat parched her throat dry as a desert. For two seconds there, Quinn had really thought they were home free. With Kayde sprinting across the arena towards her, leaving all of the terrifying warriors in the dust behind him, she had trusted that the two of them would find their way out without getting hurt or delayed much further.

She hadn't realized that she was still capable of deluding herself like that. The fire had shot up around her in a giant circle, and though it hurt to stare into the flames, Quinn kept her eyes trained on where it met the ground, watching to see if it moved in any closer. There was a spot in the center of the circle that was just wide enough for her to stretch her arms out where she could breathe and not feel like she was immolating her lungs.

The reckless impulse to sprint for the fire and jump through it kept trying to take hold of her. As if her troubles would be any easier if the fire were keeping all of those dangerous aliens from her. What had Mara said? Choose a champion and bring him to heel? How could she bring a champion to heel if she was stuck behind a fence of fire? Not that getting one of them to cooperate would be that difficult, not when she was sure that Kayde would be her champion, would be the victor of all of them. She didn't let herself contemplate what would happen if Kayde fell. They had come so far, even if they had known they were heading in the same direction. They couldn't be torn apart now, the injustice of that might just destroy her.

With nothing else to do, Quinn was forced to watch the battle as it played out. If she looked high enough and abandoned staring at the base of the flames, she could just make out the heart of the battle in the center of the arena. The battle that Kayde was running headfirst into. By the time he made it there, it looked like only five of the original twelve warriors were left to battle among themselves. Two had teamed up. A short orange beast that would only come up to her chest and an Oscavian were taking on an alien that looked like a mix between a tree and a dog. Every time they hacked at him, he kept coming. And when the Oscavian broke off a limb, it didn't seem to slow the treedog down.

Kayde threw himself into the melee, and if Quinn hadn't known him she would've been terrified to find out that this was her champion. He was a hurricane of action, his movements unstoppable as he took out the Oscavian from behind before flattening the orange alien and then ripping the treedog to shreds. It happened in seconds, those three hadn't seen it coming.

Excitement began to overpower the fear flowing through her veins. Quinn had never found violence a turn on, but knowing that Kayde was taking on all of these beasts for her, knowing that freedom was within their grasp as soon as he won, she found herself a little bit attracted to the danger. To his danger.

By the time Kayde had taken out the three aliens, only one was left. They faced off, snarling and growling and sizing one another up. Quinn didn't recognize the species of alien Kayde was up against. It had four arms and the fingers on all of its hands were tipped with wicked looking claws that looked even sharper than Kayde's. It was taller than Kayde, too. At least by half a head, and twice as wide as he was.

Quinn didn't want to look, but she couldn't look away. They met in a giant clash and Quinn could almost imagine the sound of bodies slapping together, could practically taste the blood that they drew in their ruthless battle to the death. Kayde's opponent was good, that was obvious even to her untrained eye. But she had to believe that Kayde was better. The crowd let out a chorus of gasps as the four-armed beast got in a particularly vicious hit, sending Kayde sprawling to the ground. Her alien, her champion kicked up to his feet just as quickly as he'd fallen and he spat on the ground, wiping dust from his face and ready for another round.

She was too far away to make out his expression, though she knew exactly how he would look. It was the same infuriatingly neutral way he looked every day. And she would pay almost anything to have him look at her that way again when they were free of the bonds that held them.

In a final flurry of blows, it was over. Kayde sent his opponent to the floor in a limp pile and at the same moment she realized he was the only one left, the flames extinguished as if they were never there, only a hint of heat reminding her of their presence. Quinn took off running, her need to see Kayde, to prove that he was all right, overriding any instinct for caution. She had to dodge two of the bodies, something that might have horrified her under other circumstances, but she was so far beyond petty concerns like that at the moment.

Kayde was breathing heavily, and his tattered shirt was covered in a dark substance that might have been his blood. When he saw her his eyes flared red, something she thought she'd seen them do once on the ship, but this time she was sure.

Raze sometimes looked at his mate, Sierra, like that.

It was a stray thought, something that normally she wouldn't pay any attention to, but with the heat of battle riding high, and the uncertainty of how they were going to get out of this mess still surrounding them, the idea that Kayde would look at her like another man looked at his mate practically brought her to her knees.

But then he blinked and his eyes were once more their normal dark color.

The crowd was as quiet as a crowd of that size could ever be, only the rustling of movement and the murmur of distant voices whispering around them. Quinn held out a hand and found that it was shaking. "My champion."

"My queen," Kayde said as he reached for her.

Chapter Eleven

The searing pain that ripped through him as his hand touched Quinn's could have been a remnant from his battle with his final opponent. He was covered in small cuts, and some deep enough to cause a distant worry, but that was all background noise to the pure relief of victory. There was no pain, not until he touched Quinn, and then it was almost enough to make him stagger and fall to his knees.

But he would not show weakness in front of this crowd, not when they were so close to their freedom.

Quinn's eyes narrowed, as if she sensed something wrong, but when she opened her mouth to say something else, Kayde gave her a quick jerk of his head. She dropped his hand and the pain dissolved, as if it had never been there at all. He filed that mystery away for later. A single touch had never hurt him like that before, but they didn't have time to dwell on it.

"I'm glad you're not dead," Quinn whispered to him, the sound almost swallowed up by the crowd.

"The feeling is mutual." His every action of the last several days had been to bring him to this moment where he found his companion. "But we are not out of danger yet."

"No kidding."

The sound of metal clanking set his nerves on edge, and he almost expected to see another monster burst out into the arena, another battle to face. But it was only the gate that Quinn had come through opening. No guards came out to threaten them with blasters, and no one shot darts at him to knock them out. It was already an improvement over his other times in the arena. If one discounted the number of opponents he'd had to face.

A light glowed inside the gate, beckoning them towards it. There was no other way out of the arena, and though Kayde hated to do as the Beznens were bidding them, they had no other choice. There was no way to get both him and Quinn over the walls and into the crowd and then through the crowd and out of the building without almost immediately being stopped and injured or killed. Some battles could only be won with patience.

He and Quinn walked side-by-side to the gate and were met by four Beznens that Quinn seemed to recognize.

"I am so glad to see you again," said the central figure.

"Mara." Quinn greeted her.

Mara nodded at Kayde. "You have chosen to serve the Queen, rather than take your freedom."

Quinn shot him a look, but Kayde didn't look back. He could explain the particulars later. He kept silent and waited for the Beznen to say more.

"The coronation is not complete," Mara continued. "But you are the first Queen among many to survive the choosing of the champions."

"Yay for me," she said, and even though Kayde didn't have a soul, he could hear Quinn's sarcasm. It was thick enough to choke them all.

Mara and her fellow Beznens led them down a narrow hall and into a room which opened with a soaring ceiling and huge doors that let out into a giant green forest. At her wave, one of the attendants removed Quinn's manacles and they dropped to the floor with a loud *thump*. "Riches beyond your wildest imagination, and the heart of our planet lie at the end of this path. The way is dangerous, and your champion is tasked with keeping you safe. Claim your crown and return in three days and you shall take your rightful place as our Queen."

"You're letting us go... outside?" Quinn quickly tacked on the last word, and her face was screwed up in a confused expression.

"Of course, you must claim your crown. You may take your supplies from this room, and tend to any wounds. Once you exit the palace, you may not return without the crown. Any attempt and you will be slaughtered on sight." She delivered this pronouncement as if she were giving them the weather forecast.

"Can we have a map?" Quinn asked.

Did she really mean to go after this treasure? Kayde would follow wherever she went, but he would not expect her to heed the siren call of riches.

"If you can find one in this room, it is yours," Mara responded. She turned on her heel and exited the room, taking the other guards with her. The door slammed shut behind them and Quinn practically collapsed where she stood, falling onto a nearby chair and letting her shoulders slump forward.

"I thought you were dead." It came out shaky, like she hadn't let herself think about the possibility until just this moment. "I was afraid I would never see you again. I didn't..." She trailed off, shaking her head, unable to finish the thought.

"I am not that easy to kill." He didn't know how to give her comfort. He thought he should touch her, pat her on the shoulder, to prove through physical contact that they were both alive and mostly well. But the outfit she was wearing exposed more than it covered, and he didn't know what would happen if their skin touched a second time.

"Can I..." She huffed out a frustrated breath and leaned back until her chair was tipped at a precarious angle. "Never mind."

"What is it?" There was no request that she could make that he would not try to fulfill.

"I think I need a hug." It came out in a small voice, the words vulnerable and desperate and very lonely. "Would you hug me?"

Kayde was powerless to resist the request. He couldn't remember the last time he had given someone a hug. Had he been a child? Had it been decades? It didn't matter. He nodded at her, and Quinn was out of the chair, throwing her arms around him and clinging tight. Kayde claimed his own arms around her back, the flat of his palm pressed against her warm naked skin.

It stung for a moment, but the pain went away almost as quickly, even as the touch shook him to his foundations. He could feel something inside of him stretching out, something that shouldn't be there trying to dig hooks deep into him and to bring him out of the shadows and into the light. The longer they touched, the more that sense grew, and the more Kayde's survival instinct beat at him to pull away, to pull back, to stop touching Quinn.

But there were things more important than survival, and at this moment comforting Quinn was one of them.

Her hands climbed up his back until she was clutching his shoulders and nuzzling her face into the crook of his neck. Physical sensation washed over him, the echoes of something he hadn't felt since he'd given up his soul. The soulless were incapable of physical desire, lust a forgotten remnant of their life before. But right now it echoed through him, not enough for him to do anything about it, but a strong enough reminder to make him question everything he knew was possible.

Was it possible to witness two miracles in a single lifetime? Even when Raze regained his soul, Kayde had known that such a thing could never happen to him. The time for him to meet his denya was long past, and hoping for something he couldn't change would only make him deteriorate faster.

But with Quinn in his arms, a flutter of impossible hope flew through him. Could she be his denya? Could he be that lucky?

* * *

This was a comfort cuddle, a security snuggle. Yeah, Quinn was pretty sure that Kayde was going to get fed up with her and pull away at any minute, but she had to soak up as much of the contact as possible until then. She'd never understood touch hunger before. Who needed contact so bad that their body cried out for it? Outside of sex, of course. But now she was beginning to figure it out.

This connection right here, it wasn't sexual. Well, not entirely sexual. This was about affirming they were alive and mostly safe. Though from the way her body was reacting and the way Kayde's scent was sinking into Quinn's pores and practically marking her, if they kept this up for much longer it would take a decidedly sensual bent.

Reluctantly she pulled back, and when she glanced up at Kayde, her breath caught. He was checking her out like he wanted to devour her, like he needed to *worship* her. His eyes had flared red again and the color held as the seconds ticked by. This wasn't a trick of the light like back on the ship or a momentary slip in the heat of battle. No, this was all about her, and him, and them.

He reached a hand up tentatively and two fingers stroked the ridge of her cheek. It occurred to Quinn that this was the first time that Kayde had ever initiated contact between the two of them, but she kept that to herself, afraid to break this magical spell.

She leaned into his touch and her eyelids wanted to flutter closed, but she forced herself to keep eye contact with him. She didn't want to miss a second of this.

Was he going to kiss her? All she had to do was lean in and close that tiny gap between them and all the mystery, all the anticipation would explode into one moment of pure perfection. But she held herself completely still, transfixed as if she were held in a spider's web.

Was this some sort of Detyen power? To enchant women until they were held helpless in a warrior's grasp? Maybe, but if they all had this power, then Quinn was only vulnerable when Kayde was using it. She didn't want to stare at anyone else all day, didn't want to dream of kissing and touching them until she was breathless with want. For her it was only Kayde NaDetya, and she was almost certain she saw that exact desire in his eyes.

And then he pulled back.

The spell wasn't broken. She could feel a tenuous connection reaching out between the two of them, not quite physical nor quite spiritual, but there all the same. It anchored them to one another, but she was afraid that if either of them gave it the slightest resistance it would dissolve into nothing, just unmoored gossamer threads.

So how did they make that connection real? Permanent?

"We need to get back to the sh—"

"Shh!" Quinn cut Kayde off with a harsh sound. As she cleared her throat, she did her best to say "cameras" so that only Kayde could make it out. She didn't know if the Beznens could hear them as well as see them, but she wasn't going to risk whatever daring escape they were about to undertake on the hope that they couldn't. "Let's gather supplies like Mara told us to. I don't know how long it is 'til sunset."

They worked quickly and stuffed two bags full with various protein bars and hydration packs. By the time they were done, they had enough for weeks of survival, along with waterproof blankets and sturdy shoes for each of them. Quinn was frustrated that she couldn't find an outfit to replace what she'd been dressed in, but she satisfied herself by finding a sturdy jacket that fell down to her thighs. It was better than nothing.

What neither of them found was a map. That wasn't exactly surprising, and Quinn hoped that one of Kayde's secret warrior skills would include finding their way back to their ship.

Quinn slung her pack over her shoulders and found Kayde waiting for her near the door. "Do you have everything you'll need?" she asked him.

"We will make do," he replied.

Quinn looked around the room one last time. It held no special significance to her, but she'd been forced to stay in this building for days and in a strange way it felt like her home on the planet, almost like it was safe. Now that had to be crazy. Kayde was still half-covered with blood and gore from the people he'd been forced to fight, to kill. And if he hadn't been victorious, she would have been another body lying on that sand. There was no safety here, just the veneer of it, and not even a particularly good one.

And so they set out, stepping through the wide door and onto the soft grass of the meadow right outside the door. And just as soon as they were outside, Quinn could feel those same eyes looking at her that she'd felt in the market. Was there some kind of mass surveillance on this planet? Was it something in the atmosphere?

"I really don't like this place." Quinn couldn't keep herself from saying it out loud. There was a chill in the air and she shivered despite her jacket.

"I am beginning to understand what you mean," said Kayde. They both spoke quietly. The only way someone would hear them was if they were standing very close, and from the looks of it, she and Kayde were completely alone. But Quinn didn't trust anything she saw on this planet.

They started to walk, Kayde in the lead. "Any idea where we are?" she asked him.

"That Mara person mentioned that we were in the palace. Based on the mountains in the distance and that faint buzzing sound, I would suggest we are just outside the Governor's palace. Which means," Kayde paused and closed his eyes before turning slightly toward the right and continuing on, "the markets and the shuttle station are this way."

"You think it's going to be that easy to get back to the ship? We just walk there?"

Kayde didn't stop moving, but she didn't need to be facing him to hear the weary tone. "No," he said. "I am sure this won't be easy at all."

Chapter Twelve

He was right, though Quinn tried not to hold that against him. The first trouble came from the guards. They mostly stayed out of sight, but every time she and Kayde strayed too far from the direction of the forest they were meant to be heading to, a patrol of guards conveniently came within hearing distance. She and Kayde never saw them, but that was for the best. She didn't want to think what the guards could do to them if they thought she and Kayde were breaking the law.

They probably *were* breaking the law.

So even though they knew where the market was and where their ship should be, they were slowly herded out towards the woods which were in the opposite direction of where they wanted to go. Darkness was falling, the sun setting in the distance, and the shadows from the trees reaching out like long grasping fingers to release night from their grasp. If it weren't for the fear of impending death or the memory of recent captivity, the place would've been idyllic in its own way. It almost reminded her of home, of Earth. The grass was green, the trees tall with brown bark and green leaves, but the fruits were different, in bright jewel tones and shapes that looked nothing like anything she'd seen back home. She was tempted to taste, but wasn't fool enough to give in to that.

No, there was only one temptation she wanted to give in to, and he was walking right beside her. They'd been walking for hours, and Quinn's everything ached, her toes, her feet, her calves, her thighs, and all the way up the rest of her body. Who knew that walking at a steady pace could give a girl a headache? Had she known that it was possible for her earlobes to hurt? But she was doing her best to keep her complaining to a minimum. Kayde had the heavier pack, he was the one who had to find the path out of here, and he had been forced to fight in the arena for his life multiple times. He hadn't told her what the Beznens had done to him, but he had begun to limp a little as if he had an injury on his leg, and she knew his leg hadn't been injured in his most recent fight. It wasn't a difficult leap to make, to figure they had made him fight other captives in the arena.

She stumbled over a large rock embedded in the dirt and it was only Kayde's grasp on her arm that kept her from face planting. Her companion came to a stop.

"We should rest for a while, we've covered a lot of ground." He took his pack off and let it fall to the forest floor, where it landed with a dull thump. How many kilos did that thing weigh? Twenty? Thirty? His shoulders had to be killing him. Quinn's only weighed half that and her back practically cried in relief when she let her bag fall to the ground.

"We've covered a lot of ground in the wrong direction." It came out snarky and Quinn flinched at her own tone. This wasn't Kayde's fault, but he was the only person around, and she had to take her frustration out on something before she started screaming and forgot how to stop.

Kayde didn't respond. He was like that, she noticed. Most of the time he only spoke when directly addressed, when he was asked a question. No one would accuse him of being a sparkling conversationalist.

Quinn lowered herself down to the ground and as soon as her butt hit the dirt she knew it was a mistake. She wasn't going to want to stand back up for all the riches in the world, and even the promise of a ride off this planet wasn't doing much to the hard comfort of the cold ground. She braced a hand by her side, certain that if she fell over and lay down she wasn't going to get back up. She couldn't expect Kayde to carry her out of this place; he was already doing all of the heavy lifting, so the least she could do was carry herself.

Kayde dug a hydration pack out of his bag and tipped his head back, letting the vitamin infused liquid flow down his throat. Not a drop escaped his lips, and Quinn was fascinated watching his throat work as he swallowed. Heat lit through her body and she found a reserve of energy she hadn't realized she'd been holding back. Had she thought she couldn't cover another meter? If Kayde gave her one hint, she would cross the distance between them and be on him in a second.

But her stoic alien warrior seemed oblivious to the effect he had on her. She was beginning to think that moment that they'd shared back at the palace had been all in her imagination. All one-sided. She had just about managed to convince herself of that when Kayde finished drinking and lowered his chin, looking at her with those fathomless dark eyes of his and lips wet from the memory of his drink. His eyes flared red and Quinn sat up straighter, leaning forward until she came up on her knees and crossed half the distance between them.

"Why do your eyes do that?" she asked. It had seemed like too intrusive a thing to ask the other Detyens she knew. But she didn't feel the same reluctance when it came to Kayde. She wanted to know everything about him, almost like she had the right.

"Do what?" he asked in response.

"Turn red." It was like they were on fire, or he was possessed by a demon, something sinister and yet so seductive she couldn't stop herself from reaching out and touching him.

Their fingers wove together as she grasped his hand. "They shouldn't."

"They are. You're a mystery, you know that?" The longer she spent with this man and the more she learned about him, the more she wanted, no needed, to know. And the more questions she had.

"I am no mystery, I am merely a... remnant." His fingers squeezed hers and Quinn thought he was going to pull back; instead he tugged her forward until she was practically splayed across his lap. One of his hands came to rest on her hip, the heat of it burning through the thin material of her jacket.

"A remnant of what?" The red hadn't faded from his eyes and Quinn felt like she was trapped beneath the gaze of a hunting beast. A predator's prey with no hope of escape.

"It is not my secret to tell," Kayde said after several long moments. "And certainly not here."

For a few seconds Quinn had managed to forget just how much trouble the two of them were in, but those words were like a bucket of cold water dousing any ideas she might've had. She pulled out of Kayde's grasp and returned to sitting across from him. "So is there a plan?" she asked. She desperately wanted to follow up on whatever secret he was hiding, but he was right, this wasn't the place to share.

Kayde nodded. "Get your rest, you'll need it."

When darkness fell, they moved. Kayde had no doubt that the forest around them teemed with danger, with deadly animals and traps laid to catch the unwary. It would be wise to confine their movements to daylight, but with the guard patrols and the possibility they were being monitored ever present in his mind, Kayde knew that their only chance at making it back to the market and then to the ship came from moving by night.

Quinn had managed to fall asleep and Kayde waited until the last moment possible to rouse her. He told himself that his decision was completely logical. The more rested she was, the faster they could move. But he suspected that his real motivation came because she looked so peaceful with her eyes closed and her breathing even.

She woke with a start and Kayde had to cover her mouth to keep her from crying out. Her eyes flashed with fury, but as soon as she saw it was him, they softened and that chasm deep inside of him shrank just a tiny bit more.

He handed her the cloak he had fashioned out of spare blankets, leaves, and dirt and used a series of gestures to instruct her to put it on. From his silence, she gathered that they both needed to be quiet and it only took her a minute to get dressed. He had struggled for several minutes about the decision to leave their packs behind. Those supplies could be the thing standing between life and death, but they also weighed him and Quinn down, tiring them out and making them move slower. He stuffed as many hydration packs and protein bars into his pockets as he could manage and decided to leave the rest. Speed and stealth were the two most important things at that moment, and if they were stranded out in the wilds long enough to need their provisions, they were already dead.

He and Quinn had not discussed the possibility that the ship might not be waiting for them. They hadn't spoken of the ship at all out of fear that whatever surveillance was watching them would hear and the Beznens would figure out their plan of escape.

Kayde was a skilled pilot and as long as there was a single ship at the shuttle port, he would get them off of this planet. Quinn had placed her trust in him, and he would not fail her.

Kayde held out a hand and managed not to flinch at the wave of sensation when Quinn took it. It hurt to touch her, but at the same time his body craved it, and every time they touched the need to do it again only grew. Could she really be the woman for him? Every hour they spent together the emotions he shouldn't have been feeling got stronger and stronger, and Quinn said his eyes had gone red, which was something impossible for the soulless. But he had known Quinn for months, had first seen her when she was recovered from Fenryr 1 with the rest of the women that they'd collected. Back then, Raze had gone from soulless to mated in the course of a week. He must've recognized Sierra almost immediately. How could Kayde have known Quinn for so long without suspecting what she was to him?

Then again, he reasoned, he had attempted to flee a planet to escape the emotions she roused in him, fearful that he was destabilizing. That was some sort of recognition, even if the conclusion was incorrect.

Kayde buried all thoughts of denyai and mating. They could dwell on that possibility when they made it back to the ship and escaped from Beznifa. Until then he had to cling tightly to his training and use every sense and skill that he possessed to get Quinn away safely.

With their hands clasped, they moved as quickly and quietly through the forest as they could. During the day, Kayde had barely noticed the sound of Quinn moving beside him, her footsteps blending in with the calling birds and the wind whistling through the trees. But the darkness seemed to amplify everything and every footstep she took was like the crash of boulders in the quiet night. But he knew that his own footsteps weren't featherlight. He had training on how to move quietly, but he wasn't accustomed to moving with stealth through foliage this dense.

They couldn't stick to the path, as it was sure to be monitored, either remotely or by guards, but Kayde didn't trust his instincts enough to stray too far. Even during the day, the forest around them was dense and he lost sight of the landmarks that told him where they needed to go. The palace and the city were behind them, but in the dark it was disorienting, and they moved slower than he would have liked. It took more than an hour to cover a stretch of forest that had taken them a quarter of the time to traverse when they could keep to the path. But guards and surveillance weren't the only dangers in the woods at night.

Quinn had mentioned several times that she felt like she was being watched. Though he believed her, Kayde's own instincts hadn't been tripped. Until now. In the darkness, off the path, and far from safety, he could practically feel the eyes of some dangerous beast following them. Stalking them. They were being watched, hunted. By what, he didn't know, but given all of the dangers that he and Quinn had faced while indoors, he didn't want to meet the kind of trouble they could find in the wild.

The safest move would be to find a secure place to stay for the night and light a fire to keep beasts away, but that wasn't a possibility, not if they wanted to escape the planet. Kayde hoped that the creature on their tail couldn't find exactly where they were. They were disguised in cloaks covered in dirt and leaves, and that would help disguise their scent. But tricks like that would only work against something born to hunt these woods for so long.

Quinn sped up beside him, perhaps sensing the same danger. Branches crunched around them as they broke past them and they still couldn't move fast enough to satisfy the sense of urgency riding both of them, but before long they made it to the edge of the forest and within sight of the governor's palace. It was only a few kilometers on to the market, and a few kilometers beyond that to the port, but the ground here was open, easy to surveil, and had to be crawling with guards.

"Are we really just going to walk out of here?" Quinn breathed the words against his ear and Kayde had to work to suppress a shiver.

He took his time, trying to see any hint of danger peeking out from the streets or the buildings beside them. It didn't make sense to him that the Beznens would just leave them alone, out in the open, where they could make a move to escape the second the guards' backs were turned. Was the call of the riches so great? What kind of people did they usually abduct?

Kayde kept his guard up, but he led Quinn out of the forest towards civilization. They stayed off the roads as best they could and crossed them with caution when it couldn't be avoided. By the time they made it to the edge of the port, the sun was already starting to crest the horizon and it would not be long until someone noticed the two of them.

He used his claws to cut a hole in the fence surrounding the space port and he and Quinn sprinted for their ship, which sat, practically gleaming, right where they'd left it. He was so focused on the risk of guards that he almost didn't register the growl that went up around them, making the hair on his arms rise at the threat.

Then Quinn screamed and everything got a whole lot worse.

Chapter Thirteen

A rush of air was Kayde's only warning as a giant mass of angry animal barreled into him, knocking him sideways with a growl sinister enough to make his hair stand on end. Kayde kept moving, rolling away from the beast and flipping back to his feet, getting into a ready position to fight. He spared a quick glance for Quinn, but didn't see her. His claws flashed out, but sharp as they were, it would take a lot to damage the thing in front of him. It was large and black, on four legs, with a head as big as Kayde's entire upper body. It had to be at least five times his size, and he was certain that this was the beast that had stalked them out of the woods. How had it been so quiet? Its paws were as big as the wheels of an automobile back on Earth, but it slunk forward with a liquid grace that made it seem almost unreal.

Kayde didn't see it move; there was nothing, no bunching of muscles in its legs, no gathering of air in its chest, nothing to hint that it was about to spring forward and attack. It was just there, and Kayde was covered by its daunting weight. He swung out with his claws, but the beast's skin might as well have been made with some combination of metal and leather. No matter how hard he hit, he couldn't pierce it. All he could do was try to avoid the beast's own wickedly sharp claws and its mouth, which looked strong enough to bite Kayde in half.

The beast grunted as Kayde got a good strike in with one of his feet. He was practically pinned, but had just enough space to shimmy completely under the animal and escape from between its feet. He never stopped looking for a weak point, and the beast gave a mighty yowl as his claws struck the tender flesh of its belly. Before Kayde could dive back and hit it again, it screeched at him and retreated several meters. Kayde took stock of his own injuries, but the beast hadn't managed to do any more than give a few bruises and make the wounds he already had a little worse.

Bright lights flashed all around him, ruining what was left of Kayde's night vision and momentarily blinding him. He dove for cover, taking a position behind a small vehicle that looked like it was made it to haul supplies from the market to the port. He expected the guards to start shooting at any moment, using the strobing lights to keep him disoriented, but he waited several seconds and nothing happened. He risked a glance up from where he was crouched behind the vehicle and saw that Quinn had managed to climb on top of a maintenance tower and was manually turning the bright lights off and on with the press of a button.

"I think that cat thing is gone," she called over to him, her voice echoing through the open port. There wasn't much use in remaining quiet now; if any guards were around, they would've seen the flashing lights. They didn't have much time.

"You scared it away, good thinking." He didn't know if he would've been able to defeat it by himself.

"Yeah, yeah, we'll congratulate each other later." Quinn lifted her hand from the button, leaving the lights off before climbing down the metal scaffolding that formed into a ladder on the side of the tower. The sun had risen higher while he fought, casting the entire port in eerie morning light. Quinn came to his side and leaned back against the vehicle. "The ship is just over there." She nodded past a wide open swath of tarmac. There was no cover, no vehicles, no trees, nothing to obscure them from view. "What are the chances that guards start opening fire the second we break cover?"

"Almost certain." The cat-like creature's attack had been lucky in its own way. By pure chance, they were covered by two large ships, the maintenance tower, and the small vehicle that he and Quinn were currently leaning against. The second they broke out from under the cover of one of the ships they'd be dead. Already Kayde could hear the stopping footsteps of guards getting closer. Either the lights or the cat's screams had summoned them to check out the disturbance.

He might have considered stealing one of the two ships that they were trapped under, but both the doors were sealed tight, and he didn't know what kind of security measures they would find aboard. He knew his own ship, and as long as he could get himself and Quinn safely on it, he would find a way to get them off this planet.

Quinn tapped her hand against the sturdy roof of the vehicle they were leaning against. She pressed her face up against the window and nodded to herself before testing the door. It opened easily and she slid behind the driver seat. The passenger-side window came down and she leaned over. "Get in. I'll get us to the ship."

Kayde wasted no time following her instructions. As long as the guards were just using blasters, this little transport vehicle would give them the cover they needed to cross the distance. Quinn took off and they were both jolted back in their seats by the unexpected speed of the vehicle. It wasn't incredibly fast, but definitely faster than either of them were counting on. They jetted across the tarmac and just as expected, the guards began to open fire as soon as they were exposed. Quinn dodged the shots as best she could, sending the vehicle spinning in mad circles before righting it again and heading for their ship.

"Don't worry about the blasters," Kayde told her. "They can't get us through the metal."

"I know that," Quinn grit out, her fists gripping the steering controls tightly. "That doesn't mean they can't fry the electrical."

They crossed the open space much faster than they could've hoped to on foot, but when Quinn swung the vehicle so that the passenger side faced their ship and got a little cover from it, they could both see that the hatch had been sealed shut and was locked with an impressive looking device that Kayde had never seen before.

"Get that door open," Quinn commanded. "I'll keep them distracted."

* * *

She had to be going fucking insane. Sure, Quinn knew how to drive. It wasn't like it was all that difficult, but until today the most dangerous obstacles she'd had to overcome were angry rush-hour drivers, and one angry farmer who'd been upset that she and her foster siblings stole eggs from his farm. None of that could have prepared her for today, and none of it would've suggested that this was almost fun.

Yeah, exhilarating, edge of your seat, heart-pounding fun. As Kayde rolled out of the vehicle and slammed the door behind him, Quinn let out a whoop of triumph and sped away, wheels squealing against the pavement. She was sure that one of the switches in front of her would engage the anti-grav, but she didn't want to risk stalling out by hitting the wrong button. She headed straight towards the guards, drawing their fire away from Kayde and praying to whatever god was listening that none of the guards got off a lucky enough shot to fry the engine.

At the last minute, she swerved away and headed back towards where Beznifa's answer to a saber tooth tiger had tried to rip Kayde to shreds. In a perfect world, she would've been able to find the cat and lure it towards the guards, setting her two enemies against one another. But given all of the noise and lights coming from the port, she would bet the cat was long gone, and so far nothing about Beznifa had been perfect.

How long would Kayde need to get inside the ship? A minute? Five? She could drive in circles all morning, but eventually the guards would realize what she was doing. Already they were beginning to divide their fire, sending shots towards Kayde, a few of the braver guards even beginning to advance on his location.

Quinn wasn't about to let that happen. She spun her vehicle back around and charged straight for them, ready to batter them to the ground if that was what she had to do to protect her warrior. The guards must've figured out that she meant business. They scattered as she got close, one missing being pulled under her wheels by a few scant centimeters.

A minute had never seemed so long in her entire life. That was strange to consider when she was driving so quickly, but no one thing could hold her focus while she was so worried about Kayde. Her heart was there with him, cheering him on and trying to give him a little bit of her strength, as if he needed it. He had been the one to get them this far. She knew she was practically dead weight when it came to this escape, so she was determined to be useful now, using this one skill that she had.

She couldn't fire a blaster for shit, her hand-to-hand combat was laughable, and she hadn't been able to plan any kind of escape, but she could drive, and she could ignore the fear burbling in her veins and head straight into danger if it meant keeping Kayde safe.

The hum of a ship starting up was loud enough for Quinn to hear it over the sound of the blasters and the skating of her vehicle. Laughter bubbled out of her throat and if Kayde had been sitting beside her rather than getting their ride prepared to take them home, she could not have stopped herself from kissing him.

She'd have to save that for later.

It felt like she should throw some glib comment over her shoulder at the guards, but nothing came to mind, so she didn't waste her breath. She swung the vehicle back around to make her final pass across the tarmac. The guards redoubled their efforts to take her out, but Quinn thought she was home free. She could practically taste her escape.

And it was at that exact moment that the smell of smoke tickled her nose and her vehicle lurched to a sudden stop ten meters from the waiting hatch of the ship. She was so close she could taste it, but there was no way to cover the distance and avoid getting hit. Acrid and chemical smoke filled the cab of her vehicle so quickly that Quinn barely had time to stumble out before she choked. She slammed the door shut behind her, but that did little to deter the air around her from being polluted.

Flames licked up the side of the vehicle and Quinn knew, just knew, that the main battery had been compromised. Depending on what the Beznens used to power that thing, that could mean she was seconds away from an explosion. She had two choices. Die by blaster, or be incinerated. The opening to the ship was so close that the injustice of it all overwhelmed her and tears pricked at her eyes. Though she could just as easily blame them on the smoke all around her. She hoped she was far away enough that if the car exploded it wouldn't damage Kayde's ship. At least one of them needed to get off this damned planet. He was the one with the mission, he was the one who needed to make it. He was the one who deserved to live.

A sense of peace stole over her as it sank in that this was the end of the line. She was pinned down with no hope of escape. If she had a blaster, things might've been different. But all she had were her wits, and she'd already used them to steal enough time. She could have died at any moment when those slavers held her captive, but she had stolen almost an entire year from them. And then the impossible happened and she was rescued, and in being rescued she met the man on that ship who had fascinated her in a way she'd never known was possible.

She had regrets, tons of them. And the biggest regret was that she'd never know the taste of Kayde's lips. But it was something she could live with—well, die with—as long as he survived.

The sounds of blaster fire were even closer now and Quinn risked a glance around the vehicle to see if the guards were coming. But the smoke and the flames were holding them off for now, and they seemed to be falling back, taking cover, as if they themselves were under attack.

No, they *were* under attack. The blaster shot was coming from the other side of the ship, and there was no way Beznen guards were shooting it.

Kayde. He was giving her a chance, Providing the distraction and cover fire she needed to make it to the ship. She didn't hesitate, didn't give herself a second to doubt that she could make it. She sprang to her feet and sprinted for all that she was worth, paying no attention to the guards who could lay her flat with a single shot. At the moment they were too occupied with avoiding being hit to hit her.

She scrambled through the hatch and threw it shut behind her, sprinting through the ship to find Kayde, who had taken position behind a different hatch near the ship's main storage section. She wanted to launch herself at him, to wrap her arms around him and never let him go, but she wasn't about startle a man holding a giant blast rifle. "I'm on board," Quinn panted from a safe distance away. "Let's get out of here."

At first she thought he didn't hear her. He calmly let out two more shots before pulling back and slamming the hatch closed. He put his rifle to the side and turned towards her, his eyes blazing red.

Quinn's breath caught and though it shouldn't have been possible, given the excitement of the last few minutes, her heart started beating even faster, and she was distantly concerned that she might pass out. Kayde stalked towards her, every bit the dangerous alien warrior that she was completely obsessed with. She expected him to yell, to be commanding, to be demanding, and conquering. But he reached up and cradled her cheek like she was something precious, something breakable, and irreplaceable.

"You put yourself at risk." There was a ragged edge to his words, emotion like she'd never heard from him before in every syllable. "For me."

"Yeah, I did." She couldn't break away from his gaze, like he held her under some kind of spell. What was this power he had over her? This connection that spring up between them?

"Why?" He sounded truly puzzled.

"Because your..." She couldn't finish that sentence, she had no right. And though they were still in danger, still sitting in the middle of the port that they needed to fly away from right this second, there was something Quinn needed more, something she needed to give to Kayde, to share with him. She leaned forward and sealed her lips over his, taking that taste and marking it so deep on her soul that she could never forget.

Chapter Fourteen

Sensation, emotion exploded through Kayde as Quinn's lips moved against him. Any lingering question about who she was to him dissolved as they shared their first kiss in the heat of battle, moments away from danger, and as far away from home as either of them had ever been. It was perfect. *Denya.* He could sense it in his bones, and the remnants of his soul that was trying to piece him back together and make him a man worthy of Quinn.

The need to claim her rose within him, almost overpowering everything else. He backed her up against the wall and deepened the kiss, sweeping his tongue against hers and imprinting her taste on his being. She arched against him, letting out a moan that shot straight to his cock, and her hands gripped his sides almost hard enough to bruise. He wanted it that way, wanted to take her rough and fast before slowing down and doing it all again, this time worshiping her like the goddess she was.

It was only the defense system coming online and alerting him to the blaster fire currently threatening the shield that made him pull back. Quinn looked up at him, pupils blown, eyes dazed, and sucked in a deep breath before her tongue darted out to lick her lips. "Hello to you too." She smiled at him. "That better be a thing we're doing now, cause if it was only one time I think I'm going to go crazy."

There was time for one more kiss, and Kayde stole it. "Later," he promised.

"Later," Quinn repeated.

They both ran for the cockpit. There was no more time for greetings, and no knowing what kind of defense system Beznifa had in place. Kayde slid into the pilot seat while Quinn was buckling herself into the co-pilot's station beside him. They shared a glance filled with hope, lust, and just a little bit of fear. That stolen moment in the back of the ship could be the only time they had together, and they both knew it. The ship could be blown out of the sky in a matter of minutes, but neither of them mentioned that possibility. There was nothing they could do to change it.

"Next time," said Quinn, "I get to choose the vacation spot."

For the first time in two years Kayde felt the urge to smile, his lips twitching at the corners. "Next time," he agreed. He started up the ship, abandoning half of the safety protocols in favor of speed. As soon as he confirmed that their fuel levels were satisfactory, Kayde took off, shooting straight up as fast as the vehicle would allow them to go. The shields were at full capacity, ready to take the laser blasts headed their way. The ship rocked with the first impacts, but quickly stabilized as the defense system began to predict the attack pattern.

"Should we be firing back or something?" Quinn asked. Her hands were gripping the arms of her chair tightly, so hard that her fingers had to hurt.

"Not unless we have no other choice. Our goal is to escape, not escalate the situation." It rankled his newly blooming emotions to not punish the people who had harmed his denya. But the more important thing at this moment was to see that she escaped.

Quinn nodded and flinched as something bright flashed across the view screen in front of them. She opened her mouth as if she were about to ask a question, but clicked it closed again almost as quickly.

Kayde didn't know how to comfort her, and most of his focus was on making sure they didn't get blown up. But Quinn was trembling and she had lost a lot of color in her face. That couldn't be good. "Close your eyes," he instructed.

Quinn did the opposite, her eyes widening to an almost impossible degree as she jerked her head towards him. "Seriously?" She practically yelled it.

"Seriously. I give you my word that we will both get out of this, but you should shut your eyes right now." If she couldn't see what was happening, she couldn't panic about it. It made perfect sense to him, so why was she having such a terrible time understanding it?"

She still didn't shut her eyes. "I'm just going to be imagining something worse. Focus on flying this thing, I'll be fine."

She didn't look fine, but right then flying got a whole lot more difficult as two speeders launched into the air, giving chase. Kayde engaged evasive maneuvers, but the speeders had been expecting that and the ship rocked as one of them got a good hit on the shield outside of one of their engines. Quinn couldn't bite back her yelp, but she just gripped her chair harder and clenched her jaw.

"Can't we jump to FTL?" she asked, voice quavering.

"Not until we break atmo." There were too many variables when it came to engaging in faster than light travel, and jumping to it before they hit the vacuum of space was a guaranteed death sentence. It was coming up close, but the shields were already weakening and it would only take a lucky shot by one of those speeders to take them out. "Ten more seconds," he promised. One way or another it would all be over then.

"Okay," said Quinn, her breath unsteady. This time she did close her eyes while she sucked in deep breaths, trying to keep a hold of herself.

Kayde increased their speed as much as he dared. He put a little distance between them and the speeders, but they were still easily within range of the blasters. He keyed in the coordinates on the FTL controls and left them there, ready for the second they broke away from Beznifa and could safely get a move on. The ship rocked as they went higher, but this time it wasn't blasters trying to stop them, it was the gravity field of Beznifa letting them go.

Kayde waited one more second before engaging the FTL and jumping them away from Beznifa and on their way to safety.

Quinn opened her eyes and let go of her death grip on her seat. "We made it?"

Kayde nodded, unsure of what to say now that they had finally arrived at safety after their week in hell.

Quinn took a deep breath. "Good," she said, repeating the word several times, mostly to herself. "I'm going to go..." She waved her hand towards the back of the ship before unbuckling her safety restraint and standing up on unsteady feet. "I just need a..." She shook her head, maybe unsure of what she needed.

"Go," said Kayde. "Do what you need to do. I'm going to set the auto nav and then take a shower." He had never before announced his schedule for the day to her, but she seemed at a loss and he hoped that something mundane like that would help her find her footing.

She nodded absently. "Okay." She shuffled back towards the cockpit door and climbed carefully down the ladder. Kayde heard her footsteps retreat into the heart of the ship and he had to quell the urge to chase after her and promise her that everything was going to be okay. It only took a few minutes to set their coordinates before Kayde was pushing himself out of his chair, his muscles heavy with exhaustion as the last week caught up with him. He could collapse into his bunk and sleep for several days, but the grit and grime of the arena in the woods covered him, making a shower his first priority. His stomach rumbled and clenched, a bit of queasiness rising in his throat, making a meal the next item on his list.

He was just past the galley when footsteps pounded coming towards them and Quinn burst through the door, a practically maniacal smile lit up on her face. "You're never going to believe this," she said.

"What?"

"Our supplies actually made it to the ship. They loaded them just like they were supposed to. I thought for sure we were meant to be stuck rationing whatever meal bars we could scrounge up, but we've got plenty of supplies to get all the way to HQ and back. I really think we're going to be okay."

Kayde had thought about their supplies while they were making their journey to the ship. He'd forgotten about their day in the market, it seemed so long ago. But Beznifa was a legitimate trading planet, and it was completely possible that the market traders had little or nothing to do with the people who had taken them prisoner and use them for their entertainment. He felt light all of a sudden, his muscles unclenching and his breaths suddenly deeper. Relief, that was what this was. "I agree," Kayde finally said. "We're going to be great."

* * *

Kayde only took a few minutes in his shower and Quinn barely had time to gather some toiletries before he was turning the water off and leaving the now humid chamber for her. She didn't see him get out of the shower, but she could imagine the water streaming down his neck and back, over every muscle and down to the floor. God, even the thought of his *feet* made her shiver, and she'd never been into anything like that before. No, this madness all just came from Kayde. There wasn't any part of him that she wasn't attracted to, from his dark hair to his color shifting eyes to his hidden claws and the emotions he kept buried so deep she had at one time been worried that he didn't feel anything at all.

But there was no way on earth, or in space, that a man could kiss like he did and not feel anything. If they hadn't been under imminent threat of explosion, she wasn't sure where that kiss would have ended. She wasn't sure she ever wanted it to end.

She set the water temperature to scalding and climbed under the stream. It wasn't very strong, but the fact that she could take a shower on a ship, or at all, was a blessing she wasn't about to reject. The slavers back on Fenryr 1 had been stingy with the bathing, and though they'd let her wash on Beznifa, she'd never escaped that oppressive sense of being watched. There was none of that here, only blessed warm water and complete privacy.

And it was with that privacy in mind that Quinn found her fingers drifting lower as she let her mind wander back to the thought of Kayde occupying this same space, letting the water run over his muscles and thoroughly soaping himself until he practically sparkled. If she were a little braver, she might have offered to join him, to help him clean his back and make sure he didn't miss all of those hard to reach places.

For as long as they were on the ship, that would have to remain a fantasy. She barely fit in the shower stall alone, and she was sure that Kayde had to duck to get under the spray and his shoulders probably brushed the walls every time he moved. Yes, they'd be pressed up tight against one another if they tried anything in the shower, but there wouldn't be enough room to get clean, let alone enough space to get dirty.

But if the shower were just a little bigger... Quinn bit her bottom lip as her fingers brushed that sensitive point at the juncture of her thighs. She imagined a rougher hand, one that had gripped her close as they ran through the night, one that had promised her with a touch that everything would be alright. He would be gentle with her the first time, she was sure of it, treat her like she was made of something breakable, something that needed to be handled with care. But not broken. He never looked at her like she needed fixing, no he saw her strength.

Her nipples tightened as her fingers played against her sex and Quinn trembled. She kept her mouth stubbornly shut, not wanting to be heard, even as she imagined her only companion's lips raining down on her neck like the spray of the shower, even as she imagined his fingers replacing her own, preparing her for him and lighting her up in an explosion of pleasure.

It had been *so* long since she'd felt free enough to do this. She pressed harder, almost defiantly, as she remembered why she hadn't felt the urge or the right to take pleasure for herself. And as those thoughts invaded her mind, the release at the tip of her fingers fizzled out, leaving her cold and frustrated.

She shivered and realized the cold was coming from the water, not her psyche. She made quick work of cleaning herself off and stepped out of the shower before chilly transformed into freezing. Quinn was glad the mirror was too fogged up for her to catch a glimpse of her own reflection. She could feel the tears pricking at her eyes and if she saw that vulnerability that had to be naked on her face she knew she would scream, or cry, probably both.

She reared back a hand to punch the wall, but flattened her fist at the last moment, transforming it into a weak slap instead.

Weak, just like she was. There was a hot guy out there who kissed like sin and looked at her like she was the last life support suit on a failing ship, and even as she spent her nights dreaming of him and all the wicked things he could do to her, she couldn't even get herself off to the thought of him. All because of some stupid assholes who thought she'd make a great piece of property, who took and took and took things that weren't theirs until she couldn't remember what it was like to want to give.

A harsh sound escaped her throat and Quinn collapsed against the door behind her, the small latch digging into her kidney. She didn't care, she welcomed the pain. Anything was better than the stupid *shame* that she knew she didn't deserve. She hadn't done anything wrong. She'd fought every second of every day to keep her sanity, and she'd done everything she had to do to survive. And now that she'd finally found something that was worth living for, not just surviving, she didn't know if she could grab and take it without breaking down and pushing it—him—away because of something she couldn't control.

Before climbing in the shower, Quinn had been playing with the idea of hunting Kayde down and seeing if he wanted to explore where that kiss could take them. Now she wanted to lock herself in her room and not come out until she made it back to Earth.

But she couldn't do that. Even in the midst of her pity party, her inner survivor was stirring, demanding that she get back out there and take what she needed, that she not roll over and let those men who had tried to take everything from her win. Quinn groaned and dried herself off roughly with the towel she'd found. It was rough enough to have been made of sandpaper, but the abrasive surface was distracting enough to momentarily clear her mind. By the time she was dry, she hadn't figured out what the hell she was going to do about Kayde and the attraction she didn't know how to act on, but she was no longer on the edge of a panic attack, so she called that a win and did her best to not think about it anymore.

Sleep. Sleep in a bed she knew was safe, knowing that tomorrow she'd wake up on a safe ship with no one that meant her harm. That was what she needed. She could deal with the rest in the morning.

Decision made, she stepped out of the shower and almost ran into Kayde who was holding two trays, both of them laden with some of the best food that their dinky food processor could make. Her mouth watered and she had to clench her fists by her side to keep from reaching out and grabbing one of those trays away from him. Did he really need to eat *that* much? No wonder he'd been insistent they make the supply stop.

"I loaded the foodstuffs into the processor," he told her. "I thought you might be hungry, so I was going to leave this by your room." He nodded to one of the trays.

Quinn's heart cracked, and this time it had nothing to do with lust. She'd never had someone take care of her like that, and she didn't know what to do with everything that it made bubble up inside of her. "Thank you," she finally choked out. She tried to reach for the tray, but with her dirty clothes and toiletries, she needed an extra arm if she was going to manage carrying it all.

Kayde saw her struggle and kept the tray to himself. He hesitated for a moment, the look something she'd never seen from him before. As a matter of fact, she realized that he hadn't been wearing that neutral expression she was used to since they'd stepped on the ship. It was like something in him had caved and all of his emotions had come rushing out, showing themselves on his face just like he was a normal person. On someone else, what she saw from him would have been subtle. On Kayde, he might as well have been announcing everything he was feeling with flashing lights and noisemakers. "There is a small table in my room," he said. "We could eat together." He offered it cautiously, like he expected her to say no.

They hadn't made a habit of sharing their meals, and before her shower and her freak out, Quinn would have jumped at the chance to spend more time with him and to see where the night would take them. But now she was about ten seconds away from exhaustion and she knew she only had enough energy to stuff her face and then collapse. "I don't think I can do more than eat," she admitted. "The day, everything, it's all catching up, you know?" That was as close as she could manage to come to admitting what was actually wrong.

Maybe another person, a human, would have let her deflect the invitation gracefully, but Kayde wasn't that man. "Then just come eat. There's no need to talk."

"Just eat?" she asked. "Not..." She couldn't bring herself to list off all the things she both wanted and was terrified of doing.

Kayde held up one of the trays. "Just eat," he promised.

"Let me drop this in my room." She held up her clothes. "I'll be there in a minute."

And, true to his word, they just ate. The silence was loud around them, all the little sounds of the ship filling the spaces where they weren't talking. But it wasn't uncomfortable. And when Kayde took the trays away, they still hadn't said anything to each other, but Quinn couldn't make herself leave his room. He came back and stopped short when he saw that she hadn't left. "I thought..."

"I *am* really tired." She felt the need to justify it, more to herself than to him. "My brain, it's all jumbled up right now. And I feel—" She made a sound of frustration, unable to articulate what she was trying to say, to ask.

"Would you like to sleep in here?" her alien offered, nodding towards his bed. "I can sleep on the floor, and this way we can be sure that we're safe together. No one is separating us again."

When he said it like that, Quinn heard a promise she wasn't sure he meant to make and her heart hurt with the want that pooled deep in her soul. "You don't have to sleep on the floor," she barely whispered. "I think I'd like if you didn't." It was one thing the slavers hadn't managed to take from her. For all the horrors they'd inflicted, they'd never made her sleep beside them.

It was a tight fit, but when Kayde slung an arm over her and she let their legs tangle together, they managed to find a comfortable position, and before Quinn knew it, she was drifting off, feeling safer than she'd felt since before she'd been stolen from Earth, and restful in a way she couldn't remember managing before. If she could spend every night like this, her sleepy brain thought, she just might call that heaven.

Chapter Fifteen

"Has anyone seen Quinn lately?" Sierra Alvarez asked her gathered team at the Detyen suite in Washington, D.C. Her mate, Raze NaFeen, sat by her side, his arm slung casually over her shoulder as each of them reviewed data they'd been gathering about possible sightings of Ambassador Yormas of Wreet. Dryce was fixing lunch in the kitchen and looked up over-the-counter, shaking his head slightly. Iris Mason, Toran's mate, sat on the floor surrounded by printouts of all of the data they'd managed to extract from Yormas's partner, Nyden Varrow. Toran leaned against the wall and watched his mate, a small smile on his face.

He shook his head at Sierra. "I don't think so. She was supposed to come to dinner earlier this week, but something must've come up."

"She didn't call to cancel?" asked Iris. She didn't look up from her papers while she spoke, sorting them into neat stacks.

Everyone in the room thought for a minute, and no one could remember hearing from Quinn. "The last time I saw her," said Dryce, bringing a plate of food out from the kitchen, "was when she had that thing with the other girls from Fenryr 1."

"They're not from Fenryr 1," Sierra interjected. "It's not like they shared a sorority."

"What's a sorority?" Raze asked quietly, but not quietly enough to keep the question from being heard from everyone else.

Dryce's expression lit up. "I'll tell you later," he promised.

Sierra glared at her mate's brother and Dryce blew her a kiss, unrepentant. "When was that? That meeting?"

Dryce thought for a moment, chewing on a carrot in delicate bites. "A bit more than a week ago, I think. Yeah," he nodded to himself, "it was before Kayde left."

A tense silence hung in the air at that pronouncement. After Toran had announced Kayde's departure, he and the other Detyen men had gotten into a huge fight about it. Toran had pulled rank, but Raze and Dryce had the numbers and they had gone a few days without speaking to one another. They still didn't agree with

Toran's decision to let Kayde go, but they were moving past it as best they could. With Kayde already gone, they all realized, arguing was pointless.

"You don't think..." Iris didn't finish a thought, but it caught the attention of everyone.

"What, denya?" Toran asked, his voice going soft.

That tone got Iris to look up and she shot her mate a bright smile. "I don't know." She shrugged. "Is it possible she went with Kayde? Dryce just said that no one has seen her since he left the planet. Maybe she decided to tag along."

Toran's expression turned stony. "I hope that's not the case."

"Why?" asked Raze. "Do you think he's a threat?" Raze had grown protective of Kayde in the months since Raze had regained his soul. He and Sierra had spoken about it several times. Kayde was a reflection of who Raze had been and who he would still be if he hadn't met Sierra. It broke Raze's heart to see everything that Kayde missed out on by sacrificing his soul, and it was his most secret wish that Kayde could find his denya and be saved just like Raze.

"Kayde wanted to leave the planet for a reason," said Toran. "He said it was loud here. Too distracting for his senses. And I suspect there was a specific person he was trying to avoid."

Quinn. No one said it, but it was obviously Toran's conclusion.

"Kayde was stable," Raze insisted. "Even if she went with him, he wouldn't hurt her."

"You can't know that," said Dryce. "The soulless... They..." He couldn't seem to find the right words to say what he wanted to say. Probably as he remembered at the last moment that his brother knew more about the soulless and Dryce ever would.

"I know Kayde," said Raze, stubbornly.

Sierra squeezed Raze's thigh in silent support. "Let's not get ahead of ourselves," she broke through the growing panic in the room. "There's no reason to think that Quinn and Kayde are together right now. Yes, it's strange that Quinn hasn't contacted any of us, but that doesn't mean that anything bad has happened. She's an adult, and we're not her keepers. I'm going to call some of the

467

other survivors and see if any of them know where she is." She kissed Raze on the cheek and took her communicator into the room that had been assigned as his when he and the Detyens had come to Earth. Raze's main residence was in her apartment, but sometimes they crashed in the Detyen's suite when they worked too late and were too tired to make the drive home.

Valerie was the first of the survivors to come up in the list of Sierra's contacts, but she scrolled quickly past that information. She still got a bad taste in her mouth every time she remembered the look Valerie had given her when she discovered that Laurel wasn't on the ship while they were escaping from the Detyen HQ. If Valerie hadn't been the one to come up with the idea of leaving Laurel behind, she didn't have a problem with it. CJ came up next and Sierra was more than happy to talk to her.

CJ confirmed that she hadn't seen Quinn in more than a week, not since the night where she and her fellow survivors had met up over drinks. "She got weird at one point," CJ remembered. "Not drunk weird but weird weird."

"Weird how?" That was too many weirds and the word was starting to lose meaning.

"She cut out the back of the bar and went to the alley for some reason. Then the rest of the night she was looking around like she expected someone to be watching her."

"Did you see anyone watching her?" Sierra asked. Why had no one said anything before now? Then again, she wasn't friends with most of the survivors, she was just a reminder of all the trauma they'd been put through.

CJ thought for a moment. "I thought there might've been an alien, he kind of looked like one of those Detyen guys. The scary one."

There were only four Detyens, was it really that hard to remember their names? "Which one is the scary one?"

"The blue one." CJ only paused for a second, not giving Sierra time to interject that three of the four Detyens they knew were blue, including her mate. "The one who always looks ready to cut somebody."

Kayde. The default expression of soulless Detyens could be a bit violent-looking, especially if someone didn't know why they looked that way.

"So you haven't seen her since that night, and Kayde might have been there?" Sierra asked to confirm. "And did she say anything about her plans? Was she going to go anywhere?"

"That's right. Wait," CJ said like Sierra had anywhere to go. "She said something about getting a gift for Muir. That kid is messed up."

Sierra bit her tongue to keep from saying anything about the degrees to which all of the survivors were messed up.

"I think she wanted to go back to the ship that brought us to Earth. I know it was like a week ago, but that's the last thing I remember her saying. I hope it helps."

Sierra disconnected the call. She rested her communicator against her forehead and considered her next move. She really hadn't thought that there was any possibility that Kayde and Quinn were together. Why would they be? But given what CJ said, and Toran's concern that Kayde had been fixating on Quinn, it was looking more and more possible by the minute.

Sierra wanted to put a call in to the field where they had been storing the ship, but she didn't have the authority to request the security feeds that would tell her if Quinn had shown up. Instead she scrolled down to another contact and barely hesitated to add to the list of favors she could never hope to repay. "Dad?" she said when he answered. "I need your help."

* * *

In a perfect world, Quinn would've slept through the night cuddled up tightly in Kayde's arms. It didn't happen exactly like that. For one, the bed really was too small for two people. No matter how she wedged herself, at least one limb was hanging off the side and she always felt like she was one deep breath away from crashing to the ground. Maybe if she'd been willing to plaster herself up against Kayde, clinging to him like they were glued together, it might have worked out better. But she had never been a clinger; she got too hot when she was sleeping, and waking up covered in sweat was the exact opposite of sexy.

In that same perfect world, sleeping beside Kayde would have cured her insomnia. Knowing a giant warrior lay right beside her should have made her feel safe and protected and able to turn off. Consciously it did, when she was asleep? Not so much. She would drift off, content in the knowledge that Kayde was right there and he wasn't about to be taken away. But then came the nightmares and that sensation of hopelessness, of knowing that no one was coming for her. They weren't memories, not exactly. Instead she'd find herself in a deep hole, unable to climb out, or stuck in a bricked up wall, with no way to call for help. Sometimes she could see the people who put her there, but most of the times they were just shadows and distant laughing voices.

She'd wake with a start, and when she woke the miracles promised by Kayde's presence finally made themselves known. She wasn't disoriented, wasn't panicking on the edge of an attack. When she woke, she knew she was safe, and the remnants of her nightmares were blown away like they were nothing more than dust. Then she'd settle back onto the bed and the whole cycle would start again, drifting off to sleep knowing she was safe, drowning in a nightmare, then waking up assured of Kayde's presence. It happened three or four times, until the last time she woke up and Kayde wasn't sleeping beside her.

A glance around the room settled her almost as quickly as sleeping beside him. There weren't any knickknacks to remind her of Kayde's presence, but his scent had permeated the place, and it was almost like the air was hugging her. She was about to throw the covers off and escape to her own room when the door opened and Kayde stepped inside. He looked at her for a long moment, and his expression gave nothing away. Were they back to that then?

"I had hoped that you would sleep longer," he said, standing in the doorway as if he wasn't sure he should enter his own quarters. "It's only been a few hours since we jumped to FTL. I was just checking to make sure everything was in order."

His expression might've been shuttered, but he was talking more than he had before they'd been detained. That was good, Quinn liked that. It was no fun to travel with an android that had a malfunctioning communication chip.

"A few hours is more than I usually manage," she confessed. "I actually slept pretty well."

"You woke up several times," he said, revealing that he hadn't slept as soundly as she'd thought. Then again, he was a trained warrior, and probably slept lightly by default.

"It happens, I'm used to it. Have you had breakfast?" She didn't want to talk more about why she couldn't sleep. They both had to know the reason, and dwelling on it wouldn't fix anything. She couldn't quite bring herself to look at him. The memory of the kiss and everything that came after hung in the air between them, and Quinn didn't know how to handle it.

"No, my scheduler notes that I do not need to eat for another ninety minutes."

"But are you hungry?" How was that a complicated question? "Why does your scheduler need to tell you when to eat?" Maybe he really was an android, though she had never heard of one that could bleed before.

Kayde stared at her, and though his expression didn't shift from the same blank look he always had, she thought she saw thoughts flashing through his eyes, a hundred a minute, as he came to some sort of conclusion, making her realize that she had asked a much more complicated question than she thought. He finally entered the room and let the door close behind them. He took a seat at the small table beside his bed and faced her. "I am soulless."

Quinn remained quiet. She had no idea what he was talking about, but she could tell it was a big deal, that this confession was something momentous, and maybe something he shouldn't be telling her. But she wanted to know, desperately needed to know. In their short time together something had shifted within her, had rearranged her priorities until finding out everything she could about Kayde was up there with her need for food and water, and definitely above sleep.

"Have the others told you much about the Detyens?" he asked after it was clear she wasn't going to respond to his confession.

Quinn knew a little; the information would've been difficult to avoid given that she had been working around the Detyens for quite some time. "I know that your planet was destroyed, and that you've been searching for the people who did it for a hundred years. I know there aren't that many of you left, and that some of you have mates. Human mates, like Sierra and Iris."

"So no one has told you about the denya price?" he asked.

Quinn shook her head, not liking the sound of that.

"You're right that we take mates, the recognition is immediate. And until recently no one knew that humans could be mated to Detyens. There aren't many Detyen females left. Since the destruction of Detya, more men have been born for some reason, and in the immediate aftermath of the destruction, many of our women were lost in a tragic ship crash. It's been killing us slowly ever since. Without mates, Detyens are doomed to die at the age of thirty. Without that bond, we cease to be. When Detya still existed, the price was more of an inconvenience. There were entire systems created to ensure that mates found one another. Only a small percentage of the population failed to find their denya. But it was still tragic."

Quinn's mind reeled at this confession. Dead at thirty? That was so young. How did they live like that? She didn't know what she would do if she knew her life would be cut short just because she couldn't find the right person in time. And Kayde... She didn't like to think of the world, of the universe, without him in it. Even if she wasn't his mate, she'd rather someone else have him than see him die.

Her mind drew up short at the thought. When she started to hope that she might be his denya? But now she knew it was impossible. If they recognized their mates on sight, wouldn't he have said something by now?

"How old are you?" she managed to ask, and was proud that her voice to tremble. She was really asking a different question. How much time did he have?

"I'm thirty-three," he answered, confusing her even further. "I'll get to that," he promised. "A long time ago, long before Detya was destroyed, a scientist had several children. One by one they reached their thirtieth birthdays, and one by one they perished. None of his children could find their mates, and the scientist was desperate to find some way to save them. When he had only one child left, a daughter, he made a breakthrough. On the night before her thirtieth birthday he performed a procedure and the next morning she woke up, even though she didn't have a mate. Except something went wrong. She murdered her father, destroyed his laboratory, and then killed herself after leaving a message saying that what had been done to her should never be done to anyone else. What she didn't know was that the scientist had sent his data off to one of his friends. The friend was so horrified that he never did anything with the information he had. And the story became a legend, barely more than a myth, until Detya was destroyed and my ancestors grew desperate. They had no hope of finding mates, no one on the military ship was compatible with anyone else. They searched for survivors as best they could, but one by one they began to die off. Until someone discovered the scientist's research. They took a vote and agreed to try the procedure out on a few candidates. It worked, removing what the scientist had called the soul. Creating the soulless allowed the soldiers to live longer than they should have. But it did come at a price. For the Detyens, the soul is the seat of our emotions, and the heart of the denya bond. Those who allow their souls to be removed sacrifice all emotion, all joy, all hope, all pain so that we may serve our people for a little bit longer. And none of the soulless had ever found their denya. Until Raze."

"Raze? Your Raze?" Quinn was trying to make sense of this story, but her heart ached as she realized everything that he had sacrificed for his people. It was greater than his life. It was something she couldn't imagine giving up.

"I think he would refer to himself as Sierra's Raze," Kayde said wryly.

Quinn sat up straighter. He didn't sound like an emotionless robot anymore. "And is Raze the only one who has found his mate?" She tried to keep the hope out of her voice, tried to speak neutrally, but she feared she failed miserably.

Kayde's eyes met her and they glowed red. "Not anymore."

Chapter Sixteen

"I don't know if I can have sex." Quinn didn't mean to blurt it out, but panic bubbled in her and her thoughts cascaded in the wake of Kayde's confession. Mate? Her? Him? She'd barely begun to hope it was possible before all the reasons it wouldn't work started shouting at her. What kind of mate would she be if she couldn't even get off by herself? "You shouldn't pick me, you should find someone better. Someone who isn't broken." Tears threatened to fall and Quinn wanted to scream. She thought she was over this shit. She was safe from the slavers, she didn't have to worry about going back there, so why was all of this crap hitting her now?

She didn't see Kayde move, but suddenly he was beside her, one hand tentatively resting on her shoulder. She leaned into him, unconsciously at first and then she burrowed in tightly, seeking his warmth, his scent, everything about him that settled the disquiet in her bruised psyche. "Even if I could choose," his voice rumbled around her, "there's no one else I would want. Since the moment I saw you, you've been in my thoughts. At first I thought it was some kind of curse, a fixation hounding me that could lead us both to ruin. But now I know that there is no place in this universe I belong, except for at your side."

She cried just enough to get Kayde's top wet, but not enough to get all blotchy, thank God. With Kayde sitting right there it was impossible not to calm down eventually, but it was still a lot, almost too much, to take in. "Why did you do it? Was it your choice?"

For a second she thought Kayde wouldn't understand what she was asking, but he caught the thread of her thought easily enough. "Yes, all of us who sacrifice our souls choose it. There is an application process and not all applicants are accepted. We need to fall into certain diagnostic parameters for the safety of everyone involved. And I chose to do it because my people needed me. There aren't enough of us left and I never thought there was a choice. I was a prime candidate for the procedure, it would be a dereliction of duty to pass on the opportunity."

Had she ever felt that strongly about anything? Quinn might have agreed to a devil's bargain like that in the darkest days of her captivity, but she didn't think anything could convince her to give up her emotions, whatever passions she possessed, when she had an entire life to live. Then again, Kayde hadn't had a life to live, he'd been given less than half of a human's. "Did you ever regret it?"

His hand moved, stroking her hair, playing with the thick strands. "Once it was done, I felt nothing, so even if I wanted to second guess my decision, I couldn't. And now that I am beginning to feel again, now that the bond is reaching out from you and pulling me out of that darkness, I can't regret a moment of it. It's brought me to you."

Quinn wanted this to be the perfect moment. They'd found each other, had saved each other in their own ways, and now they could come together and celebrate the connection that had been blossoming between them for some time now. She'd felt it long before she climbed on this ship and embarked on this journey, and every day she spent with Kayde only strengthened the bond that she'd never before realized could exist between two people. This wasn't love, not like she'd been taught to recognize it. It was something deeper, something cosmic. They'd been born on different planets, to different species, and yet here they were, holding each other and revealing secrets they didn't share with anyone else.

But just because she yearned for this connection, didn't mean it solved her biggest problem. "You deserve a mate who can let you touch her." It stabbed at her heart to imagine someone else with Kayde, and even as she was trying to make a noble sacrifice, Quinn didn't think she could give him up.

Kayde tilted her head up and brushed his lips against her forehead. "I'm touching you now," he pointed out.

"You know that's not what I mean." She wanted to believe that he had a point, that any apprehensions she had would dissolve so long as she was with Kayde, but wounds like hers didn't heal just because she wanted them to, just because she really liked a guy and wanted to be with him. Trauma like that couldn't be fixed with a mind over matter attitude. Suddenly she regretted not going to those therapy sessions she'd been prescribed after she'd made it back to Earth. Maybe then she wouldn't be in this situation.

"We don't need to do anything you don't want to do," Kayde assured her, even as she could feel a line of tension in the way he held her.

Quinn barely stopped herself from scoffing. "I've seen how the others act around one another. I'm pretty sure they start humping the second we turn our backs." It came out bitter and Quinn hated herself for it. She hadn't realized that she was jealous of that connection they had, but now that the same bond was within her grasp and she was scared to reach out and take it, she found that the thought of the other mated pairs made her angry.

"Believe me, they don't always wait for privacy." Her alien was definitely learning the finer points of sarcasm. She wondered what he'd been like before. Would he be that man again? Or something new? He hesitated before his next words, his hands rubbing idle circles on her back as if soothing a wild animal. "Have you... tried anything since you've been back? With—" he swallowed and Quinn was almost certain he was trying to bite back a possessive urge to growl, "anyone else?"

The jealousy he was trying to suppress should have scared her. It should have turned her off. It wasn't sexy, and others did shit like that as a sign of ownership. She'd been owned before and she'd rather die than let it happen again. But when Kayde got that look in his eye, it was different than the humiliation of captivity. It was a kind of protection that she'd never known she would want. "There hasn't been anyone I wanted to do anything with." *Except you.* She caught his eye to make sure he understood those unsaid words. She swallowed hard before continuing. "I tried... in the shower... I was thinking of you." At that confession, Kayde practically purred and the sound sent a shiver down her spine and straight to her core. Quinn didn't try to bite back the gasp of want that escaped. She wanted to give him whatever reactions she could, even if she couldn't give him everything. "But then I remembered what *they* did to me and it ruined everything. I don't want to invite them into bed with us. I don't want to remember the things they did when I just want to feel you." She didn't cry that time, thankfully. She'd never been one for tears, and the last few days had wrung her out until she had nothing left.

"I will never push you," he vowed. "If you tell me no, tell me to slow down, tell me to get out of the room and not come back, I'll do as you say. You have my word. If it's never more than this..." He paused for a long moment, making Quinn wonder what he wasn't saying. "Then we will only do this."

"You're holding something back," she accused. "You can't just be happy about this."

Kayde's arms tightened around her and she settled in against him, lying against his back. "The denya bond needs to be sealed," he said. "That is normally done through sex. But there must be another way. I can already feel the bond inside me," he took her hand and placed it just under his heart, "right here. It isn't fully set yet, but it's calling out to you, connecting us already."

That sounded nice, sounded perfect, and it explained the knot that Quinn could feel in her own chest. But it brought up an even bigger question. "But what if it never happens? Are you in any danger? You gave up your soul to gain a few more years. I'm not letting you do that again. Knock me out and fuck me if you have to, but you don't go back to being that robot that I first met. That... that would break my heart."

Kayde nuzzled her. The longer they kept in contact, the more he seemed to kiss her, to claim her, like he couldn't help himself. He'd gone from cold machine to cuddly bear so quickly that she was still reeling, trying to catch up. "I will always hold your heart safe," he promised. He pushed up as if he planned to rise from the bed.

Quinn shot a hand out and gripped his arm. "Wait."

He froze.

"I want to try," she said, finding a well of bravery that had been hiding somewhere deep inside of her. "I don't know how far I can go, I don't think I can let you... that we can go all the way, but I want to test the limits. To see where I am right now. To see where we can go from here. Will you let me try?" She felt naked, half sitting, half laying on the bed, a raw nerve exposed and vulnerable.

Kayde sat back down. "Anytime, denya. We will do what you want, and I promise, no further."

That should have settled her nerves, made her feel better, like she was completely in control, but Quinn practically shook as she made room for Kayde on the bed. It wasn't really necessary, as he'd made his own space when he'd been sitting before, but she needed to do something or she might just jump out of her skin. They sat side by side, both looking forward, barely touching. Quinn was transported back to her teenage years when she hadn't had a clue what she was doing, and she'd been doing it with boys she shouldn't have been giving the time of day. Everything was so good between her and Kayde when they'd spontaneously kissed, when they embraced. But now that she was sitting here, deliberately inviting him to do more, she wasn't sure what she could handle.

She glanced at Kayde and he looked back at her, patient, his eyes simmering with want but tempered, holding himself back. There was a wild beast buried inside of him, she'd seen it when he'd fought, felt it when he held her against the wall and plundered her mouth. It thrilled and terrified her, and she wasn't sure how she would react if it escaped. He said he could control himself, but could he really? Even then? He was a being of passion and strength, one who'd basically cut off a limb out of loyalty to his people. Could something that powerful really be caged?

Yes, she could see the reassurance he was trying to tell her silently. It could. He was power... and control. And if he had to hold himself back to give her what she needed right now, she was absolutely certain that he would. He could give this to her, let her find herself again. Quinn vowed that she would; she made the promise to herself, afraid to voice it just now and hear whatever reassurance Kayde would give her. She was going to get better, was going to find a way to give every part of herself, no matter what it took. He deserved it, and so did she.

She waited for him to do something, but realized he was waiting for her. This was her show. Kayde wouldn't make a move until she said it was okay. Quinn took a deep breath, breathing in the smell of his soap and the underlying scent of his skin, letting it wrap around her until it sank into her pores and reminded her that she wasn't alone, that she was safe. "Kiss me," she commanded, proud at how steady her voice sounded, even as she was still unsure of this whole endeavor.

He was gentle, but there was no hesitation in the way Kayde's lips covered hers. Quinn opened under him, yielding as his tongue plundered.

It was wonderful and horrible. Everything she wanted, yet so far from enough that Quinn could have cried in frustration if her mouth weren't otherwise occupied. Her hands grasped at the air around them before she reached out and let her fingers burrow into Kayde's hair, feeling the thick strands wrap around her digits. Once she touched him, he mirrored her action, resting his palm on the back of her head and wrapping another around her shoulders. He didn't move his hands, just let them rest, let her set the pace even as he kept control of the kiss. It was a dance, one Quinn didn't know the moves to, this exchange where they were both follower and leader. It shouldn't have worked, should have been confusing, but Quinn could only give silent thanks for the way her alien warrior was holding her close. He kissed her like she was precious, like she deserved to be kissed for hours every day until her lips were swollen, but he didn't hold her like she was fragile. Yes, he touched her with care, but his tight grip and the firm press of his lips and sweep of his tongue told her that he saw her as anything but broken.

Even if she didn't know if she agreed.

Kayde leaned into her and Quinn found herself lying back on the bed, covered by Kayde's weight. She could feel his hardening cock pressed against her through all the layers of their clothes and her breath caught, half arousal and half fear. Her heartbeat kicked up and she tried to tell herself that it was just the excitement of the moment. She was in Kayde's arms, where she belonged, where she wanted to be, and she didn't need to fear what would happen. They were only going as far as she wanted. He promised.

But somehow his leg ended up between hers and that spiked Quinn's fear, tipping her over the edge until she started to struggle beneath him. She pushed at his shoulder, slamming her mouth shut and almost biting his tongue in the process. It only took Kayde a moment to figure out what she was trying to do and he backed up, putting a little space between them, lifting himself off of her.

But his leg was still between her thighs and that was the problem. Quinn batted at it and scrambled back until she was sitting up. She let out a sound of frustration and curled her hands into fists, wrinkling the sheet under them.

"What the fuck is wrong with me?" She didn't mean to yell, but she was too angry to modulate her voice. She couldn't bring herself to look at Kayde. She buried her face in her hands and muffled her next scream. At least she wasn't crying, she told herself. At least she was spared that humiliation. She'd already made out with Kayde once before. Why couldn't she handle it now?

She didn't want to look at him, didn't want to see the disappointment that was sure to be dancing across his face. He was probably wishing for some better mate right now, someone who could handle him. Or, even worse, he was wishing that she'd never awakened this part of him so that he'd never know what he was missing.

"I'm sorry," she finally muttered. "Maybe this was a bad idea." No maybe about it. This was *definitely* a bad idea. "You should probably just leave me alone."

But Kayde didn't move away. Quinn finally braved a glance at him and saw him studying her like he'd looked at his opponents in the arena. Nothing about him screamed violence, though. No, he was looking for some weak spot, analyzing what they'd just done and looking for a way to fix it.

"I'm not leaving you," Kayde said, and Quinn knew that he was talking about more than what was happening in the room. "But I do have an idea. If you'll let me?"

* * *

Kayde's newly growing soul ached at seeing his mate in pain, especially when she was torturing herself over something that she had no control over. He knew that she'd been a victim, that she'd been used by some of the cruelest creatures in the universe. And he knew that healing was a process he couldn't expect to happen overnight, or even over the course of a few months.

Yes, his body yearned for hers and there was an ancient creature lurking inside of him who urged him to claim her no matter the cost, but he was not some base beast. He would give his mate care and time, but he would not let her retreat into herself or pull away from him out of some misplaced sense of self-sacrifice. She was *his*. He'd traveled the universe, given up his soul, lost all hope, and yet he still found her. He could wait as long as she needed before they claimed one another.

At least he thought he could. He was only the second among the soulless to find his denya, and he could not know what it would do to him to regrow his soul past the age of thirty and not claim his mate. Raze had claimed Sierra quickly, before there was any time to analyze what was happening to him. But, Kayde rationalized, he had already known Quinn for months and he still lived. He would not share these doubts with her. Not while she was so wrapped up in her own mind that she would only use the information to torture herself further.

"What's your idea?" she asked, voice thick with apprehension.

He grabbed her hand and pulled her gently towards him. Quinn leaned in, but she didn't move much closer. "Come here," he said, as if enticing an Oscavian jungle horse. "Sit close," he patted his lap with his free hand.

"You really think me being on top is going to get rid of all of my brain crap?" Quinn's eyebrows shot up, and though she was clearly skeptical, at least she no longer seemed afraid. It was a miracle to Kayde how easy it was to read her emotions now. Before it had been like a thick wall of glass separated them; he could see the gauzy outline of what she was feeling, but had no hope of deciphering it. Now he understood as if there'd never been any obstacle at all.

"I think you need all the control you can get," he told her. He didn't suppress the hum of satisfaction that purred from his throat as she slung a leg over his and straddled him.

Quinn's eyes clouded for a moment and Kayde thought she would pull back. She sat back, perching near his knees, most of her weight on her own legs on either side of him. "It was your thigh," she confessed.

"What was my thigh?" He wanted to reach out and run his hands down her arms, to pull her close until she was flush up against him and could feel the evidence of how much he wanted her, but she needed the distance and Kayde could content himself in looking at how the shadows of the room played across her skin. The pale illumination from the ship's morning lighting program gave her a golden glow, her brown skin gleaming under it.

"That's what set me off last time." She reached down and stroked her hand across his upper thigh, her fingers lightly skimming over the fabric of his pants.

It was a brand, the heat he imagined from the contact searing him deep. His cock twitched, hardening further, but he kept himself still, let Quinn lead even if it felt like it was killing him. He'd endured pain before, but he'd never known that pleasure could be such torture.

"It's not as bad now," she said, fingers drawing patterns on him.

Kayde had to bite the inside of his cheek to keep from reaching for her until she was ready.

"I think it's okay, as long as I know I can pull back anytime I want." Her face grew concerned, a line appearing between her eyes as she thought. "I mean, I know you're stronger, that you could hold me in place..." She gulped. "But I think it's okay." Her voice began to tremble and she seemed ready to spring off of him.

"Would you feel better if I couldn't move my hands?"

That suggestion replaced all of the lingering apprehension on Quinn's face with intrigued surprise. Kayde struggled to keep his own face placid as he imagined what that would look like, him bound underneath his mate, a supplicant to her pleasure. It wasn't something he'd ever done or wanted to do before, but if it was what his denya needed, he thought the idea might have some merit. And some fun.

"You want me to tie you up?" Quinn finally managed, completely incredulous. She looked him up and down, finally poking a finger at his chest. "You're all..." she waved a hand, "*you*. I can't believe you're that into giving up control."

He covered her hand until it was lying flush against his chest. "I am into whatever you want, denya, and I will do what it takes to see to your needs. If you wish to tie me up and use me for your pleasure, we will try it. If you wish to torture me with your touch for hours, I am yours to do with as you please." He could have given her more options as his brain spiraled out, providing a surprising list of fantasies he'd never even considered. It seemed that his denya had opened the creative portion of his mind, and he looked forward to seeing what he could get Quinn to agree to do with him.

She bit her lip and eyed him once more. "Maybe we save light bondage for another day." She smiled and leaned in closer, ghosting her lips over his for a moment. "Just having you suggest it kind of helps. But I'm not ready for that yet."

Yet. That hung as a promise between them for a moment before lips covered his in earnest and all thoughts of what they might do in the future dissolved as he gave the present his total focus. She tasted earthy, human, and sweet, welcoming him into her arms as her hands danced over his skin. Kayde wanted to reach out and touch, but he'd already moved too fast once and he wasn't about to ruin this a second time, not when she was still willing to try.

Though the call to mate beat inside of him, he let his mate lead, let her set the pace of the kiss and decide where and when to touch him. His fingers ached to touch her, a similar feeling to when his claws threatened to burst from his skin, but at the same time completely different. He would never hurt her, never threaten her with his claws. They existed to protect her, to protect their clan, their people.

Despite the ache, he kept his hand at his side, determined to take only as much as she gave to him and ask for no more. But when one of her hands circled his wrists and pulled it towards her, placing it just above her breast, he groaned. Her skin was soft, even through the fabric of her top, and he wanted so badly to feel the smoothness of her skin that he almost asked before thinking better and deepening the kiss.

Quinn writhed on top of him, scooting closer every time their tongues danced. She tugged at his top, letting her lips trail down his chin until she lapped at his neck, tracing the patterns of his clan markings and making him shiver as lust stabbed through him. "Take this off." Her hands squirmed until they pressed against naked flesh.

"Your wish is my command." Kayde reached over his head and pulled the shirt off, tossing it aside. He wanted her naked too, but for the moment he was satisfied to watch her look at him. Her eyes couldn't go red, but they sparkled with an inner fire, something uniquely human, full of light and hope and lust, everything Kayde wanted to see when his mate looked at him.

Her eyes were a caress as they raked over him, pausing to study the way his clan markings climbed down his side and practically pawing at the muscles over his abdomen. Everywhere she looked, he could feel it, and his cock strained in his trousers, begging to be free. His hips jerked, an unconscious move, but it drew her eye.

Quinn gulped and reached out, tracing her finger down the ridge of his muscles as if she could cut him open with a single claw. Her nail was just long enough to scrape, but she didn't press hard enough to hurt, just enough to make him feel it. Kayde leaned into it, wanting to wear her mark, no matter how small. Her hand stopped at the top band of his pants, right above the clasp, and the air grew thick with promise. All she had to do was lower her hand another few centimeters and she'd be resting it over him, but after a moment she drew back, flattening her palm against his stomach and pressing him back against the wall behind the bed.

She leaned her head to the side, giving Kayde the perfect opening to place his lips against her pulse, to taste the way her life beat within her. He kissed a trail, tasting her and loving her, finally letting his hands roam as she made her own exploration.

Time drifted away while they learned each other, taking and giving, teasing and surrendering to the heat of the moment. At some point Quinn's shirt came off and Kayde lavished attention everywhere she let him, her breasts, her stomach, her shoulders. She giggled and gasped when he played with the small indentation in the middle of her stomach and she moaned when he took his time swirling his tongue against one stiff nipple and then another.

When her fingers finally landed on his cock, Kayde practically jumped and bucked against her before freezing in place, worried that he'd scared her off. But Quinn's grin was wicked as she played with him through the thin material of his sleeping pants. She stroked him with abandon, her eyes lit up with every groan and growl that came out of his throat. He no longer sounded like a rational being and he didn't care. He writhed under her caress and had to keep himself from begging her to remove his pants and palm his naked cock. If he did that, he knew there was no way he'd be able to hold himself back from begging her to let him fuck her.

It was delirious torture, and Kayde wouldn't have it any other way. He could hear himself saying things in Detyen, making vows and promises that even he wasn't sure if he understood. Quinn's eyes were hooded with lust the more he spoke, even though he was almost certain she couldn't understand his meaning. Almost no translators knew Detyen anymore, there weren't enough people left to speak it.

Not even that dreary thought could pull him out of the moment. With a gasp he came, still wearing his pants and making a sticky mess. A sticky, wonderful mess brought on by his mate, who was now looking at him like she'd pulled off a particularly neat trick.

Kayde was out of his mind with satisfaction and the only thing that could make it greater would be to watch his own mate fall apart with him. He reached over and tugged her close, his hands skimming against the band of her pants before she stopped him with light fingers on his wrist.

"I..." She was hesitant, as if she didn't want to break the spell between them. "I don't think I'm ready for that."

He wanted to push ahead and show her that she was stronger than she knew, but Kayde had made a promise, and even as his resolve was weak with pleasure he knew that it was paramount that he keep it. "Show me what you look like when you fall apart," he urged. "I promise I won't touch you." To make it clear he laced his fingers behind his head and leaned back, leaving his chest completely exposed.

Her cheeks were flushed with arousal, eyes dark with want. She was close to the edge, he could tell, and she needed this, needed to take back this moment and see just how good things could be between the two of them.

Quinn bit her lip and hesitated, but then their eyes met and she must have seen something she liked from him.

She didn't push down her pants and it was sweet torture to watch her fingers move under the fabric once she dipped them inside. She groaned and arched her neck, but she never broke eye contact with him and Kayde couldn't look away, even as he wanted to witness her entire body come.

It didn't take much, just as he'd predicted. Her breath hitched and then she was rippling with pleasure, a guttural sound echoing around them as she brought herself to her peak and crested.

With deep breaths, Quinn fell against his chest, pulling her hand out of her pants and resting it on the bed. Kayde reached for it and pulled her fingers into his mouth, tasting her arousal secondhand. If he couldn't have her, he would satisfy himself with this small taste to tide him over until she was ready for more.

Her eyes widened and darkened, and he could see that she might just give in as he pushed. Already Kayde was recovering, ready for a second round. But he let her hand fall and wrapped his arm around her, simply being with her, content for the moment.

If he should have said something, he couldn't find the words, but as silence wrapped around him, he knew they sat in the perfect moment, and he wasn't ready to let it go just yet.

Chapter Seventeen

Over the next few days, Quinn and Kayde fell into a pattern of testing her boundaries, making out, and sharing their time together while they sped through space, neither of them outright saying that they might be flying into the aftermath of a massacre. She could tell that it hit Kayde sometimes. He'd go quiet, even quieter than usual, and look at the control panel as if he wanted to punch in a command to turn them around and head back to Earth before he could find out if his people no longer survived.

She tried to bring it up with him once, but he'd deflected until she somehow ended up sitting on his lap in the kitchen, both of them writhing together until they were spent. Eventually she did manage to let him take his pants off and she got her hands on his naked cock, what she was coming to think of as her new favorite toy. And she'd even managed to let him put his hands on her. But not in her—they'd tried that exactly once and it led to a huge freak out and a small panic attack.

They weren't having sex, not like she'd known it before. But the moments they shared were more intimate than any experience she'd had with anyone else. Because of her limitations, she and Kayde had to communicate. They couldn't just fall into bed together and go at it until they were both satisfied. She'd never been one for talking much in bed, and she'd been too guarded to even articulate her likes and dislikes much beyond telling someone when they hit the right spot.

Not with Kayde. He tortured her with care, taking things almost agonizingly slow until she had to beg him for more. His offer to use restraints had only sent her mind reeling with dozens of ideas of the things they could do to one another, but she hadn't yet been brave enough to bring that up again.

Putting the sex aside, their trip after leaving Beznifa was much more companionable than before. They spent their time together, they talked, they shared meals, they developed something between them that Quinn wanted to last long after they stepped off the ship. Maybe it was the weak, incomplete bond holding them together, or maybe it was just Kayde and the way he was her anchor. She wanted to go anywhere with him, do anything, but another part of her was afraid that when they landed everything would change, that he would go back to being that wooden, robotic man who'd intrigued and frustrated her all the same. She didn't want him to pull back, to stop showing affection when they were around other people.

But she also knew that where they were going, the people would expect him to be soulless. And he'd told her of the harsh penalties that came when the soulless acted out. If they thought he was unstable, if they didn't believe that she was his mate, they might execute him. When he'd told her that, she'd insisted that they try to seal the bond. She'd been determined that she wanted him to make love to her, to claim her fully. That had been the night of the panic attack, where he pressed one finger inside of her and she showed him just how much of a head case she was. He never let her see if this bothered him, never made her feel bad about her limitations.

And because he was so considerate of all of that, she didn't let him know her fears. If he closed off from her when they landed, she'd find a way to deal with it. She'd handled rejection before, she could take it again.

Though Quinn had practically moved in with Kayde, spending every night since their first together in his bed, she still kept her things in the room she'd claimed for herself. It was more of a storage issue than anything else. Rooms on the ship were *tiny*. There was only one drawer where Kayde could place his belongings. Her own simply wouldn't fit beside his.

She rolled out of bed on the sixth day since they'd first made out and got dressed. A look at the clock told her it was late morning by ship time. Kayde had no doubt been up for hours already, and normally he would have woken her up with kisses, even if they only had time to make out for a bit, not enough to take it further. Before boarding the ship, she would have thought they'd be able to make their own schedules, to take all the time in the world to do what they wanted and to fit any necessary duties in around their moments together.

But though Kayde had his emotions back, he was still a warrior, still trained to make a schedule and stick to it. He was up with the dawn—metaphorically, seeing as they were far from any star system—and doing his exercises, checking their coordinates and fuel levels, doing everything that it took to run the ship. Quinn, in contrast, slept a bit later and mostly puttered around when she wasn't at Kayde's side. The ship still wasn't designed for entertainment, but that mattered less when she had a Detyen warrior to keep her company.

After getting dressed Quinn made her way to the cockpit to find Kayde sitting in the pilot seat, a blank expression on his face. Her heart stuttered for a moment, all her fears rushing back, but when he saw her he gave her a small grin and everything was right again. "You should've woken me up earlier," she said, taking her seat beside him. She automatically reached out for his hand and they laced their fingers together, letting them hang in between the seats.

"You seemed peaceful. I didn't want to wake you if you were going to get a full night of sleep."

Quinn's insomnia hadn't gone away, even if she was sleeping better than she had in a long time. But now that Kayde mentioned it, she realized he was right. She had gotten several hours of uninterrupted sleep and felt more rested then she could imagine. "You're going to spoil me. No one's ever—never mind."

He looked at their joint hands and kissed hers. "It is my responsibility and pleasure, denya." She thought he was going to say something else, but he let their hands fall back between them and they lapsed into silence. They'd had many moments like this over the last few days, sitting silently, enjoying each other's company with no need to talk. Conversation still didn't come easy to Kayde after years of barely talking to anyone, and Quinn didn't feel like she needed to fill the silence. It wasn't that they didn't talk; they'd spent hours doing that, but they could also sit quietly by one another without any awkwardness. She kind of loved it.

But the silence was different; there was something loaded about it and she realized that Kayde was holding something back. He practically thrummed with tension and while she had discovered a great way to get him out of his own mind for a bit, that wasn't going to work for the moment. "Is something wrong?" Her instinctual urge to add *with me* or *with us* still sprang up, but she managed not to say that part out loud.

"We should be within communications distance of headquarters. I've been sending out encrypted messages for the past few hours and I've heard nothing back." She knew it was bad when he used that emotionless, even tone. He was trying to be better about it, but at a moment like this she understood the urge to suppress every emotion, to keep the hurt at bay.

"How long 'til we get there?" She never wanted to land, never wanted to give up this magical world she was living in with Kayde, but that was selfish and she wouldn't want to stop him from reuniting with his people.

"Three or four hours. I have the ship's cloaking on high, which means we have to move slower. If their defense system picks us up, they might think that we're an enemy scout. But we can't go in without cloaking in case..." He trailed off, but Quinn understood what he wasn't saying. They couldn't go in without cloaking because it might not be a Detyen military contingent waiting for them. They could be flying directly into enemy territory.

"What do you need me to do?" They had talked about what might happen when they met the Detyen Legion, but now that it was about to happen Quinn couldn't get over how real it felt. In a matter of hours they would answer the question that had been haunting Kayde and his team for months.

Kayde squeezed her hand. "Just sit with me," he requested. "There's nothing to do now but wait and see."

* * *

Two hours later, they received their first communication from Detyen HQ. Kayde offered his identification information and was ordered to drop the ship's cloaking and proceed with caution. He could read the apprehension thrumming through his mate, but he had no way to comfort her. They didn't know what they were flying into, or what his people would choose to do to him once they realized he was getting his soul back, and Kayde could not lie to Quinn and offer her false hope. Things could go very wrong very quickly, but no matter what they did to him, he trusted they would keep her safe.

When Detyen HQ, or the moon it was housed on, rather, appeared on the horizon, Quinn stiffened. She shot him a look and a smile. "One last chance to turn around," she offered.

"At this point they could easily chase us down," he replied. And they would. Detyen HQ was a closely guarded secret. Toran hadn't been sure that the Detyen leaders would let the rescued human women off the planet when they were forced to take shelter there after their escape from Fenryr 1. But with battle raging around them, they hadn't been in a position to argue when it was time for the women to go.

"No matter what happens, I don't regret coming with you." She had a half smile on her face, and it took Kayde a moment to realize that she had been teasing when she told him they could turn around. She understood just as well as he did what the outcome of the next few days might be.

"We will be okay," he promised, even as they both knew he could easily be wrong. "I won't give up on this, no matter the obstacles."

Her smile turned sad, and her eyes got a little watery. "Me too."

He leaned in and kissed her. It was meant to be a small peck, but her hands came up and held his cheeks tightly, and his own arm wrapped around her. They kissed with desperation, with a depth of emotion that Kayde hadn't known was possible. This wasn't about sex, wasn't a prelude to anything. It was a kiss they both gave knowing that it could mean goodbye. But Kayde refused to let it hold that meaning. He gentled his grip on her and made himself pull back as the exchange between them softened. They were both breathing hard when they separated, and Quinn's cheeks were flushed.

"I want to try sex again." It burst out of her, the words running together in a panicked confession.

If they weren't minutes away from breaking atmo, Kayde would've been tempted to pull her back out of the cockpit and take her up on her offer. Instead, he forced himself to give her an eager smile. "Tonight," he promised. "Once we've been assigned quarters and have a proper bed."

Quinn blew out an unsteady breath and nodded. "Tonight," she agreed.

Kayde turned to his controls. Now he had to make sure that whatever happened, they spent the night together. They approached the moon at a steady pace, and though Kayde was looking for the defensive satellites that normally circled HQ, he saw nothing artificial in the sky around them. They must have been destroyed in the battle a few months ago and not yet replaced.

If he were the praying type, Kayde might have said one before beginning his final descent to the planet. The lack of satellites didn't bode well, even though he was in communication with Detyens over his comms. He prepared himself for destruction, knew that he could be flying into a situation where he might encounter only the few survivors of his kind, those lucky enough to survive the battle, but unable to repair headquarters or find a way to leave.

Cloud cover was heavy, and they came in through a thick snowstorm, the weather a cold reminder of home. Sierra and Iris had both promised the team that winters on Earth could be just as dastardly, but the heat of summer back there had been worse than any frigid night he'd spent at home.

As the snow cleared, he could see evidence of the battle with the Oscavian warship everywhere. Outbuildings sat in tatters, the destruction looking so fresh that Kayde would not have been surprised to see black smoke billowing from the decrepit piles of stone. But among the evidence of destruction, there were also signs of growth. A crew in full winter survival gear operated heavy machinery that was busy clearing one of the destroyed buildings, and a separate group was building up a communications tower that had fallen. Kayde counted at least ten Detyens on the ground, and there were sure to be dozens if not hundreds more inside.

His hands unclenched from where he was gripping the controls too tight and he let out a breath he hadn't realized that he'd been holding. His people were alive, damaged, but unbroken.

At his side, Quinn was silent, but she let out her own relieved breath only moments after him, as if she had been waiting to see how he would react to the state of his home.

They were directed to land in a field outside of the central administrative building. The snow was densely packed, mixed with ice and some kind of rock to give them a hard enough surface to set down. It made the landing a bit tricky, as the field was actually a plateau with a steep drop off at one end. The wind outside buffeted the ship, whistling around them and welcoming Kayde home. But when he looked over at Quinn, he realized that this little moon had stopped being his home a long time ago. His home sat next to him. And wherever she went, he belonged.

"Are they going to freak out about you?" she asked in a tone that told him this was one of the things that had been bothering her for some time.

"They might." He could not offer her a comforting lie, especially when his people's reaction would be evident in a matter of minutes. "Trust me."

Quinn gulped. "Always."

He reached over and squeezed her hand before bringing it up and swiping a kiss across her knuckles. If they had time, he would've given her a proper kiss, the proper reassurance that they would make it out of this. He'd tell her with his actions, even if he couldn't manage it with his words, that his people would see her as the hope she was, that they would do nothing to harm her. But already Kayde could see a line of warriors coming towards their ship armed well enough to take out a fleet of Oscavians.

"Why do they look like they're about to shoot their way on board?" Quinn asked. Her hand squeezed against his, possibly to keep herself from trembling.

"It's just a precaution," he hoped. "Go and put on one of the survival suits. It will keep you warm enough until we get inside, it's too cold for your regular clothes."

Quinn looked at him for several beats before nodding and getting up from her chair. She went back to do as he said while Kayde radioed the communications tower and let them know that both he and Quinn would be wearing survival suits, their faces obscured by the helmets meant to keep them safe. The operator on the other end of the communication acknowledged his information and instructed him to remain unharmed while exiting the ship. Kayde gave a final confirmation before disconnecting communications to join Quinn in getting into a survival suit.

When they were ready, they went to the main door and stood side-by-side. Kayde hesitated, even if there was no point to it. His people were fair, he knew. But they had firm rules, especially when it came to the soulless, and if they thought he had gone mad, become unstable, he knew exactly what would happen to him. But it was too late to turn back. He pushed the button beside the door and began to open with a hiss, a ramp extending out and sloping down gently to where it met the icy, snowy ground.

Kayde and Quinn walked out with their hands raised in a universal sign for peace.

All the warriors wore full body armor, their faces covered to make them unidentifiable. Kayde thought he could identify two of the six people in front of them based on the modifications to their uniforms, but he didn't recognize the other four.

"Identify yourselves," the leader of the warriors commanded, his voice muffled by his helmet.

"My name is Kayde NaDetya, warrior of the Detyen Legion. I bring with me my denya, Quinn Porter of Earth." He said it loudly, proudly claiming Quinn as his in front of his people, even if she was not yet fully his in truth.

The warriors froze in shock, and even the wind died down at Kayde's declaration. Every single one of those warriors knew who he was, knew *what* he was, and unless word of Raze's mating had spread throughout the Legion, they would all think his claim impossible.

As one, the warriors lifted their blast rifles and aimed them all directly at Kayde. Beside him Quinn stiffened, but if she said anything it was muffled to silence by her survival suit.

"Repeat your identification," demanded the leader.

"Kayde NaDetya, and my denya, Quinn." Not a single rifle moved as he repeated who he was. Whatever these warriors have been expecting from him, this possibility had clearly never crossed their minds.

Before he could reach out to stop her, Quinn stepped in front of him and two of the rifles twitched, as if unsure what kind of threat she posed. "What the hell do you think you're doing? He's one of you." The words were a little muffled by her survival suit, but the emotion came out loud and clear.

"Step aside," said the leader of the warriors.

Quinn's spine stiffened in determination. "No."

A whisper of surprise threaded through the warriors, and based on the reaction to Quinn's declaration, Kayde was able to determine which of the six were soulless. Only two of them, the one to the left with a blue patch on his shoulder, and the one directly next to the leader. They wouldn't fire unless directly ordered, but any of the other four might take initiative.

Kayde lifted his hand to pull Quinn back, but stopped moving when the warriors shifted their focus to him.

"Step aside, human," the leader repeated. "We mean you no harm."

"And I will not let you harm my mate," Quinn told them all, and despite the gravity of the situation Kayde's heart flew free. He did not know what he had done to deserve this woman, but he would spend every day of his life making sure that he was worthy of her.

"Step. Aside," The leader repeated again, losing patience with Quinn.

He knew his mate well enough to know that she would not back down, so Kayde stepped up beside her and grabbed her wrist to keep her from doing anything dangerous. He spared her a half second's glance and gave the slightest of nods to try and reassure her that everything would turn out all right.

A flurry of movement at the entrance to the administrative building caught his attention and Kayde turned to see a group of three men dressed in survival gear, but not holding weapons, approaching them. A tribunal, elders of the Legion who were responsible for maintaining its laws and protecting its people. They alone could pass judgment on Kayde, and one way or another he and Quinn were about to be judged.

Chapter Eighteen

The first time Quinn had landed at Detyen HQ, it seemed like a paradise. Then again, sitting inside an active volcano would've seemed like a paradise compared to Fenryr 1. Back then she hadn't cared about the snowstorms, especially since she and her fellow survivors been confined to the inside of the compound from the moment they set foot on the planet. But now she was already tired of this place and wanted to go home.

They were pointing blasters at Kayde. One of their own people. What the hell had he done to them? Anger burned within her and she wanted to scream, wanted to charge of the warriors in front of them and give them a piece of her mind, and more than one piece of her fists. It didn't matter that they could cut her down in a second, her anger had transported her to a place beyond logic and pain, a place where she would do anything to defend Kayde.

And that thought steadied her. The only thing she could do to defend him right now was remain calm. Or at least *seem* calm. She couldn't quite manage to actually *be* calm when people were aiming weapons at her mate. The rightness of that word settled within her and despite the anger, despite her fear, she couldn't suppress her smile. At least her helmet kept anyone else from seeing in. Smiling at this moment was so far from appropriate she wouldn't be shocked if they shot her on principle.

A commotion from the entrance to the squat building behind them seized the attention of everyone around them. She tried to gauge Kayde's reaction to the newcomers, but he was almost impossible to read in his survival suit. He had one hell of a poker face, but it was even worse when she couldn't see his face at all. At some point in the past weeks she'd learned to read him, and she wanted to rip his helmet off his head just to make sure he still thought everything would be okay. Though, clearly, they had much different levels of 'okay' if he was fine with half a dozen blast rifles being pointed at them.

"Stand down, Commander," the man at the center of the trio said. He had a calm voice and was half a head shorter than all the warriors around him, but he wore authority like a second skin and even Quinn found herself standing up straighter at his command.

The head warrior lowered his weapon and the rest of his people followed suit. "Sir?"

"Take your team to the debriefing room. You'll be met shortly."

The commander took a second or two longer than Quinn thought he was supposed to and the air was charged with the possibility of disobedience, but after a moment he led his people away, leaving Kayde and Quinn alone with the three newcomers.

"Let's all get inside," the speaker said. He beckoned them forward with a wave of his hand and Kayde started moving as if he were on a leash. Quinn trailed behind, unsure that she really wanted inside, but sure that it was too cold to wait outside much longer.

They were led by the trio through dark gray corridors which were brightened by colorful artwork hanging on the walls. It depicted a planet that looked almost like Earth, but Quinn was almost certain it was Detya. The planet Yormas of Wreet had destroyed for some reason. The home that Kayde would never see.

At one small room, they were instructed to change out of their survival suits and given thick jackets. Their escorts also changed, but they wore hooded cowls once they were done and Quinn still couldn't get a good look at them. It disturbed her that they were working so hard to keep their identities hidden, but since Kayde didn't say anything about it she kept her mouth shut. This was his planet, and he knew the customs. If he thought it was weird, she hoped he would have said something. Then again, it occurred to her that he might keep it to himself if he thought she might freak out.

Quinn's feet started to hurt as they moved, the discomfort climbing up her legs as they trudged on. Just how big was this building? It hadn't looked that imposing from the outside, but the snow flurries might have been hiding a lot, and she suspected most of the building was underground. The distance and quick pace combined with her adjustment to real gravity had her almost wincing with each step, but she tried to put on a strong face so she didn't make Kayde look bad.

Just as she was about to break and complain, the trio leading them stopped and a door beside them slid open revealing a conference room that wouldn't have looked out of place on Earth.

Quinn almost did a double take. But when the hoods came off their guides, it was clear that they were a long way from home. The alien in the center was greenish, his skin holding a silvery tint. One of his companions was gold and the other red. They bore dark markings similar to Kayde's clan markings on their necks and one even had them climbing up his cheek. It was hard to determine their ages, but the red one was clearly older, with graying hair at his temples and wrinkle lines near his eyes. The gold one had the same expression on his face that Kayde used to wear. Soulless, Quinn would bet a hundred dollars. The greenish one in the center seemed younger than the rest, but he also seemed to be their leader.

"Sandon," Kayde finally greeted as they took their seats.

The leader smiled at him. "This is a surprise." He and his companions sat across the table from Kayde and Quinn and suddenly this felt more like an interrogation than a greeting. "I am Sandon," he said to Quinn. "My companions are Tyann," he nodded to the soulless gold Detyen, "and Gren," that was the older red one. "It is our pleasure to meet you."

Meet her and judge her? Quinn asked silently, but she tried to keep a lid on the instinctive negativity. Now that Kayde was no longer wearing his survival suit, she could read him like a book. He was cautious, unsure of what was coming next, but he wasn't tense. Whoever these men were, she and her mate weren't in any immediate danger.

Immediate being the key word.

"I was not expecting a full contingent to be fielded upon my arrival," said Kayde, bypassing any small talk. "Are things really so dire?"

"It has been a... trying few months," Sandon replied. "And you are an unexpected complication."

Quinn did her best to keep her lips tightly shut. She knew that 'complication' was just another word for problem. Something, maybe everything, about their presence bothered Sandon and she had no clue how this was going to be resolved.

"Things have settled down on Earth," Kayde reported. "Raze and his denya are happily bonded, and Toran has found his own mate among the humans. We have also found a suspect in the matter of our home's destruction. Unfortunately that investigation has hit a stalling point. In light of that, it was decided to send me here to determine what happened to HQ. Our messages have gone unanswered and there was a concern as to whether or not the Legion survived."

Quinn noticed that Kayde hadn't spoken at all of his own thoughts. His expression remained hard and emotionless, and the pit in her stomach opened up as she feared her greatest worry was coming to life. He had called her his mate in front of all of those soldiers, but now he was slipping away, sloughing off his emotions as if they'd been an uncomfortable second skin.

And then he looked at her and smiled and her fears scattered as if they'd simply been made of smoke. "In addition to all that," he continued, "I am happy to report that I have discovered my own denya among the survivors from Fenryr 1. I did not expect to be blessed like Raze, but this development gives me hope for all of our people."

Tyann, the soulless Detyen, didn't move an inch, but something about the way he wasn't moving drew Quinn's attention. She looked over at him and their eyes met, his dark and completely empty, broken. Fear pulsed in her as he examined her like she was a particularly boring rock, but she was prey caught in his gaze. After a second he looked away, but the knowledge that he'd let her go, that she hadn't escaped, settled into her bones. She didn't want to encounter Tyann alone. She didn't know what he would do and she didn't want to find out.

Sandon breathed deep, almost sighing. Gren leaned in, placing his elbows on the table in front of them to get a better look. "In light of Raze's departure from the Legion, we decided that it was better to keep news of his mating confidential, said Sandon.

"He didn't *leave* the Legion," Kayde said in his friend's defense. "He followed an order to evacuate with more than a dozen non-combatants."

Sandon nodded, acknowledging the point. "True. But as we could not offer him as an example, we deemed it best to keep his development quiet. We didn't want to upset the..." he glanced at Quinn. "I take it you've told her?"

"She's my mate," was Kayde's confirmation.

Every time he said that Quinn's stomach grew a dozen butterflies and she had to bite the inside of her cheek to keep from smiling. She felt she should be saying something, but with tensions running high, she didn't want to make things worse. Kayde seemed to be doing just fine.

Sandon sat back and the trio conferred in whispers for a moment. Rather, Sandon and Gren conferred while Tyann sat silently and observed. It went on for so long that Quinn was ready to burst, but Sandon finally turned back to them. "The tribunals need to convene to discuss this development. So right now you have a choice." He looked at Kayde, challenge in his eyes.

Kayde looked back silently.

"We will place you and your... Quinn in quarters for the time being and see to your needs as they arise. Or we can place only you in quarters until a decision is made regarding your claims. The vote to keep quiet about Raze's mating was nearly three to one in favor of silence. We cannot simply ignore the spirit of that ruling right now. Not when things are so volatile." Sandon actually seemed regretful of the things he was offering them, but Quinn's anger was starting to burble again and she couldn't bring it in herself to care.

"So our choices are prison together or prison apart?" she snapped.

Kayde placed a hand on her thigh under the table and out of view from the other Detyens, but it certainly didn't go unnoticed.

"How did the vote fall?" he asked.

This time it wasn't Sandon who answered. "The soulless thought the news of the mating should be shared," said Tyann flatly. "Most of the others disagreed."

Kayde's gaze snapped to Sandon and Gren, but neither man revealed anything about his personal opinion. "I gave my denya my word that no harm would come to her here and she would safely be returned to Earth." There was a request in there somewhere, but Kayde didn't state it explicitly.

Sandon nodded. "No matter what, that will be arranged."

"No matter what, what?" Quinn demanded. She would have shot out of the chair if Kayde still hadn't had his hand on her leg. As it was, she leaned forward, practically sprawling across the table. "Why would—?" She didn't know how to finish the question and stumbled over her words.

"What will it be?" Sandon asked when she settled back down.

Kayde opened his mouth, but Quinn spoke first. "Together. We stay together."

* * *

They were back in prison. And this one wasn't even as nice as where Quinn had been kept on Beznifa. The fact that she now had enough experience to rank her stays in captivity made her gnash her teeth. It didn't look like a prison cell, but neither had her room on Beznifa, and this one even had a door, an upgrade from her previous accommodations. The room was smaller, but the bed was big enough for her, Kayde, and a few of their friends, if they'd been into something like that.

Which she wasn't. No, thank you. She still wasn't sure she could handle her mate alone, and she would get violent with anyone else who tried to take what was hers. The place looked like a simple room that could have belonged to anyone on the base. There was an entertainment console on the wall, a communications hub where they could request anything they needed, and a bathroom tucked away in the corner with a large shower that made Quinn feel a bit experimental.

But it was still a prison. There wasn't a guard at the door, the door wasn't even locked, but they weren't allowed to leave. She'd call it the worst vacation ever, but it wasn't technically a vacation, and she had Kayde by her side, which made the whole thing almost tolerable. Almost.

"Do they have cameras in here?" She shuddered as she thought about it. She'd been under constant surveillance on Beznifa and if she found out the Detyens were no different she'd scream.

Kayde stood by the room's single window looking out at the frozen tundra of his home. "No, the inside of all quarters are private except for the detainment cells."

Detainment cells were not what she wanted to think about at the moment. She flopped back onto the bed and bounced up once before landing with a huff. It startled a laugh out of her and once she started, she couldn't quite stop. Her hysterics got Kayde to turn away from the window and he studied her for several long seconds, his expression blank, as if he couldn't understand why she had gone crazy.

Fair enough, he was still new to this whole emotion thing.

He was haloed in the bright light coming in from outside and Quinn's breath caught. She could almost forget how handsome he was sometimes. She spent so much time looking at him that he became another constant in her life, but then there were moments like this where the light hit him right and her heart started beating hard as she remembered that he was hers, that she was the only one who got to see him in these unguarded moments. The only one on the receiving end of the faint smile that graced his lips.

She should probably be grilling him, asking him exactly what he thought what was going to happen once the tribunals convened. But Quinn had spent the last weeks ricocheting between anxiety and hope, and she was learning when to worry about the future and when to seize the present. They were confined to this room for the next little while and there was nothing they could do to make the situation better. If they tried to leave, it would surely only make things worse.

So seizing the moment was the only option, really. That, or go crazy.

Kayde's eyes flashed red as Quinn started to unzip her jacket. As she cast it aside and reached for the hem of her shirt he crossed the room and loomed over her, standing at the edge of the bed. A few days ago that would have sent her into a panic, but now her heart beat hard from excitement, not fear. She was still figuring out how to get all of her actions under control, but it wasn't Kayde who caused her to fear, it never had been.

"What are you doing," he growled, his fingers grazing her wrist and sending goose bumps racing up her arm.

Quinn shivered and grinned at him. "I told you what I wanted before we got off the ship." She worked her shirt up centimeter by centimeter, teasing him with a growing naked band of skin. Kayde's fingers remained on her wrist, but he didn't try and stop her from removing her top. He only let go for a moment when she managed to get the fabric over her head, but once that was done and the shirt lay on the floor, he laced their fingers together. She still wore a bra, but she might as well have been naked from the way his eyes raked over her skin.

She sucked in a deep breath as her stomach clenched in desire and she tugged on his hand until he was forced forward, placing one knee on the bed beside her and leaving one foot stubbornly on the floor. That wouldn't do at all. Quinn reached up with her free hand and looped it behind Kayde's neck, pulling him closer for a scorching kiss. They ended up with her flat on her back, his free hand propping him up beside her, their two hands connected, and still he held himself off of her in some feat of strength and coordination that Quinn would have admired if she hadn't yearned for the press of his flesh against hers.

She tugged at him again and Kayde resisted. "What's wrong?" she finally asked, forcing her lips to the side even as her body protested. She could taste the memory of him with every word, but she didn't want the memory when the real thing was *right there*.

"The last time I was on top of you didn't go so well," he said. "I don't want to do anything to hurt you."

Sweet, caring, *stupid* man. Quinn knew her smile was a bit dopey, heart-struck and helplessly falling for him. "This," she said, pulling on his hand, "is me saying that I want to try again. I'm not letting those bastards take you from me." She wasn't sure *which* bastards she was talking about, but she wasn't going to dwell on it for the moment. It was only her and Kayde in this room, in this bed, and she was determined that it would stay that way. She wanted to make love to her mate, and nothing was going to stop her. Not tonight. Not as long as he was with her every step of the way.

Any other man would have taken her invitation and run with it, but Kayde was still her caring gentleman warrior. He crowded her slowly, leaning forward and giving her plenty of time to escape. By the time his second knee came up and he straddled her, Quinn was breathless with anticipation. She wanted this, wanted him, more than her next breath, and right now the worry of apprehension was only a tiny whisper buried deep in her mind, easily set aside and ignored.

Their lips met and it was nothing like the first time. Then they'd been high on the heat of battle, celebrating survival and falling towards one another in a fit of excited passion. There was passion here, excitement too, but the way Kayde's lips moved against hers, and the way his tongue dipped into her mouth to taste her held nothing of the desperate edge they'd first come together on. Now this was a dance they'd both learned, they were still learning it and always would be, but the first steps flowed easily, the way he touched her side, the way she yielded under him and arched against him, the way his eyes would snap open to watch her, as if he couldn't believe that they were really here together.

It wasn't a perfect kiss. Their noses bumped together, and for a few seconds Quinn forgot to breathe, but the kiss was perfect for them, a perfect expression of the connection they were building. There was still trial and error, but no room for judgment, only pleasure and fun.

Need built hot within her and soon Quinn was tugging at Kayde's shirt, needing skin, needing contact, needing him. They wrestled it off and he cursed at the fabric when he momentarily got tangled in it. He startled a laugh out of her when he took his claws to the material and cut it off like it was a vine trying to suffocate him.

"That's better," he said with an air of satisfaction. He was on his knees, towering over her, and that whisper of fear grew a little louder, even as her desire mounted. He was straining against his pants and Quinn wanted to touch the hard length of him, but the part of herself that had been holding her back all this time urged caution.

If she opened herself up to him, it whispered its vile poison directly into her psyche, then he could do anything he wanted to her. He could hurt her like no one before had managed.

She knew the doubt was showing on her face and she didn't know how to make it go away. But Kayde sensed her shift in mood before she could make a sound. He swooped in and flipped her over until he was on his back and she was the one kneeling over him. Now she could feel the hard ridge of him pressed against her abdomen and she couldn't stop herself from writhing against him until they were both groaning. It was too much. It wasn't enough.

"Don't stop," Kayde urged, and Quinn didn't. Her lips found his neck as their lower bodies moved together, the friction of all their clothes not quite enough to get either of them to the edge, but more than enough to leave them both gasping and desperate for more.

Kayde's fingers found the clasp of her pants and he flicked his red eyes up to her, the question as clear as day in those demonic depths. Quinn had to swallow hard against the sudden lump in her throat and her hand covered his for a moment before she managed a shaky nod. They'd gone this far before, farther even, but Kayde didn't take her consent for granted, he made sure she was with him every step of the way until he left her a wet, writhing mess of desperate need.

She loved him for it.

She'd taken her shoes off before she lay down, so her pants and underwear came off smoothly enough. Quinn handled her bra, slipping out of it with sure fingers, becoming strangely more confident the less clothing she was wearing. She didn't quite understand why she felt more in control the more exposed she became, but it was a blessing she wouldn't question.

"You're a bit overdressed," she said, laying her own hand against the clasp of Kayde's pants and sliding her fingers down until she cupped him through the thick material.

He groaned and arched up into her grip, his eyes falling shut as she felt him up. She ran her hand over him, fondling his length and imagining what it would feel like inside her. There were ridges along the length unlike any human, something uniquely Detyen that she knew she'd feel imprinted on her once they got that far.

And they were going to get that far. She needed him now.

Kayde covered her hand with his, joining her as she brought him close before stilling her. "Not yet," he managed, breathless. "Not until you're ready."

"Oh, I'm ready," she promised. It was half lust, half bravado, but they were doing this tonight, she wouldn't let anything short of an alien invasion stop them.

"Let me watch you," he said. She'd found he liked that, watching her touch herself, seeing what she liked. His eyes were a caress, she could feel their heat even when he kept his hands plastered to the bed, as if he was worried that if he touched her, he wouldn't be able to stop. "Get yourself ready for me."

Oh, the promise in those words coiled deep within her. She wanted him now, but the thought of being caught in his gaze made her short of breath and caught a plea in her throat. Yes, she could do that. But not completely alone. Quinn reached out and dragged one of his hands up off the bed until she plastered it against her hip. The other came up against her other hip like a brand. She'd never known that to be an erogenous zone, but wherever Kayde touched her, she was set alight. And she wanted more. She canted her hips on top of him, moving against his body and trying to use him to bring her to the edge, but it wasn't enough. He gripped her tight and she knew that it wouldn't take much to get him to let go, to get him to give her exactly what she was begging for.

But not yet, not when he'd asked for something of his own.

She started with her breasts, teasing them, touching them, hiding them from Kayde before she leaned in close and let him swipe his lips against the sensitive skin. His tongue darted out and the sound that escaped her throat was inhuman. And it only made Kayde harder beneath her. He loved to bring out this desperate side in her, she could see it in his reaction, he loved it when she let go and let the lovemaking take her, no longer concerned about her past or what she *should* want. All that mattered was the two of them and the things they did to one another, the pleasures they gave.

It was a perfect moment, one she didn't want to resist.

Her fingers trailed lower, drawing a line down her chest and stomach, giving Kayde a trail to follow with his eyes. And his lips. He stayed flat on his back, but she was already leaning over him and she could feel his resolve breaking with every flick of her fingers that preceded one of his kisses. But he didn't touch anywhere that she hadn't already, and she couldn't help but wonder what she'd do when her fingers were buried deep in her sex, opening herself up and preparing for him.

As her fingers brushed against her folds, she imagined it was his tongue doing the work, playing with her until she was dripping with pleasure, ready to welcome him into her and make love to him all night. She pushed one finger inside of her wet heat and swallowed hard. The last time he'd tried this, she'd already been riding the edge of panic. And this was the first time he'd deliberately told her to use her own fingers like this. But panic didn't come this time, whether it was because she was doing this to herself or because they'd moved beyond it, Quinn didn't know and she was beyond caring. She could care later, right now she was trembling with the need to *feel*.

"Another one," Kayde demanded. His own thumbs made circles on top of her hip bones, keeping them connected and reminding her that she was the one in control here. He'd only put his hands where she let him, would only taste where she'd already touched.

She did as he asked, adding a second finger and groaning as it stretched her muscles. It had been a long time since she'd willingly taken something inside of her, and Kayde wasn't exactly small. Her mouth watered to think of his naked cock, but while she loved to look at him, the thought of letting him inside of her was a little intimidating.

"You're so beautiful," he praised her, the words torn out of him. "I could watch you for years and never tire of it."

Words caught in her throat, something she'd never known she wanted to say, but she couldn't force them out. All she could manage was, "Now, *please.*" She wasn't above begging, not when she was scorched through with heat and desperate for his touch.

And finally her mate showed mercy. He gently laid her down beside him and took care of his pants, coming back to her completely naked and hard with want. He climbed carefully over her and placed one hand on top of hers, sliding a finger in alongside her own. Quinn felt the stretch and gasped, but no terror accompanied it, nothing but desire and lust, all her red hot emotions crying out for this man.

"Good?" he asked, his eyes twin rubies.

"Great," Quinn responded, barely coherent enough to get the word out.

The blunt head of his cock teased her entrance once they'd removed their fingers and Quinn arched up into him, wordlessly begging him for more. When he pushed into her, Quinn knew she'd come home. He filled her to the hilt and for a moment the stretch hurt, but as her body adjusted it became perfect. And then he began to move and she moved beyond perfect, beyond all thought, until there was just sensation, just pleasure. They moved in sync, their bodies tangled in an ancient dance that spanned light years and brought them to this moment of joining together, an impossible inevitability that neither of them had ever known to wish for.

Time blurred; it could have been hours or seconds, but then she was convulsing around him, her orgasm sweeping her away on a tidal wave of sensation. Something clicked into place within her, a bond anchoring deep inside where she knew it could never be excised. And with a final thrust, Kayde came, emptying himself into her with a possessive growl, bringing her over a second time and turning her mind to mush.

Quinn collapsed back against the pillows, her thoughts all quiet and muddled in the best way possible. She wanted to reach out and pull Kayde close, but she wasn't sure she'd be able to move for the next week. Beside her Kayde's breaths were heavy. She managed to turn her head and look at him. Was she imagining a glow around him? He looked somehow *more*, and she didn't know what it meant.

She reached out and placed her hand over his chest, right over his heart.

Kayde flinched and his gaze snapped to her. His eyes looked wrong. At first she thought they were their normal black, but it was his pupils that were so dilated that she could barely make out the strip of red that glowed like fire.

Quinn's lassitude vanished and she was up like a shot, leaning over him and looking for what could have set him off. "Are you okay?" she demanded. She tried to keep her voice even, but panic shot through her. She'd been so concerned about what making love would do to her that it had never occurred to her that something could go wrong with Kayde.

His breaths were heavy, labored like he was hyperventilating. His eyes widened for a moment and his lips opened in a silent scream. Then he went limp as he lost consciousness.

As Quinn jumped out of bed to go to the communication station and call for help the room lit up with flashing lights and an alarm sounded. She ran to the window to see what was wrong, sparing a glance for Kayde. In the distance she could see bright lights flying in over the horizon. Two ships sped overhead going out to meet it, their defensive shields turned on bright enough to be visible to the naked eye.

Her blood ran cold in her veins. They were under attack.

Chapter Nineteen

Kayde tried to open his eyes, but was forced to squeeze them shut almost immediately. Everything was too bright, and for some reason flashing, and loud. It took him several moments to realize that the warning sirens were going off and it wasn't his senses that had gone haywire. That was only a distant comfort. The tsunami of sound and light was too much for his battered mind to handle and he reached for one of the pillows at the head of the bed and used it to cover his face and ears, trying to drown out the light and noise.

Everything burned too bright, everything hurt, except for the anchor point of reality that he could feel nestled in his chest, just under his heart. The denya bond. Had he thought his emotions were back before? What he had begun to feel since Quinn awakened him was like trying to interpret sound and sight underwater. And now he breached the surface and was shocked by the crystal clarity around him. He hadn't realized before just how much losing his soul had cost him. Everything was brighter, louder, more, and he didn't know if he could handle it. His ears felt like they were about to bleed, and his eyes hurt, aching like they were about to fall out of his skull. Too much, too soon, how did people live like this?

Where was Quinn?

Kayde cast aside the protective shield of his pillow and braced himself against the bed before he opened his eyes. The strobing brightness of the flashing light intensified his headache, but he spotted Quinn frozen by the window and the harshness all around him softened, the edges blinded by his mate's presence. His heart thumped hard in his chest, and he could not have looked away from her if a battalion of soldiers had busted through the door and tried to attack. She was haloed in the faint light coming in through the window, unselfconscious of her nakedness like a goddess.

Lust ripped through him followed quickly by something more tender, something he couldn't begin to define but that was sustaining him right now while his mind and body were caught in a riotous confusion of emotion and sensation.

Reality snapped around him and Kayde realized what the sirens meant. He scrambled off the bed and started to reach for his clothes.

While he was pulling them on, Quinn spun away from the window and rushed over to him, her hands landing on his arms, and warmth suffused him. Her hands came up to cradle his face and she tilted his head up until their eyes met. Her concerned expression sent a ripple of fear through him. His mate shouldn't fear anything, and he'd do whatever it took to make sure that she remained safe.

Except, in this instance he was almost certain that *he* had been the one to put that look on her face.

"What happened?" she asked, her fingers curling against his cheeks until she was pressing almost painfully hard. "Are you all right?"

Kayde reached up and placed his hands over hers. "I've never been better, my denya," he responded. And despite his overstimulated senses, he meant every word. They were together, they were bound, and nothing would tear them apart again. No matter what threatened the base, or what his fellow Detyens wanted to do to him.

Doubt clouded Quinn's eyes, but after several moments she nodded. "There's a ship flying in, I can see it from the window. I think we're under attack."

Kayde stood up and linked their hands, walking with her towards the window. He saw exactly what she was talking about almost immediately, a small speeder moving quickly and getting closer. Two Detyen ships were moving towards it, but they had yet to engage. "If it's only the single ship," he said, "there's no reason to worry." But he couldn't just sit here while his people were under attack, while his mate was threatened by some unknown force.

"But it's never just one small ship," Quinn responded. "That would be suicide. Even I know that."

"I have to go out there, I have to help." Kayde let go over her hand and hurried back to the clothes he piled on the bed, pulling them on quickly with the same efficient movements he'd used every time he'd gone into battle before.

Quinn gathered her own clothes and pulled them on as well. "You can't go out there," she insisted. "We don't know what's coming, and your own people might stop you, might—" she cut herself off.

"There are never enough soldiers in the Legion." Kayde knew that well. "I am certain of my welcome."

"Please don't go." She was looking at the floor, rather than at him, and the pleading note in her voice almost stopped in his tracks. Almost.

"I have to go out there. I have to protect you." He would not let anyone get close enough to harm his mate, he would destroy anyone who tried.

"It's dangerous."

"This is who I am. I promise that I'll return to you." He could see his mate's fear, and her concern, but Kayde could not sit in this room and wait for trouble to come to them. By then it would be too late. And he had never been a coward.

"You better," Quinn said after a long moment.

There was more to be said between them, and the last thing he wanted to do was dash out of this room less than half an hour after claiming his mate, but the base was under attack and he had no other choice.

Kayde stuck his feet into his boots and tightened them quickly before standing. He turned back to Quinn and offered her what he hoped was a reassuring smile. She rushed up to him and crushed her lips against his, holding him tight, as if her love could be his shield. It took more effort than it should have to pull away, but the call of his duty finally spurred him into action and Kayde was out the door with one final glance back at his mate.

There was no guard to keep him and Quinn in place, and though the flashing lights and siren might have sent others into a frenzy, the Detyen Legion lived and died by its discipline. The Hall was deserted as everyone had already moved to find their places in preparation for battle.

It wasn't long before Kayde found Sandon heading straight for him. "Suit up," he said. "I want you out on the field in ten minutes."

Kayde was ready in nine and found himself reporting to the same commander, Kendryk, who had leveled his blast rifle at him and Quinn when they landed their own ship earlier in the day. His new emotions were swirling within him, caught between amusement and resentment, but he pushed it all down to focus on the problem at hand.

They stood in a column just inside the main hangar and waited while the two Detyen defense ships escorted the Oscavian speeder to a landing point. It hadn't made any attempt to attack, and while its communications weren't coming in, it had flashed its light in a Detyen code indicating it was friendly. Something didn't add up. The Oscavians were no allies of the Detyens, but the ship that attacked them months ago had been acting alone, had not represented the Empire in any way. So why had they fallen under the attention of the Oscavians once more? And why would these new Oscavians be friendly?

The ship landed while the two Detyen ships remained hovering in the air, their guns trained directly on the Oscavian speeder, ready to shoot if anything seemed off. Kayde and his fellow soldiers marched out, blast rifles at the ready, and went to meet whatever friend or foe was waiting for them.

The door opened on the speeder and a ramp descended. A short human woman wearing a thick jacket in an Oscavian style stumbled out onto the ramp quickly followed by a giant of a Detyen man wearing a similar coat. He was too far away to make out the fine details of either of their newest visitors, but Kayde was almost certain that the Detyen man was Druath, a warrior who had disappeared during the battle a few months ago.

"I am *not* your mate," the human woman screamed at the Detyen. She turned around and clutched her head before collapsing down onto the ramp like a broken doll.

"Laurel!" the man who might have been Dru yelled. He rushed up to the woman, Laurel, and scooped her up, walking towards the Detyen defenses as if he were immune to blaster fire. "She needs medical attention," he said, his voice rising to the edge of panic. "And we don't have a lot of time. They're coming."

Commander Kendryk led Dru into Detyen HQ and Kayde followed close behind, his newly born curiosity fully intrigued. A team of medics met them near the entrance and Dru bared his teeth at the head of the team as he tried to take Laurel from him. He used his body to shield the fallen woman and refused to let the medical team touch her until a female medic that Kayde didn't know by name convinced him to let the human woman go and that the team would treat her with the utmost care. Dru took an unconscious step after them, but Kendryk herded him down the hallway towards the command center where their leaders would be waiting.

Most of Kendryk's team had fallen away, off to follow standing orders or enact protocols, but Kayde was under no such restrictions and simply kept back a step, out of the commander's direct line of sight, on the hope that the man wouldn't dismiss him if he wasn't looking right at him. It worked. In a matter of minutes, Kayde, Kendryk, Druath, and a handful of other soldiers were huddled into a conference room in the heart of the command center. A star map of the system that HQ's moon sat in was broadcast on one wall, the handful of planets all around them silent sentinels, witnesses to the battle Dru claimed was to come.

Sandon sat with Gren and Tyann and motioned for Kendryk and Dru to take seats opposite them. Kayde plastered himself against the wall, and when Sandon nodded at him, he knew that his presence was sanctioned. He wasn't about to be cast from the room.

"Tell us what you know," Sandon commanded.

Dru sucked in a deep breath and ran his fingers through his hair. It was longer than regulation length, had grown down around his ears as if he hadn't been able to trim it since he'd been gone. He still wore the Oscavian jacket, and after a moment he slipped out of it, revealing that he was wearing a thin black, wraparound top that had been torn near the neck. Kayde caught sight of a bandage under his clothing and a healing wound danced from his wrist to his elbow. Whatever had happened to him since he disappeared, he'd seen battle.

"Laurel and I were held at an Oscavian research station. She... she's—" He couldn't bring himself to speak of the injured woman. "They performed tests on us. And—"

Sandon cut him off. "You can give the full report later. Who is coming?"

"Brakley Varrow. He's a butcher that claims he's a scientist, and he has an entire fleet. They could flatten the base in a matter of minutes, and that is if our defenses were at a hundred percent."

Kayde stiffened at the name. He didn't realize how obvious it was until everyone in the room looked at him. "Do you have something to say?" Gren demanded.

"Nyden Varrow was an Oscavian of a similar nature working on Earth with Yormas of Wreet." When everyone looked at him blankly, Kayde realized that he'd never given them the man's name. "My team back on Earth has evidence that he was involved in the destruction of Detya."

That sent the room into a frenzy. Half of the occupants turned to Kayde, wanting more information, while the rest turned on each other, trying to find out who knew what. They were only silenced when Sandon slammed a fist down on the table and brought the room to order. "You might have said something before," he said pointedly.

Kayde had to bite his tongue to keep from pointing out that Sandon and his cohort had been too busy imprisoning Kayde and his mate to listen to his report. "Nyden Varrow is dead," Kayde said. "But he said that Yormas wasn't working alone, and he did mention a brother."

Sandon acknowledged that with a nod and turned back to Dru. "What do you know?"

"They're coming," Dru repeated. "Laurel and I pissed them off, and they knew that we'd come here. She heard them. They haven't attacked again because the base wasn't a threat. They knew you couldn't pursue them, and they've been monitoring things since they left." Dru flattened his fingers on the table and his jaw was set as if he could barely keep from lashing out at anyone.

"How are they monitoring us?" asked Gren.

"I don't know. But we found reports. They know things they shouldn't be able to know. Laurel thinks there's a mole. Brakley *liked* her," he sneered out the name. "He didn't think she'd turn against him."

"Are you absolutely certain that they're coming?" Sandon asked, his eyes flashing red for a moment.

Dru just nodded.

Sandon sat back in his chair. "We have to evacuate. Our defenses are too weak. They'll kill us in an instant."

"They know about our secondary rendezvous," Dru said, hanging his head. "There's already a force waiting there."

The secondary location was meant to be a place to gather in the event of an evacuation. It was little more than a dusty rock near a little used jump point, but it was good enough for the desperate.

"We have other contingencies," said Sandon.

Dru pulled a data chip out of his pocket and placed it on the table. "And they know all of them. This information isn't kept on any server. It's memorized by those on the recovery teams. The second we leave this place they'll pick us off one by one. Varrow has been waiting for months to do this. Laurel and I barely escaped. We managed to stall them, but they're coming."

"If we can't run, then we have to fight. We have no other choice."

But that wasn't exactly true. Kayde leaned forward and took everyone's attention again. "I have an idea."

Chapter Twenty

Quinn couldn't stop pacing. Her nerves had been strung tight from the moment the siren went off, so things should have gotten better when everything went silent and the lights stopped flashing. Somehow that only made it worse. She didn't know how long a battle was supposed to take, but she was pretty sure something should have been going on outside her window. But all she saw was snow. No soldiers, no Kayde, no nothing.

Minutes ticked by into hours and two or three must have passed while she waited. How she didn't tear her hair out, she'd never know. At some point in the endless time of waiting she used the communication station on the wall to try and figure out what was going on. But though the controls looked simple enough, she couldn't find anyone who would speak to her.

The denya bond pulsed in her chest, a reassuring cord that bound her to Kayde even though they were so far apart. Wherever he was, she was sure that he was okay. If the bond were telling her anything differently, she would have gone crazy.

She wondered if she should leave the room and try and track him down, but that was the move of a desperate woman. If they really were under threat of battle, she knew she would be helping no one by getting in the middle of it. She could barely shoot a blaster, and she remembered too well her scuffle with Kayde when she had first boarded his ship. It felt like a million years ago; she didn't recognize the woman she'd been back then, and if she told that woman that she'd been going crazy hoping to be reunited with Kayde, that Kayde was her mate and she was in love with him, the Quinn of a few weeks ago would have laughed in her face.

The comm screen on the wall came to life and Quinn rushed over, hoping someone was about to give her answers. But it was a prerecorded message, something she figured out with a little bit of embarrassment when she tried to speak and was completely ignored.

"Emergency evacuation procedures are in place. Please proceed to exit three to board your waiting vessel. You are authorized to carry with you one bag of personal belongings. All food and medications shall be provided by the fleet. Proceed immediately. This is a full evacuation. Proceed to exit three." The message repeated three times before going quiet. Quinn tapped on the screen to try and call someone, anyone, to get more information about what was going on. Unsurprisingly, her calls went unanswered.

But if this place was being evacuated, she wasn't going to get left behind. Especially since Kayde was out there, and surely she could find him if she wasn't stuck in her room. She didn't have anything to carry with her. They'd been forced to leave their belongings on the ship with the promise that things would be delivered later, but that had never happened. She pulled on her coat and gave the room one last look to make sure there wasn't anything she should take with her.

There wasn't.

She had no idea how to find exit three, but as soon as she was in the hall it became clear that wouldn't be an issue. Lights on the floor guided her in the right direction and a few Detyen families with small children walked in front of her. They had to be going to the same place. Quinn got disoriented as she followed the lights in the people. It wasn't like she had a map of Detyen HQ, and Kayde had never gotten around to explaining the layout.

Quinn passed by two huge doors with small windows set into them at eye level. She looked over and saw the infirmary, almost completely abandoned, two rows of beds empty except for a single occupant. A human occupant. Quinn gave the families she was following one look before she pushed through the infirmary doors to see what another human was doing at Detyen HQ. She got close to the bed and had to bite back a shout surprise when she saw who was sitting there.

Laurel. The lost survivor, the one who had been abandoned. She was here. She was alive. Was she okay?

Quinn wanted to touch her to reassure herself the woman was real, but she kept her hands close by her sides and loomed over the bed. Laurel wasn't hooked up any machines and she seemed to be breathing steadily. Whatever was wrong with her, Quinn hoped the Detyens could fix it. She'd been through enough bad things for several lifetimes, and Quinn was sure whatever had brought the young blonde woman here, she'd had a hard path to follow.

A bright green Detyen rushed into the room and shooed Quinn away from the bed. "You shouldn't be in here. We're evacuating."

"She was my..." Quinn wanted to say friend, but she hadn't earned the right. "Is she okay?"

The Detyen sighed and gave Laurel a quick look. "We're doing everything we can," she said. "I'm optimistic. Now get out of here."

Quinn didn't argue. She turned around and went back the way she came, almost slamming into a golden colored Detyen who seemed ready to enter the infirmary. His eyes widened when he saw her. "You are well?" he asked, failing to keep a hint of shock out of his voice.

"Yes?" It came out more of a question, but, Quinn realized, she was coming right out of the infirmary in the middle of evacuation and that could confuse anyone.

The Detyen recovered quickly. "Good, good," he said. "Your mate sent me to get you. I'm to make sure you stay safe."

Warmth suffused her, even if she wished that Kayde himself had come for her. Still, she couldn't stop the smile that spread across her lips. "Really?"

The Detyen looked at her for a moment before finally nodding.

"What's your name?" If he was here to escort her back to Kayde, it would be nice to know what he was called.

"Denmen," he said. "Come, we must move quickly."

He took off and Quinn followed close at his heels. They didn't go in the direction she'd been heading, but maybe Kayde was waiting for her somewhere else. Besides, Denmen surely knew this place way better than she did. They walked for several minutes and something tickled at the back of Quinn's mind, something wrong. They'd passed by two families, both of them heading in the opposite direction, and each time they got close, Denmen turned to her, giving his back to his fellow Detyens, as if he didn't want them to catch a glimpse of them.

That was weird.

He led them to a door which had a bright red warning sign on it in a language that Quinn couldn't read. "Are you sure we're supposed to be here?" It felt like they were deep in the building and far from any exit, far from the evacuation ships. She didn't like this at all. Why would Kayde not be on or near one of the ships?

"What exactly did my mate want you to do?" she asked slowly, refusing to take another step. She really didn't want to go through that door.

Denmen turned towards her. "I'm to see you safely to the ship. Dru will meet you there."

Dru? Who the hell was Dru? "That isn't my mate's name. I think I should go back."

The confusion was back on Denmen's face. "Aren't you Laurel? You're human."

"What do you want with Laurel?" And since when did Laurel have a mate?

Denmen reached towards the side and Quinn was sure he was going for a blaster. She didn't give herself a chance to hesitate, turning on her heel and running away before he could grab her or get a shot off. Something was wrong. She needed to find Kayde.

* * *

The evacuation was going smoothly, but Kayde could feel a growing sense of dread in the back of his mind. He was working to load up one of the supply ships, and once the final crate had been secured he ran down the ramp and straight to where Sandon was standing, coordinating the evacuation. "The eastern wing of family quarters has been completely evacuated," he told Kayde. "We're sending all of them to the ships at exit three."

"Is Quinn with them?" They'd been placed in that part of the family wing, so she should be near an evacuation ship by now. He had wanted to get her out of their quarters himself, but to undertake an evacuation this quickly, all hands were needed. They ran these drills once a month and had all of the supplies on standby, but the real thing was always more difficult.

Sandon consulted a tablet he was holding, his face grim. "No, she hasn't been counted at the exit yet." He tapped on the screen several times before shaking his head. "I just reloaded the roster and she's not there."

"I'm—"

"Go," Sandon agreed. "You won't be able to focus until you know she's safe. I understand." He couldn't, Sandon was still unmated, but at least his sympathies lay with Kayde. "We're closing in on the end of evac. Once the ships start to go, you know what's going to happen."

Kayde nodded. They couldn't stop the Oscavians from coming, but they could make sure there was nothing useful for them to find. Once the ships were in the air, the fleet would engage the self-destruct mechanism and level HQ to rubble. "I'll confirm we're safe once we're on a ship."

Sandon nodded and let Kayde go. He ducked into one of the buildings and ran toward the exit where Quinn was supposed to be waiting. His sense of anxiety grew with every step he took and he wished he had a vehicle to cover the distance faster. He was sweating under his coat, but he hadn't bothered to remove it. All of the heating systems had been turned off in preparation for the evac. They didn't want people lingering indoors when they were supposed to be outside.

At exit three all of the families of the Legion were standing in straight lines, waiting to be waved onto the waiting ships. Even the children stood at attention, tiny would-be soldiers who had been forced into this life just as Kayde had been. Would his and Quinn's children face this same fate? Or would they be able to build something better for their family once the threat of Yormas of Wreet was dealt with?

They hadn't had time to discuss it, newly mated as they were, but Kayde wanted that family with Quinn, a passel of children, a safe place to live, and a bright future not bogged down by the debts of the past. Perhaps another man might have been disappointed that the place he'd called home for his entire life was about to be destroyed, but Kayde couldn't mourn. This place was as much a curse as it was a shelter. It wasn't a place to settle and grow, it was a place to remember and plot revenge against a generational wound that couldn't be healed.

It was time for the Detyens to move on, time to make a new home, a true home.

Kayde greeted the commander and asked about Quinn, but the man hadn't seen her and he didn't have time to chat. Undeterred, Kayde walked among the families, trying to see if his mate was there and simply hadn't been counted yet.

"But what kind of alien was she, mama?" a child's voice asked, stopping Kayde in place.

"I'm not sure," his mother replied. "I've never seen one like that before."

"How could she be on the base?"

Kayde approached them slowly. "Did you say you saw an alien on the base?" It was almost strange to think of Quinn in those terms, but they were both alien to each other in their own ways. If the Detyens had never seen humans before, they were in for a shock.

The little boy backed up against his mother but gave Kayde a wide-eyed nod. "It followed us to the infirmary."

Kayde looked up at the mother for confirmation and she nodded. "Don't call them 'it,'" she told her son. "I think she was a woman."

"Thank you," Kayde told them, and they both looked at him like he'd grown a second head. He left them there waiting to board their ship and headed back indoors. By the time he got to the infirmary, the only human he saw was Laurel being placed onto a gurney by the medical team, who had her tied down and had placed a large bag of supplies between her feet.

"You need to get out of here," the head doctor told him. "The ships are leaving soon."

"Have you seen another human?" he asked. Where in all the hells was Quinn? Was it possible she was still in her room?

The doctor nodded. "I told her to head to the ships," she said. "We need to move this one. Excuse me." The team took Laurel, leaving Kayde alone in the room with no hint of where Quinn had gone off to. He needed a sign, a hint, some kind of trail.

A newly formed sense tugged at him and Kayde placed a hand on his chest, rubbing at the spot below his heart where the denya bond nestled deep inside him. A spike of pain shot through him and pulled him deep into the heart of the compound.

Quinn was there and she was in trouble.

Chapter Twenty-One

Quinn didn't have the best sense of direction and she really didn't need the Detyen HQ to prove it to her. She took turns at random, just trying to put distance between herself and Denmen. He wasn't firing his blaster, but that was only a small blessing. Why the hell had he lured her away from the infirmary? Why had he lied to her? What did he want with Laurel?

Thoughts swirled around in her head, but she didn't have long enough to get a firm hold on any one of them. She was too busy concentrating on the sound of her feet pounding against the concrete ground and the way it was shaking her teeth. She sounded like a wild animal and any soldier worth his rank would be able to track her by hearing alone. She was screwed.

Kayde, where are you? She wanted her mate so bad that she could scream. If he were here with her at least she wouldn't be alone. He would be more than able to handle one treacherous Detyen.

Oh God, she hoped there was only one. What if Denmen had friends?

No. No time to think about that now. She'd only dealt with him, and if someone had been waiting for them beyond that door she didn't want to know. She could only deal with so much at once.

She rounded a corner and her eyes widened as she almost ran straight into Denmen, who was running right at her. On instinct she ducked and rolled, pulling off a maneuver she never would have been able to manage if she thought about it. She sprang back up to her feet and kept running. Her heart was going fast enough to give her a headache and her lungs were about to explode, but she couldn't stop.

She needed a break if she didn't want to pass out.

Quinn wedged herself into a little alcove full of building supplies and ducked behind a pile of bricks while she tried to catch her breath. It echoed in her ears and she was afraid that Denmen could hear her. She had to keep moving, had to get away from him, but she was shaking from the force of her exertions and didn't know how far she could make it. Could she even find the exit from where she was? Where was everyone else? Had they all evacuated already?

Footsteps echoed down the hall and fear shot down Quinn's spine, freezing her in place. She snapped herself out of it. If she froze, she was dead. Denmen hadn't hesitated to reach for his weapon and she knew the second he caught her this was all over. Quinn looked around. She needed a weapon, something that would flatten him in one go. She gulped as she saw the pile of bricks right in front of her, but she couldn't bring herself to pick one up. She didn't know if she had it in her to bash someone over the head.

She almost fell over and her hand shot out, landing on a pile of wooden beams just big enough for her to get a good grip on. She grabbed one with both hands and tested the weight. It was heavy, thick enough to do some real damage. And Denmen was almost on her.

She held tight onto the board and waited, letting her breathing even out and her muscles relax. She couldn't swing too early. She only had one shot. She was no fighter, but with this weapon and the element of surprise, she didn't need to be.

Denmen's shadow crossed her path and Quinn stepped out and swung. The blow took him by surprise and he went down with a grunt, his blaster flying out of his hand and lying somewhere in the pile of bricks behind her. A trickle of green blood flowed down the side of his head and bile rose in Quinn's throat. She'd done that to him. His eyes were closed and his body limp, but he still breathed. Quinn held the board up over her head, but she couldn't bring herself to finish the strike. Even knowing he was a threat to her, she couldn't hit an unconscious man.

She threw the board away and took off running. There was no telling how long Denmen would be out, and she didn't want to wait for him to wake up. After she'd turned several corners and completely lost her way again, Quinn realized that she'd left Denmen's weapon back there and if he woke up, he'd be more than ready to shoot her. She was pretty sure it had fallen behind the bricks and she had to hope that if he looked for it, it slowed him down enough to let her find her way out of here.

Wherever here was.

She was going to die lost and alone on this hopeless little moon. The thought rose from the depths of her dread and Quinn stumbled at the force of it. She'd come all this way, she'd found Kayde, and she'd begun to heal from the harms done to her, and now it was all going to be for nothing because she couldn't find the right damn hallway to lead her out of this maze.

If she just stopped and slid against the wall until she was sitting on the floor, would that be any worse than running until she collapsed? Would it really be so bad to give up? Hopelessness speared through her and she didn't realize that she was crying until she took a deep breath and discovered just how clogged her nose had become.

God, she was so pathetic.

The urge to give up was so strong that Quinn forced herself to move. It was ironic in a way. If her doubts had crept up on her she might have given up little by little until she was convinced that it was the right thing to do. But the force of it was so great that it was like being hit with a battering ram and her instincts to fight back were triggered before she'd even realized she'd begun to fight her fears.

She could do this. She *had* to do this. She had to find Kayde and get off this godforsaken moon and go home. They had a life there, together, and she was going to seize it with both hands and carve it out of destiny no matter what she had to fight. If Denmen had shown up right then she could have taken it, she was sure, her determination blazed so brightly within her.

When she turned the next corner she came to an abrupt halt as a Detyen stood in her path. *Her* Detyen.

"Kayde!" She flung her arms around him and held on for dear life.

He clamped her tightly in his embrace. "What are you doing down here?" he asked, his face buried in the curve of her neck.

"Long story." She wanted to tell him what happened, but she wanted to do it when they weren't under imminent threat of treacherous Detyens. "We should get to the ships." She'd tell Kayde what happened soon, but she was more than happy to leave

Denmen on the moon while the rest of them escaped. She might not have it in her to hit him over the head, but leaving him like this was no hardship. The floor rumbled under their feet and Quinn's ears popped. Her eyes snapped to Kayde's as she let go of him and reluctantly stepped back. "What's that?"

He looked back over his shoulder. "That was the first evac ship firing its thrusters. We need to go now."

The time for talking was over. They ran.

* * *

There was no good reason for Quinn to be in this part of the compound, but they didn't have time to dwell on it. Whatever had gone wrong, they could fix later. But they had to get to the ships first. The ground was a constant rumble under their feet as all the evacuation vessels began to lift off. Kayde pushed as hard as he thought Quinn could go, but he feared that they were still not moving fast enough. They were deep inside the bowels of Detyen HQ and even at a sprint it would take precious minutes to get to one of the exits.

It didn't escape Kayde's notice that Quinn kept shooting worried looks over her shoulder. "Is there something we should be concerned with?" he asked his mate.

She opened her mouth to reply, but seemed to reconsider after a moment and shook her head. Kayde didn't have time to press, but he did speed up a little and though Quinn was breathing heavily, she kept up.

They made it to exit three just in time to watch the last of the evacuation ships break atmo, the sound cracking all around them.

Quinn doubled over, her heavy breaths making white puffs in the cold air around them. "They couldn't wait five more minutes?" she panted.

Kayde surveyed the land around them, hoping the final fleet ship was still there, still waiting. But they were alone. All hope was not lost. They'd come to HQ in their own ship, and though the plan was to abandon it in the escape, it would still be waiting outside the administration building where they had landed earlier that day. "Come on," said Kayde. "We need to get back inside."

Quinn's teeth were already chattering and she didn't argue.

They moved a little slower through the eerie silence of the abandoned compound. Kayde had never before realized just how much life his people brought to the place, gloomy as it was. They didn't have time for memories, not when the self-destruct sequence could be engaged at any moment. Kayde kept that piece of information to himself, not wanting to worry Quinn. They had plenty of time to get to their ship and get away, it would only be a few more minutes.

"Are you going to miss it?" she asked as she ran her fingers along one of the walls.

"No," Kayde answered truthfully. "This isn't my home."

She gave me a funny look. "It isn't?"

Kayde leaned in and stole a kiss. "No, you are."

Her lips compressed and her eyes widened, and for a moment Kayde thought she would cry before a burst of laughter broke free. She flung her arms around him buried her face in his neck, holding him tight as amusement wracked her body. "I'm sorry, I shouldn't laugh. Really, I know what you mean. I promise I do."

Her laughter was light to his newly formed soul and Kayde promised himself that he would find the right words to express what she was to him. No matter how long it took. "We must hurry." He pulled her along and they made it to the entrance to the administrative building without any more delays. Their ship was waiting exactly where they had left it and Kayde knew they were home free.

He could see the valley beyond the ship, the sharp drop off of the plateau giving HQ a perfect natural landing site. But it wouldn't be long until the entire compound behind them sank into that valley and the plateau itself would most likely disappear in the blast. Kayde's thoughts on the upcoming changes to the landscape were scattered when he spotted a dark figure standing outside of his ship, trying to open the door.

"There's another survivor out there," he told Quinn as they stood at the final door that would lead them out of the compound. "He must have somehow missed the evac ships." Though how all of the protocols to make sure no one was left behind had missed him, Kayde didn't know. Then again, the ships had left *him* and *Quinn* behind as well, so they clearly had a level of acceptable loss. He only hoped no one else had been abandoned.

They stepped out into the cold and Quinn got a good look at the survivor by their ship. She shouted something at Kayde, but the wind roaring around them swallowed up her words. When she threw herself on him and tackled him to the ground he wanted to ask what she was doing, but when a blaster started firing it all became clear. The man at their ship was who Quinn had been checking for. He'd tried to harm Kayde's mate, and for that he would pay.

"Take cover!" Kayde yelled. Quinn nodded and Kayde was off, trusting her to do as instructed.

As he got closer to the ship, dodging the wildly fired blaster, Kayde recognized the Detyen warrior attacking them. Denmen was an older warrior who had been denied his application to become soulless and would die on his thirtieth birthday in the coming months if he didn't find his mate. The left side of his face was swollen and turning an ugly gray and a trickle of dried blood was plastered along his temple and down his cheek as if he'd been struck by a large object. Quinn's work? Pride for his mate swelled in him, along with anger that Denmen had threatened her.

"What are you doing?" Kayde demanded, crouching behind one of the boulders that ringed the edge of the landing pad. He was within easy range of the blaster now and he didn't want to give Denmen a target.

"Fulfilling my end of the bargain," Denmen yelled back. "They promised to find me a mate if I gave them the human that escaped."

Who? Rage surged in Kayde and he saw red, forgetting the question before it had been asked. "You can't have her."

Denmen fired a shot beyond Kayde, back to where Quinn was taking cover. "I don't care about your bitch. They want the other one." He shot again, all his fire going wide. "It's all her fault I'm stuck here like this."

Kayde didn't know which 'her' Denmen was talking about and he didn't care. Whoever he was working for, it was clear he'd betrayed the Legion and wanted to harm Quinn and, presumably, Laurel. Kayde wasn't about to let him get away with that. But the blaster posed a problem. He'd stored the weapons he'd been issued when he went to meet Dru's ship, and his own blaster was safely stored in the lock box on his own ship. He had no weapons but his wits and his claws, and though he knew he was the better fighter than Denmen under normal circumstances, he wasn't immune to a blaster.

"Hey, asshole!" Quinn's yell made Kayde's heart stutter. He'd run in front of blaster fire to protect her, but he needed her to stay down if he was going to win this fight. For some reason she didn't want to do that. Rocks flew overhead, lobbed farther than he would have thought her capable. Denmen gave a rage fueled yell and spun towards her, advancing on her position with no thought to where Kayde was standing.

Fear for his denya's safety warred with pride for her wit, but Kayde tamped them both down as the calm of battle overtook him. He stepped out, meeting Denmen with his fists and grabbing at his wrist to isolate the blaster. Kayde might have had more skill and experience, but Denmen was still a Detyen warrior and it was no easy task to hold him back.

They fell to the ground and a quick jab at a pressure point in the younger Detyen's wrist loosened his grip on the blaster enough for him to drop it. Kayde couldn't let go well enough to grab it himself, but he did his best to toss it out of reach of both of them.

He jammed his knee into Denmen's side and his opponent grunted and bucked at him, slamming his head against Kayde and unsheathing his claws at the same moment. They fell apart and Kayde staggered, his vision going crosseyed for a moment until he recovered. Denmen eyed the ground near their feet and found his blaster, but Kayde was faster, kicking it out of range and almost beyond the ship, near the edge of the plateau.

It was a dirty fight, claws swiping for anything they could hit, teeth bared, eyes red. They both rode the hard edge of rage, Kayde defending his mate, Denmen fighting for his life.

Denmen slipped on a patch of ice and Kayde pressed the advantage, sweeping his leg out from under him and sending him crashing to the ground. He bashed his head against the snow, but it was too soft to do much damage and Denmen was already fighting back, his grappling skills surprisingly sharp.

But he was getting tired. His chest heaved as he tried to pull in breaths and he was slowing down. All Kayde had to do was wait him out and not let Denmen get lucky. The fight was already over, his opponent just didn't know it yet.

They scrambled back to their feet and Kayde saw his opening, saw exactly how it would happen. Denmen would lunge; he didn't see the small dip in the ground in front of them. His foot would get caught, and when Kayde caught him, he'd flip him back down and use his claws to end this once and for all. In his mind it was already over, the future set in stone.

Denmen lunged, but the ground under their feet rippled with the sound of a distant blast, distracting his opponent enough to pull back at the last moment. The smell of explosives tickled Kayde's nose and he knew they didn't have much time before the self-destruct mechanism reached them.

"Quinn!" he yelled behind him. "Get on the ship!" He'd hold off Denmen, but he needed his mate moving *right now*. He couldn't look back to see if she did as he bid; the ground rumbled under his feet and he had to end this.

Now.

***

Quinn could see smoke rising in the distance and her fingers and nose were numb from the cold. Had the attack started? Shouldn't she see ships in the sky? There was no time to question it. As Kayde's words sank in, she was already running, trying to keep low to the ground in case either of them had a blaster she didn't see. It looked like the ship was way far away, but she covered the distance between the edge of the landing pad and it faster than she thought possible. Her feet slid on the icy surface under her, but she managed not to fall over.

She made it to the ship and flipped open the control panel next to the entrance, but paused before pressing the button to open the door and extend the ramp. She didn't want Denmen getting on the ship, but the ground was rumbling underneath her feet and the sound of explosions in the distance was getting closer. She had to trust Kayde to take care of him. She trusted her mate with her life, he'd do anything he needed to make sure that they got off this moon alive and together.

The hatch opened slowly enough to make Quinn bite her lip and start to gesture with both hands, hoping that might make it move a little faster. She heard a cry of pain behind her and looked to see Kayde clutching his side as green blood pulsed out under his fingers. His name died on her lips as Denmen came up behind him, a mad look in his eyes.

No. This couldn't be happening, she wasn't going to let him win.

Her eyes locked with Kayde's and she saw resignation in them. He nodded towards the hatch, urging her to get on board, to not see what was about to happen. To hell with that. She abandoned her post and dove under the ship, looking for something, *anything* that might turn the tide of this battle.

A blaster would do.

She practically tripped over it. It must have been kicked this way at the beginning of the fight. Quinn scooped it up with unsteady fingers and ran back to where she could see the two men fighting. They'd stumbled back until they were practically on the edge of the plateau. One wrong step and they'd go tumbling over. Kayde was fighting hard, but she could see the pain in every line of his body. Whatever Denmen had hit, it had been vital.

Quinn raised the blaster, but the way they were fighting meant that she could just as easily hit Kayde as his opponent, and she was no crack shot. She cursed and lowered the weapon, running closer to them. Denmen caught sight of her movement and an evil smile overtook his face, freezing the blood in her veins more effectively than the air around them. He was going to kill Kayde, she could see it perfectly. And once he killed Kayde, he would come for her. He may not have given a shit about her before, but now that her mate had hurt him, had put a damper on his plans, he was ready to take his frustrations out on her.

To hell with that.

Determination steadied her nerves and it was like she and Kayde were connected, mind to mind. He pushed Denmen, heaving him back and stepping out of the way while Quinn raised the blaster, practically in slow motion. She squeezed the trigger and watched as the bright blast of light hit Denmen in the center of his chest. His eyes widened, as if he hadn't realized she had the blaster, and he stumbled back. His arms waved madly and he let out a yell before falling backwards, tumbling off the side of the plateau and disappearing from sight.

She should have felt something about killing a man. But as Quinn engaged the safety and stuffed the blaster in her pocket, all she could think of was Kayde. As the explosions crept ever closer, she ran towards her mate and got her shoulders under his arm, helping him across the landing pad and practically dragging him up the ramp as he staggered.

"We didn't make it this far for you to crap out on me now." She infused as much steel into her voice as she could manage, trying to mask her fear.

Kayde tried to say something, but it came out little more than a muffle of unintelligible words.

"Please tell me you can fly this thing." They didn't have much time until the blasts reached them, and she didn't know how to launch the ship.

Kayde nodded weakly. "Get me to the cockpit," he slurred.

Oh, that wasn't a good sign, but they didn't have time to delay. She led him straight there, settling him into his seat before finding the first aid kit that was set up against the wall. Kayde moved sluggishly, powering up the ship and engaging the launch sequence. Quinn found an injector filled with painkiller and reached for Kayde's arm, giving him the medicine without asking for permission.

He growled at her and she had to suppress a smile. Of course he was a surly patient, she shouldn't have expected anything less. "How bad is the bleeding?" she asked, digging around for bandages and regen gel. She let out a little shout of victory when she found an almost full tube.

Kayde's breath was shaky, but his hands on the controls were steady. "It will hold while I get us in the air."

She could see the blood seeping into his top and wanted to fix him up right then, but she had to trust her mate. They were his injuries, and he knew his body. She sat back in her seat and stashed the first aid kit between her legs before buckling up. The nav screen in front of them was clear and they weren't far from the gate. They could catch up with the fleet in no time and this little setback would be no more than an unpleasant memory.

They lifted off and Quinn finally got a look at the destruction all around them. The Detyen compound was gone, completely leveled. "What happened?" The words burst out, even as her mind scrambled to find an explanation.

"Self destruct," said Kayde, his focus completely on the controls in front of them. "Can't leave anything behind."

"For who?" She still didn't know why they'd evacuated, or what was going on.

Kayde groaned and a shadow passed over head. "For them," he said as a giant warship came into view, and Quinn's heart sank.

Chapter Twenty-Two

Kayde was on the verge of passing out, and he'd had enough of battle to last him for the next several years. He'd spent days, weeks, in the trenches before and it had never been this bad. But he'd never had his mate at his side, and keeping her safe was more important than everything else.

The first of the Oscavian ships broke through the atmosphere and Kayde reached forward, reprogramming their trajectory and turning around 180 degrees. They were the last ship on the moon and he wasn't about to let them get captured. He punched the speed, going as fast as he could manage while still bound by the moon's gravity. A warning alerted him that they'd been spotted, but the giant Oscavian ship was much too slow to catch them. It could have flattened the compound in a minute, but one little speeder could outrun it with room to spare.

And he did.

The second they broke atmo he made the jump to FTL, the maneuver similar to how they'd escaped Beznifa. They left the Oscavians behind with no trail to follow and Kayde slumped in his chair, the buzz of the painkiller simmering in his veins even as it felt like his guts were on fire.

Quinn didn't wait for his okay to scuttle out of her seat and start tending to him. She gasped when she revealed the blow that Denmen had dealt him, but she slathered on regen gel like a pro, giving him murmuring reassurances that everything would be okay. With her by his side, he could almost believe it.

"Who was that attacking? How did Laurel get on the base? Why did we have to leave?" Now that they'd reached some modicum of safety, the questions poured out of her and Kayde was more than happy to answer, but when he opened his mouth, his brain gave out and he slumped in his chair as everything faded to black.

He couldn't have been out for long. Quinn's hands were clamped tightly on his shoulders, but she didn't shake him, too aware of his wounds to rattle him too much. Kayde sucked in a deep breath as the blood pounded hard in his veins. It felt like he'd been thrown out of a high-flying speeder and was about to plunge down onto hard land with no parachute. Something dropped out of Quinn's hand, but he was too busy trying to breathe to look at it.

"You're okay," she told him, her voice firm. "We're safe. You protected me." Her lips brushed against his forehead, heedless of the sweat and grime he'd accumulated in the fight. "You're all bandaged up and I gave you a stimulant to keep you awake."

That must have been what fell out of her hand. Kayde managed a nod as his breathing evened. His heart still beat wildly, but that too was starting to get better. "I feel like I got kicked in the chest. By a fighting bot."

His ever so caring mate smiled at him, a laugh in her eyes. "That's what you get for scaring me like that." She leaned back, letting her hand slowly trail down one of his arms before letting go. "I don't like seeing you injured."

"Believe me, denya, I do not like *being* injured. But I would take a hundred wounds every day to keep you safe." It was only now truly setting in that they'd escaped. He'd been moving so fast since Druath and Laurel showed up that he hadn't had time to sit down and think. Hadn't had time to realize just how close he'd come to losing his mate and his life.

Quinn's eyes softened. "I love you. And I don't want you to take a hundred wounds for me. Let's just avoid the fights all together."

"I love you, too." He might not have said it in so many words, but he tried to show it to her in his every action. "But there are many battles yet to come, the Oscavian ships that found our base will not be satisfied with a ruin. They will pursue us."

Quinn bit her lip and sighed. "Is the fight ever going to be over?"

She'd only known battle for a year or so, while Kayde had lived it every moment of his life. But for the first time since he could remember, he had hope. "It will," he promised, "and soon. The people who attacked us might be connected to Yormas of Wreet." He told her all that had happened, from Dru and Laurel arriving on the planet, up through the battle, filling in the blanks of the last few hours.

"You think that Laurel is Druath's denya?" was Quinn's first question.

Kayde shrugged. The regen gel burned on his side, but the painkiller he'd been given when they first boarded was doing its job, and he was able to focus. "Perhaps," he conceded. He could remember the fury in her voice when she'd denied Dru, but that passion had to come from somewhere. "She said she wasn't his mate. But I don't know where she would have gotten the idea that she was."

Quinn looked thoughtful. "I hope she figures it out. She's been through so much, she shouldn't need to suffer anymore."

So had his own mate, but she had found a core of inner strength, and even though she'd been put through all the hells she'd shown that she had the heart of a warrior. But even warriors needed rest. "You can go and sleep," he offered. "It will be some time until we rendezvous with the fleet."

Quinn reached out and placed her hand over his. "I'd rather stay here."

Kayde couldn't help his smile. "There's no other place I want you to be."

"Where are we going? The fleet, I mean. You didn't say."

There was only one place in the galaxy that they had a chance of making a stand, one place where they'd already begun to lay the groundwork of a life and a potential alliance that could save them all, and the planet that had the best chance of saving the young of the Legion from the Denya Price. Kayde squeezed his mate's hand before leaning forward to program in the coordinates to find the fleet, then he turned to her. "We're going home. To Earth."

She met his eyes and smiled. "Everything's going to turn out alright now, isn't it?" It was a question, but she asked it with confidence.

And for the first time in a long time, Kayde felt the truth in his answer. He had his mate by his side and a real home on the horizon, a place where his people could be safe. "It is."

Detyen Warriors

Soulless

Ruthless

Heartless

Faultless

Endless

***

***

Mated to the Alien

Ruwen

Tyral

Stoan

Cyborg

Krayter

Kayleb

Shayn

Braxtyn

Doryan

Detyen Warriors

Soulless

Ruthless

Heartless

Faultless

Endless

Paranormal Romance

Marked

Bear in Mind

Alpha's Mercy

Gemma's Mate

Stealing the Alpha

The Alpha Heist

Entangled with the Thief

In the Alpha's Bed

Find more by Kate Rudolph at www.katerudolph.net

About Kate Rudolph

Kate Rudolph is sci-fi and paranormal romance author who lives in Indiana. She loves writing about kick butt heroines and the steamy heroes who love them. She's been devouring romance novels since she was too young to be reading them and had to hide her books so no one would take them away. She couldn't imagine a better job in this world than writing romances and sharing them with her fellow readers.

If you enjoyed this story, please consider leaving a review.

CPSIA information can be obtained
at www.ICGtesting.com
Printed in the USA
BVHW040946060321
601818BV00012B/1717

9 781393 688396